Emerald

ALSO BY ELLE CASEY

ROMANCE

Red Hot Love (3-book series)
By Degrees
Rebel Wheels (3-book series)
Just One Night (romantic serial)
Just One Week
Love in New York (3-book series)
Shine Not Burn (2-book series)
Bourbon Street Boys (4-book series)
Desperate Measures
Mismatched

ROMANTIC SUSPENSE

All the Glory
Don't Make Me Beautiful
Wrecked (2-book series)

PARANORMAL

Duality (2-book series)
Pocket Full of Sunshine (short story & screenplay)

CONTEMPORARY URBAN FANTASY

War of the Fae (10-book series)
Ten Things You Should Know About Dragons (short story in The Dragon Chronicles)
My Vampire Summer
Aces High

DYSTOPIAN

Apocalypsis (4-book series)

SCIENCE FICTION

Drifters' Alliance (3-book series)
Winner Takes All (short story prequel to Drifters' Alliance in Dark Beyond the Stars Anthology)

To keep up-to-date with Elle's latest releases, please visit www.ElleCasey.com
To get an email when Elle's next book is released, sign up here: http://www.ElleCasey.com/news

Emerald

ELLE CASEY

Montlake Romance

This is a work of fiction. Names, characters, organizations, places, events, and incidents are either products of the author's imagination or are used fictitiously. Any resemblance to actual persons, living or dead, or actual events is purely coincidental.

Text copyright © 2018 by Elle Casey
All rights reserved.

No part of this book may be reproduced, or stored in a retrieval system, or transmitted in any form or by any means, electronic, mechanical, photocopying, recording, or otherwise, without express written permission of the publisher.

Published by Montlake Romance Publishing, Seattle

www.apub.com

Amazon, the Amazon logo, and Montlake Romance Publishing are trademarks of Amazon.com, Inc., or its affiliates.

ISBN-13: 9781542047067
ISBN-10: 1542047064

Cover design by @blacksheep-uk.com

Cover photography by Matthew Hegarty

Printed in the United States of America

To Joka, my artistic, adventurous, and lovely friend.

CHAPTER ONE

I wrap my shawl tighter around my shoulders as the late-morning chill sends a shiver through my body. My basket is full of warm, fresh eggs that I've collected from my girls in the coop, and I'm headed back to the house. All the animals have been fed and now it's my turn.

I wave and smile at Harold, a man who pitched a tent out in the yard last week and who is now hanging his socks to dry on our communal laundry line. He seems content to pull weeds in the garden in exchange for the free living space.

Harold comes every year about this time. He says autumn is the best season for reflecting and resetting his priorities. I don't know much about his other life, the one outside our little intentional-living farming collective. I think he's a businessman in Washington, DC, but we don't ask a lot of questions here. People are free to do what they need to do and be who they need to be in order to find happiness.

Reflecting on Harold's personal journey makes me think of my sister Amber. She left for New York City a little over three months ago to set the record straight with some men who claim to be our fathers—men who, for twenty-five years, should have been a part of our lives but weren't. My other sister, Rose, and I fully expected Amber to come back as soon as she was done giving them a piece of our collective minds, because she had a flight booked out the same day she arrived, and because other than telling them we weren't interested in the thirty-million-dollar inheritance they were offering, she had no reason to be in Manhattan. But she didn't come back that day or in the days or weeks after either. Not permanently, anyway. She got wrapped up in their business and the guy she connected with romantically—Ty, the lead guitarist in their band—and we haven't seen her since in any meaningful way. She stopped off for a few days once, but that was it. She was more a visitor than a resident on that trip, and it was really strange.

Of course we still chat by phone almost every day, but it's not the same thing as living together, side by side. I miss her terribly. It's hard for me to understand how she could so easily and completely abandon our life here on the farm for the one she's now living in New York City. I don't think the environments could be any more different. I get it that she has the right to live her life how she wants and needs to in order to be happy and feel fulfilled, but the problem is that her choices have changed my life also, and I didn't ask for that. I didn't want anything to be different from how it's always been, and I'm not comfortable with how it's worked out . . . with all of us having to work a little harder and our neighbor Smitty being more involved in the farm's operations. I wish Amber would come back so things could return to the way they used to be, before the band Red Hot came into our lives.

None of us three girls were raised to be big-city types. For twenty-five years, we've been participants in the vision our mothers realized when they quit being groupies of Red Hot and settled down on this two-hundred-acre farm in central Maine. We've had a peaceful life promoting the beauty and bounty of our natural world, creatures both large and small living together in harmony and doing harm to none. I love it. It's where I'm meant to be.

We are all one: This is the message we've grown up hearing, which I took to heart from the moment I understood what it meant. But if I'm being honest, I have to say that I'm having a hard time feeling the *oneness* with a sister who's so very far away.

Amber hasn't told me a whole lot about what she's been doing in Manhattan, other than meeting a lot of people and staying very busy. Her new job is in public relations, but she says she's learning a lot about band management too, now that their longtime employee Ted is thinking about retiring and isn't really on the best of terms with the band. After it was discovered how much trouble he caused in their lives twenty-five years ago, he's kind of on their poo list. I don't know what band management actually entails, but Amber seems to enjoy doing it.

If I were in her shoes, working in that big city for Red Hot, I'm pretty sure I'd feel like I was living on an alien planet somewhere, interacting with extraterrestrials. I'm much more comfortable with the people who visit our farm; they're all searching for peace and quiet, a place where they can center themselves and discover or rediscover their life's purpose. The craziest thing that happens around here is someone wandering around naked, but I'm used to hippies doing their thing, so it doesn't even faze me anymore. My life is completely tame compared to Amber's. She actually laughed as she told the story about a man yelling sexual innuendo at her when she was trying to eat a hot dog. If that happened to me, I'd hide in the restaurant's bathroom and never want to come out, but she just took it in stride, like it was entertainment and not aggressive, scary behavior. I just don't get it. Amber has always been bolder than I am, but it's almost like she's a different person now. I don't know her anymore, and it makes me sad.

I kick a stone off the path and watch it roll into the woods, shuffling some leaves out of its way as it passes through and crushing the more delicate ones beneath it. That little rock reminds me of Red Hot and the men who make up the band. They just bouldered into our lives three months ago, messing everything up; sometimes I feel like I'm being crushed under the weight of it.

I was angry and sad when I found out I had a father who was alive and well out there, playing in a famous rock band whose music I'd been listening to almost every day of my life for twenty-five years. I'd believed from things our mothers said as I was growing up that they didn't know who our fathers were—a partial truth, as it turns out—but I'm even angrier now that these men are pretending to be innocent, trying to say they were ignorant of the fact that they had children growing up just a short plane ride away. In my opinion, not bothering to find out the truth of why our mothers left them years ago doesn't equate to ignorance . . . it means they're coldhearted. They cared more about the music than our mothers. And one of these men is supposedly my father. I don't know which one it is, and I don't want to know. As far as I'm concerned, the past can stay in the past where it belongs.

Our mothers never would have left the band and the life they had together if they'd felt wanted and loved. I'm sure, like most groupies, they were being used as a distraction . . . for sex and partying. I hate thinking of the women who raised me, who sacrificed so much for my sisters and me, being cheapened like that. I'm glad they left that life behind and took us with them. Men who treat women like that don't deserve us.

The band members expect us to believe that they didn't know their manager, Ted, arranged for our mothers to disappear twenty-five years ago here to central Maine, where they bought this farm with money provided from the band's coffers. *Puh-lease.* How could they *not* know a couple hundred thousand bucks were missing from their bank accounts? I'd have to be a complete nincompoop to believe that nonsense.

Before Amber related this story to us, we'd been kept in the dark about our mothers' shared past, not knowing how much the three of them cared about the band and the men in it or how special their time together was. It might have been only two years, but to them, it seemed like it lasted a lifetime. I was never told that these rockers I'd grown up seeing on well-worn album covers had fathered us, but there had to be a good reason why our mothers chose to leave that part of their story out. If their relationships were so great and full of love—as our mothers would have us believe now that they're confessing all their sins—why didn't they tell those men the truth before they left? Why did they leave without saying anything at all about being pregnant?

Asking these completely legitimate questions of Carol, Barbara, and Sally—who raised my sisters and me together as one group-mom, even though Carol is the one who actually gave birth to me—gets me nothing but answers that make no sense. They say life with the band had a very casual atmosphere, where people came and went for no reason and without explanations; there were never any promises made, no commitments. And they claim they didn't want to screw up the music. They didn't want to interfere with the band's creative process.

What a bunch of baloney. If some man ever got me pregnant, he would know about it before anybody else did, and I certainly wouldn't let him be absent for twenty-five years before he showed himself to my child either. That's just wrong, no matter how you look at it. I'm having a hard time believing my mothers' version of events and still respecting them at the same time, so I choose to believe they were duped by users and just don't want to admit it. They can be stubborn sometimes. And they were young . . . younger than my sisters and I are right now. I made several dumb decisions when I was in my early twenties. Dating our childhood friend Smitty was one of them. *Ugh*. What a mistake that was. Just thinking about our one disastrous night together is enough to turn my mood completely sour. He's a nice enough guy, but we have very different ideas about how a first date should go. *Never again*.

I push the bitterness away. It's pointless to be working myself up over choices I made before I knew better or choices my mothers made when they were young and silly. They made their beds—choosing to leave and set up our lives here—and we've been lying in them ever since. And by the way, those beds are *comfortable*. My life is *good*. No, my life is *great*. I love how everything turned out. I just wish those men had stayed gone. But nooo . . . they had to send their lawyer out here to offer us a huge inheritance and mess things up. And now Amber is gone, and I'm left to pick up the pieces without one of my two best friends at my side.

Nope. I'm not bitter at all.

I walk up the front steps to the farmhouse, picking up a couple of beautiful orange and red leaves that have blown onto the porch. I sigh loudly, letting all the stress leave my body. It's the simple things that make me happy, like autumn leaves drifting randomly into my day so I can appreciate their gorgeous colors and textures. I'm a creative person and, truthfully, not very social. I don't like crowds and I'm not keen on strangers, except for the ones who come here to find peace with us; they tend to like space and are cool about giving it, too. My sister Amber might go so far as to say I have social anxiety, but I'm not sure I agree with that label. I mean, I've never had any trouble selling items we grow and make here on the farm at the local farmers' market. I've dealt face-to-face with literally hundreds of strangers, and I've never suffered more than a racing pulse or a flushed complexion as side effects.

Okay, so I'll admit that I like more controlled environments, where there aren't any big surprises. But does that make me socially inept? Weird? I don't think so. I just prefer peace to chaos, and there's nothing wrong with that. There are plenty of people out there like me. I just haven't met them because we all prefer to stay on home ground.

I pause to contemplate my world, turning around so I can appreciate the beauty surrounding me. The trees look like they're on fire with red, yellow, and orange leaves ready to drop to the ground. Wind scatters the already fallen ones left and then right, collecting them in piles next to the various outbuildings. A three-legged border collie—affectionately named Banana because he's always been a little crazy—has his nose to the ground as he hops along, chasing anything that moves. He glances up at me for a few seconds, verifying that I don't have any snacks for him, before he continues on his mission.

I love having my family close and my work right outside the front door. I take care of the animals on our farm—chickens, goats, cows, pigs, and horses—and help my sister Rose at her veterinary clinic when she needs it. And when I'm in the mood, I paint. Granted, I'm not in the mood to do it very often these days, but that's okay because it's not how I make my living. The products we sell from our farm provide enough for all of us, and I have boundless love here: unlimited support, hugs whenever I need them, and a listening ear from any number of women who understand and get me. How could I possibly want more than that? And if I need a little extra something, if I'm in the mood for some music, for example, I can go into town and listen to the older, retired gentleman who plays guitar at the local pub, or I can turn on the radio. If I want to go out with a guy, I can pick one up at the bar—it's too small and hole-in-the-wall-y to be called a club—or I could call up an old flame . . . Smitty, for example. Not that I would. But I could.

I've experimented with sex, like my sisters have, and although I enjoy it, I really don't see what the big deal is. I've read romance novels that have leading men who knock women's socks off with orgasms galore, but that hasn't been my personal experience. Do I regret that? No, of course not. How can you miss what you've never had? It's not in me to do that.

All I care about is waking up every day, being a hardworking member of this intentional-living community my mothers started, and doing my part for the family. What I receive in return is priceless: I get to live and work in paradise with wonderful people and animals who do nothing but love me back; I have a front-row seat to a visually stunning changing of the seasons four times a year; and I'm part of a strong, supportive sisterhood that I share not just with Rose and Amber, but with our mothers too. What's not to love? Reflecting on my life makes me feel warm and sunny inside, even on this chilly autumn day. Some people wait their whole lives to find happiness, but I was born into it.

Am I upset with Amber for leaving? It might sound like I am, but I'm really not. I would never want to hold her back from her dreams. What's hard or confusing for me, though, is understanding how her dreams could be in New York City, because she never said anything about wanting more than what we had growing up. She always seemed as happy as I am. And that scares me, maybe. Because I realize it's possible that she didn't know she wasn't happy until she left here. Amber woke me up to the idea that a person might not know what she's missing until she sees or experiences that *other* thing—hot sex, for example.

But that wouldn't happen with me . . . not like it did with her. I'm sure of it. We're close, but we're very different. She was always the take-charge older one. It doesn't matter that she was born only a week before I was; it's always felt more like years. Whenever there's a problem, she steps forward and fixes it. I'm more the look-the-other-way type when things get hairy, and Rose is always too busy to bother with other people's problems; she's more into animals than humans. I think the farm might have been too tame for Amber . . . not enough conflict to keep life interesting or something.

Unlike her, I don't relish conflict, and I definitely don't enjoy butting heads with people. Not that she loves those things, but she doesn't shy away from them either. Whenever things in my life get ugly or even just uncomfortable, I prefer to disappear into my painting studio. Even if I'm not in the mood to create anything, I can always rearrange my tubes of acrylic colors, clean out the dust, build canvases, or make frames that might someday hold new pieces. I don't always need to be creating to feel satisfied; sometimes just being in that environment soothes my soul.

I leave the porch and my melancholy thoughts behind as I enter the house, walking into the kitchen and placing the basket of eggs on the counter. There's a recipe book resting open on a wooden stand a guest made years ago from wood on the property, which means Sally will be mixing up something delicious today. I leave the eggs out so she'll know that they're here for her. She can be a little scatterbrained sometimes and forget that we put them in the cupboard these days to keep them safe from the stray kitties that sometimes wander in and think eggs are fun toys to knock off the counter.

"Is that you, Emerald?" Sally's voice sails from the living room into the kitchen.

Speak of the devil. "Yes!" I say, turning to shout through the doorway. "I have some fresh eggs for you. I'm leaving them on the counter."

Her voice is closer now, coming from the front room. "Thank you. I was thinking about making some cream puffs."

"Yummy." I love Sally's cream puffs. She and her daughter, Rose, have one thing in common: they're both healers of a sort. Rose heals animals with medical care, and Sally heals sad feelings with delicious baked goods. Amber's mother, Barbara, is a pretty good cook too, but I'm a huge fan of Sally's stuff especially. I search for the cream puff recipe in her book and leave the page open to it. I don't want her forgetting what she just promised.

She walks into the kitchen, her salt-and-pepper hair not caught up in braids for a change, creating a fuzzy frame for her face. It always strikes me how different Sally looks compared to her daughter Rose. Sally has frizzy gray hair that used to be brown, and Rose's hair is blond and straight. It makes me wonder if Rose takes after her father, if he has blond hair too. I immediately push that thought out of my head. I don't want to think about those men right now. I'm already feeling emotional enough as it is.

I walk over and give her a hug. "Good morning, Momma Sally."

"Good morning, my darling." She holds my face between her hands. "Look at those pink cheeks. Are you cold?"

I shake my head, sliding my shawl off my shoulders. It's warmer here in the kitchen with the wood stove going. "No, I'm okay."

She frowns. "You look sad. Is there something wrong?"

I back away from her touch. I don't like the idea that she can see into my head and read my thoughts about Amber being gone. "No, I'm fine. Really."

"Your sister called while you were out," Sally says.

"Amber?" Even though Rose lives here and it's still morning, wondering which sister called is justified; Rose is at her clinic up the street more often than she's home. She slept there last night to keep an eye on a critically injured owl.

"Yes. She has some exciting news, but she didn't want to share it until we were all together. I called Rose already, so she's on her way."

Dread fills my heart. "What's going on? Is it good news or bad?"

"Amber sure seems to think it's good."

That doesn't reassure me. These days, my sister's idea of good news doesn't always jibe with mine.

The front door creaks open and a female voice calls out from the foyer, "Is anybody home?" The door slams shut.

"We're in the kitchen," I say loudly so Rose will hear me.

She walks into the room and stops, her hands on her hips. "Where's the emergency? I got here as quickly as I could."

I roll my eyes, pointing at Sally behind her back. "Apparently, Amber has news."

"Since when is that an emergency?" Rose drops her alert stance and comes over to give me a quick hug. We're big on hugs in our family.

Sally is busy pulling a mixing bowl and saucepan out of the cupboard. "I just said it was really important; I didn't say it was an emergency."

"Please, Mom, you acted like the house was on fire."

Sally shrugs, smiling through her hair explosion. "What can I say? She sounded excited."

The telephone on the wall rings, interrupting the conversation. I stare at it, mistrust filling my heart. I know I'm overreacting, but I can't help it. So many changes have happened in Amber's life, and it feels like her personal evolution is spilling over into our house. I don't like change. I want things to stay the same as they've always been: three moms, three daughters, lots of love and laughter, and no one here to break us up into little pieces.

CHAPTER TWO

Rose walks over and grabs the handset off the wall. "Hello, Glenhollow Farms." There's a pause as she takes in the caller's response and smiles. "Hey, Amber. What's going on? I hear you have some big news." After listening for a few seconds, Rose looks at me. "She says she wants to tell us all at the same time. Go get the other moms."

I leave the kitchen without a word, walking over to the staircase and resting my hand on the wooden rail as I shout: "Barbara! . . . Carol! We have an important phone call downstairs! It's Amber!" My heart rate picks up as I try to imagine what my sister is going to say. *Is she getting married? Pregnant? Leaving the country and never coming back?* Knowing her, it could be anything.

Floorboards creak above my head as the women move to respond to my summons. I go back to the kitchen without them, my feet dragging. I have a really bad feeling about this.

Soon enough, we're all together standing by the phone. It's the old-fashioned kind, with a long spiral cord and a rotary dial. We try to fit our five heads over the earpiece so we can hear at the same time, but fail miserably—Sally's hair tickles my nose so much it makes me sneeze. I back away, giving the rest of them room. Listening to Amber's news firsthand isn't going to change anything.

Amber's voice comes out sounding tiny. "Can you guys hear me? I'm yelling so you can all hear me!"

"Yes, we can hear you," Carol says, also shouting.

"What's going on, baby?" Barbara asks. "You've got us on pins and needles over here." She's grinning broadly, the pride she has in her daughter shining out from her every pore.

"I have really big news," Amber says. "You guys are going to totally pee your pants."

I shake my head, my face going warm. This is not good. I don't want to pee my pants over anything she might say. It's going to involve the band. The men. The ones she shouldn't even be talking to. *We had an agreement.*

"Don't keep us waiting; tell us," Rose says.

I search Rose's face. She doesn't sound any more excited about this than I am, which makes me feel like I'm not totally alone. A trickle of relief comes in. It's good to know that not everything has to change.

"Okay, the big news is that the band is going to Japan for two weeks, and they want our moms to go with them!"

I'm not sure I heard her correctly. *Japan?* "What?" I'm asking anyone who will answer, but everyone is too stunned to respond.

All of a sudden, Barbara stiffens, her eyes opening wide. She speaks in whispered tones. "We're going to Japan. With the band."

I hear Amber's voice off in the distance, but my ears are ringing, making it impossible to understand what she's saying.

"You guys are going with the band to Japan?" Rose asks. She presses her ear closer to the phone, effectively blocking our moms out. "Are you serious? Red Hot wants to take them along?"

I don't hear the rest of it. I don't want to. I move over to Sally's recipe book and start pulling ingredients out that she's going to need. My stomach feels like it's rolling and flipping around inside my abdomen, making me nauseated. Our mothers are being dragged into this fantasy too. First Amber has left, and now they will too. *Will Rose go next? Will I be left here all alone?*

I look over my shoulder. Our mothers are going crazy, giggling and crying, hooting and hollering. They don't seem to care that the invitation is coming from Amber and not the actual band members. If it were me, I'd insist on a little more respect than that. But my mothers are not me. Twenty-five years ago they left these men behind for good reason, yet now they want to go running back. I just don't understand it *at all*.

I turn away so no one will see my tears. I pull out the flour and then the sugar, placing them on the counter.

"That's really exciting, Amber. I don't know if you're the one who put this together, but thanks. The moms are super thrilled." Rose sounds grateful, her tone matching her words.

I hold on to the edge of the counter, a wave of dizziness hitting me. Rose doesn't care. She doesn't care that these men are snapping their fingers and our mothers are running back like puppies craving attention. She's happy. She's okay with this. I want to scream with frustration, but I don't.

Of course I don't, because I know I'm letting my emotions get away from me again. I'm out of line. *What the heck is wrong with me?* Obviously, I need to get a grip on myself. It's just a two-week trip to Japan. It's not like my moms are selling the farm and leaving me forever. And besides . . . they're well into their forties; they should be able to make decisions about how they're going to live their lives without any fear of me judging them.

I take out the salt and place it on the counter next to the flour. A few deep breaths help take the edge off my runaway emotions. I make a mental note to go out into the trees later, to our meditation area, so I can re-center myself. I hate feeling so off-kilter, but even more so, I hate that it's those men again who are causing me to feel this way. They don't deserve to have that kind of power over me. I don't care what anyone says . . . they are not my fathers.

"When do we leave? What should we pack?" This is Carol who asks these questions—my mom, ever the practical one of the group. She's always been the take-charge type, and anyone who meets our family of women always assumes she's Amber's mom because they're so alike. But nope . . . she gave birth to me—the girl who'd rather run into the woods than deal with conflict face-to-face.

"Less than a week. Here . . . you take the phone and talk to her yourselves." I hear footsteps, and then Rose is next to me, her hand resting on my shoulder. "Are you okay?"

I nod vigorously, trying to convince myself as much as her. "Of course. Why wouldn't I be?" I don't need my anxiety to upset Rose. She has enough on her plate with all the sick animals in her clinic.

"I'm not going anywhere," she says. She's another woman in this house who's way too adept at reading my thoughts.

I try to smile away her worry. "Of course not. But if you want to go, you can." I shrug. "It's no big deal."

She looks at me funny. "I have no desire to be anywhere but here. And we can talk about this more later if you want, but I really need to skedaddle back to the clinic. Duty calls."

"No, I'm fine. I'll take care of their chores while they're away; it's no big deal. We have a couple of our regular, seasonal guests coming soon; they can help out with the laundry and household stuff that the moms usually do."

Rose leans in to give me a hug. I force myself not to cling to her in response. Instead, I withdraw to pull a wooden spoon from the drawer. Sally will need it to make those cream puffs.

"It's only temporary," Rose says. "They'll be back in no time."

"Yeah, sure. Of course." I focus on the recipe book in front of me, squinting my eyes to read the tiny print, hoping I'm being convincing at not caring.

Rose leaves my side and walks back over to the mothers, who are signing off the call. As soon as the phone is back on the cradle, I force myself to turn around and smile. I don't want to be a downer. This is a really exciting moment for them, something they've been dreaming about for over twenty years, probably. I know they've been feeling very sad and mixed up with all the things Amber's been telling them about the band, and this is their chance to get it straightened out and have all of their questions answered. They didn't get a chance to see the men when they were in New York helping Amber move in with Ty, but I know they wanted to really badly. And when the band was here for a short visit in the summer, none of them had the guts to get into any deep conversations about the choices they made way back when. They deserve this time together, and I'm not going to stand in the way of it.

They're holding hands, gibbering on and on about what they're going to pack, who they're going to hug first, and how they'll finally be backstage again. And then they start moving en masse through the door without a backward glance.

"What about the cream puffs?" I call out at Sally's back.

Her hand goes up above her head to wave as she disappears from view. "Sorry! No time for cream puffs. Gotta go to Japan!" They all shriek with laughter, the sound fading as they gain distance. Rose leaves behind them, on her way back to the clinic.

I turn around and start putting the necessary cream puff ingredients into the bowl, crying as I realize there's really no point in going through these motions when I'm going to be the only one left here to eat the damn things.

The phone rings again, and I turn to glare at it. Amber must have forgotten to give them some details about their trip. I wish I could ignore it and let the call go, but I can't; it's my sister, and I'd never abandon her.

"Hello."

"Hey there, Grumpy." Amber's tone makes her sound as excited as our mothers.

"I'm not grumpy. Just . . . tired." *Even though I had a solid eight hours of sleep.*

"I wanted to talk to you too, but they hung up the phone."

"They're a little excited."

"I should think so. Can you believe it? I'm finally getting them back together. It's going to be amazing."

I don't want to lie by agreeing or burst her bubble by telling the truth, so I say nothing.

"Anyway, listen . . . I need your help."

"Don't worry. I'll cover everything while they're gone."

"No, not that. Something else. I need you to come here."

"What?" She's not making sense. She wants to shut the farm down completely? She must be insane. "Come *there*? Why?"

She laughs. "To visit me. Duh."

"Oh." I imagine myself getting on a plane and flying into JFK like she did three months ago, and goose bumps jump out all over my skin. "I can't, really. It's going to be way too busy here without them."

"Rose can help out and so can Harold. I know he's there."

I chew my lip. "But there's the hives and . . ."

"Oh, please . . . Don't act like you're doing anything with my hives, you big fat liar. You'd let the honey overflow and the colonies swarm before you went anywhere near them. I get weekly reports from Smitty on the bees, so don't even try it."

I sigh. "We have animals, you know. Lots of them. Who's going to take care of them?"

"Harold and friends. I know for a fact there are at least four tents pitched out there right now. Our visitors love helping with the animals. And besides, it's not rocket science; you feed 'em, water 'em, and call the vet if there are any injuries. Done."

I glance out the window and scowl at all *eight* tents just beyond the window. "Why now?" I ask, trying not to be offended by her casual dismissal of my contribution to our farm's operations. "Why don't I wait until they get back from Japan?" If I can stall, it'll give me enough time to come up with a better excuse. I should have known the bee thing wouldn't work.

"Because, while the band is gone, this is the one short period of time where I don't have any work to do." She switches to her pitiful voice. "I'm all alone in the middle of New York City with no one to share it with."

"Why don't you come here, then?"

"Because! I still have to keep up with things. And I have to be here in case there are any emergencies. Shit happens all the time, without warning, and I'm the one who has to straighten it out. I can't do that long-distance. Besides, don't you want to see my new life? See my new apartment? It's huge, and I'm going to be all alone up here." She sounds pitiful.

I'm surprised by this; to hear her talk, you'd think she has a hundred new friends by now. "Why not Rose?"

"Because I know very well she has at least ten sick animals that need her there at the clinic or they'll die."

She has a point. No one will die if I'm not here. And it's not that I want anyone or anything depending on me for their lives, but it makes me feel very . . . expendable.

"I don't know . . ." The idea of going to that city literally makes me sick . . . sicker than I was already feeling over the Japan news.

"Pleeeease? Pretty please? I'm so lonely. I miss you. I miss *us*."

Her words grab me by the heart and squeeze. I can't breathe for a few seconds. To imagine that she could be missing me as much as I'm missing her is too much to ignore. "Fine," I say, sighing loud and long. "When?"

"I already booked you a ticket out in five days. You have a little time to make arrangements."

Typical Amber. She knew she was going to convince me. Asking me was merely a pretense. "I can't stay long."

"Ten days."

The thought of ten days off the farm makes me panic. "That's a long time."

"It'll fly by. And you'll love it here, I promise." She pauses and then talks over my response. "Oh, shit, Ty's here. I have to go. Kiss, kiss! Love you! See you soon!" And then she's gone. Just like that, she disappears from my life again.

I hang up the phone and stare at it. I just got railroaded into spending ten days in Manhattan with my sister, who I am now totally convinced is as crazy as a soup sandwich.

I worry what this little trip is going to do to me. Will I be crazy too by the time I return? Will my life get turned upside down and inside out like Amber's was when she went there? I don't want anything to change. I like my world to be comfortable and predictable, and this trip represents the opposite of that.

It only took a week for that city to change Amber's thoughts and plans for her future. I pray the effects of being in Manhattan for ten days won't be lasting on me. When this trip is over, I want to come back to my life here—taking care of the animals, selling our products weekly at the farmers' market, and maintaining a home that people love to visit. That's it. I don't need a fancy job or fat paycheck to see value in myself. No way, José. New York needs to *stay* in New York and leave me out of its nonsense. I resolve then and there to make sure nothing about me or my outlook on life changes as a result of my visit with Amber.

CHAPTER THREE

I can't believe I'm actually here in New York City. Our mothers already came out for a week to help Amber move in to her apartment, so why does she need me? Surely she's already seen the Empire State Building and all those other places that Manhattan is famous for. And she has new friends that fill up this new life of hers. Why doesn't she just go out with them? Why did I need to leave *my* life behind? I can't quite drown out the mean-girl answer that echoes faintly in my head, saying my life is the less important of the two.

Maybe I should have insisted she come to the farm instead, but our mothers were so excited when they left, I didn't have the heart to do it. I'm never the one to raise a fuss or create conflict, so it was no surprise to anyone including myself when I got on the plane in Maine and headed to JFK, despite the fact that I have no desire to live in the Big Apple, not even temporarily. And now here I am, waiting for my sister to pick me up. My plane was early, so I'm at the curb with my bag, searching for signs that my ride has arrived.

Someone taps me on the shoulder. I turn, praying it's not a stranger asking me for directions. I wouldn't know how to tell someone to find a bathroom, let alone anything else around here. Besides, I really don't like talking to people I don't know. *Stranger danger.*

"Surprise!" a woman shouts, throwing her arms out.

I almost don't recognize Amber at first. *Is she taller?* Her hair is different... shorter and wavier. She's wearing jeans with a very stylish and colorful top, and her smile is so big it's nearly blinding.

I embrace my sister, holding her close. She even smells different. "It feels like it's been forever since I've seen you," I mumble into her shoulder. My heart hurts.

"It *has* been forever. Three months forever, and you are in *big* trouble for not coming to see me sooner." She squeezes me harder, taking my breath away.

She has invited me to visit a couple times before this trip, but I've always said no. I love my sister more than anything in the world, but I'm not a city person. I like fresh air, peace and quiet, and space. The things that she's been describing herself doing are exciting for her, but for me they sound like anxiety-inducing catastrophes I'd rather avoid.

Case in point: she regularly buys hot dogs for a homeless stranger who asks her if she's going to have sex with her food. Who says that kind of thing? Weirdos. And who hangs out with that kind of person? Apparently, my sister does. Like I said: soup sandwich.

"Look at you . . . fresh off the farm." She pinches my cheeks and then squishes them together, leaning in to kiss me right on the mouth. "Gosh, I've missed your pretty face."

I can't deny that Amber's welcome is warm and loving. Even if she is turning into a New York cuckoo bird, at least she hasn't lost her love for her family, and for that I'm grateful. "I think somebody's a little bit lonely in New York City." I smile at Amber, her excitement infectious. Now I see why she wanted me here. If this is the greeting I'm getting, she must be feeling very out of her element, alone in a strange city filled with people she doesn't understand or who don't understand her. Maybe there's hope that she'll return to the farm instead of making this place her new home. I *could* try to work that angle with her while I'm here . . .

"Just jonesing for some of my Emmie sugar."

"What?" *Dang*. She's more than lonely . . . she may actually be going Jack-Nicholson-in-*The-Shining* crazy. "Do you think it's possible you're working too hard?" I ask. I pray that's the explanation and not that she's actually changing into a person who comfortably uses the terms *Emmie sugar* and *jonesing*.

She waves away my concerns. "Nah. Just go with it, Emmie baby. Where's your stuff?" She looks around me.

"It's right here." I pull my wheely bag up to my side so she can see it better. It was a gift from Rose. She found it on sale at the local drugstore when she went into town for veterinary supplies.

"That can't possibly have all your stuff in it." She looks at me, confused and maybe a little cranky. "You know you're staying here for longer than two days, right?"

I roll my eyes at her insult. "Yes, I know I'm here for ten days." I shrug. "I don't have a lot of clothes, but it doesn't matter because it's not like I'm going to a fancy ball or anything."

She wiggles her eyebrows at me. "Ooh, you're already giving me ideas about fun things we can do." She loops her arm through mine and starts pulling me down the sidewalk.

I can't tell if she's joking or not, but just in case, I need to set her straight before her crazy mind goes any farther down that road. "Just so you know, I am *not* going to any ball or other fancy-schmancy event, so you can get that thought out of your head right now." I swear if she tries to make me, I'll lock myself in the bathroom and refuse to come out until my plane is scheduled to leave.

At this point, I wouldn't put it past her to try and set that up. Amber has become this whole other person since moving to New York City. She's always going out, attending events and parties, meeting important and famous people. I don't know how she does it. Our lives up until just a few months ago were all about being on a farm and taking care of animals and the occasional lost soul. Now she's running a business empire, second in command only to the band manager, who's been in that job for thirty years. Two days ago, my mother showed me a magazine article that had Amber's face next to it with the headline MOVERS AND SHAKERS IN THE MUSIC INDUSTRY. I have only one word for that: *insanity.*

"We're going to do all kinds of fun things together; don't you worry your pretty little head about it." She stops next to a limousine.

"What's this?" I ask. I'm pretty sure she's pulling my leg.

A man comes out of the driver's-side door to open the trunk. Then he walks over and takes my bag without a word.

"This is your ride. And that is Mr. Blake." Amber switches to her military commander voice that she used to adopt when imitating an angry parent. "He does *not* like using first names."

I glance from my sister to the driver. I sense some sort of joke between them, but I don't get what it is. "Okay, if you say so. Nice to meet you, Mr. Blake."

"Likewise." He comes over and opens the back door for us and then stares off into space.

My sister nudges me on the shoulder and whispers loudly, "This is the part where you get into the car."

I lower my voice. "You brought a *limo*? Why on earth would you do that?" She knows I don't like drawing attention to myself. She might as well have picked me up with neon lights wrapped around her head. She kind of did with that shirt she's got on, now that I think about it.

I can't ignore her pushing on my shoulder anymore, so I climb inside and slide across the smooth leather seats. It smells like a new car. I've only ever experienced that ambiance once before in my life, when Amber and I hitched a ride into town with someone who was visiting the farm to buy some of her honey and three dozen of my freshest eggs for his restaurant. I was worried I was going to leave sweat stains from my legs on the seats; it was really hot that day and I was wearing shorts. I would never have done it if not for Amber insisting it would be faster than walking or riding our bikes. She was always getting me into uncomfortable situations, disregarding and overriding my anxiety with her sense of adventure. It feels like it's happening again. Right now. *Ugh, I hate this.* I hunt for my seat belt.

"All the other cars were being used, and taxis can be a problem sometimes if the press follows me," she offers as explanation. "I don't like it any more than you do. Come on, get in, get in."

"I *am* in." I reach over and tug her hair.

"Don't start that." She points at me. "Buckle your seat belt."

I pause to do as she orders, mumbling my response under my breath. "Somebody got bossy while she was away." *Extra bossy, that is.*

Amber lets out a long sigh and stares out the side window, all her spark disappearing instantly. It's like watching the end of a Fourth of July fireworks show, when all the colors and light fade to black.

Guilt threatens to choke me. I'm letting my fears bleed over into frustration at her, and I shouldn't. She's just being Amber, which isn't a bad thing at all. I reach over and take her hand, wiggling it a little. "Don't be mad at me. I'm only messing with you."

She shakes her head and looks at me as Mr. Blake gets into the driver's seat. "No, you're right. I am super bossy. I need to stop."

"Don't worry, I'm used to it; you've always been that way."

She leans over and pokes me in the ribs to tickle me. I fend her off with some solid girly slaps. She's never been able to defeat me once I get those going.

"Quit," she hisses. "Mr. Blake will never take me seriously if he sees you slapping me."

The man glances in his rearview mirror, rolling his eyes before he looks away. I'm not positive, but I think he likes my sister, even though he's trying to pretend he doesn't. But who could blame him? She's the funnest, silliest, most exciting person I know . . . And now she's gone from the farm, and I miss her so much it makes my heart ache.

I love my sister Rose too, of course. And even though she's so busy with her animal clinic I hardly interact with her these days, at least I see her more often than I do Amber. Rose will never leave the farm for sure. She won't even *visit* this city. Lucky for her, she has a great excuse—any number of sick and dying animals in the clinic that need her tender and expert ministrations. If I didn't hate to see their suffering so much, I'd work there more often, and then maybe I could use it as an excuse to force Amber to come to us. It's seriously tempting.

As we make our way around the airport traffic, I glance at my sister, older than I am by a week and more experienced in the big world by a mile. She's busy answering someone's text, her fingers flying over the buttons of her new phone. I'm glad to be with her, but this trip is a reminder of why I have to come all the way to New York City to do that: she's gone for good. This is her new home. There's no way I'll be able to convince her to come back to the farm, and I was fooling myself to even entertain the idea. A melancholy descends on me that I have to work to keep hidden.

The drive from the airport into the city slowly helps me to forget my problems, though. I've seen pictures of Manhattan before, but photographs cannot do this place justice. The buildings are so high, it's impossible to see the top of them from inside the car. We're surrounded by myriad sounds, smells, and hard surfaces. So far I've seen nothing cheerful or soft about New York besides my sister, but because I wasn't expecting anything different, it doesn't bother me. Like Amber said, this place is electric.

At home, if I were to see a limousine driving by, I would stop and stare at it, trying to figure out who was inside. They must be pretty commonplace around here, though, because nobody is looking at us as we make our way through the city or stop for traffic. The windows are tinted black, so for all they know, I could be the president of the United States, or Oprah, for God's sake. But they don't care.

I think everybody is too busy minding their own very important business to worry about somebody else's. Everyone looks like they're on a mission to get somewhere fast. Several women are wearing running shoes with their office clothing. They look a little silly—all-business from the ankles up and all-athlete from the ankles down—but they're probably more comfortable than they would be running in stilettos.

I glance at my sister's feet. She has heeled boots on. They're not as high as some of the shoes she's told me she's been wearing, but they're more fashionable than any I ever saw her in on the farm. Her outward appearance has changed so much; I wonder how much of her insides have changed.

I look down at my casual slip-on shoes, wondering how I'm ever going to fit in here. Are these even legal? The fashion police are going to arrest me if they see me in these well-worn, scuffed flats. It doesn't really matter that I'm not wearing the latest styles, because I'm only visiting, but still . . . it would be nice to not stick out like a sore thumb. I promised to stay for ten days, and I will do that because I love my sister and I want to support her while her boyfriend and our mothers are out of town, but if she thinks she's going to bring me to a party, she'd better think again . . .

"The first thing I'm going to do is take you to Gray's Papaya for a hot dog. You're gonna love it."

A trickle of worry leaks into my heart. "Isn't that where that guy is? The one who says all those perverted things to you?"

"Ray?" She laughs. "Yeah. He'll be there. I bought him a present. I can't wait to give it to him."

"What did you buy him?" I can't even imagine what she'd buy a person like that.

She pats me on the leg. "Just wait and see. It's silly."

I shake my head as I look out the window. My sister is full of surprises. And to be honest, I'm not so sure that I am going to be able to appreciate the gift she bought for this man Ray. She said it's silly. What could that mean? Silly as in it'll make me laugh or make me cringe? I'm afraid it's the latter. It's clear I don't know Amber that well anymore, and I don't think she knows me either. It's more than depressing.

As we wind through traffic, I have to fight back tears that I can't really explain. *Am I crying because I miss the girl she used to be or because she's left me behind?* Regardless, it either makes me a whiner baby or a selfish brat, and neither is any good at all. I spend the rest of the ride to her apartment scolding myself for being a boob and forcing myself to cheer the heck up.

CHAPTER FOUR

The chauffeur takes us around the back side of my sister's huge apartment building and drives into a parking garage with a big metal gate that closes automatically behind us. After carefully negotiating twists and turns that put us several levels belowground, he drops us off at a door that has a digital code-reader box on the wall next to it. He takes my suitcase from the trunk and sets it down beside me.

"Thank you." I feel like we should tip him or something, but my sister doesn't make a move toward her purse.

He leaves with a nod, getting into the limo and driving out of the garage.

I feel like such a rube. Of course you don't tip a personal driver. *Duh.* I haven't been out in the world much, but I have seen the movie *Pretty Woman*, and there was never any tipping of Darryl the limo driver.

My sister digs into her bag and comes out with a small black key fob. When she touches it to the code-reader box that has a red light on it, the indicator turns green and the door clicks open.

"This place is like a prison," I say, wondering if the key to her apartment will be as big as a jail keeper's.

"That's right. We keep all the bad guys *out*, though." She pulls the door open and leads us into a small antechamber in front of some elevator doors. It smells like damp concrete and paint in here. My suitcase bangs over the threshold, and the noise of it echoes out behind me into the garage.

"Is all this security really necessary?" I know there are some strange people in New York City, but it seems like my sister is being a little overly paranoid.

She presses the call button for the elevator. "You probably won't have the opportunity to see Ty or any of the rest of the band on this trip, but when you come back another time, you'll see why it's necessary. If you see them in public, anyway."

I'm getting the distinct impression that my sister hasn't been giving us the whole story about her life here. "That sounds pretty scary, actually."

The elevator arrives, and she holds the door open so I can get through with my bag.

"Not really. You get used to it."

I'm not sure I could ever do that. My sister is tougher than I am, though, so it's not surprising to me that she's adapting so easily. She single-handedly managed the beehives at our farm from the age of twelve, something I could never do, even at twenty-five. Being stung by a bee once as a kid was all I needed to know about honey harvesting—it's definitely not my thing. But Amber doesn't let what she considers minor setbacks to keep her from meeting her goals. Once she decides to do something, it's done. Take me visiting her in Manhattan, for example. Like most people, I'm powerless when standing in the face of her determination.

One of our neighbors, Smitty, has taken over her hives—thank goodness, because I wasn't crazy or stupid enough to do it myself. I understand my sister wanted to leave and that bees are critically important to our life on Earth . . . and I'm supporting her as much as I can . . . but those bees? *No way.* Thank goodness for Smitty. I just wish I hadn't slept with him that one time. It makes it awkward to see him around the farm when he's there checking on things. I keep an eye out for him, and so far I have always managed to be busy in the house whenever he comes by.

The elevator doors shut, ready to take us up to the top floor—the penthouse. My sister has to slide a plastic card into the control panel to make the buttons work. I shake my head at this additional security measure. A person might be able to break into the garage and that electronically controlled door, but they'd be stuck here in this elevator without the proper access credentials. This is such a completely different world from the one I'm used to. We don't even lock our doors at Glenhollow Farms.

"Once we get you settled into your room, we can go out and grab some lunch," she says.

"At the hot dog place?" I try to sound enthusiastic.

She throws her arm over my shoulders and squeezes me up against her. "Exactly."

After a very long and slightly nerve-racking trip up and up and up, the elevator finally opens into the foyer of my sister's apartment. The opulence hits me like a slap in the face—marble, silk, peacock feathers, gold, sparkling things, artwork that reminds me of a Jackson Pollock rip-off . . . It looks like an interior decorating warehouse exploded in here.

"Wow." The word pops out of my mouth before I can filter it. I hope she doesn't take offense.

"Pretty swanky, huh?" She puts her hand around my waist and pulls me into the foyer because my legs have forgotten how to work. "Home, sweet home. It came already professionally decorated. Come on . . . follow me. I'll show you where your room is."

Professionally decorated by a blind person, maybe. That would explain all the crushed velvet and silk, anyway.

I walk behind her down a long hallway, passing door after door. Some of them are open to various living spaces: one of them is a cinema, another is an office, and two more are bedrooms. None of them have that wow factor I saw in the foyer, thank goodness. I was starting to think an alien had taken over my sister's brain and caused her to forget that gold lamé is something that should be avoided.

"This is your room." She stops in the entrance and waits for me to go in first.

I step into the space. Considering what I saw in the foyer, it's not overly decorated. In fact, I may go so far as to say it's pretty in its simplicity. And it's large too—almost the same size as our living room back home.

"Wowie, wow, wow. This is really cute." I leave my bag by the door and walk in slowly. The carpet is thick and soft, a shade that reminds me of the pale peachy-pink flowers that grow on vines up the side of our house. The dark wood bed has four smooth posts that are really tall but not high enough to reach the vaulted ceilings outlined in several stacked layers of crown molding. Pink silk drapes hang on the wall opposite the door, matching the rose-and-green coverlet folded at the foot of the mattress.

"Look out the windows. Check out your view." Amber is beaming as she ushers me forward.

I walk over and push one of the drapes aside; it's heavier than I was expecting, with a thick white liner weighing it down and ensuring that sunlight can't penetrate. What I see beyond the window takes my breath away. "Is that the Empire State Building?" I never imagined it would be this imposing in person, and I'm still miles away from it, I think; it's hard to tell from up here.

"Yep." Amber sounds proud, as if she put it there herself.

"This is really incredible." Now I'm getting an inkling of why she might want to live here; it is pretty impressive. If I never had to leave the apartment, I might actually be able to stay here too. Not forever, but for ten days? Sure. No problem. Some of the heaviness lifts from my heart. Maybe New York won't be quite as terrible as I feared.

"Why don't you take fifteen *seconds* to unpack your bag and then come with me into the kitchen?"

I turn to look at her smarty-pants face. She's smirking at me.

"Ha, ha, you're hilarious." *Fifteen seconds.* My sister thinks she's so funny. Now I feel like a hick, having brought only two outfits.

She won't leave until I prove her right, so I put my bag on the king-size bed and unzip it. I pull out the small stack of clothing from inside as my sister opens the top drawer of the dresser for me. I put everything inside it and close it with my hip.

"See?" She looks at her watch. "Oh, even less. Ten seconds. I totally called it."

I roll my eyes and go back to my bag. "I have toiletries too, you know." I deliberately slow my movements. I'll be damned if it's only going to take me fifteen seconds to unpack my sad, sorry little suitcase.

She walks over to another door and opens it. "This is your bathroom. You don't have to share it with *anybody*."

I collect my toothbrush, mini toothpaste, and hairbrush, and walk over to join her, peering inside. What I see is more opulence packed into a space larger than anyone could need.

"Holy mackerel. This bathroom is the biggest one I've ever seen in my entire life." The walls and surfaces are all marble and glass. Thick nubby cotton mats lie on the floor in front of the shower, bathtub, and sink. I can see everything beyond where I'm standing thanks to the angled mirrors; farther back, there's a desk and chair for putting on makeup—something I won't be using because I don't wear any—and large walk-in closets to the left and right.

"And it's all yours." She leans in very close and stares at me. "And you don't have to *share* it."

I have to chuckle. The number of times we've fought over access to our one, tiny bathroom at the farm is not lost on me. "Okay, I have to admit, it's awesome." I place my toiletries on the counter. They look so tiny all by themselves on the massive marble slab.

She claps with happiness. "See? I told you you'd love it." She grabs me by the hand and pulls me out of the room. "Come on. I want to show you the kitchen."

I follow her down the long hallway and pass through a family room big enough for twenty people, before I find myself inside a kitchen that could easily cater a large dinner party. The appliances are huge, and all of them stainless steel or black. The counters are gray-and-black granite, and the windows have views as spectacular as those from my bedroom.

"Do you actually cook in here?" I'd be afraid of leaving a stain on something. The countertops are cold against my fingertips—so different from the wood ones at the farm that have always felt warm to me, even in winter.

"To be honest, not often. We order in a lot." She walks over and opens the fridge. "Look. We're stocked up for weeks."

Every single shelf in her refrigerator and freezer is jammed full of clear glass containers with colorful plastic lids on them, and they're all labeled. I read a few of them aloud: "Butternut squash lasagna. Red curried lentils with baba ghanoush and pita on the side." I look at her, flabbergasted. "Did you *make* this stuff?" I don't know my sister *at all* anymore.

She grins. "Are you kidding me? You know I don't cook."

The relief that flows through me is almost dizzying. I thought my entire world had just turned inside out.

She shuts the doors to the refrigerator and freezer. "It's a service. They have a menu for the week, we order what we want, and then they bring all the fresh groceries in here and cook it, box it up, put it in the fridge, and leave."

"Wow. You have your own personal chef." I can't even imagine what that must be like. I've cooked so many lunches and dinners for our family at the farm, I've lost count. I started when I was eleven, which means I've been doing it for more than half my life now, and I know exactly how much work and prep time went into making those meals in her fridge. They must have cost her and Ty a fortune. But I guess since they're making the big bucks now, they can afford it.

A very unkind voice creeps into my head and speaks my inner, most hateful thought: *Sellout.*

I immediately tamp it down. My sister is not a sellout. She's working hard and earning her money. The band offered her a ten-million-dollar fortune and she turned it down, just like Rose and I did.

Amber continues her explanation, clueless to my inner battle. "No, not a personal chef, really; close, but not quite. This way, we have some of the benefits of a personal chef, but they don't live here with us and invade our privacy."

"I'm starting to get the impression that your privacy is pretty important to you." This is so strange to me, considering we were both raised on a hippie commune where anyone and everyone was welcome to live, no questions asked. All a person ever did to be a part of our extended family was be kind and work on the farm somehow—harvesting, planting, building, cleaning . . . Our mothers were always very generous and accommodating.

Amber pulls two glasses from a nearby cupboard before grabbing a bottle of wine from the refrigerator. It's a little early in the day for drinking, but today is not a normal day. I will happily drink whatever she's offering . . . anything that will make this easier for me.

"It is *very* important," she says, nodding. "I never realized *how* important, though, until I kept having it taken away from me." She pulls the cork out of the bottle with a pop. "There's one thing I've learned after being around the band for these last few months: you always pay a price for fame, and the first thing to go is your private life."

The word *fame* makes me think of how proud Barbara is of her daughter. "You know your mom is saving all the clippings that mention your name or have your face on them. There're already two huge scrapbooks in our living room next to the new television." The television was a gift from Amber, so we could stay current with the band. I never watch it. We had a TV before, but not the pretty flat-screen or the satellite plan we have now.

"I know. Believe me, she's told me all about it." Amber rolls her eyes.

"They're really proud of you. I am too."

She smiles distractedly, making sure she doesn't spill the wine as she pours. "I'm proud of me too. I feel like I'm doing a really good job. Things are going great for the band and Ty."

I take a full wineglass from the counter and hold it up for a toast. "Here's to you and all of your amazing success that you totally deserve."

"Thank you, sweetie." She touches her stemware to mine and takes a sip. "So what are *you* going to do with the rest of your life?" She asks this with a twinkle in her eye, oblivious to how it will affect me.

Her question throws me for a complete loop. I wasn't expecting it. I should have an answer ready for her, something that just slips right off my tongue, but I don't. After seeing all the evidence of her success around me, I have to ask myself the same question she just did: *What do I want to do with my life?* I know she didn't mean anything cruel by it, but it hurts that I don't have an answer. Do I have a plan? I thought I did, but now that I think about it for two seconds, I realize my goal all along has been to just keep doing what I've always done. Does that count as a plan? I fear in Amber's world that it doesn't. And now I don't even know if it counts as one in my world. *Dammit.* Just two hours into my visit, and I'm already questioning my life's purpose. *What. The. Hell.*

She uses her glass to point around the room. "All this could be yours, you know."

I'm confused. "Why? What are you talking about?"

"Well, you could come and work for the band, or you just take the ten million bucks they offered you."

My jaw drops open in shock. "Did *you* take the money?" *Is that how she affords this place with all of its prison-like security?*

She frowns. "No, of course I didn't."

"Then why would *I* take the money?" I'm getting angry. It's like she's suggesting something about me that's not very nice.

"I'm just saying . . ." She puts her hand on my arm. "I know you don't like to get out much, and the farm doesn't have a lot of . . . opportunities. So if you need some money or want to get some things for yourself, it would be really easy to do that."

I back away, breaking contact. "But you know what that money means."

She looks at me and shakes her head, almost as if she pities me. "It's not like that. I've gotten to know them a lot better since I've been working with them."

I feel completely betrayed. Maybe it's a bit overly dramatic, but we've been put through the wringer these past few months back at Glenhollow, and apparently she either doesn't get it or she doesn't care. "We've talked about this so many times, Amber. Why are you acting like everything has suddenly changed?"

She sighs and puts her wineglass down, picking at her perfectly manicured fingernails. Her gaze drops. "You know, when we agreed not to take the money, it was because we thought it was some sort of payoff . . . like a super-lame apology for ignoring us for twenty-five years."

I work really hard to not growl at her. "Which is *exactly* what it is."

She looks up at me. "But I've told you what they and their attorney, Lister, told me. You remember, right? They didn't know about us until just recently. They found out through Darrell. He's the one who's trying to cause them all kinds of trouble—the guy who used to be the bass player back in the beginning."

The more she talks, the angrier I become. I know she's trying to explain herself, and I'm trying to listen, too, but all I'm seeing is red and all I'm hearing is *blah, blah, blah.*

I work to keep my temper controlled. "I realize that Darrell is the one who outed you as a daughter of one of the band members to the press, and he's the reason why you had to move into this place and get all the security to protect your privacy, but that doesn't change the fact that those men tried to give us that money because they felt guilty."

Her lips press together for a few seconds before she responds. "I don't see it that way anymore."

Be fair. Listen. This is your sister. My conscience is trying so hard to keep me on track, I have to at least try to obey it. I inhale deeply and exhale completely before I continue. "Okay, so . . . tell me how you see it." I take a generous sip of wine, almost finishing the glass, trying to stall her inevitable argument. Maybe it'll help to have her explain to me how suddenly thirty million dollars from absent fathers isn't guilt money. I'm not going to run from this, as much as I might want to. I shouldn't have to fear my sister just because she's sharing what she considers to be the truth with me.

"Let's go sit down." She points to a smaller room off the kitchen. "It'll be more comfortable."

I consider arguing but decide against it. Refusing to sit down would be childish, and we're beyond that—at least when we're having serious conversations. I follow her into the room and sit down next to her on the couch with a few cushions between us. She turns sideways and rests her wineglass on her leg.

"Our fathers, whichever band members they are, did not find out about us being alive until the band manager, Ted, finally confessed to what he'd done, just a few months ago, which he did after Darrell threatened to blackmail the band with the information. The money is an apology . . . not for being bad people, but for all the missed opportunities, for the child support they would have paid if they'd known we existed. They aren't bad men, Em. They're really nice. They feel as robbed of the relationship as we do. They also respect and love our moms, so they're not interested in casting blame or causing arguments over it; they just want a chance to be the fathers they are or could have been."

I take a moment to let that digest. My short conclusion is that I don't really believe it, and I don't think Amber does either. "So, if it's all hunky-dory now, how come you're still not taking the money?" I stare her down, daring her to answer.

She shrugs. "I'm . . . not comfortable doing that at this point in time. I prefer to just work for them for now."

Relief flows through me. She hasn't totally been brainwashed, at least. "Yes. Exactly. I'm still not comfortable with it either, regardless of what you call it." I pause, taking a few breaths to calm my emotions. My sister is not the enemy here. "You told us before that Ted was behind everything . . . that he gave our mothers the money to pay for the farm. I'm still not quite sure why he did what he did—kept our mothers' pregnancies from the band and forced our mothers out. He pretty much admitted he completely messed with their lives. What did he expect to gain by that, by hurting all those people? How is he even keeping his job now that they know what he did—if they're supposedly all mad about it?"

Amber traces the rim of her glass with her finger. "At the time, Ted thought he was doing his job . . . keeping the band on top and focused on building their fan base . . . meeting contractual demands by their record label, which he truly believed they'd no longer be able to do if they were focused on babies and wives. The band members themselves said enough times that families were not welcome on tour and that they weren't interested in having families at that point in their careers. That's how he's justifying his actions now."

"And you forgot those facts, I guess, when you forgave them?" Seems pretty convenient to me; for them, anyway, but not so much for us or our moms.

"No, I didn't forget anything," Amber says, clearly annoyed with me. "I realize they carry some of the blame here, but it's minimal. The fact is, they were never told about us."

I hate that Amber has become their advocate. Doesn't she hurt inside over this like I do? It sure doesn't seem like it. "But they never tried to contact our moms either," I point out. "If they had, things would have turned out a lot differently." We would have had *fathers*, and that's no small thing, especially to three little girls who dreamed and talked of these mysterious beings often over the years. Amber is forgetting that part of our shared past, I guess.

"Maybe. But is it fair for us to crucify them for something they *should have* or *might have* done?"

I shrug, not exactly comfortable with saying my answer out loud, which is *Yes, I do think it's fair to blame them.* Amber will become angrier about it than she already is if I continue to call her out on this, but I do think it's fair to call a spade a spade. They rejected our moms in word and deed. Three precious and pregnant young women—our mothers— were willing to give these men their hearts and souls, and yet, they were rejected . . . and then a henchman sent them packing. What kind of men allow that to happen? Amber has just confirmed that's what went down, so it's no longer just conjecture. No. Sorry. The kind of men who would do something like that are not welcome in my life.

"What about Ted?" I ask, not yet willing to totally let this slide. "Seems like they'd be pretty angry at him." Or they're not, because he did exactly what they wanted him to do. *Ha!* They have Amber so bamboozled . . .

She pauses, shrugging as she stares into her glass. "Who knows? He may have lost his job now that they know the extent of his treachery; the jury is still out on that." She sighs. "The fact is, now that I know his job a little more, his dedication to the music, I can kind of see in a *tiny* way why he might have thought he was doing the right thing."

I feel like I'm having a heart attack . . . *She understands how he could do it? What?*

"But that's not important. The important thing is, once Darrell started making waves, they got the whole story from Ted and Lister, and

Ted came clean. Call it a crisis of conscience, maybe . . . I don't know. But as soon as they found out that these women they still remembered fondly had left under false pretenses and pregnant, they immediately hired a private investigator through their attorney to find them. To find *us*."

It all sounds too neat to me. Too convenient. There are too many holes in the story. Normally, Amber is so sharp, but she obviously has blinders on in this situation. "I'm not sure I can believe the band knew nothing about our mothers or us all this time. Why didn't they ever try to find our moms before? How could these men not have known our mothers were pregnant? Didn't anyone stay in touch? Didn't they hear rumors, at least? Two men totally involved with the band—the manager and their bassist—knew, but the rest of them didn't? That's a pretty big secret for people to keep for all that time, don't you think?"

"I don't have all the answers. Not yet, anyway. Nobody's been talking about this stuff very much because they've been so busy getting Ty up to speed and preparing for their trip to Japan. And you know our mothers . . . The only thing they're thinking about right now is being groupies again. Explaining and rehashing their pasts is probably the last thing on their minds. Heck, knowing them, they'll never bring it up. You know how they are about letting bygones be bygones. They've always been about forgiveness and not judging."

"Yeah. I guess now we know why," I say bitterly.

"You don't begrudge them this second chance, do you?" Amber asks, a hint of censure in her voice.

I smile sadly, shaking my head at the image of our moms finding out they were going with the band to Japan. I wasn't there to see their reunion, but I can picture it perfectly in my mind. Sally probably lost consciousness. "No, I don't. Not really. They are so crazy. They're going on fifty but acting like they're twenty."

"I know." Amber pauses, searching my face. "Are you mad at them?"

"No." I sigh, long and loud. To be mad at my mothers for being in love, for making stupid decisions when they were just kids . . . now that would be unfair. "Why would I be? They're happy."

She shrugs. "I don't know. I'm just not getting the impression that you're happy about any of this." She uses her wineglass to indicate the room, and maybe her life along with it.

I pull in a deep breath and let it out slowly, hoping I can calm my nerves and my emotions enough to be fair. "I will admit . . . I am very confused and unsettled right now."

My sister scoots closer to me on the couch. "What can I do to help? You know I don't like to see you sad."

I shake my head. "There's nothing you can do. I just need time to adjust. I guess maybe I'm one of those people who has a difficult time dealing with change."

"Rose told me you were painting again a while ago, but then I didn't hear anything more about it, and I haven't seen any of your new work. How's that going?"

"It's not." And I don't want to talk about it, so I hope she takes the hint when I stare at the wall and don't say anything else. My sisters are usually pretty good about being sensitive to my creative issues. The moment I realized our lives were going to be drastically altered by Amber's decision to go to the city, my creative vibe vanished. But I don't want her to feel bad about that; it's not her fault that my emotions are so tightly strung sometimes.

"What else is bothering you?"

I look at her, wondering how she could be so clueless. She used to be tuned in to my emotions and unspoken thoughts. "I guess what's bothering me is that this is all so easy for you."

She frowns. "What's so easy for me?"

"All this!" I throw my arm up, losing my tenuous hold on my temper. "This place! This life! You're in love with this guy Ty, but you hardly know him, you two have this ultra-secure, high-rise prison apartment, and you're living like the Prince and Princess of Wales." I want to stop, but I can't. "And you're working for these *men*, who for twenty-five years and with unlimited funds never bothered to check up on the women they supposedly loved? And you're, like, best friends with them now? How does that happen?!"

Silence descends between us, and the only things I can hear are the hum of the refrigerator in the next room, the pounding of my pulse in my ears, and my heavy breathing. I cannot believe I just said all of that out loud. My chest is burning.

"Wow. That was a mouthful." Amber sits deeper into the couch cushions, no longer smiling at me.

I wilt and my voice comes out as a whine. "Why did you ask me if you didn't want to hear the answer?" Now I'm mad at both of us. I should have kept my mouth shut. I'm never one to make waves, and this is why; I hate it when I don't get along with my sisters. I always regret speaking my mind; it causes conflict and hurt feelings . . . two things I hate being responsible for.

"I *did* want to hear the answer. I just wasn't expecting that *particular* answer. Don't get mad. I'm not angry with you, I'm just processing."

My response is to pout, to keep from bursting into tears. "Process it with a nicer look on your face, would you, please?"

She gives me a half smile. "You are such a brat sometimes."

I feel like crying, but mostly it's just emotional exhaustion fueling that desire. I had no intention of coming here to confront my sister over things that don't really matter in the long run. Whatever I say about these men is not going to change the trajectory of either of our lives. Amber is too stubborn to move off the track she's taking, and I'm too smart to fall for the baloney being served around here. Regardless, it won't change the fact that she and I love each other and will always be close sisters . . . and that relationship is far more important than any other. "I'm not a brat. I'm just telling you what I think and what I feel. I'll shut up about it now."

She nods. "That's fair. You don't have to shut up about anything. I do think it would help you to talk to the band, though. It really helped me. They've tried so many times to contact you, to set up a meeting, but you never take their calls. They'd come to see you, you know, if you didn't want to come here."

I shake my head. "I'm not interested and neither is Rose. We've told you several times, Amber. You need to let it go. We sent you here to handle everything, and you did. You told them exactly what we wanted them to hear: we're not interested in their money, and we're not interested in DNA tests or father-daughter relationships. Nothing has changed." I plead for forgiveness with my eyes, not wanting her to feel bad about the things I've said. "I know you're working for the money they pay you, so that's not the same as taking ten million dollars from them for nothing other than sharing genes."

She nods. "I get it. But you know, I like this place. I like this life. I think it really suits me. I don't think it makes me a bad person."

"It *does* suit you." I reach out and touch her arm. "Perfectly. I'm not saying otherwise. And I'm not saying it's a bad thing that it suits you either. I'm actually kind of jealous that you found something that makes you so happy." *I can't believe I just said that. Is it true?*

Unfortunately, I think it is. I think I *am* jealous of my sister. Not that I want her life, because this lifestyle is totally not me and I wouldn't want it to be, but I'm envious that she's found her *thing* . . . the thing that makes her jump out of bed in the morning with purpose in her heart and a smile on her face. I'm not exactly sure I have that. I do love the farm and all the animals . . . but I'm not sure I ever leap out of bed. It's more like I lie on my back and stare at the ceiling for a while before I can manage to drop my feet to the floor. I always thought that this meant I was content. Is it possible it means that I'm not? That I'm lost? Amber's very clear and definite declarations about her happiness with her new life have me questioning everything.

I knew it was a mistake to come here.

"Oh, sweetie, you don't have to be jealous of me. You have so many wonderful things going on in your life." She puts her hand on mine, giving me puppy-dog eyes.

I wave her off, pulling my arm away. "I know. I don't know why I said that. I have a beautiful, perfect life, and I am not sad about it at all."

She stares at me long enough to make me uncomfortable. I finish off my wine and stand up, going into the kitchen to pour another glass. If we're going to continue this conversation, I'm definitely going to need more alcohol. *What did you say, Mr. Clock on the Wall? It's not quite noon yet? Oh, well . . . screw it.*

"What would you like to do while you're here?" she asks. "Now that the band is gone, my schedule is pretty much clear for a few days. We can go to some museums, see the Empire State Building, Times Square, a Broadway show . . . We'll do anything you want."

I fill my glass and take another sip of the wine, imagining myself fighting crowds of strangers to visit things I could easily read about in books or see on the Internet. "Just hanging out here could be fun." I look around and nod, pretending like this place is the best place on earth to be, which it is when compared to that stinky, loud, impersonal, and pollution-filled city beneath us.

She twists around to stare at me. "In here? Are you kidding me? You can't come to Manhattan and just sit in my apartment the whole time."

I shrug. "Why not? It's awesome."

She slowly shakes her head, frowning at me. "If you stay here, I'm buying you some painting stuff. We're getting some canvases and some brushes and paints, and you're going to create something, dammit."

I laugh. "Is that so?"

"Yes. You need to earn your keep if you're not going to be any fun." She points at a blank wall. "I've got a spot for your next masterpiece right there."

I know she's only joking about being so demanding and she doesn't mean to be rude, so I won't take offense. Besides, it could help my situation to have something to do, to take my mind off all this . . . stuff. And if it buys me more time in the apartment rather than out there in that loud city, good. "Fine. I'll paint something." It'll get her off my back. My studio is the one place I can find complete and utter tranquility, and I might be able to recreate that ambiance here in one of these rooms she doesn't use. When I paint, everyone leaves me alone. Maybe I could make it work here.

The problem is, I've never been able to use my gift as an escape or a cop-out. I can only create when I'm feeling inspired. And as my sisters have both noticed, I haven't been feeling that way lately. I wish I knew why, because I miss it. My muse has taken a vacation to parts unknown, and I don't know when I'm going to see her again. Maybe I could just splash paint all over the canvas for two weeks and call it done. Amber doesn't seem to mind the fake Jackson Pollock look. The very idea makes my artist's soul sick, though.

I started to work on something when my sister first left for New York, but when I found out that she was staying, it killed my motivation. Rationally, I know that what she has going on in her life shouldn't have anything to do with mine; we're adult women, and none of us made any kind of plan to stay together forever. We're close, but we're not the Siamese triplets our mothers accuse us of being. Not really. But her news still managed to make me sad enough that painting was no longer fun.

"Okay, then, we have a mission," Amber says. "We're going to find an art supply place."

"You know . . . ," I say, fiddling with the label on the wine bottle, "you could probably order all of that stuff online and have it delivered, just like you do with your food."

"Forget it," she says, cutting me off with a sharp tone. "We're not doing that. You are going to get out of this apartment at least *once* in the ten days you're here, and that's final."

I drink some more of my wine. "Fine." I know hiding out up here in this tower is weird, but that doesn't stop me from wanting to do it. If I get out once, though, I can say I'm not a total recluse.

"And I'm buying you some clothes, too, and don't try to argue with me about it. I saw what you pulled out of that suitcase. You were planning on wearing the same outfit over and over again, weren't you?"

"So?" Amber has never had a problem with that before, especially when she was the person in charge of doing everyone's laundry.

"You can't do that here," she says, sounding a little outraged.

It makes me laugh. "Why not?"

"Because! You're not on a hippie commune, you're living in Manhattan now . . . for the next ten days, anyway. And I say you're going to have fun and buy new clothes here, whether you like it or not."

I can't stop smiling. "Damn, you are *twice* as bossy as you ever were back at the farm."

"Believe it, sister." She finishes off her wine and holds her glass above her head. "Come over here and fill me up."

I grab the bottle and go back into the sitting room, refreshing her glass and then mine, taking the spot on the couch right next to her as I place the bottle on the coffee table.

I face her, an apology in my eyes. "I love you a lot . . . you know that, right?" *I'm sorry I'm so lame, so afraid of change, so uncomfortable in your new world. I'm sorry that I fear losing you, my sister who I love so much, because we no longer have anything in common.*

She leans her head against mine and touches our glasses together. "I love you too, little sister. Even if you are slightly agoraphobic, afraid of strangers, and a terrible dresser."

I don't say anything; I just sip my wine. I hate that her description of who I am is accurate, and I wonder if it's possible that New York could work its magic on me like it worked its magic on my sister . . . or if I even want it to.

CHAPTER FIVE

Amber's in the bathroom when the phone in her kitchen begins to ring. I remain in the sitting room staring at it, wondering what I should do. This isn't my house, so I don't feel comfortable answering a call without permission.

Her voice comes from another part of the apartment. "Would you grab that? It's the doorman downstairs."

I hop up from the couch and stride over, feeling bad that I made the caller wait so long for a response. I pick the handset up from the hook, and it's so light, I nearly hit myself in the head with it because I'm expecting it to be like the one we have at home. I gingerly place it against my ear, not even sure it's going to work. It feels like I'm holding a hollow child's toy. "Hello?"

"Hello, Ms. Fields? You have a visitor downstairs named Sam who says you're not expecting him until a few weeks from now but you're going to want to see him anyway." The voice is that of a young man, but since we came in through the garage, I have no idea who he is. *What if he's not the doorman? What if he's one of those paparazzi people trying to sneak in?* Panic starts to seep in.

"Hello? Ms. Fields? Is everything okay?"

I glance to my left and see a second phone right next to the one I'm using—the real telephone. *Duh.* Of course this call is coming from the reception area downstairs; I'm on an intercom. And now I've got the doorman worried about me. I can't believe I'm being so paranoid.

I clear my throat, forcing the panic away. "Okay, hi, um, this isn't Amber. This is her sister. She's not available right now." *Where in the heck is she?* She left me in the sitting room five minutes ago saying she'd be right back.

"Oh. Hello, Amber's sister." The doorman's voice drops to a near whisper. "To be honest, he doesn't seem like the patient type. Could you get Amber on the line or ask her if it's okay to send him up?"

"Yeah, sure. Hang on a minute; I'll go ask her."

I let the handset dangle from its short cord and rush through the apartment. "Amber? Where are you?"

"I'm in here," comes her muffled voice from the hallway.

I stop outside the door that I assume leads to a bathroom. "There's somebody downstairs named Sam. He wants to come up. He says you're not expecting him yet."

"Did you say *Sam*?" She sounds stressed.

"Yes."

"Are you sure? You have to be sure."

Now I'm doubting myself. Did he say Sam, or was it a word that rhymed with Sam, like *a man*? Or *Dan*? Or *a lamb*? Okay, I know there's not a lamb down in the lobby, but now I can't even be sure he said something that rhymes with Sam. That wine is seriously kicking my butt. "I'm pretty sure."

"We have to find out who it is for sure, no second-guessing. We can't let just anybody up here."

I should've known that. *Rookie move*. "I'll be right back."

I run back to the phone, grabbing it and speaking breathlessly. "Who is it again?" I realize how rude I sound and try again immediately. "Amber wants to know who it is exactly. First and last name and all that. Sorry for being so abrupt."

There's a smile in his voice. "I can tell you're Amber's sister." He's a lot calmer than I am.

"How? I mean, why? What?" I'm too distracted to remember what he said now. *How much wine have I had?*

"Because you're so polite, just like she is. The guy says his name is Sam Stanz. He's Tyler's brother. He does look like him, and his ID checks out."

I search my memory for any mention of this name: *Sam*. I think my sister said that Tyler has a brother and that he's supposed to be working with the band. "Hold on just another minute. I need to go tell her and see what she says."

"Okay. No problem. I'll wait."

I rush back to the bathroom and place my hand on the door, slapping it lightly. "It's Sam Stanz. Tyler's brother."

"What?" Her surprise is obvious.

"You weren't expecting him?"

"Not for another three weeks! What's he doing here now?"

I fiddle with the bracelets on my wrist, not sure what to do. "Do you want me to ask him?"

"No." She sounds cranky. "Just give him the go-ahead."

Go-ahead . . . give him the go-ahead . . . "You want me to let him upstairs?"

"Uh . . . yeah . . . that's what 'give him the go-ahead' means."

I'm going to let her get away with her rudeness because I know she's not mad at me, and it's not her fault the wine has somehow destroyed fifty percent of my brain cells.

I suppose this means her plan for us hanging out together is over. It's not like she can ignore him while he's here. As much as I didn't want to go sightseeing around town, I am a little sad about it. I was finally wrapping my head around the idea that if I was going to have to be in New York City to spend time with my sister, I might as well step outside my comfort zone a little and try to enjoy it the way she wants me to.

I walk swiftly back to the phone and pick it up. "Amber says to let him up. I assume you've checked to see that he is who he says he is." I'm so proud of myself for thinking of this. *Total security expert.* I'm not as small-town as Amber thinks I am.

"Yes, ma'am. Like I said, his ID checks out. We always check identification before letting anybody up."

Oh damn. Missed that one. "Oh, yeah. Oops. I forgot you said that. Thank you. I didn't catch your name? Or maybe I did and I forgot it already? And if I did, I'm sorry for that too." I'm sweating now. *Perfect.*

He laughs. "No, I didn't tell you before. I'm Jeremy. I should have introduced myself. I met your sister when she first came to New York City, and then I came to work here after she moved in."

I fan my face, trying to cool it down. "Yes, I remember her mentioning you. She said that you were always really nice to her."

"Cool. That's great to hear. Okay, so, I'll send Mr. Stanz up. You have a nice day."

"You too." I place the phone that's not really a phone back on the hook and stare at it. It's a simple plastic machine that somehow has both the power to transmit voices and the power to ruin my day. *Stupid phone thingy.*

I walk from the kitchen to the foyer and back again. I don't know what the standard protocol is here. Am I supposed to greet him while my sister is stuck in the bathroom or leave him to his own devices? Hiding out in my room sounds really good right now. And what is Amber doing, anyway? She's been in there for ten minutes already.

I abandon my pacing for the spot outside the bathroom door. It's still shut. "Hey . . . what are you doing in there?" I pause and then giggle, remembering the standard question any of us sisters would ask the other when locked outside the bathroom door as kids. "Building a log cabin?"

"Stop. Now is not the time to be teasing me about pooping. I'm serious."

"Why not?" I tap on the door more firmly. "Open this door right now." I've spent enough moments in the bathroom with my sisters to know that there's nothing she needs to hide from me.

"Give me five more minutes. I'm just . . . dealing with something."

Uh-oh. Irritable bowel syndrome strikes again. "I hope you've got some spray in there, because your boyfriend's brother is coming up." I walk away smiling way too hard. Sad to say, there's nothing like a little poop joke to cheer me up. I'm twenty-five on the calendar but sometimes still ten years old in my head when it comes to my sisters. Amber and Rose are my own personal fountain of youth.

I hear the sound of a bell, and the heavy doors of the elevator opening. Abandoning the idea of hiding out in my bedroom—my sister would kill me if I let her first meeting with her boyfriend's brother happen outside the door of a smelly bathroom—I walk quickly back to the foyer and stop just outside the entrance. I have a moment before I'm discovered to drink in the details of the man before me.

Sam Stanz is not very tall . . . more like brawny. His shoulders and arms are thick with muscle. He's wearing a plain white T-shirt that fits him exactly right, perfectly outlining his chest muscles and slim waist. His jeans ride low on his hips and bunch up a little at the bottom of his black boots. He's got a big dark-green backpack that's seen better days, full of stuff, and a guitar case in each hand. Tattoos run the length of his right arm but the other is bare. His hair is dark brown and looks as if it hasn't been brushed in a couple days; it's neither overly long nor very short. His face is boxy, with a bold jaw and nose, deep-set eyes, and strong brow ridges. His aura is dark and broody.

All of this together adds up to one hell of a sexy look, but it stops at the beard. Oh, man . . . that beard. Do I like it? I'm not sure. It suits him in a strange way . . . kind of bringing the whole caveman look into the twenty-first century. It's long and thick, reaching almost to his chest . . . a shocking addition to the other parts of this package that were pretty much straight-up musician. He looks like a mix of rock 'n' roll and hippie love child. I don't know what to make of the mingling styles. I think I like it . . .

He looks up and sees me standing there evaluating him. His expression doesn't change except maybe for a tiny tightening of his brows. He doesn't look particularly happy to see me, but why would he be? He doesn't even know who I am, and he just arrived from who knows where.

"Welcome to Ty and Amber's place." I open my hands in what I hope is a graceful gesture of goodwill.

He puts his guitar cases down and slides the pack off his back. It falls to the marble floor with a thud. His voice is deep and a little gruff. "Do you always talk about yourself in the third person?"

I have to think about that for a couple seconds, but even that moment of reflection doesn't help. I have no idea what he's talking about. "Excuse me?" I wring my hands, wondering if I've said something rude without realizing it. I probably should have followed my first instinct and hidden in my room.

He walks toward me. "Amber, I presume."

Amber . . . third person . . . Now I get it. "No, actually . . ." I hold out my hand to shake his, surprised by how rough his palm is when we make contact. "I'm not Amber. I'm her sister Em. It's nice to meet you."

He works hard and not just at playing the guitar; I can tell by his calluses. It's a little thrilling, to be honest. I've always liked watching a man hard at work. His hand slides away from mine, leaving me feeling weirdly alone. Normally, I relish the moment when I can stop touching a stranger's hand out of social obligation, but not this time. *Strange.*

"M? As in the letter *m*?" He backs up and sticks his hands halfway into his front pockets.

"No. Like *e-m* . . . short for Emerald."

He nods, his beard going up and down as his eyes roam the space. "Nice place."

I wince as I look around the foyer with him. "Sure." *If you like that kind of thing.*

"Kind of tacky, actually," he says.

I have to smile at our shared opinion and his boldness. "No comment."

He blatantly looks me up and down from head to toe, making my smile disappear in a flash. I feel my ears going red at his evaluation. I have to look away, not bold enough to meet him stare for stare.

"You live here too?" he asks.

He's done ogling me, so I look at him again. I focus on the beard. "No. I'm just visiting. Amber didn't . . . know that you were going to be here yet, so she invited me. She said she was lonely." I immediately feel bad about revealing my sister's emotional state. This guy is going to think we're both a couple of weirdos—one who decorates with feathers and one who has a brain made of them.

He shrugs, looking around the room again. "Some things went down. It was better for me to come now rather than later."

"Okay." *Some things went down? What does that mean?* I look at his unkempt appearance and his tough-guy stance and wonder if it was some kind of criminal activity that *went down*. Maybe I shouldn't be so judgmental, though. He's got two guitars, and I seem to recall hearing that he's quite talented. Perhaps he just suffers from an artist's temperament like I do. We both have the same opinion about interior decorating, at least.

"Where's your sister?" he asks, pulling me out of my thoughts.

"She's temporarily indisposed. But she'll be out in a minute." I sure hope she has some bathroom spray. That door isn't very far from where we're standing, and I'm pretty sure we have to pass by it to give him a tour of the place . . . something it seems manners would dictate we do since he is Ty's brother, after all. This thought makes me wonder if he's planning on staying here. He is family, and he does look like he's ready to settle in by the size of that backpack. He has way more clothing with him than I do.

"Are you going to be staying here?" I ask.

"If it's okay." He shrugs, his gaze focused on a mirror across the hall. "I don't really have the funds for a hotel. Figured I could get more stuff done just working from Ty's place." He looks around the room again, his expression unreadable. "I'm not planning on staying very long."

Not very long? One part of me is relieved to hear that, but the other is a little bummed. I'd just gotten back to thinking that not stepping out of my comfort zone and hanging out here in the apartment for ten days was a better idea. He was going to be my excuse for not going out and doing all those touristy things Amber was thinking of making me do, but if he's only going to be here for a couple days, that's not going to work.

But . . . if he can stay for a week or two, she'll have somebody who can do that stuff with her, and I can stay home and paint all day and then have wine and yummy food made by her personal chef in the evening with her. It could turn out to be perfect. I wonder what the chances are of me successfully convincing Sam to stay long enough to be my tourist surrogate. I also wonder if I could work up the lady-balls to even open my mouth and suggest it.

"If it's cool with Amber. And you," he says, as if he's expecting me to respond.

Oops . . . daydreaming again. "I'm sure it will be fine. There's plenty of room here."

We stand in awkward silence for way too long. Sweat pops out between my shoulder blades. *What should I say? Should I ask him what went down that made him come here sooner than planned?* No, that would be rude. *Should I ask him about his family?* No. Amber said something about things being strained between him and his brother. *Should I ask him where he came from?*

"You mind if I get myself something to drink?" he asks, interrupting my inner dialogue.

I instantly feel bad about my lack of manners. "Of course. I'm sure it's fine if you help yourself. Come with me. The kitchen is just in here."

Sam leaves his things in the foyer and follows me out of the room. Thankfully, I manage to find my way without taking any wrong turns. I open the fridge and point. "Help yourself."

He stands in front of the offerings, and I back away to give him space. Maybe he doesn't need it, but I sure do. Every time I look at him, I start to sweat again.

"Wow. There's a lot of food in here."

"I know. I'm looking forward to trying some of it." *Because it means I won't have to go out. Yay!*

He takes a beer from the fridge and twists the top off as he shuts the door. "Wouldn't your sister rather eat out? I hear they've got some good restaurants around here."

"I guess not." I wander over and retrieve my wineglass from the sitting room, pouring myself a couple sips' worth from the bottle that's nearly empty when I return to the kitchen. *Did I really drink all this wine?*

Sam takes a swig of his beer and we stand in the kitchen, saying nothing. The hum of the refrigerator seems to gain volume in the awkward silence. I finish my wine way too quickly and stare longingly at the bottle, wondering if I can afford to put any more alcohol into my system. I haven't started slurring my words yet, so I'm probably good for another glass . . .

"So, what do you do?" Sam asks.

"Do?" This question makes no sense to me. *Does he mean right now? For fun? On a day-to-day basis?*

"Yeah. For a living. Do you do anything?"

"Oh, yeah. I do." Now I feel silly. Of course I do something for a living. I mean, it's not like I make a million dollars and live in a high-rise apartment, but I do work. My face is burning with embarrassment. I can't even have a normal conversation with this guy. I think it's that beard. It makes him look a little scary. Very intimidating. Not like a regular guy. Not like the ones I meet at the bar back home or have ever been with.

"Do I get to know what it is, or is it a secret?" The slightest hint of a smile turns up one corner of his mouth.

Oh my god, I can't believe I'm acting like such a dingbat around this guy. It's just a beard! I've seen hundreds of beards on the farm! My goats have beards! Even one of my chickens has one!

"Oh, yeah, sorry. I'm spacing out. I think I've had too much wine." I brush the hair away from my face and lean on the counter. "I work as part of a farming collective, in an intentional-living community."

I pause for his reaction. All I see is a blank stare that tells me I've already lost him. This is normal for anyone who's not actually at the farm asking me this kind of question.

I sigh, sad that I can't dress up my life and make it sound more interesting. "I'm a hippie. I grow and raise stuff to sell at the farmers' market."

He nods. "Okay, I get it now. That's cool."

What do I say to that? Yes, it's cool? No, it's not very cool, but I do it anyway? I think he's just being polite, so I say nothing.

"What kind of stuff do you grow?"

"This and that."

He stands there expectantly, waiting for more detail.

I continue under duress, knowing that the more I explain, the more of a backwoods hick I'll become to him. "Vegetables, some fruits."

"That it?"

I sigh. "No. We have eggs from the chickens and ducks. Goat's-milk cheese. We have some beehives, so there's honey, too." *Aaaand that's my exciting life as a hippie chick extraordinaire.* In other words, I always have dirt under my fingernails and I rarely wear shoes.

"Bees scare me," he says.

I have to smile at this tattooed tough guy with his big old beard being afraid of a little bee because I totally get it. "Bees scare me too. A lot."

His hand freezes partway to delivering the beer bottle to his mouth again. "Why do you have hives if they scare you so much?"

"They're not my hives, actually. They were Amber's before she moved to New York."

He nods, staring at me. I get the impression he's trying to see inside my head, and since I already have enough people in there reading my thoughts, I don't want to add him to the mix. I turn around and give myself another healthy serving of wine. The bottle is now officially empty. *Screw staying sober.* I might as well go whole hog at this point because it's not like things could be any more awkward than they are now. *Let the word-slurring begin!*

"Bees and I don't get along," I say, taking a big sip of my drink with my back still to him. He'll probably think I'm a lush, but oh well, what the hell. It's not like I care what he thinks.

"You're not taking over the bee stuff for your sister while she's here?" he asks.

I shake my head as I turn around to face him, liquid courage firmly in hand. "Nope."

"She's going back? To the farm?"

I shake my head again. "Nope. I don't think she's coming back." Now my brain space is being taken up by the idea of my sister leaving home never to return, and my mood shifts into a new, all-time-low gear. I take a big slug of my wine at the same time that Sam downs a healthy swig of his beer. I wonder if he's using the alcohol to help fuel the conversation too.

"So, your sister . . ." He looks around the kitchen and tries to see into the nearby sitting area. "She's still indisposed?"

"Yeah," I say, thinking about how much I already miss her. "She's busy building a log cabin right now." The words are out before I can think to stop them.

Oh, shoot! I cannot believe I just said that out loud! Oh my god! What is wrong with me? I put the wineglass down and push it far away from me. I've obviously had way too much.

"What did you just say?" Sam is smiling for real now. It makes my heart burn for some reason. *Indigestion. I have instantaneous indigestion. Or a heart attack. I might be dying.*

I can't speak, but he's standing there expectantly, waiting for me to stop acting like a freak. My face is on fire. I force the words to come. "I know you heard me."

"No, I'm not sure I did." His eyes are practically twinkling right now, lighting a fire in my belly.

The words rush out of me like a waterfall of awful. "I said she's building a log cabin." *Oh, god! I said it again!* Why is that challenging look on his face making me do this horrible thing?

He tips his head back and laughs really loudly.

Amber is going to roast me alive for this. *Unless she never knows about it.* Desperation seizes me. *She can never find out.* I have to get him to shut up before she comes in here and asks us what we're laughing about. "It's not that funny." I'm trying really hard to make him feel stupid for laughing at something so juvenile.

"Oh, yes it is. Trust me." He rubs his chest and takes another long drink of his beer.

The chances of me getting any real sophistication back are pretty much nil at this point, so I do my best to fake it; I smooth down my hair and lift my chin. "I have to go check on my sister and take care of a few things. Feel free to help yourself to more beer or whatever you want in the fridge. I hear the food is pretty good." I start to leave the room, but his voice stops me when I'm halfway through the door.

"Emerald."

I turn my head to look at him. *Time to face the music.* "Yes?"

"It was nice meeting you." He tips his beer bottle at me before he finishes it off in one long pull. And now I know he is entirely too aware of how incredibly good-looking he is.

"It was nice to meet you too." I leave him in the kitchen and walk as quickly as I can back to my bedroom. As soon as I'm inside, I shut the door behind me, lock it, and run over and throw myself down on the bed face first.

I cannot believe what a dingleberry I am. My sister is going to kill me when she hears what a great first impression I made on her boyfriend's brother.

CHAPTER SIX

A few minutes after I've settled into the idea that my trip to New York City is completely doomed, there's a tapping at my door and my sister's voice follows.

"Are you in there?"

"Yes." I'm lying on the bed staring up at the ceiling. It's not the one I'm used to seeing. *Strange. Why am I here? Oh, yeah. Too much wine.* If I were at home staring at the ceiling above my bed, I'd know what I'd be doing next: I'd be getting up for the day; going outside to collect eggs; feeding the goats, dogs, cats, and horses; and then going back to the house to do my part to clean it up and make it look nice. I'd help with cooking breakfast, lunch, and dinner. I'd visit with people at the farm and maybe in town, too. I'd share lots of hugs and get into occasional tiffs with my sisters. I'd help out at the clinic if Rose needed me. I'd do what I always do, day after day after day . . .

But I am not doing any of that today. This is not my bedroom at Glenhollow Farms. My life before this moment was so predictable and common and *nice*, but here in this high-rise apartment, I have no idea what's going to happen to me next. Am I going to go out to a big restaurant or a fancy party filled with movie stars? Will I visit the Empire State Building? Will I hear a homeless man named Ray ask me if I'm going to have sex with my lunch? Or am I going to tell a guy I just met that my sister is pooping in the bathroom down the hall? Anything could happen at this point. I don't like how unpredictable and out of control my life is right now. I don't trust it.

"You okay?" she asks.

"I'm just resting." I can't tell her everything I'm thinking right now; she'll feel guilty for inviting me, and it would be mean to do that to her. She didn't come right out and say it, but I know she needs me here for moral support. She might be full of sophistication and big-city life now, but I know when my sister is feeling out of sorts. Up until now she's always had someone she knows around her here, like the band or our mothers. This two-week period would have been the first time she was in the city totally alone, so I get why she called me and begged me to visit.

"Could you come out? Sam's in the living room, and I've got to figure out what we're going to do."

I get up and walk slowly over to the door. My feet feel like they're encased in concrete, they're so heavy. I really, really don't want to deal with any of this. My social anxiety is seriously rocking the party.

After I release the lock, Amber enters and closes the door behind her, leaning against it and staring at me. Her complexion is on the pale side. She doesn't look angry . . . more like stressed.

I force myself to forget my problems and focus on hers. "You weren't expecting him, were you?"

She shakes her head, wrinkles appearing between her brows. She looks even worse than she did two seconds ago.

"He seems nice enough," I say, trying to ease her mind. "But I think he wants to stay here." I cringe, knowing this is not good news for either of us. Houseguests, no matter how nice they are, bring complications . . . and I'm not even sure how nice Sam is. My first impression of him was not that encouraging.

"He does. I guess he doesn't have the money for a hotel."

"Do you have room for him?"

"Yes. It's just going to be . . . awkward."

Maybe I'm imagining things, but it seems like she's looking meaningfully at me. She's probably worrying that my stranger-danger issues will be a problem for her. I need to let her know that it's fine . . . that he can stay and maybe—if I'm lucky—even be her plus-one for all the touristy things she wants to do. A spark of hope lights up in my chest.

"Why will it be awkward?" I ask, trying not to sound too bright and cheery. Amber reads my thoughts way too readily as it is; I don't need to make it easy on her. "I'm fine with it. Don't worry about me if that's what the problem is." *Crud.* I sound too eager. She'll probably think it's because I find him attractive. But maybe that's better than her realizing I'm hoping his presence will get me out of playing tourist. I mean, he is cute, but it's not like I want to live here with the guy, even temporarily; he's a stranger, after all. But I'm not going to encourage Amber to kick him over to a hotel just because it makes me feel uncomfortable to be staying in such close quarters with a man I don't know very well. We do it all the time at the commune, so it shouldn't be any different here. I'm going to keep telling myself this until I actually believe it.

"Are you sure?" Amber asks.

"Yes, it's fine, really."

"I could offer him money for a hotel room, but I don't think he's going to appreciate that very much. He seems a little . . . touchy."

"Yeah, what's up with that?" Touchy is a great way to describe his vibe, now that she mentions it.

"There's history there, between him and Ty. I don't know all of it yet, but I get the impression it's going to be a little weird around here until they figure it out."

I shrug, walking over to rub her upper arms in an effort to calm her down. "We can handle it. Nothing needs to change. Just set me up with an easel and some painting supplies, and I'll get busy on that masterpiece you want for the other room. And maybe you can show Sam around the city. That'll be fun, right?" *Just ease her into it . . . Easy does it . . .*

She shrugs me off, pointing at my face. "Ha! Faker! I knew it. You think you're going to pawn your sisterly touristing duties off on Sam, don't you? Well, think again, scammer, because you're not getting out of it that easily. You're still coming with me to do some stuff, and that *includes* clothes shopping."

"Yeah, sure, no problem." I lift a shoulder all casual-like, acting like it's no big deal that she just completely and totally read my mind. *God, I hate that I'm such an open book.* I still have hope that I can weasel my way out of it, though; I don't care what she says. And besides . . . she didn't totally shut down the idea of showing Sam around, right?

She rolls her eyes up to the ceiling and sighs. "What else could go wrong today?"

"Hey, what's going wrong? Nothing at all. I'm here to hang out and have some fun with my sister, and Sam is here and he's going to have some fun too. Easy peasy, lemon squeezy."

She shrinks down, deflating like a balloon as she looks at me with her head tilted to the side. "Are you going to pretend that you're happy to be here now?"

I envelop her in a hug, guilt assailing me. "Stop. You know I'm happy to see you. There's nowhere else I'd rather be than right here with you." I'm not lying either. I love my sister so much, and I can see she's stressed out. If I can help her with that, I'm going to. There's no question about it. And I realize this means that I'm probably going to have to do some shopping, but that's the price I must pay for being a nice person. *Ugh. The things I won't do for family* . . .

She hugs me back. "Do you mean that?"

"Absolutely. Let's go get Sam and do something fun." I squeeze her extra hard.

She laughs. "You want to go have a hot dog? I have a serious craving."

My heart trips with fear. *Perverted strangers . . . processed food . . . Sam . . .* "Absolutely. I can't wait to meet your friend Ray and see the present you bought for him."

She pulls away and stares at me suspiciously. "Why do I think you're messing with me right now?"

I look as innocent as possible. "I have no idea. I'm being totally sincere."

She grabs me by the face and kisses me, first on the left cheek and then the right. "I love you so much. You have no idea how much I've missed you and how much I need you right now."

"Oh, yes I do . . . About half as much as I've missed you." I knew she needed me. I'm so glad I didn't turn her down. As difficult as this is for me, it would be worse to know Amber was suffering alone. I just hope that whatever is bothering her is garden-variety loneliness and not something else. I'm not as good at reading minds as she is, and Amber isn't the best at being vulnerable and letting people in.

She opens the door and steps out, pulling me by the wrist with her. "Let's go get our hot dog on."

I stop in my tracks, forcing her to turn and look at me.

"What's wrong now?" she asks.

I bite my lip, knowing I have to tell her this but hating it. "I kind of have to confess something." If she finds out from Sam what I said before she hears it from me, she will die of embarrassment. I can't let that happen to her; she's already freaked-out enough.

"What?"

"Don't get mad at me."

She puts her hands on her hips. "The more you warn me off, the more upset I'm going to be."

"Everything's fine." *Kind of.* "I'm just telling you . . . first . . . that it wasn't intentional, okay? I panicked. You know I'm not good in social situations."

She folds her arms over her chest. "I'm waiting."

I cringe as I tell her. "When Sam and I were waiting for you to come out of the bathroom, I might have let it slip that you were building a log cabin."

Her arms drop like deadwood to her sides as her jaw falls open. She probably wants to say something to me right now, but I think she is physically incapable of it.

I hurry to patch things up. "I promise I wasn't trying to be mean or silly. It just popped out. I think I've spent too much time on the farm."

She answers in a loud, angry whisper. "I think you have too, you goofy hippie!" She grabs the hair on either side of her head and squeezes. "You are in *so* much trouble! I can't believe you'd *do* that to me!" Her face is bright red.

I should be scared at her reaction, but now that's she's dropped her hands and has two big clumps of hair sticking straight out from the sides of her head, it's taking all my internal fortitude just to hold it together. She looks like a deranged chicken, and I should know, because I have a few back home. I start giggling at her beet-red face. I can't help it; it has to be the wine making me think she looks like Agnes, my Gold Laced Polish hen. "It just came out. I don't have any control of my mouth sometimes."

"If I didn't love you so much, I'd march straight into that other room right now and tell Sam about the time you pulled your pants down and touched the electric fence with your bare butt cheek and fell facedown into a cow pie."

My laughter falls away as I gasp. "No! You double-dog dared me to do that! That was your fault!" I'll never forget that totally humiliating moment for as long as I live. I had no idea the shock would make my body spasm like that. And for the record, cow pies taste twice as bad as they smell.

"I swear, I'll tell him." She stands straighter, asserting her older-sister-with-a-secret dominance over me.

I blanch at the idea of that hulking man in the other room hearing about me getting cow turds up my nose and between my teeth. He'd never picture me as anything but a hayseed hippie after hearing that story. "You'd better not. He already thinks I'm a great big hick as it is, but at least he doesn't picture me with my face covered in cow shit."

She frowns. "Why? What did he say? Did he say something rude to you?"

Oh, dang. She thinks he insulted me. I feel bad that I'm making a poor impression for Sam before he's even had time to really get to know my sister.

"No, he didn't say anything. He's been perfectly nice." *And perfectly sexy and perfectly hot and perfectly dangerous, too.* I've only talked to him for twenty minutes, but I already know he's trouble. I just need to stay clear of him so I don't open my big mouth and share any more way-too-personal information.

"Come on," I say, urging Amber down the hallway. "We're not getting anywhere with this silliness. We've left him alone for too long. We're being terrible hosts." She mumbles something under her breath, but I push on her back, keeping her going forward. "I'm not listening to you. Just keep moving."

Amber, normally the take-charge type, is suddenly dragging her feet. But it's my sisterly duty to make sure that she's at least polite to her houseguest, just like our mothers taught us to be with people all our lives, so I continue, even though I'd love nothing more than to lock myself up in my room and take a nap to sleep off the effects of the alcohol.

"How bad can it be?" I ask, using my most cheerful voice. "He's the brother of the love of your life, right?"

She stops just outside the living room and leans in close, whispering in my ear, "Yeah, but you're my sister and you just told him—a perfect stranger, I might add—that I was pooping in the bathroom. So yeah . . . *That's* how bad it can be."

I nod, imagining being in her shoes right now. "Mmm, yeah. You might have a point. It is pretty bad." I think about it for a second. "It's possible I might need to crack open another bottle of wine to survive this day."

She rolls her eyes and takes my hand. "No way, lady. No more wine for you, you stinkin' lightweight. Come on."

We walk into the living room and stop, side by side in the entrance, to view what awaits us. Sam is on the couch with his legs splayed open and his arm thrown over the back cushions. He's leaning far into the corner of the furniture with his mouth hanging open as he snores.

I didn't think this man could ever look adorable with that caveman beard, but damn . . . there he is, doing it. I squeeze my sister's hand, wondering if she thinks the same thing I do.

"Oh my god," she says, sounding repulsed. "Would you get a load of that hipster beard? *So* hideous."

I elbow her in the ribs. "Shush! He's going to hear you." And she is so wrong about his beard, but I'm not going to argue where he'll hear me.

He lets out a loud snore and then stops, smacking his lips together as he slowly opens his eyes. For the briefest of moments, I have an impression of what he might look like when he rolls over after having sex, with those half-lidded eyes and that sleepy look on his face with a slight grin. It sends a thrill through my entire body, and I feel like I've just inhaled a giant balloon full of helium. If I talk right now, I'll surely sound like Mickey Mouse. I clamp my lips together just in case they're thinking of flapping around again.

He sits up straighter and slides his feet down to the floor, moving to rest his elbows on his knees. He swipes at his mouth with the back of his hand and then strokes his beard a couple times before he looks up at us and speaks. "You must be Emerald's sister."

CHAPTER SEVEN

Amber walks farther into the room and straight over to Sam with her hand out. "I sure am. Amber's the name. And you're Sam. We're so glad you came." None of her earlier misgivings about his presence are evident; she seems genuinely happy to see him. It's pretty impressive, actually. I wish I could be that easily social. There will be no more awkward pauses now that Amber is in the room, *thank God.*

He stands, rubbing his palms on his jeans before he shakes her hand. "Sorry to drop in on you like this. I had to come out a little ahead of schedule. Things came up."

Again, the mysterious event that got him here three weeks early . . . It's burning me up inside, wondering what it is. *Bad breakup? Drugs? Bank robbery gone wrong? Running from the law?* He's looking more dangerously sexy by the second.

"Not a problem at all," Amber says, seemingly nonplussed by his empty explanation. "You're welcome to stay here, or we can put you up in a hotel. It's totally your choice. You're Ty's brother, so I'm not going to kick you to the curb by any means." She looks over at me. "My sister's here for ten days, but if you don't mind sharing the apartment with two girls, you're welcome to stay."

"If you don't mind, I think I'd rather do that. Hotels around here are a little pricey."

"Excellent . . ." She pauses, looking slightly uncomfortable. "Of course . . . but just so you know . . . not that I'm trying to change your mind or anything . . . but this would be an expense the band would take on . . . if you wanted to stay at a hotel, I mean. We don't expect you to pay out-of-pocket for expenses you incur while working for the band. Anything you have to spend while you're here is on them."

I shift my weight from one leg to the other, feeling a little weird about hearing this conversation. I'm not involved in the band's business, and I don't want to be. Just the idea of it makes me want to throw something breakable or kick a hole in something. *I'll start with that fake painting in the foyer.*

"That's cool," Sam says, his face blank and his voice on the stern side. "But I'd rather just stay here if that's okay with you. I won't get in the way."

"Oh no, not at all. You could never get in our way." She looks over at me with this crazy grin on her face, trying to convince everyone in the room that she's perfectly relaxed and happy when I can see that she's clearly not. "We're just going to head out to Gray's Papaya to have a hot dog. You're welcome to join us."

I can tell by the look on his face that he's not sure if Amber's invitation is genuine, but I also see him rubbing his stomach like a man who has an empty tank that needs filling. I don't think he was very thrilled with the gourmet offerings in the fridge earlier either. Maybe he's more of a hot dog kind of guy. I'm kind of hoping he is; it matches the bank robber fantasy I have going on in my head right now a lot better than someone who would dig into a butternut squash lasagna.

"I hear they're pretty awesome," I say, trying to sound enthusiastic. "Amber has a friend there named Ray, and she's bought him some kind of surprise, so if you like hot dogs, it might be worth going just to see what it is." My sister can be very creative with her gifts.

She looks over at me and glares, but I can't figure out why, so I keep smiling.

"If you don't mind me tagging along, I really could go for a hot dog. I hear the ones in New York are pretty good."

Amber walks into the kitchen and grabs her purse off the counter. "They're the best. Trust me. You'll love them. I eat way too many of them. Come on, let's go." She runs out of the kitchen like it's on fire. Sam and I are left standing there looking at each other.

"I guess she really likes those hot dogs," he says.

"Maybe. Maybe a little too much, if you know what I mean." I try not to laugh. It's not fair to make my sister the butt of our jokes.

Instead of laughing like I expect him to, Sam looks at me funny.

Oh, shit. I just realized . . . it sounds weird that I'm discussing my sister's preference for hot dogs. They're so . . . phallic. Sam probably thinks I'm trying to be sexy with him. *Yeah, I love to eat hot dogs too, big boy, they're my favorite . . . Mmmmm, hot dogs . . .*

Jesus. Could I be any more ridiculous? *No. I could not.*

He walks across the room, coming toward me. I know I should turn and leave ahead of him, but I don't want him to look at my butt, so I just stand there like a doofus. He stops right in front of me, staring me down. His warm brown eyes look like melted chocolate. The beard that my sister thinks is hideous actually looks quite soft up close. I would love to reach out and stroke it, but I know that would be completely weird and not something I would ever do.

He holds his arm out.

I look down at it in a panic. *Does he want me to hold his hand?* The hot dog conversation has definitely given him the wrong impression.

"After you," he says. He lets his arm drop to his side.

Oh God, what is my problem? It's like I've never been around a guy before. Of course he doesn't want to hold my hand. I don't want to hold his hand either. Who cares if he sees my butt, anyway? I'm wearing a skirt, for God's sake. He can't see anything but layers and folds of material.

I turn and head out the door, part horrified and part fascinated by my complete lack of social skills. I've obviously been out on the farm for too long. Maybe it's a good thing for me to be in the city a little bit, so I can learn how to act like a normal human being.

I walk into the foyer with my head held high, trying to decide if I'm swinging my hips too much or too little. I don't dare look at him over my shoulder to get his reaction. I've never thought about how I walked before this moment, but now I'm wondering what I look like. *Do I look like an old lady? A sexy young woman? An elephant? A penguin? An awkward, immature girl who has no idea what she's doing in the presence of a handsome stranger?*

Amber is waiting by the elevator with the doors open. "Are you okay?" she asks in a low tone as I saunter in past her.

"I'm perfect. Perfectly perfect." My voice echoes around the foyer.

She comes in after me and slides her plastic card into the panel as we wait for Sam to join us.

"Good, because you were acting like you were all hot and bothered in there."

I grab her arm and whisper-yell in her ear. "Be quiet! He's going to hear you!"

He walks into the elevator just moments later. It's possible he overheard the conversation, but I don't dare look at him to find out. Instead, I stare straight ahead and try not to grab on to the railing inside the elevator when it starts its descent with a lurch.

"Lived here long?" Sam asks Amber. I'm glad for any small talk that I don't have to participate in.

"About three months or so. We really love it. The guys down in the lobby are great, and we never see any neighbors. It's like we own the entire building, even though we don't."

"They're vigilant." Sam doesn't sound very happy about that fact.

"Oh, yeah. Trust me, it's needed. I know it's a pain having to explain yourself when you're down there, but nobody from the press has ever penetrated our fortress." She finishes with a laugh.

Well, at least she's admitting the fact that she lives in a fortress. Amber was never one to deny the truth, though. She's always been pretty straight up, and I do love that about her.

"Do you think we'll have any trouble when we leave the building?" I ask, a bit of fear trickling into my heart at the idea of paparazzi accosting her. I glance at Amber to gauge her reaction.

"No. With the band out of town, nobody pays any attention to me."

"I guess that's good." I'm not sure if she's making this up to calm me down or if it's true that she only has value to the outside world when she's attached to Ty. The idea makes me kind of sad.

"Where are they?" Sam asks.

I look at him, checking to see if he's trying to be funny or not. *How could he not know where his brother is?*

"In Japan for two weeks. Ty just left. I'm really sorry you missed him."

"That's cool. I'll see him when he gets back."

Sam will be here for the entire time I am. When a silly thrill runs through me at that thought, I realize that my libido and my brains are definitely not on the same page. This could be a problem.

We ride the rest of the way down to the lobby in silence. When we reach the ground floor and the doors open, there are two young men at the reception desk who both smile at Amber as soon as they see her.

"Hi, Jeremy. Hi, James." She points at me as we get closer. "This is my sister Em. You should let her in any time she comes to the door, no questions asked."

James grabs something and comes around the desk, walking over to us and stopping just inside the front doors that lead out to the sidewalk. "Do you mind if I take a picture?" He's staring at me.

I look at him like he's just grown two heads. *Why on earth would he want a picture of me?* I'm not the famous one in the family; that's Amber, public relations manager of Red Hot. "What? Why?"

"So that the other employees will know who you are and won't bother you when you try to come in," he explains.

I feel completely and totally foolish now. "Of course. Take all the pictures you want." I stand with my hands folded in front of me and a closed-mouth grin. I hate my natural smile, so I always try to rein it in for photographs. It's too big. Once a little kid who came to visit the farm said I had horse teeth, and I never forgot it.

"Great. Thanks very much." He takes the shot and then stares at the camera as he walks away.

"Wait," Amber says. "Take a picture of Sam, too. He's going to be staying here for a while."

James looks up. "What? Oh, yeah. Sure." He comes over and gets a picture of Sam scowling. Maybe he doesn't like his smile either. I don't know why, though; every time I've seen it, it's made me feel like I'm melting, and he doesn't have a single horsey tooth in his entire head.

Sam is out the door the moment James is done. I don't think he's a fan of the attention. Amber shakes her head slowly, giving me a look that means we'll talk about it later. I'm cool with that, because I'm not here to enter into any of their drama. I don't even want to meet the band. As far as I'm concerned, Amber took care of all of our issues with them when she came here three months ago, and there's no need for me to get involved.

Just thinking about this dredges up recent memories that refuse to back down: *mothers . . . fathers . . . abandonment.* I do not care who my father is. It doesn't matter if he's a guitar player, a drummer, or the lead singer for Red Hot. I already know all I need to know about him: he's the type of man who lets a woman he supposedly cares about, someone who has no money of her own, disappear from his life . . . and he doesn't bother to worry about her welfare or her happiness after he's done with her. What girl needs a father like that in her life? *Not this one.*

I walk out the door and follow in Sam's footsteps to the curb. We wait for Amber to catch up. When she gets there, she raises her hand and lets out the loudest whistle I've ever heard in my life.

My hands fly up to my ears, and my eyeballs bulge out at her. She turns around and catches me staring at her in shock.

"What?" she asks, sounding annoyed. "Do you want to get a cab or not? This is the fastest way, believe me."

I nod, silently in awe of this person before me. I realize that as comfortable as I am with my sister when we're tucked away in the apartment, I really don't know who she's become out here in the city. She's bold, she's loud, and she is unapologetic about all of it. A piece of me is envious of her ability to take charge of her life like this, to be fearless in the face of so much that can intimidate. I don't think Amber has suffered a single moment of social anxiety in her entire life. I guess I'm doing enough of that for the both of us.

I look over at Sam, expecting him to be admiring Amber too, jealous of his brother that he has such a beautiful, smart, intelligent, and capable woman as his girlfriend. But I find him staring at me with the strangest expression on his face.

I turn away quickly, not wanting to know what it means. I'm afraid it's pity and sympathy mixed with humor. It's probably completely hilarious for him to see me—this weird hippie girl—trying to fit into the big city and failing at it so spectacularly. I mean, who could blame him? Five minutes after I met him, I told him my sister couldn't come greet him at the door because she was too busy pooping. Who does that? Apparently, I do. Ten days is way too long for me to be sharing living space with this man. Who knows what I'll be saying tomorrow after I've gotten to know him better?

As a cab pulls up to the curb and Amber opens the back door, Sam is suddenly at my side. He leans down and whispers in my ear, "Maybe she has some stomach cramps or something. Don't hold her mood against her."

My heart flips over in my chest. I turn to face him, my mouth hanging open. I giggle for a second before I can stop myself to admonish him. "Shush! That was supposed to be a secret! She'll kill me if she hears you say that."

He gives me a half smile as he ushers me toward the cab. "I never said your secrets would be safe with me."

CHAPTER EIGHT

Apparently, hot dogs are a big deal here. There's a line out the door of this restaurant, which doesn't make a whole lot of sense to me because there are hot dog vendors standing with their carts on almost every block. I guess these dogs are special. Amber is looking around the sidewalk outside, a frown marring her features.

"What's wrong?" I ask.

Sam watches us, waiting for Amber's response.

"I'm looking for Ray. He's usually here this time of day."

I look around too, not that it's going to help. I have no idea what the guy looks like. "Maybe he'll be here later," I offer. I'm actually glad he's not around. Amber says he likes to put people on the spot with his rude comments, and I'm already feeling self-conscious enough. I'd rather not have to worry about the crazy things he's going to say that will throw me off and remind me once again how much I don't fit in here. Amber can handle that kind of thing like it's nothing, but I'm likely to pee myself and run for the hills. And if it were only my sister witnessing my humiliation, that might be okay, but Sam is here now, too. He's already seen enough of me being a goofball.

"Is that him?" Sam points.

I follow his gesture over to a man handing out leaflets near the curb.

"No," Amber says, sounding disappointed. "He's too well dressed to be Ray."

Sam's eyebrow goes up, and I get why—this man's outfit doesn't look like it's seen a washing machine in at least a month. Ray must be something to behold.

My sister opens up her handbag and looks down into it with a sigh. "I guess my present is going to have to wait for another day."

"What is it?" I ask, trying to keep the conversation going as the line moves forward.

"Just something silly." She closes her bag. "You'll see when I show it to him."

"How do you know this guy?" Sam asks.

"He's usually here, hanging around inside or outside the restaurant. We struck up a conversation one day, the first time I ate here, and every time I visit, we continue that conversation."

"What's it about?"

I try not to stare at Sam's face, but I'm really curious what his reaction will be when he hears Amber's answer. I know what mine was—something bordering on disgust.

"He asked me if I was going to have sex with my hot dog."

Sam just looks at her, blinking a few times.

She shrugs like it's normal for a person to speak like that to a perfect stranger. "He likes to say stuff for pure shock value. It cracks me up."

Sam nods a couple times and then turns to face the front door of the restaurant.

His non-reaction makes me think he's judging my sister harshly, and now I'm mad at him for it. If Amber wants to have a conversation with a derelict about sexy hot dogs, that's her prerogative. It doesn't make *her* strange. Okay . . . so maybe I'm not the best person in the world to judge what's strange or not, but I know the kind of person she is. She might be bold and unapologetic, but she's not a perv. I feel the need to rush to her defense as I stare at his unyielding back.

"My sister doesn't take baloney from anybody."

"That's one way to put it," he says, not looking at either of us.

Amber and I share a glance. She shakes her head at me slightly, telling me not to say anything more, but I can't keep my mouth shut. Sam is still being way too judgy for my liking. "Better that she stand up for herself than hide in a corner and be afraid to go out anywhere."

He looks over his shoulder at me. "You know anybody like that?"

My face burns red, and my frustration level skyrockets. I wish I could answer his obvious challenge out loud, but I can't; I'm too chicken. In my head I can, though, no problem. The answer is, *Yes*, I do know somebody like that. *She's standing right here behind you, you big dope-head. So what of it?*

If that guy Ray asked me if I was going have sex with my hot dog, I would've immediately walked—no, *run*—away, abandoning my lunch with the solid plan of never returning to this part of the city. I'd mentally cordon off a three-block area in all directions and never venture inside it again. Avoidance—that's my game. *Surrender. Retreat. Hide. Abandon ship.* I sure as heck wouldn't have answered his question and then bought him a gift. But I'm not Amber. I don't have her lady-balls or her generosity.

"So what made you come out to New York early?" Amber asks Sam, a dare in her voice.

I reach over and take her hand, shaking it a couple times before letting it go. I don't want her to think she has to jump to *my* defense now. This is her boyfriend's brother, and they need to get along, which will never happen if she does the big-sister act trying to protect me.

He shrugs, not looking at either of us. "Some personal stuff."

"Anything I need to know about?"

She's not going to back down. I feel my blood pressure creeping up because I don't think he's the type to retreat either. Are we going to have a showdown at the G. P. Corral? This is New York . . . Will people join the fray and start throwing hot dogs around? With my luck, I'll get hit right in the face with one, and then that's all Sam will ever see when he looks at me. Not that I care. Or . . . upon further reflection,

I might care. I don't want to be known as the girl who took a wiener to the forehead. I look left and right, searching for a place that might serve as cover in the event things get out of control. There's a nice little niche right next to the garbage can to my left . . .

Sam slowly turns to face Amber. "Why would you need to know about something going on in my personal life?" One of his eyebrows goes up. He doesn't look happy.

I stare at my sister, wondering which version of her I'm about to see: the girl I grew up with in Maine or the new and improved, badass New York version. My fingers and toes feel like they have pins and needles attacking them as the tension rises.

"Because I'm the one who's handling your contract." She shrugs, taking some of the sting out of her words. "I'm a detail-oriented person, what can I say."

"It's not a detail you need to worry about." He turns around and starts walking forward, filling up the space created by the advancing line.

Her expression morphs into one of anger as she glares at his back.

A movement catches my eye, and I see a man who looks like he could be my sister's friend. I've never been so happy to see a homeless man in my life. "Look! It's Ray!"

My outburst has the desired effect. Amber turns to follow my gaze, and Sam moves forward again, putting more space between us.

"That *is* him," she says. "How did you know?" Her voice sounds a lot more cheerful now.

Phew . . . crisis averted. "He looks just how you described him." *Like a man who doesn't have a home and who's mentally ill.* He's big and broad shouldered but stooped over and shuffling. His clothes look like rags hanging from his large frame. He's wearing a bright-red knitted hat—the only thing of any distinguishable color on his body. The rest of him is the same dark shade of gray as the dirty street, including his long, knotted hair.

Amber grabs my hand as she speaks to Sam. "Hold our spots; we'll be right back." She abandons the line, pulling me with her. I so wish she had taken Sam instead, leaving me to stand in the line alone, but alas . . . here I am, running on tiptoes so I can keep up with my sister and not fall flat on my face as she rushes over to greet her friend, the hot dog pervert.

"Well, well, well. Look what the cat dragged in," he says in a gravelly voice when he recognizes her. I wouldn't say he looks particularly happy to see my sister, but he doesn't look angry either. I think his face has this expression permanently affixed to it.

"I thought you weren't going to be here, you old grouch." She's smiling as she delivers her insult.

"It's lunchtime. Where else would I be? Your bedroom?" He laughs at his rude joke.

She snorts. "You wish. How about the park? The grocery store? You know, hot dogs are terrible for your health. You should go hang out at another restaurant sometime."

"Who says I don't?" He's not laughing anymore. I don't think he likes her lecturing him.

She shrugs, digging into her purse. "All the spies I have watching you tell me."

He narrows his eyes at her. "You'd better not be surveilling me. I told you how I feel about the government." He looks left and right, suspicion darkening his expression.

She pulls a silver packet from her purse, thrusting it out at him. "Here. This should help keep the government from being able to find you. Consider it a tinfoil hat for your whole body."

He takes it from her and turns it over, confusion drawing his eyebrows together. "What's this?"

"Open it up and you'll see." She sounds proud of herself.

He pulls the plastic cover off and holds up the flat, folded-up piece of silver in his hand. It's about a half-inch thick.

"Open it," Amber urges.

He slowly unfolds it, one square at a time. When he's done, a shiny silver sheet as long as he is and twice as wide is revealed.

He grunts as he stares at it, turning it left and right to see it from all angles. "Are you sending me into space?"

"Yeah. I'm sending you into space. This is the first thing you're going to need: it's a blanket."

He points at his head. "You already gave me a hat."

She rolls her eyes. "Yeah, and winter is coming, dummy. You're going to need more than a hat to stay warm."

My jaw drops open as I realize she just called this monster of a man a dummy. Is she insane? I ready myself to grab her and pull her out of harm's way. He doesn't look like he could move too fast, thankfully.

He smiles at her. "Who's the dummy? Where'd you get this piece of junk? China?"

Amber holds her hand out. "You don't want it? Fine. Give it back."

He hugs it to his chest immediately, his expression suddenly very possessive. "No. Go away. You already gave it to me." Ray turns and starts shuffling away.

She shouts at his back. "Don't trade it for anything. It's Mylar. You're going to need it when it gets cold. It's good for shade too!"

He waves his hand over his head, his dirty fingers sticking out of the ends of cut-off gloves. "Yeah, yeah, yeah," he says. "Nag, nag, nag."

I look at my sister, fascinated by her smile. Ray smells really bad and is obviously three different kinds of crazy, but she's actually enjoying this relationship somehow. We've dealt with a lot of interesting characters out at the farm over the years, but none of them came even close to this guy. I'm even more in awe of my sister's metamorphosis now than I was before. This city has turned her into the most tolerant person I've ever met. I don't think even our mothers could handle this Ray person as well as she has.

"That was really nice of you to buy that for him," I say. "The hat too."

She shrugs, looking down at her purse as she rearranges things inside it and then closes it more fully. "Winter is coming. I have no idea where he sleeps."

I look over at him. "Do you think he's out on the streets full-time?" He's setting up a little spot next to the exit door of the restaurant, a bag of belongings on either side of him. He leans against the building with the silver blanket now wrapped around his waist like a skirt. He looks hilariously bizarre. I almost admire his style; no one could say that he cares what people think, at least . . . and in a city like this, that means something. It seems like everyone else is dressed like they're hoping to be scouted for a fashion magazine.

"There are a few shelters and some churches that take people in when it's really cold, but I haven't gotten to the point with Ray that I can ask him where he stays."

Interesting . . . they can talk about sexual relations with food items but not sleeping accommodations. I really don't understand New Yorkers.

We make our way back over to the line. Sam is just at the entrance to the restaurant, and there are only five people ahead of us now.

"That was nice," he says, looking down at my sister.

She stares straight ahead. "It's nothing."

He shrugs and turns to face the front of the restaurant along with her. "He'll probably appreciate it in a few days. I hear a cold front is moving in."

"Yeah, I heard that too."

I'm behind Amber and Sam, looking at two really stubborn, prideful people who *may* be calling a truce. It's hard to say. Observing behavior, both animal and human, is one of my favorite things to do, something I've had a lot of practice with at the farm. It's funny to me how similar these two people in front of me are. I like that they're managing the conversation around me, though, and that my sister is in control, never backing down or admitting defeat . . . never saying anything embarrassingly silly because she's panicking and doesn't know what else to say. She makes me proud.

The line moves forward again, and now I can see a menu. I stare up at it, trying to figure out what I'm in for. A stomachache for sure . . .

"We're each getting two dogs with a drink." My sister points to the menu board. "Those are the different drinks you can get. Tell me what you want on your dog, and I'll order it for you."

Sam and I speak at the same time: "Ketchup."

Amber looks first at Sam and then me. "No cheese? No chili? No onions? No mustard, even? You guys are in the hot dog capital of the world and you're getting plain old ketchup?"

Sam rubs his abdomen. "I don't want to get an upset stomach. I hear these things are murder on the intestines." He winks at her and then looks up at the menu.

Her eyes narrow as she stares at the side of his face. Then she turns and glares at me.

I'm trying really, really hard not to laugh; it's making me look like I have gas pains, I'm pretty sure. As soon as Sam turns away more fully, Amber mouths a sentence at me: *You are going to pay for that log cabin comment.*

I throw up my hands and lift my shoulders, trying to express my innocence, when Sam turns around and catches me. I immediately drop the pantomime and stare at the floor, praying for the moment to be over. I'm torn between laughing and wanting to run all the way back to the apartment. Once again, I am the dingbat in the room.

Amber is going to kill me as soon as she gets me alone. I owe her a big, fat apology for embarrassing her in front of her boyfriend's brother with that whole log cabin comment, and I don't relish the dressing down I'm going to get, so I vote for staying put and eating one of these horrible-looking hot dogs that probably aren't even made of real meat, so I can delay the inevitable as long as possible.

CHAPTER NINE

"Well, that was an experience," I say as we walk out of the restaurant. My sister leaves me standing with Sam just outside the exit and goes over to talk to Ray again.

"You want to go over there with her?" Sam asks.

"Not particularly. I don't really understand their relationship, to be honest."

"That was nice of her . . . Getting him that blanket." His voice is gruff.

I look up and find him staring at her.

"My sister is very kind. Both of my sisters are."

"You have two?" He looks at me, those chocolate-brown eyes of his very engaged.

His gaze is so intense, I have to look elsewhere. I focus on his earlobe as I respond. "Yes. Rose is our sister. She's back in central Maine where we grew up."

"That's where you live?"

I nod, looking him in the eye again. He seems genuinely interested.

"What do you do there again?"

I sigh. "Didn't we already cover this?" I smile so he knows I'm not mad.

He shrugs, smiling a little bit too. "I'm not sure I really appreciated your answer like I should have last time."

I guess my life is so boring it doesn't even sound like a life. Talk about deflating. I shrug, brushing off the hurt feelings. "I just take care of the animals and sell stuff. It's nothing more complicated than that."

He looks at Amber again and then back to me. "So, how does your sister become a PR manager for a band like Red Hot if she grew up in the middle of nowhere in Maine?"

"You really don't know the story?" I stare at his facial expression, searching for clues of deceit, but see nothing there.

"No. Should I?"

"You don't talk to your brother very much, do you?"

He shoves his hands down into his pockets and rounds his shoulders. "Nope."

I nod my head politely, curious about his life but loath to dig deeper. To push for more would make me feel as though I were interrogating him. I like my privacy, and I'm going to assume he likes his too.

"You guys have plans after this?" he asks.

I'm grateful for the change of subject. "I don't know. You'll have to ask the boss."

"You're in the Big Apple. Don't you have anything *you* want to do?"

I shake my head and stare at the ground. "Not really. I prefer to hang out at the apartment."

"With all those ostrich feathers and stuff?" He half-smiles and it's utterly charming. Sharing a secret over my sister's home decor is way more fun than it should be.

I hold in the laughter that wants to fly out. "Those are *peacock* feathers."

"Ostrich . . . peacock . . . whatever. Feathers are feathers. Do you like them?"

"No, I'm not a big fan of those or the gilding." It seems slightly traitorous to admit that, but when he sighs and tips his head back, smiling, I don't feel bad anymore.

"Thank God . . . I thought I was alone in that nightmare."

I'm really enjoying the twinkle in his eye. He can be really handsome when he's happy. "My sister said the place came professionally decorated."

"By who? Willy Wonka?"

"Shush!" I say, looking over at Amber. She's turning around and heading our direction again. "She's going to hear you."

"I've got nothing to hide. I'll tell her right now to lose those feathers."

I think he's teasing me, but I can't be sure. "Shush." I glare at him and he smiles. He knows he's making me nuts.

"Is there anything *you* want to do while you're here?" I ask. Now it's my turn to challenge him. My pulse is pounding at my boldness. I meant the question as a distraction, but now that I see the look on his face—darkness and unspoken thoughts—I really want to know his answer. There are hidden depths to this man, and normally I don't bother with people's private thoughts because I don't want anyone to bother with mine, but he's different for some reason. I want to know all about him. Unfortunately, the chicken-hearted girl in me needs to find out what makes him tick from another source, because I don't have the guts to ask him to his face for the answers to the questions I have. He's too intense for me.

"I have work to do," he says, all traces of humor gone. "I'm not here to be a tourist."

I nod. "Yeah. Me too."

He gives me a sassy look. "You got some chickens to feed up in that high-rise?"

"No, Mr. Smarty-Pants. But I have a canvas I need to paint, so . . ."

"A canvas for . . ."

Suddenly, Amber is there and the moment is gone. He never finishes his sentence. She stops at my side and smiles, full of cheer. "You guys ready to go to the paint supply store?"

I expect Sam to beg off, but he shrugs and answers, "Sure. Why not?"

I shrug too, feeling shy and off-balance again. The art supply store is my special territory . . . I'm not sure I want to share it with him. Amber is one thing, but Sam is something else altogether. I'm afraid of him watching me and getting into my head, into my world. My life has been safe and the same for so long; it's *comfortable*, and I like it that way. Sam makes me decidedly *uncomfortable*. He makes me feel . . . antsy. Unsettled. Like I'm longing for something more, but I don't know what that something more *is*.

"Let's go," Amber says, ignorant of my inner conflict. Sam walks away, headed for the curb.

She hails a cab in no time and gives the driver directions to a place she finds on her phone. We're soon weaving our way through traffic, Amber humming away to a tune on the radio.

I stare at the back of Sam's head, wondering what's going on inside it. Is he wondering what I'm going to buy? What I'm going to paint? Or is he thinking of his life in California? His work? The trouble that sent him to New York three weeks early? His girlfriend or wife?

The idea of him having a special woman in his life sends a sharp pang of jealousy through me. *What the heck . . . ?* What do I care if he's taken? It's not like he's my type, and it's not like I'm his. We're just sharing an apartment for ten days. *Ugh, get a life, Em.* I hate that I'm acting like a hormonal teenager. I can be an adult woman sharing a living space with a hot guy without imagining anything happening between us. I know I can. I just need to concentrate . . .

Amber speaks softly so he won't hear. "Are you cool with him coming with us?"

"Sure. No big deal." Although it feels like a big deal, I know it shouldn't be. *Come on, Emerald, woman up!*

"Do you feel like seeing anything else while we're out? Maybe the September 11 Memorial?" she asks.

I'm about to shake my head no, but then I see the side of Sam's face as he turns his head toward the driver. He's definitely interested in the conversation. "Sure. Why not." I might not want to do the touristy things for myself, but I can do them for Sam. Besides, I'm an American citizen; I should go see the memorial while I'm here. It's the right thing to do, to honor the people who died or suffered.

"We'll go to the memorial first; it's closer." A somber mood descends over the taxicab as Amber instructs the driver to take us there.

CHAPTER TEN

We stop at the curb a few minutes later, and Amber quickly pays for our ride with her credit card. She's an expert at working the computer to take care of the bill. She gives the cabbie five dollars in cash and waves at him in the rearview mirror. "Thank you."

Sam is waiting for us when we get out. Together, we move toward the memorial, mingling with the crowds. There are a lot of people here, even though there's a chill in the air. The sound of falling water rises above the murmur of voices.

"Have you ever been here before?" Amber asks Sam.

"Nope. Never been to New York City."

"You guys go ahead. I'm going to grab a brochure." Amber goes over to an information area while Sam and I walk to the edge of the first structure: a huge, deep pit in the ground continually filling with water that disappears into a hole in the middle.

I'm not sure what emotion this memorial is supposed to invoke in me, but all I can think about is how the water just keeps disappearing and there's nothing left to show for it. It seems so . . . hopeless. Is it supposed to represent the cycle of life, with things going in, going down, disappearing, and then somehow magically coming back again? I don't see how that has anything to do with the deaths that occurred here. No one who died on that day is coming back. It makes me sadder than I already was.

People all around us are crying. I have an ache in my chest. I feel a hand on my shoulder, and it confuses me for a moment because it's too heavy. And then I notice that Amber is still several feet away. It's Sam who's touching me as his jaw clenches over and over again. He's staring out into the water so intently, I'm not sure he even realizes what he's doing.

My chest tightens, and I shift just the slightest bit away. I don't mean to reject him; it's just that his presence is so incredibly intense, I can't handle it without my heart racing and my pulse running away from me. It's silly to be so affected by a near-stranger.

His hand drops away. "Sorry," he says softly, still staring at the water.

"Don't apologize. I get it."

"It's really sad here." His voice is gruffer than normal.

My own voice is strained, higher than it should be. "Yes, it is."

"Did you know anyone who died here?"

"No. It was kind of before my time. I was just a kid."

"Yeah, me too."

I study his face, looking for signs of his age. His beard covers up too much of his skin to be able to gauge it correctly. "How old are you?"

"Twenty-seven." He pauses and then looks at me. "You thought I was older, didn't you?" He sounds slightly offended.

I shake my head at his vanity. *Silly man.* "Don't worry. You don't look a day over forty with that beard."

He strokes it as he returns my gaze, his sadness slipping away to be replaced by pure chemistry. "Not into the beard?"

I try not to smile, I really do, but the way he's petting himself and looking at me like that . . . it's getting me *all* riled up. My lips move up into a sneaky grin despite my best efforts to remain serious. I hope my sister doesn't look over at us. I hope *no one* looks over at us; this is a completely inappropriate emotion to be having in this place.

"The beard's . . . okay," I say, lying. In truth, it's nice. Too sexy, really. He should probably shave it off so I can lose the urge to stare at him every five seconds.

I turn my attention back to the memorial. There are engravings on the edges of the ledge surrounding the water. I run my finger over one of them. *Jonathan.* A man named Jonathan died in this place where we're standing. He will never grow a beard or flirt with a girl from central Maine or worry about how scary and confusing it can sometimes be to make connections with people you've just met. Suddenly, I feel very, very lucky to be alive, standing in this place with this beautiful man next to me. Tears well up in my eyes. I quickly brush them away before Sam can see me riding this emotional roller coaster straight down to its lowest point.

"How old are you?" he asks.

I'm glad for the distraction and wonder if he did it on purpose to spare me my embarrassment. "Twenty-five."

"Huh." He slowly nods, staring off into space. That single syllable is loaded with meaning, but I can't translate what it is by reading his body language. He just keeps bobbing his head up and down.

I face him. "Huh? What's that supposed to mean?"

He turns his head and looks me up and down. "I was just thinking . . . you don't look a day over forty in that skirt."

My heart does a double flip. *He's flirting with me!* I have to bite the insides of my cheeks to keep from saying anything as my face flames red again. *Oh my god, he is too much.* How on earth are we going to live in the same apartment for ten days? If he's this intense after just a few hours, I can only imagine . . .

"Do you like the music?" he asks out of the blue.

I'm confused for a moment, wondering what music he's talking about. The only thing I can hear is water and people talking. "Huh?"

"Red Hot's music. Sorry. Totally random subject change."

"Oh. Yeah. Okay."

"Things were getting kind of heavy," he says by way of explanation.

"Yeah. No. No, I get it." It takes a second for my brain to come back online. *He didn't mean to flirt. He regrets it. He's taking it back.* "Yeah. I guess I'm a fan." I don't want to offend him and tell him that I couldn't care less about their music. After all, his brother is their guitarist, and I'd heard that Sam is supposed to be writing new stuff for them. It would be like him telling me he dislikes farm animals.

"You don't sound very convinced," he says, smiling slightly, the emotion not reaching his eyes.

"My mothers were big fans." I shrug.

"You have more than one?" He looks at me quizzically. He probably thinks his silly beard is throwing me off again.

I shake my head and stare down at the water. "It's a long story."

He glances over at Amber, who is now wandering around the other fountain. "I think we have some time."

I'm not sure how much of my family's dirty laundry I want to air in front of Sam, so I take two steps to my left, pretending to be interested in another perspective of the fountain. "Maybe another time."

His jaw tenses and he looks straight ahead. "I get it." His half smile looks forced.

"You get what?" I worry I've offended him somehow, and I don't want to do that. Not here. Not anywhere, really.

"Who am I, right?" He glances at me, vulnerability in his eyes. "Some jackass who wandered into your vacation and ruined it."

I shake my head at him, taking two steps back to the right. I'm being rude for no good reason. My mothers would be so disappointed, especially considering who he is to the band. "No, it's not like that. I'm not here on vacation, and you didn't ruin anything."

"You sure about that?" He nods in Amber's direction. "I'm pretty sure your sister thinks you're here to play tourist."

"She might think that, but that's not the case. She was going to be lonely with Ty gone, so I came to keep her company . . . That's it."

His jaw tenses again. "You're a good sister."

"Because I'm visiting when she's lonely?" If he only knew how much I *didn't* want to come, I'm sure his opinion of me would change in a heartbeat.

"Yeah. And you're doing it in a place that you don't really like."

Huh. Maybe he does somehow know. "What makes you say that?" *Do I have another mind reader in my life?* How horribly inconvenient that's going to be.

His gaze is piercing. It's like he's seeing right through my façade. "It's obvious you don't like being here. You don't like crowds. You don't like talking to strangers." He shrugs. "You're reserved. Like me."

I nudge him with my elbow as I look out over the water, trying to lighten the mood. "What are you talking about? You're no stranger. We're practically related. My sister is dating your brother, and they're living together."

He doesn't say anything to that, so I risk sneaking a glance at him. He's staring out ahead, not seeing the memorial or anything else as far as I can tell. He's got a faraway look in his eye. His shoulder muscles are tense, and his jaw is bumping out over and over again.

"Are you okay?" I ask.

He shakes his head and turns around, slowly walking away. "Yeah, I'm fine."

I'm torn; do I stand here by myself, or do I follow him? I hate the idea of looking like a desperate fool by running after him—he'll take it as a sign that I like him, no doubt—but I also know what it's like to be sad and to feel alone . . . like I'm an inconvenience to everyone around me.

He thinks we're alike. *You don't like talking to strangers . . . like me,* he said. And I know that when I'm feeling down, I just want everyone to leave me alone. He probably wants that for himself too. I watch him go, the slump of his shoulders making me feel bad about my decision to stay.

I'm not good in situations like this. Not good *at all*. Terrible would probably be the most apt description. Analysis paralysis. Too shy to fly. Too school for cool. Would following behind him be creepy, sad, or compassionate? I have no clue.

He looks upset. I don't think it's the memorial doing it either. Maybe this place is prompting his sad thoughts, but there's something else going on, too. I hesitate to take action, not just because I'm not sure how to react, but also because I don't want to open up the door to him asking me a bunch of personal questions, and I risk that by volunteering to get involved with his problems. Rather than making a mistake by doing something, I decide I'd rather make a mistake by doing nothing. There will be less embarrassment that way, at least. And so I let him walk away . . .

Suddenly, Amber is by my side, taking any further decision out of my hands. "Why do you look so forlorn? Is this place making you sad?"

"Of course it is. I think that's the whole idea." I'm trying to make a joke out of it, but it falls flat.

She puts her arm around my shoulders and hugs me to her. "I'm sorry. I just thought . . . if you're going to see anything in the city, this should be it."

"No, you're right. Thanks for bringing me here. I should see this. Everyone should see this."

"We'll skip the museum part," she says. "You could spend hours in there, but maybe another time." Amber looks over at Sam. "Is he pissed I brought him here?"

"No. I think he's sad about something else."

"Did he tell you anything?"

"About what?"

"About his life. About what his deal is."

I shake my head. "No. He said some stuff went down back where he lives and that's why he's here early. That's all I know."

I can practically see the wheels turning in my sister's head as she stares at him. "Sam and Ty had a hard time growing up. Their father wasn't a very nice person."

"They can join the party, I guess." I can't keep the disappointment from my tone.

"Don't start," Amber says, pinching my cheek lightly. "Our fathers are not mean people. It's a totally different thing with Sam's father, trust me."

"Whatever you say. I don't want to talk about it."

"Why not?"

I sigh. "Since when are you so nosy?"

"Since when am I *not* nosy?" She's back to staring at Sam.

"Aren't you worried about upsetting Sam and Ty by digging into their past?"

She looks at me. "Why would being interested in their lives upset them?"

"Maybe they'd see it as pushing when they don't want to be pushed."

She sighs. "Not everybody is as hyper as you are about people knowing their personal details."

I laugh at her boldness. "I think people are more worried about them than you give them credit for." Her teasing strangely makes me feel better. She's accepted me as who I am. Acceptance means a lot to someone like me, a girl who never feels like she belongs anywhere beyond the end of her driveway.

"Whatever. Let's go get a cab."

Amber and I walk arm in arm to the curb where Sam is waiting for us. He throws his hand up, and a cab veers over in response.

"Well done," she says, giving him a thumbs-up.

He nods at her compliment, saying nothing.

She leans in and speaks quietly in my ear. "I think he's the strong, silent type."

I jab her in the ribs with my elbow. "Shush." Now she's just looking for trouble. I'm pretty sure he heard her, because his back tenses up as soon as the words are out of her mouth. I don't think he's one for teasing, which means we could be in for some trouble over the next ten days. There's one thing my sister knows how to do well, and that's how to get under a person's skin.

CHAPTER ELEVEN

The cab brings us to the art supply store, where I allow my sister to buy me some primary acrylic colors, a few brushes and palette knives, and a large canvas . . . even though the last thing I feel like doing right now is painting. Hoping for inspiration, I also put a box of rubber gloves on the pile at the cash register. They aren't something I've ever used with my work before, but I read an article a few months back about this other artist who does use them and I feel inspired to give her technique a try.

Amber holds up the box. "What are these for? Protecting your manicure?"

I take the gloves from her and put them on the counter with the other supplies so the man can ring everything up. "No. It's a secret."

"Oooh, I like secrets." She leans in close and wiggles her eyebrows. "Tell me all of yours."

I push her on the shoulder. "No. Go away."

Sam is waiting for us at the front of the store, about ten feet away, his expression beyond bored. I'm not going to feel bad about it, though, because he didn't have to come. We offered to drop him off somewhere, and he turned us down.

"I'm going to pay you back for all of this," I say. I left my purse in my room, thinking we were dealing strictly with hot dogs.

"Don't worry about it. I have loads and loads of money now." Amber grins big at me.

I roll my eyes. She knows I don't care about money. "Good for you."

"We're still going clothes shopping, I hope you know."

I glance up at Sam, who's busy staring at his phone. "Not now. Sam would kill us if we asked him to do that."

"You are correct on that," he says without looking up, making my heart jump. I was thinking he wasn't paying us any attention when he was actually hearing every word.

Amber sticks her tongue out at him before she responds. "No, he's not invited to that outing. We'll go tomorrow or the next day."

"Can we go back to the apartment now?" I ask quietly as the clerk finishes bagging up our purchases, hoping Sam doesn't have superhero hearing. "My stomach is bothering me." I rub it, seriously regretting my lunch choices. No wonder my sister spent so much time in the bathroom today. Those hot dogs are murder. I'm glad I didn't order the chili or the onions.

"Yeah, we'll go back right now."

I look at Sam and drop my voice even lower. "Do you think he needs anything before we get back? Like at the grocery store or whatever?"

"I don't know . . . let me ask." Amber raises her voice. "Hey, Sam! Em wants to know if you need anything while we're out!"

I could seriously kill her right now. I hold in my reaction, trying to act like being outed by my sister isn't totally embarrassing. Now he knows I'm afraid to talk to him.

He shakes his head, his expression getting darker and darker the more he stares at his phone.

"Looks like he got a text or an email that's not making him very happy," Amber whispers over my shoulder as I reach for my bag of goodies. "I wonder what it says."

"Whatever, Nosey Parker. Mind your own business." I pray he can't hear us digging into his life.

He turns abruptly and exits the store, stopping outside on the sidewalk. Amber and I stare at him through the window as he punches in somebody's phone number and then starts talking rapidly. He is not happy at all; that much is clear.

"I hope he doesn't cause any trouble while he's here," Amber says under her breath.

"Why would you say that?" We walk as slowly as we can toward the door, giving him time to have his conversation in private and giving us time to gossip about it.

"Think about it . . . ," she says. "He got here three weeks early because something was going on in California? That can't mean anything good."

I won't share my crazy ideas of him running from the law and whatever else my imagination was cooking up earlier. He doesn't seem like the type, now that I've gotten to know him a little bit more. At least I don't think he does. Not that I have any experience with criminals or anything. Jesus, what am I thinking? For all I know he could be an ax murderer. "I'm sure it's nothing," I say, trying to reassure Amber and myself.

"He's a tortured soul."

"Really?" I pause to look at her, my hand on the door. "What does that mean?" I can't tell if she's being facetious or not.

"We'll talk about it later." She pushes the door open, mumbling under her breath, "Let's go. I don't want him taking off and running around the city with a chip on his shoulder."

"What do you mean? Why would you say that?" I'm hurrying to catch up to her. She's making no sense.

She's bearing down on Sam as he takes a couple steps away from us. "I know the look of somebody who's about to rabbit off."

He looks perfectly calm to me—maybe a little angry, but not like he's about to run away. "I think you're imagining things."

She stops suddenly, causing me to bump into her as she turns around to face me. "I've been living with *you* for twenty-five years, Little Miss Scared of Her Own Shadow. Trust me . . . I know when somebody is about to take off because they're freaking out about something."

"What? You're crazy." I can't tell if she's joking around, but I sure don't appreciate being called *that* name.

And then Sam starts to walk quickly down the sidewalk away from us.

"See? Told you." Amber starts to jog after him, and I hurry to follow. My heart feels heavy as I realize she was right about him, and that she could be right about me, too. *Am I really afraid of my own shadow?*

CHAPTER TWELVE

"I'm going to grab a cab," Amber says, running short of breath. "You get Sam and bring him back here." She leaves me standing on the sidewalk with my mouth hanging open.

"But . . ."

She's already gone, stopping half a block away with her arm out.

Sam is quickly disappearing in the other direction.

What to do, what to do, what to do . . . Amber's words echo around in my head: Little Miss Scared of Her Own Shadow . . .

Scared, my butt. I start running after him without another word. My sister needs my help and I'm going to give it to her, even though Sam is a big boy and I'm sure he can handle wandering around the city by himself. He did look upset. It might be good for him to have somebody nearby just in case. And I'm not afraid to talk to him, or run after him, or do what needs to be done, *so there!*

"Sam!"

He ignores me.

I kick my pursuit into higher gear, my feet slapping on the pavement with my all-out effort. I'm a-huffin' and a-puffin', my arms pumping madly while my skirt flies way out behind me—a sad imitation of a superhero's cape. *It's a bird . . . it's a plane . . . it's Super Hippie!* I can't believe I'm doing this, looking completely foolish with so many potential spectators. What is wrong with that man, anyway? He knows I'm chasing him; why doesn't he stop or at least slow down?

His strides are really long. He's in a heated discussion with someone, and as I draw near, I hear parts of it.

"I told you, I can't deal with this right now. She needs to get her shit together."

Who is she? Who is he talking about? What's her problem?

"I know that. I did everything I could for her before I left, like I have been for two solid years. Sadie is fine, I made sure of it, but I'm fighting a losing battle with her. At some point she's got to stand on her own two feet."

Wow. He sounds kind of heartless. After hearing this, part of me wants to stop and run the other direction, get in the taxi with my sister, and let him find his own way home. But Amber asked me to get him to the cab, and apparently she's made it her job to keep him happy until Ty gets back, so I can't let her down. I'm closing the gap between us, despite the fact that the hot dog I ate an hour ago is really kicking my butt. *Oh, the cramps.*

"I know she's a mess," he says. "She's been a mess for a long time, and I've done everything I possibly can to change that, but until she *wants* to change on her own, there's nothing we can do."

I'm nearly there . . . I reach out to tap his shoulder . . .

"Listen, I've gotta go. This is not the time for me to be having this conversation." He touches his phone screen and shoves the device into his back pocket, coming to a dead halt with no warning.

Unable to slow down fast enough, I run right into his back.

"Hey! Watch it!" he yells, jumping to the side and spinning around.

His sidestep causes me to lose my balance. When his body is no longer there to stop my descent, I fall to the ground and land on my knee, crumpling onto my side instantly with the pain that shoots up my leg.

"Oh my god, oh my god," I groan. "That hurts so much."

He's standing over me, furious. "What in the hell are you *doing*?"

"Can't you see what I'm doing?" I gasp. "I'm *dying*, you dingleberry!" I cup my hands over my knee, trying to will the pain away.

He bends down and swoops me up into his arms. One minute I'm on the cold ground, and the next I'm flying through the air. I scream out in surprise. "Whoop!"

"You okay?" He's looking down at me, either annoyance or worry lines etched into his face.

I couldn't be more embarrassed than I am right now. If my knee weren't destroyed, I'd be running in the opposite direction twice as fast as I got here. "No, I'm most definitely *not* okay. What are you doing? Put me down." I don't like his hands on my body; it's making me warm in weird places and my knee is killing me—a terrible combination of emotions. I struggle to be free. His beard tickles my cheek, and I reach up to slap it away without thinking.

"Sorry." He drops my legs and my feet flop down. I cry out as my knee buckles under me.

He catches me before I fall and props me up with his shoulder. "You're really hurt."

"No shit, Sherlock. What was your first clue?" I'm angrier at myself than I am at him. I shouldn't have been following so close. Hell, I shouldn't have been running after him in the first place. Now who's Miss Nosey Parker? Me, that's who. I was trying so hard to listen in on his conversation, I ran right into his back. What a freak.

He stops and stares at me for a few seconds and smiles.

"What are you looking at? And why are you smiling when I'm clearly injured?" He's laughing at me, I know he is. And who could blame him? *Why do I have to be such a klutz?*

"You just called me a dingleberry *and* said, 'No shit, Sherlock.' I haven't heard either of those insults since the tenth grade."

I frown, not in the mood for his happiness. "Yeah, well, I like to kick it old-school, what can I say." I stand straighter and wince. I don't think my knee is seriously hurt, but it is going to have a hell of a bruise. "Just help me get to the cab, would you, please?"

"Yes, ma'am."

"Don't call me ma'am. It makes me sound bossy." Why am I acting so rudely when I'm the one who was so busy trying to eavesdrop that I ran up his heels? *Ugh*. I wish I knew. It's possible I'm still smarting from the comments Amber said about me being afraid of my own shadow, but I hate to think that she has that much control over how I feel. One little sentence issuing from her mouth has the power to turn me into a freak of nature.

"Why not?" he asks. "I like it when you get bossy."

I roll my eyes. Trying to stay mad at him when he's being like this is impossible. It's like I can't *not* embarrass myself when I'm in his presence, and he just finds it all so funny. *Ha, ha, look at the goofy hippie, tripping on her own feet as she runs down the sidewalk.* Keeping my mouth shut is probably my best bet from now on, so I decide to zip my lips. No matter what he says, I will not respond.

"It was very graceful," he offers.

I say nothing.

"The way you fell to the side like that after you tackled my ass."

Not responding is becoming difficult. He's totally mocking me. There was nothing at all graceful about that fall, and we both know it.

"Is that your middle name? Grace? Because it should be if it isn't."

I grit my teeth to remain silent.

"Emerald Grace . . . huh . . . I didn't get your last name?" He's grinning down at me as I limp along.

I can't remain silent any longer. "And you're not going to. Could you just shut up for a little while? Your voice is making my knee hurt more."

He barks out a laugh as we arrive at the cab.

My sister is standing there with her hands on her hips. "What happened to you?" She looks at Sam. "How did she get hurt? Why are you laughing?"

"She tripped. Very gracefully, I might add."

"I was trying to catch up to Sam, *like you asked me to*, and I bumped into him." I glare at Amber. This is mostly her fault. She knows I'm not athletic.

"Did you tell her to tackle me? Because that's pretty much what she did."

Amber frowns at me. "I definitely did *not* tell her to tackle you."

"Ha, ha, very funny, you guys. Stop joking around. My knee is killing me."

"Let me see." Amber comes over and lifts up my skirt, exposing way too much of my thigh.

I slap her hand away. "Quit it! You're showing everybody my nether regions."

Sam stares up at the sky, biting his lower lip as his eyebrows come together up in the middle of his forehead, practically.

I glare at him. "I don't know why my being exposed in public is so funny to you."

"Nether regions . . ." He shakes his head slowly, lowering it to look at us. "You girls are killing me."

Amber takes over the support at my shoulder. "Come on, sister. Lean on me. Let's get in the cab and go home."

"It's not my home."

She stops. "What?"

"I *said* it's not my home. It's *your* home."

She rolls her eyes. "Whatever. Just get your butt in the cab."

Sam opens the door for us, and I do my best to slide in, wincing when my knee bumps the front seat. I move all the way over to the far side and stare out the window. I am going to pout like nobody's business, because today stinks. I've been outed as the least graceful woman in our family, my knee is aching, and on top of all that I have gas now, too, thanks to that terrible hot dog. What else could possibly go wrong?

This little trip is not going at all how I expected it to. I thought it would be just Amber and me sitting around her apartment, drinking wine and talking about the good old days, with me learning all about her new life. Instead, I'm watching my sister flirt with a homeless guy, eating food that's making me have gas so bad that I'm afraid I'm going to spontaneously combust if I don't get to a private place so I can unleash very soon, and I'm getting all hot and bothered over this dumb, moody-beardy guy who I somehow managed to tackle on the sidewalk in front of at least fifty people. I don't think this trip could get any worse, and I'm only on day one.

CHAPTER THIRTEEN

Getting back to the apartment with Amber and Sam's help is no big deal. I'm limping a little, but there's no serious injury to my kneecap. Situating my paints, brushes, and other materials in my room is also no biggie. My bedroom is large enough to set up the big floor tarp, easel, canvas, and supplies, no problem. The nap I take for the next several hours flies by like it was nothing. It's exactly what I needed to settle my nerves. But the telephone call that Amber gets while I'm relaxing into the pillows on my bed . . . now that's a *really* big deal. A really big, horrible, awful deal.

"What do you mean you need me in Japan?" she asks. She looks at me in confusion, as if I can explain what the person on the other end of the line is trying to say to her.

I sit up, my heart going cold. Somebody wants her to leave, and it sounds very urgent. I pray that our mothers are okay and that no one has gotten hurt.

"I thought everything was fine. What's going on with Ted?" She falls silent, listening to the explanation that I can't hear. I feel slightly less panicked knowing that Ted's the issue and not our moms or Ty.

I try to lean in so I can eavesdrop on the call, but I have to bend my knee to do it, and the twinge of pain I get reminds me that I really should just lie back and relax. I can wait for the news she's getting until after she hangs up the phone.

Amber, who was sitting next to me on the bed, stands and starts pacing the floor. "How could you guys let this happen? He was supposed to hang on at least through the end of this leg of the tour." As she listens to the caller's explanation, her expression morphs through several emotions: confusion, anger, frustration, and then, finally, acceptance. "Are you sure you can't handle this without me? Em is here. She came all the way from Maine."

I turn and swing my legs over the edge of the bed. My knee doesn't hurt that much. It's just a bruise. My sister is seriously stressed-out, and if I'm understanding this right, she's about to take off across the globe. I need to get up and *do* something.

"Can Em come with me?"

I nearly have a heart attack hearing that. I wave my hands at her and frown, telling her *Hell no* as best I can without actually shouting it like I want to. The day I go to Japan will be the day after Hell freezes over. I don't care that more than half my family is there. My feet are not leaving American soil. I have a hard enough time communicating with strangers in my mother tongue, so I can only imagine how I'd handle Japanese people trying to speak to me. *Holy nightmare.*

She sighs heavily, brushing me off with what looks like disappointment. "Fine. I'll book a flight out as soon as possible. I'll send you a text with the details. I assume you'll send me a car?" She nods when she gets her answer. "Okay. I guess I'll see you soon."

She hangs up the phone and sighs. "You're never going to believe this."

I try to smile. "Don't tell me, let me guess . . . They need you in Japan and you have to leave yesterday?"

She stares at her phone as if there will be answers on its screen. "Yes. Apparently, Ted just got fired, so now they're over there in Japan and everything is falling apart and they need me to help put it back together. Our mothers being there probably isn't helping. My guess is they had something to do with this shake-up." She hisses out a long sigh and looks up at me apologetically. "I am so sorry. I dragged you down here to spend time with me, and now I'm abandoning you. I feel like a serious jerk."

"No, don't say that. But don't they have anybody else who can handle this . . . whatever it is?" The comment about our moms is worrying me, but they're grown women; surely they don't need their twenty-five-year-old daughter to come to their rescue.

"They don't, actually. Ted was the guy who took care of everything, and I'm the number-two person . . . or I was the number-two person. I guess I'm temporarily the number-one person now. The band really counts on me for a lot of stuff. They trust me. They're a little paranoid about who has their best interests at heart after all the things Ted did."

Bitterness rises up in me over her prioritizing these men over our plans, burning me up. "Maybe they don't like the idea of us spending time together." That would be in keeping with the way they've acted for the last twenty-five years. They don't really care about our family; they only care about themselves and what's convenient for them. And Amber being attached to me and our home is *very* inconvenient.

"No, that's not it at all. They would never do that. They totally respect the bond we have and are happy for us. Honestly, I'm more worried about Ty than I am about the rest of them."

"Why? He's a big boy, isn't he? Can't he handle his life by himself?" My sister thinks she has the solution to every problem in the world, and normally it makes me proud of her . . . but today, not so much.

She gives me a scolding look. "Of course. He's a grown man and a professional musician, but his integration with the band hasn't been the easiest thing in the world—as you well know because I've already told you all about it—and right now with them being in a foreign country and their manager taking off and all that crap . . . and Sam being here after Ty hasn't seen him in years or even talked to him besides inviting him out here . . . It's just a lot to deal with. I think it would be easier for all of them if I were there to help smooth things over. I'm part of the team now, and that's a big deal for me."

Anger and sadness that she'd leave so easily bubble up inside me. "Since when did you become so integral to the band's success?"

"Since when did you become such an angry person?" she counters. "Usually you're very understanding. You never begrudge Rose the time she spends at the clinic doing her thing, so why are you giving me such a hard time? Is it because I'm leaving you behind? Because you could come, you know . . ."

I look at her like she's crazy, hoping to be able to deflect the truth I feel in her words. "I'm not angry, and I'm not begrudging you anything. I'm just asking you a legitimate question. You're right . . . you did ask me down here . . . or you *begged* me to come down here is more like it, and now here I am and you're leaving. Is the band more important to you than I am?"

She walks to the door, her eyes shining with tears. "I'm not going to justify that *not*-legit question with an answer. You're in a bad mood because you hurt your knee and because I'm leaving you behind right after you came to visit, and I get that. It sucks. But I don't really have a choice if I want to do my job properly and help keep the band from imploding. Now . . . I don't want to say anything in anger that I'll regret, so we can talk about it some more after I pack."

"Fine. I'm going to pack too." I move toward my suitcase.

She stops in the doorway and spins around quickly. "Pack? No! You can't!"

"What do you mean, I can't?" I'm already halfway done, and my leg is working just fine.

"You have to stay." She sounds panicked, when what she really is, is crazy.

"I'm not staying here; don't be ridiculous. You won't be here, so why should I be?"

"Because Sam is here! You can't just leave him here by himself."

I laugh. She's making zero sense. "Why not? You are!"

She sputters, at a loss for words.

A bratty, evil comment jumps from the recesses of my brain and out of my mouth before I can stop it. "What's the matter? Are you worried he's going to steal your peacock feathers while you're gone?"

"Feathers? What . . . ? What are you talking about?"

I fold my arms over my chest as my breath heaves in and out and my ears burn with the angry emotions building up. I want to stop, but the words keep spilling out. "You know that's not a real Jackson Pollock in your foyer, right?"

She holds up a hand and closes her eyes for a few seconds before opening them again. "Okay, you're obviously still suffering the effects of that wine, so I'm just going to let this stuff go. I'll be back in a half hour after I've packed, and we can finish talking about this if you want. But maybe you should take a little nap and sleep it off in the meantime."

"I already took a nap. Maybe *you* should take a little nap and sleep it off."

So, yeah . . . That was the lamest comeback ever delivered in an argument, but nothing else is coming to mind, so I'm stuck with sounding like an angry third-grader. I'm so mad at that stupid band, I can't think straight. What a bunch of jerks. They're destroying my family! Red Hot, my butt. More like Red *NOT*. They're so used to the world revolving around them that it doesn't mean anything for them to pull my sister away from her short visit with me. The fact that they'd even ask her to come when they know I'm here just to hang out with her tells me that they think they're top priority over everyone else. Who am I anyway, right? I'm just the girl who refuses to acknowledge that they're these saints who think they can buy us out and pretend like they never knew we existed before three months ago or whatever. And our mothers are just going along with this garbage, apparently. I'd say the band is doing a pretty good job of ruining everything in my life, but they're not doing it single-handedly; they're getting help from the women I love most in the world, and it's killing me.

Amber leaves without another word, so I grab my suitcase and go back to the bed, taking a seat on the edge of it with my bag next to me. What am I going to do? Pack or not? She wants me to stay here with Sam. *Craziness!* Does she actually believe that Ty's brother and I would hang out? Go do touristy things together and get along like long-lost buddies? How ridiculous can she be? Has she not lived with me for the past twenty-five years?

I know for a fact how it will turn out: I'll spend the entire time in my bedroom, and he'll either do the same or disappear into New York City and have a good old time with all the women who will throw themselves at his broody, handsome self. He doesn't need me here any more than I need to be here for him. In fact, I'll probably just get in the way of him turning this place into his own personal sex lair.

I go over to my purse and pull out my cell. After dialing the farm's number, I wait for someone to answer the phone. Our mothers aren't there, but Harold is. When I left, he moved into the house to help take care of things, but I'm sure I'm needed back there. Without me, the entire operation is going to be barely stuttering along. This doesn't have to be about Amber or Sam; this could be just about my life missing me. Harold will make the decision for me, telling me I'm needed back home. I just need to hear the words and I'm gone, gone, gone. Like *Gone Girl*, but without the fake murder part.

"Hello, Glenhollow Farms," a man's voice says. He sounds younger than Harold.

"Hi, this is Em. Who's this?"

"Hey, Em, it's Smitty. How are you? How've you been? Are you enjoying New York City?"

My stomach suddenly feels hollow. I do not want to talk to Smitty right now, but I guess I have no choice. "I'm okay. Just wondering how things are going over there. Do you need me back, by any chance?"

He laughs. "You've been gone for less than a day, and you already want to come back?"

God, he's so irritating. "No, not really." I lift my chin, annoyed that he's laughing at me. "I was just, you know, wondering about the animals."

"Everything is fine. Five of your regular long-stay visitors came in today, and they're getting settled in. All the chores have been divvied up, and everybody seems happy to do their part. General consensus seems to be that it's about time you guys had some time away from the farm."

"Oh." My heart plummets into my toes. I had no idea my life was so boring to people on the outside of it. *Am I the only one who likes my life?*

"You sound disappointed that everything is going so well." I can hear his big, fat smile in his voice. I'd so love to throw some dirty straw in his face right now. He did it to me once when we were ten years old, and his payback is long overdue.

"I'm not disappointed." I chew my lip, trying to come up with an explanation for my call that makes any sense. "Maybe just feeling a little useless." I regret the words as soon as they're out of my mouth. I don't need to invite Smitty into my private life. He'll probably see it as me making a move on him. He knows me well enough to recognize that I don't volunteer personal details very often.

"Hey, if you want to come back, come back; this is your home. But don't come back because you're afraid to be there."

I pull the phone away for a couple seconds to frown at it. *Ugh . . . that word again:* afraid.

"What's that supposed to mean?" I say when the phone is back at my ear, offended that he'd say such a thing to me. *Pfff. Like he knows me at all.*

"You know exactly what it's supposed to mean. You don't like the city. You don't like people outside of your little circle. You're probably just looking for an excuse to come home because you're afraid." He laughs. "Bawk, bawk!"

My face goes hot. What is he . . . ten years old? Why am I even talking to this idiot? "You know what, Smitty? Shut up. You're a jerk."

He laughs. "I love you too, kid. So are you coming back or not?"

"No, I'm not coming back. I don't need to come back there. I'm not afraid of the city. I love it here. I went to the September 11 Memorial today. And it was crowded. It was *loaded* with people from everywhere. Total strangers. It was very moving, too. Very emotional."

"Oh yeah? I think I've read that about that place."

I let out a long sigh at the laughter I can hear in his voice. He's hopeless, and it's pointless to be mad at him when I know it's just myself I'm disappointed in. Smitty is right: I am scared. I don't want to be, but I am. "You are such a boob. I'll talk to you later."

He laughs out loud this time. "Yeah, I'll see you soon."

I hang up. Smitty's wrong; he's not going to be seeing me soon, because I'm staying here. And then when I get back, I'm going to avoid him like the plague he is. I chew my lip as I think about the space between the rock and the hard place I've just wedged myself into. I don't want to do what Amber has ordered me to because she's not the boss of me and I'm mad at her; but I'm also not going to give Smitty the satisfaction of chickening out. *Ergh, this is so frustrating!*

I really don't have much of a decision to make. My sister wants me to hang out here with Sam? Fine. That's easy enough to do. Heck, I'm already here and totally unpacked. So I'll stay, but not because she expects me to. I'm staying because I know what it's like to be dumped in Manhattan and left to fend for myself not knowing anyone, and quite frankly, it sucks. Sam might be cool with that kind of thing, but then again, maybe he isn't. Maybe he's like me. He seems like a sensitive person who might appreciate having someone he knows nearby. And if that means I have to go do some touristy things with him, well, so be it. This has absolutely nothing at all to do with the fact that I think he's handsome either. I sure hope he won't think that. I'll have to come up with a way to explain to him why I stayed behind so he doesn't get the wrong impression.

Smitty and Amber are wrong about me. I am not afraid. Smitty and I may have gone out a few times, and we may have slept together once, but that doesn't mean he knows me. Nobody knows me. The tiny mean-girl voice in my head is saying maybe even I don't know me, but I ignore her; she's full of shit.

I leave my bedroom on a mission. I'm going to notify my sister of what's what and tell her not to worry, that everything is being handled. She can run off to be with her precious band and I'll stay behind to handle things, just like I did when she left us to live in Manhattan. And then I'm going to go find Sam and ask him what he wants to do while he's here, and we'll make plans to do it. Every single thing he wants to do, from walking to the top of the Empire State Building to inline skating in Central Park . . . it is going to *happen*. I am going to be the *best* damn hostess anyone in this city has ever seen. *Stranger danger . . . thhhppbbtt. Please.* But first, before I do any of that, I'm going to use the bathroom, because my guts are suddenly in knots.

CHAPTER FOURTEEN

My sister's door is locked, and I can hear her talking rapidly on her phone behind it, so I leave her alone. In the living room, I find Sam sleeping on the couch again. I get a glass of water from the kitchen and sit down on the chair next to him. As I swing my foot up to cross it over my leg, my toe bumps into the coffee table and wakes him up.

"Who's that?" He's instantly sitting up straight, looking out over the room in confusion.

"It's me," I say, signaling with a wiggling finger. "The hostess with the mostest." I take a sip of my water.

He looks at me through squinted eyes. "What?"

"Have you not heard the news?" I'm trying to sound friendly, but it's coming off as bitchy, so I try again. "My sister got a phone call."

"From who?" He leans forward and rubs his eyes for a few seconds before falling back against the cushions and stroking his beard. He looks like one of the cats at my house, cleaning itself out in the sun. When he runs his fingers through his messy hair, attempting to smooth it down, it only amplifies the effect. Even when I'm mad, he's cute, dammit. *So not helpful.*

"My sister got a call from somebody in the band. Their manager quit, and everything is falling apart. Apparently, she needs to go over to Japan and handle things."

He leans forward and rubs his hands together, staring at his palms as he frowns. "She's leaving?"

"Yes. She's leaving."

"Are you going too?" He presses his hands together between his legs and stares at the floor as he waits for my answer.

"No, my job is to stay here and keep you company."

He shrugs. "You don't have to do that. Unless for some reason your sister's worried about me being here alone in her apartment." He presses into his palm with his thumb, giving himself a massage of sorts.

I shake my head, anxious to get that notion out of his mind. "No, nothing like that at all. I planned to be here for ten days and my plane ticket isn't good until the fifth, so I'm stuck here anyway. Don't feel like you have to hang out with me or anything, though. You can just do your thing and I'll do mine." I should be relieved at this idea, but I'm not. I'm more . . . disappointed.

My brave notions of inline skating in the park are far, far away, now that I'm sitting this close to Sam. What was I thinking? Of *course* I'm afraid. Smitty was right about that. But he was wrong about the source of my fear; it's not the strangers out there in the city . . . it's the stranger *in here* who makes me nervous, who makes my pulse race, who makes me ready to jump and run with a look or a simple phrase. So why am I not ecstatic that he doesn't want me to show him around town?

Sam sits back deeper into the couch cushions, stretching his arms behind him and lacing his fingers behind his head. "No big deal to me either way. Stay or go."

It's a completely natural thing for him to say, even polite, maybe, but it hurts. I feel so . . . unimportant . . . unwanted. I shrug, trying to act like I don't care. "I'll be busy painting, so you probably won't see much of me."

"Yeah, I'll be writing music, so . . . yeah, I'll be busy too."

"Maybe I'll just see you at the breakfast table, then." I'm trying to put a happy spin on it, be cool about all of it, like he is.

He frowns and shakes his head. "Probably not. I'm more of a night owl."

"Oh. Okay, then." I'm not going to tell him I'm a night owl too sometimes, since he's obviously brushing me off. "Maybe I'll see you at dinner. Or not." *Ugh.* I sound desperate for his company. Hopefully, he'll understand that I'm just trying to be polite.

He shrugs. "Maybe."

Well, I did my best. Clearly, we are not going to be having any deep conversations, and this ten-day period is going to be the longest one of my entire life. Of course I'm not going to leave town just because he's rejecting my company. I don't want him to think he has that kind of power over me, especially because he *doesn't*. I'm definitely going to start out with a black background on that stupid canvas we bought today. I'm going to paint something dark. Something that matches my mood.

My sister appears in the doorway. "Did you get Sam up to speed on the news?"

"Sure did," I say with a sunny grin. "We're all set."

"I'm really sorry this happened. If I could change this at all, I would."

"Don't worry about us. We're big kids. We can handle it." It's possible Sam's words are meant to be comforting, but his expression isn't getting there at all. He looks annoyed.

It's hard to believe he expected Amber to entertain him, so I can't understand his emotion. "Yeah, we'll be fine," I say, trying to fix the weird message he's sending. "I'm going to paint and he's going to write music. We'll stay out of each other's way."

Amber sighs in relief. "Great. Maybe the two of you can help each other get your creative juices flowing. Anyway, I've got a flight out tonight, so I'm just going to grab a cab and head over to the airport right now."

"Right now?" I look at Sam, wondering if he's as surprised as I am.

Nope. He seems completely nonplussed. Cool as a cucumber, as usual. It's almost as if he was expecting her quick disappearing act. God, I hope he doesn't think this is some manufactured event, designed to get us together.

"Yeah," Amber says. "It's an international flight, so they take off in the evening. And I need to check in two hours before departure and get some things from the band's offices before leaving too, so . . ." She shrugs.

I stand, placing my glass of water down on the coffee table. "How about if I ride over in the cab with you?"

"If you want to, that would be great. But it's going to be a long trip for you. Maybe a couple hours headed back because of all the traffic."

"That's okay. I don't have anything else better to do." I realize after I say this that I just totally insulted Sam. *Yes, Sam, sitting in traffic for two or three hours is way more interesting than talking to you.* Oh, well. He'd probably say the same thing in my shoes. He's already made it clear he has no interest in even sharing a meal.

"I'm going to head out," Sam says, standing. "Do you have a spare key by any chance?"

"Yes, I do. Thanks for reminding me to give it to you." Amber walks over to the kitchen and pulls out a drawer. She starts putting things down on the counter from inside it. "Here is a key fob for you to get in from the garage, Em. You'll have access to my car and driver, who already has one, but you can also use a cab to bring you right to the back door to avoid any people outside. Also an elevator card." She slides these things in my direction and then another elevator card toward Sam. "This is the key to the apartment." She points to the plastic rectangle. "If you come in through the reception area at the front entrance, all you'll need is this key card to get the elevator to work, and it opens right up onto our floor, as you saw earlier. They know you downstairs, so there shouldn't be a problem with you getting access."

She walks over to the intercom phone and picks it up. "But just in case . . ." She pauses, waiting for someone to answer her call. "Jeremy, hi. It's Amber. I need to go out of town for a little while, so I just want to be sure before I go that you guys have it down there in the book that Sam Stanz and Emerald Collins are both allowed access to my apartment and this building while I'm gone." She nods a few times and smiles. "Thanks so much. I knew I could count on you. Bye." She hangs up the phone and turns back toward us. "Everything is all set. I'm just going to grab my bag from my room."

I nod. "Go ahead. I'll be right here waiting."

After Amber leaves the room, Sam looks at me with a half smile. "I guess you're going to get out of that shopping trip."

I think this is his way of apologizing for being slightly rude. I smile, my own effort at making amends. "Yeah, I guess I lucked out there."

"If you change your mind about wanting to go, let me know. I could go with you or whatever."

I stare at him, totally shocked by his offer. "You'd go clothes shopping with me?"

Now he looks just as shocked as I feel. His mouth drops open, and he frowns in what looks like confusion. "Uh, no. I don't know why I just said that. I hate clothes shopping. Or shopping of any kind, really."

I'm glad it's his fault that things are awkward between us this time. "Maybe you said it because you feel sorry for me."

"Why would I feel sorry for you?"

I shrug, feeling silly that I said anything. "Because my sister is leaving when we should be spending time together? I don't know."

He waves his hand in front of him. "Just forget what I said. I'm overtired." He leans forward and heaves himself up onto his feet with a small groan, stretching his arms up to the ceiling and exposing a sliver of his belly in the process.

I have to look away when it makes a spark run through me. *Quick! Think of something cool to say! Don't let him know you're imagining him naked!* "Did my sister show you what room you'll be staying in?" *Oh, God, what is wrong with you, Em?! Now he knows you're thinking about his bedroom!*

He walks through the kitchen without sparing me a single glance. "Yeah, I'm all set. I'll catch you later." He disappears into the big living room beyond, leaving me by myself with my sexy thoughts and total inability to be cool. I scared the poor guy away with my complete lack of finesse.

I stand in the sitting room looking around, wondering what the heck I'm going to do for the next ten days while sharing living space with a man who sends me riding an emotional roller coaster every time we start talking. I'm probably better off avoiding him and being creative instead. The problem is, I really don't feel like painting anything right now. In all the years I've been making pieces of art, I've never been able to force myself to make something out of nothing.

The sound of Amber pulling a suitcase down the hallway cuts into my thoughts and throws them into the back of my mind. I have plenty of time to worry about that other stuff . . . *about Sam.* For the next several hours I'm going to be chatting with my sister in the backseat of a car, and there's nowhere I'd rather be.

CHAPTER FIFTEEN

We fill the cab ride with meaningless chitchat, both of us avoiding any conversation that will get us angry at each other again, up until the last fifteen minutes, when the first airport signs come into view.

"What are you going to do with Sam?" Amber asks out of the blue.

"*With* Sam? What do you mean?" Just hearing his name makes my pulse quicken. I don't think it's because I'm afraid of him either. Some distance has clarified a few things for me, the first being that I find him incredibly attractive and the second that I find him intriguing. *Go away, complications!*

"I mean what I say. What are you going to do with him? Where are you going to go? What are you going to see? Are you two going to hang out? Are you going to do some tourist stuff together?"

She looks so hopeful, I almost feel bad shaking my head no. "Amber . . . would you get real, please? You know very well we're not going to do anything of the sort together. Or separately, for that matter."

"Why not?" She sounds genuinely disappointed. "You seemed to get along really well today."

"Yeah, until I tackled him out on the street. *That* was really impressive. I'm sure he'd love to go do that again with me."

She lifts my skirt to look at my knee. There's a purple bruise covering half of it. "That was a pretty nasty fall, huh?"

"Yes. And totally weird. I just need to stay clear of him and spare us both any further humiliation."

She puts my skirt back down, sighing. "Could you please just try? For me?"

"Try what?" She is so frustrating. I don't know what she's asking me to do, but I'm pretty sure I'm not going to like it.

"Try to . . . I don't know . . . figure him out. Sam and Ty have this totally iffy relationship. It was a really big deal just getting Sam to agree to come out here and try to do this job for the band, and he and Ty haven't even really talked yet. I can't even get Ty to give me the whole story. I'm not sure he knows what it is. If you could do something to help smooth over the situation, I would owe you . . . like, a million favors." She puts her hand on mine. "I know this is a big ask, but I was thinking if you two got to know each other a little bit, you'd feel more comfortable around him, and he'd see what a great girl you are and how sensitive you are, and maybe . . . I don't know . . . he'd respond to that." She pauses. "He's an artist too, you know. Like you. Maybe you two speak the same language. From what Ty has told me about Sam, I think it could be possible."

My heart is hammering in my chest. I don't believe Sam and I have anything in common, other than we both think he's good-looking. "If I did that . . . got him to talk about his life with Ty . . . it seems to me that it would be *the band* who'd owe me a million favors, not you." Which makes me even less likely to follow through. Not that I was considering it, anyway. Amber couldn't be asking me to jump farther out of my comfort zone than she is with this request.

She frowns at me. "It's one and the same thing. I work for the band, and as of today it is now my job to make sure their lives go very, very smoothly. It's what I'm being paid to do." Her face crumples a little. "This is my dream, Em. My dream. I thought I could live on the farm and be happy, but I realized I can't. This is what makes me want to jump out of bed in the morning. It's what I was meant to do, and they've given me the chance of a lifetime. Can you understand that?"

"What do you mean *as of today* it's your job to do all this stuff?" As far as I knew, being their PR manager wasn't that involved, but the look on her face is telling me something very different. "Did something change after this phone call?" Her words are making me sick. I hadn't realized so fully before how much she hated her life on the farm. How could I have been so clueless about my own sister?

"I just got promoted, Em. As of an hour ago, I became the band manager *and* the public relations manager of Red Hot."

I can't stand the look on her face. She looks like I do in the mirror, full of fear—and that is *so* not Amber. I grab her hand and squeeze it, realizing how big a deal this is to her, and knowing deep down that what she says is not new to me. Rose and I have talked about it many times; Amber was meant for bigger and more exciting things than life at Glenhollow can offer her. "I didn't realize . . . Congratulations. I know that's super exciting for you." Part of me is genuinely happy for her, but the other part falls into a pit of sorrow. The chances of her ever coming back to the farm are disappearing with every interaction she has with those men, and that's something I'll have to live with, but I'm worried our mothers will soon follow. Then it'll be just me and Rose, and who knows how long it will be before she leaves too. There's no way I could run that farm on my own . . .

She points to her face. "Do I look excited?"

I study her more closely. "No, actually, you look kind of cranky about it." I'm trying to lighten the mood, but the expression on her face tells me it's not working.

"I'm completely and totally stressed. Sam being here early was a golden opportunity for me to figure out what's going on between him and Ty . . . to do what I could to start the repair process between them . . . but I can't do that if I'm not *here*. What if leaving him alone here for a week ruins everything? What if he implodes and takes off?

We'll never get him back, I know we won't. You said it yourself . . . he has things happening back where he's from. Chances are whatever it is will pull him home without someone here to talk him out of it, and he won't come back for another try."

I stroke the back of her hand, trying to calm her down. It works with my chickens, and since Amber's acting like a fussy hen right now, I have every reason to believe it could work with her. "How could you not being here ruin everything? It can't; don't be silly. You going to Japan just leaves everything in neutral gear, right? Sam'll just wait for everyone to get back. It'll probably be a nice vacation for him. He said he's never been here before, right?"

"But what if he decides he hates New York? I think he's a lot like you; I don't think he appreciates all the traffic and the people. What if he freaks out and leaves us high and dry? You wanted to leave; that was your first reaction to me going. The band will never forgive me. Ty will be . . ." She stops for a moment to collect herself. "He'll be so deeply disappointed and hurt."

"Why would you think that about Sam in the first place? He's not giving off any signals that he wants to leave. He didn't look afraid of anything to me. I didn't see him acting timid or out of sorts today." And I spent an awful lot of time studying the guy—probably way more than I should have—so I should know. "He was a little emotional, but I think that's a normal reaction to have at the September 11 Memorial."

"I know all that, but still . . . he has issues with the public." She looks uncomfortable as she finishes her thought. "He can't perform . . . In front of people, I mean."

"Come again?" It almost sounds like she's talking about sex, and I know I could never perform in public either, so . . . yeah. I don't think I could even *kiss* a man where someone else might see me. All of my sexy interludes have been conducted in total privacy.

"I said, he can't perform . . . music . . . in front of *anyone*. He's a brilliant songwriter, but he cannot go up onstage."

"Why not?" I'm kind of shocked by this piece of information, actually; I never would have suspected that of Sam. "He looks like the quintessential rocker to me. Wasn't he born for the stage?"

"You'd think so, but no, because he's incredibly freaked out by all of it. He has a terrible case of stage fright. Like pathological. Maybe it's a kind of mental block or something, I don't know . . . But I'm never going to find out from Japan, that's for sure."

"Oh. That's really sad. About Sam, I mean." I can't even imagine what that must feel like. I get pretty scared going out in public and talking to people I don't know, but stage fright for a musician is totally different. Playing music is the thing Sam was born to do, from what Amber says, but he can only do it halfway? How depressing. "No wonder he's so moody."

"I know. I think it's pretty devastating for him. That's why when he was rude today, I just let it slide. Trust me . . . he's a tortured genius. He's got some serious issues, but he's got a talent that is just . . . *un*believable. I've heard his music. His songs will make you weep; I'm not kidding. He could totally revitalize Red Hot with his songs and jump-start their careers all over again."

I don't get why this excites Amber so much. All I can picture are droopy old-men butts in spandex and leather, and it ain't pretty. "Aren't they a little old for that? More ready for retirement than starting all over?"

"Come on, Em, you know age is just a number. Our mothers were acting like they were nineteen years old again just hearing that they were going to be backstage. Don't you want this for *them*? Don't you want our moms to be able to relive their youth together? Do the things they wished they had done before they walked away for us?"

Her words lance my heart like they were sent on an arrow off Robin Hood's bow. "Of *course* I want that for them. All I want is their happiness. They deserve that."

"That's all I want for them, too. And for me and you and Rose. We could all make this happen—give our moms back the thing our very *existence* took away—but only if we work together."

I let out a long, tortured sigh. It's time for me to take one for the team again. "Okay, fine. What do you want me to do? I'll do what I can, but I'm only me, you know. I'm not a miracle worker. Chances are I'll screw things up worse than they already were by getting involved."

"No, don't say that; that's baloney. You're a sweetheart, and Sam knows it. I could see it when he was looking at you today. He thinks you're cool."

"Cool? Please. No, he doesn't. He thinks I'm a complete and utter nincompoop, and based on my behavior today, I wouldn't argue with him on that."

"Stop. Don't say that about yourself or about him. Anyway, I don't have time to argue with you over it. We're almost to the airport. Just . . . keep him here. Don't let him leave. Do whatever you have to do."

"How am I going to do that?" I start laughing. She is being so ridiculous. I've never seen my sister this desperate before.

"I don't know. Figure something out. Be creative. That's what you do, right? Create things? I'm just asking you to create a solution to a problem. Let your imagination run wild. Make it happen."

Apparently, Amber has fooled herself into thinking I'm her: the solutions girl. Oh well . . . it's not like I'm going to be able to convince her otherwise before she gets on the plane for Japan.

"Fine. I will do my best to find out what makes Sam happy, and then I'll do that thing." *As if.* Right now I am lying through my teeth so my sister can relax and have a stress-free trip to Japan. Whatever happens with Sam after she's gone will happen. I'm just going to let him do his thing while I do mine. End of story.

"I knew I could count on you," Amber says, resting her head on my shoulder. "You're the best sister ever. I know you'll figure out what his buttons are."

"Buttons?" Guilt is seeping into my heart from Amber's touch at my shoulder. I'm telling her I'm going to do this thing that I know very well I can't do, letting her think I'm on board when I'm not. *Liar, liar, pants on fire.*

"What he likes. You know. What we talked about. Make him happy. Press those damn buttons. Just be yourself, and that'll be perfect."

Be myself. *Be myself?* Is she crazy? She knows I can't be myself! It'll be a disaster! The cab takes an exit and the airport appears ahead. For all my nonchalant statements to myself about not doing anything, about letting things roll out naturally, I'm still starting to panic. I thought I could be cool about this, but I can't. Amber's really counting on me. I can't just do *nothing*.

My worries tumble out of my mouth. "But what are they? His buttons? What does he like to do? How does he pass his time? And how am I qualified to be the person to make him happy?"

She grabs my hand and squeezes. "I don't know. Just figure it out. No one reads people better than you do."

I stare out the window so she won't see the tears welling up in my eyes. I can't just blow him off like I was hoping I could. She needs me to at least try. I'm not at all qualified for this very important job, but I don't want to let her down. The conflict feels like it's killing me. My head is pounding. *Amber's going to feel terrible when I have a stroke over this.*

She takes my hand and presses it up to her cheek, pulling my attention away from my impending aneurism. "Please don't be stressed, and please don't be angry at me. I love you, no matter what happens."

I look at her through shimmering eyes. "You mean as bad as I'm going to screw this up, you'll still love me in the end?"

"You're not going to screw it up, but yes; I love you, no matter what. If he leaves, it's not your fault. If things fall apart, it's not your fault. The shit between him and Ty goes back a really long way, and nobody, including me, is expecting you to change anything about that. Just . . . keep him company if you can. I'm not saying you have to hang out with him all day long, but if you could just check in with him once a day at least and make sure he's not planning on jumping off a building, that would be cool."

I nod. This I can probably do. It sounds a lot less intimidating than all the other things she was suggesting, like pushing buttons and getting into his personal business. Relief washes through me and allows my sense of humor to make an appearance. "Check . . . So, my job is to make sure that Sam does not get so distraught sharing a living space with me that he wants to jump off a high-rise."

She reaches over and pinches my cheek. "Now we're talking. *Now* you get me." The taxicab pulls up to the curb, and Amber leans over to kiss me. "I love you. You are my favorite sister, but if you ever tell Rose I said that, I will deny it."

I kiss her back. "You've already told both Rose and me that we're each your favorite sister a thousand times. We've compared notes over the years, so don't even try it."

She points at my face. "Hey! You weren't supposed to do that."

The love I have for my sister wells up in my heart and feels like it's going to spill over and flood the car. "I get it. We're both your favorites. And you're both my favorites, too. There's nothing I wouldn't do for you, including staying in this horrible city and hanging out with your boyfriend's brother and trying to keep him happy, even though I don't think he's the type that ever *gets* truly happy."

She hugs me, squeezing hard and bumping into my injured knee. I wince but keep my complaints to myself.

"I love you, I love you, I love you. Stay safe. Don't talk to strangers if it makes you uncomfortable. But still have fun. And go shopping, would you please? Your clothes are horrible."

I laugh wearily. I've spent one day with my sister, but it feels like a week. "Get out of my cab."

After she shuts the door, Amber reaches through the window to throw a bunch of twenty-dollar bills on the seat. "Pay for the fare with cash, and if you need any more money, the combination to my safe is my birthday and it's in the closet in my bedroom behind my boots."

"As if I'm ever going to take any of your money. Go to Japan, would you?"

"Fine, I'm leaving." She backs away, waving at me.

"Have a great trip!" I shout out the window. "I'll miss you! I love you!"

She blows me a kiss as she's running down the sidewalk with her suitcase rolling behind her. "Love you too!"

The cabbie looks at me in his rearview mirror. "Where're we going?"

"Back to where you picked us up, please."

"You got it." The cabbie shifts the car into drive and pulls away from the curb, a chorus of horns echoing behind us.

My heart is heavy as we slowly make our way around the cars dropping passengers off. I lose track of Amber as she quickly disappears into the crowd. I can't believe she just left me in New York City all by myself. Or with Sam. I don't know which is worse: to be all alone or to be alone with him.

I take a deep breath and let it out slowly. Then I repeat the action a second time, a third time, and a fourth. I need to steady my heart rate and respirations so I can try to enjoy this trip back into the city and not stroke out. I chant in my head to help talk myself down off the ledge of panic:

I am not going to stress about spending over a week with a stranger who makes me feel nervous and giddy at the same time.

I'm not going to stress about the crowds and the traffic and the pollution and the crime and all the strange and mysterious things that surround me.

I'm not going to freak out about the fact that my sister will expect me to be wearing new clothes when she gets back, and I'm not going to allow myself to be angry over the fact that she is rushing across the globe to be with men who don't deserve even a single moment of her attention, after I left my life to be with her, because she's chasing her dreams and I love her too much to hold that against her. If I had a dream that strong calling to me, I know she'd do the same for me.

Slowly but surely, my nerves unwind and smooth out. I love my moms and I love my sisters, so I'm going to do whatever I can to keep everybody happy. But when this sacrifice is made and the trip is over, I'm going to go back to my life—my beautiful, peaceful, tranquil, boring life—and I'm never going to wish it were different ever again.

CHAPTER SIXTEEN

Everything *should* be going perfectly. I have my easel and canvas all set up . . . my brushes, my paints . . . my palette is loaded . . . I even have the rubber gloves ready to go if I decide to do this thing without brushes. But that stupid, loud, intrusive *racket* from the other room is ruining everything. How in the hell am I supposed to be able to concentrate when it feels like a crappy high school metal band is practicing inside my ear canal?

Sighing, I put my palette down on the small table covered in plastic wrap and place the brush back in the cup I found under the bathroom sink. As I turn to face the hallway behind my bedroom, I glare. More horrible sounds are making their way under the space below the closed door.

Bwont, bwerp, bwap! Bop boop boop bwerpitty bwerp bweeeerrp!

I'm going to recommend to Amber that she get her hearing checked immediately, as soon as she returns from Japan, because if she thinks Sam's music is anything other than total crap, she's obviously tone-deaf at the very least.

Derw, derw, dow, dewp, boopa, derp, deeerrp!

My bottom jaw shifts to the left; my teeth are officially set on edge by Sam's so-called music. I turn and take a deep breath with my eyes closed. I can get through this. I can paint with him playing in the room across the hall. It's mind over matter. It's all about concentration and focus . . .

"Goddammit!" Sam yells, his voice coming through our two doors muffled but still very clear. Then something heavy hits the wall and something even heavier crashes to the floor. Several discordant twangs are involuntarily strummed on his electric guitar. I'm not sure, but it sounds like he might have used his instrument as a weapon to kill a television.

Smiling through the pain, I pick up my paintbrush and hold it poised over the blank canvas. I will paint something. I will create something beautiful. I will . . .

More crashing comes from the other room.

Then . . . *Bwooowww wow wow wowwww, weir, weeeer!*

I throw the paintbrush down on the plastic and stride over to the door. I've had just about enough of this nonsense. He knows very well I'm trying to work in here. It's like he's begging for me to come over there, so, fine! Here I go! I'm going right over there to have a word with him about his complete lack of courtesy for other people. And I'm not scared at all. My heart is hammering because I'm so *angry*.

"Hey!" I shout, banging on his door. "Do you mind?!"

Suddenly, his face is there, inches from mine. The breeze from his sudden opening of the door brushes loose hair against my cheeks, tickling my skin. My heart stops momentarily.

"What?!" he yells, his face red and sweaty.

I'm struck dumb. Seeing him there without a shirt on is enough to send my heart into overdrive. His chest is sweaty too. He has a tattoo over his heart that reads *Sadie*.

I say the first thing that pops into my head. "Who is Sadie?"

He stares at me for a few seconds, his nostrils flaring, his breathing reminding me of an angry bull. Time stands still, only starting again when he finally answers. "What do you want?"

His rudeness snaps me out of the little spell that had temporarily taken over my righteous indignation. "You know I'm trying to paint, right?"

He shrugs, his body stance relaxing a little bit. "No, actually, I didn't know that." He uses the back of his hand to wipe his forehead.

"Well, I am. And it's pretty much impossible to do with you making such a ruckus over here."

One of his eyebrows goes up. "A ruckus?" He strokes his beard a few times, moving his jaw around.

"Yes. A ruckus." I ignore his sexy beard maneuvers and lean over, trying to see around him. "It sounds like you're in the process of destroying this bedroom." I can't see anything but darkness; apparently, he plays with the lights off and his window blocked with a blanket. *Weird.* I feel bad for my sister, but I hope she's not going to blame me for the expense he's racking up by tearing holes in her walls or whatever I heard him doing in here.

He glances over her shoulder. "Not exactly. More like destroying my equipment." He has the grace to sound a little chagrined.

"What equipment? You came here with a backpack and two guitars."

"I rented a couple amps and some other stuff. It was delivered earlier."

"Oh." I somehow missed that. It must have happened while I was napping. I guess that explains the loud guitar I was hearing. "Well . . . I don't think my sister or Ty would appreciate you bringing the house down around our ears while they're gone."

"Probably not." He rests his arm on the doorjamb and sighs. "I'm just a little frustrated. I'm sorry if I was making too much noise. I'll try to be quieter."

I nod, feeling like a schoolmarm scolding a student. "Good. Thank you." I turn to go, but then he speaks and I freeze in my footsteps.

"What are you painting?"

I force my legs to get moving again and continue into the bedroom without looking back. "Nothing, because you're being too *noisy!*" I slam the door behind me, but not before I hear him laugh.

I walk over to my canvas and stare at it. It's just as blank as it was an hour ago. The big white space is almost a threat, staring out at me, taunting me: *Paint on me, chicken. Paint something . . . or are you too afraid? Make yourself useful around here, why don't you . . .*

I put on a pair of rubber gloves. I've never painted with my fingers before—well, not since I was a small child, anyway—but I might as well give this new technique a try, because this damn canvas ain't gonna paint itself. It can't hurt anything to try something different, right?

I pick up a tube of black paint and put a blob of the color on my fingertips. I use the first two fingers of my right hand to smear it around and then step back to look at it. My heart is still pounding. I don't know if it's from the painting craziness or that man across the hall.

I frown at the result of my first finger-painting attempt. *Humph.* I'm not impressed so far, but I might as well keep trying. At least I'm getting *somewhere*.

I pick up a dark-blue shade and repeat the process, covering up more of the white gesso that serves as the foundation for what my sister has deemed to be the next masterpiece for her apartment. *Pfff.* Even finger-painting, I can't do any worse than that fake Jackson Pollock out in her foyer. My energy picks up just a tad.

I select a deep-green shade next and smooth it into the blue and black. The effect isn't completely terrible. I'll probably never show this to anyone, though. I wonder if there's a place in New York City where I can safely and legally burn a canvas.

I grab another couple of colors and play around with them, warming to the idea of finger painting as an adult. What's happening on the canvas right now is nothing like my old style—it's more abstract and amorphous—but it's keeping me busy, at least. I feel the stress created by Sam's discordant destruction across the hall start to ease out of my body. I think I read somewhere that therapists use finger painting with the mentally ill. I'm not sure I want to examine too closely what this is saying about me right now.

The next color has to be exactly right. Purple maybe? I'm not sure. I select a tube and hold the color up to my fingertips. *Maybe.* This *could* be the one I need to use next.

I put a giant helping of it in my palm and place the tube down on the table. Smearing my gloved hands together, I prepare myself for this daring move that's already feeling really good in the deepest part of my creative self. I'm just reaching out to touch the canvas, fingers loaded with glorious violet paint, when a horrible noise comes from out in the hallway again.

Bana, bamp, bamp, bowowowowww, derrrr, neerrrrr neeerrr!

I flinch but move my fingers closer to the canvas anyway. This is really going to be the beginning of something special, I can feel it. I just need to get past the noise and . . .

Louda dout dout dow, de deeer deeer de deeer deeerr woww!

I cringe. Whatever creativity I was feeling bubbling up in me is now simmering down to nothing again. I cannot believe this. *What is his damn, freaking, fracking, frucking problem?!*

"Goddammit!" he shouts. I hear what sounds like furniture moving, wooden legs scraping across floors. But I don't remember his bedroom even having wooden floors. *What in the Sam Hill is going on in there?*

I close my eyes and take a deep breath, in and out. I am locked and loaded with my purple paint, ready to dive into the creative process. This painting session need not end here. I can live my life while he is living his. His problems are not my problems, and my problems are not his. This is my world, and I'm the only one in it. Peace and serenity exist inside my bubble. *Serenity now . . . serenity now . . . I can do this . . .*

I reach out with my eyes closed and make contact with the canvas. *Down and to the right. A sweeping motion, that's it, yessss . . . This is going to be so beautiful . . .*

"That's it! Fuck this shit!" Sam shouts.

My eyes fly open as his reality comes crashing into mine. I grab the bottoms of my gloves and snap them off my hands, sending purple paint across the tarped area to land on the formerly pristine wall. *Jesus H. Christ on a Popsicle stick! What the hell!*

I'm across the room in two seconds, running full out. Sam is *so* going to get a piece of my mind. I fling my door open in time to see his back disappearing down the hall.

"Where are you going?!" I shout, outraged at the idea of him missing out on the dressing down I was about to give him.

"Out."

I leave my room to follow him. "Where?" I know what my sister would say about all this: *He can't leave angry! Who knows what trouble he'll get into?* Maybe he's going to the airport to take off for LA. Maybe that girl Sadie is waiting for him. He avoided my question about who she was. She's probably the reason he left early, and now he's regretting that decision.

"What do you care?" He stops at the end of the hall and spins around to face me, waiting for my answer.

I slow down as I approach him, shrugging. I need to be cool. Amber needs my help. I can't tell him what a shitty shithead he is for being so loud and inconsiderate . . .

"I don't know. I was just thinking . . ." *Panic level ten! Quick! Say something that makes sense!* "If you're going out, maybe I can hitch a ride with you?" I have no idea where this is coming from. I don't want to go anywhere with him! What the heck? I think Amber brainwashed me with all that finding-his-buttons stuff in the cab.

He jabs his thumb over his shoulder. "I was just going to get some air."

I smile brilliantly. *Hallelujah.* This is so much better than hearing he's leaving for California or that he's going out to score some drugs or climb up onto the roof of the building.

Words tumble out of me. "That sounds great. Really great. *Phew.* I could really use some fresh air myself. Do they have that here?" I'm getting a cramp in my face from smiling so hard.

He walks toward me and stops a foot away. I don't know what to say, but my smile slips away out of nervousness. *What is he going to do? Why is he so close?*

He reaches up and gently swipes his thumb across my cheek. "If you're going to go outside, you're probably going to want to clean your face off first."

My hand slowly rises to my cheek. "Oh, no. How bad is it?" I have been known to paint almost as much of myself as I have my canvases.

His smile is almost sad, which is weird. "It's not bad," he says. "Just a couple specks here and there. I may have smeared some, though."

I hold up my finger. "Don't leave without me. I'm just going to go wash my face, and I'll be right back."

"I'm not going anywhere special," he warns as I hustle back to my room.

"Perfect. I don't like going to special places."

His chuckle follows me down the hall.

CHAPTER SEVENTEEN

When I get to my bathroom, I stare at my reflection in the mirror. "What are you doing? Where did all that come from?" I can't believe I'm being so stupid. The guy was about to leave me alone in an empty apartment where I could finally get something accomplished, and the first thing I do is what, exactly? Volunteer my services as his tour guide? How can I be a tour guide in a city I don't even know myself?

I turn on the water and pump some soap from the dispenser onto my hands. It quickly turns green. The rubber gloves did not protect me completely, but to be fair, the pigment was probably there before I put the things on. I'm a messy painter, which is why, at home, I've been relegated to doing my work out in a shed where no one else goes.

I scrub the blue and green paint specks off my nose and wipe away the purple smear that Sam spread across my cheek. As I stare at my complexion, I almost wish I had some makeup to brighten my look a little. I'm too pale. I look . . . sad or something. *Oh well, nothing I can do about it now.*

I double-check to make sure I have nothing in my teeth before I leave the bathroom and, on an impulse, grab the little pile of change I found in the bottom of my suitcase. As I head back down the hall toward the foyer, I try not to act like I'm in a hurry, like I'm not panicked that he's already left, like I'm not actually looking forward to being with him for another minute more. I pause to adjust my skirt and check my nonexistent watch, just for good measure, but I have nothing to worry about. He's standing in the same place I left him, and he's facing the elevator doors; he's missed all of my cool moves.

As I step into the foyer just behind him, he pulls a plastic card out of his pocket and holds it up at me. "You have your key?"

"Uh . . . no. Can we use yours?"

"Sure, but what if we split up? Won't you need your own?"

I nod as my heart sinks a little. "Yeah. That makes sense. I'll be right back." I go into the kitchen and grab the key fob and card off the counter, sliding them into my small purse.

So what if we get separated? I head back to the foyer. *We don't have to stick together.* I was just offering to keep him company, but he doesn't need to take me up on it. It's not really rejection. Or it is, but it doesn't matter because it's not like he's my boyfriend or anything. I'm not really responsible for him. He's a grown man and I'm a grown woman, and if we go our separate ways after leaving here, well, Amber will just have to chill about it.

We step on to the elevator together. "You have anywhere special you like to wander around here?" he asks as he selects the button for the lobby.

I think of what Amber told me to do: *Find his buttons and push them.* "No. I just got here today. I don't know the city at all." We'll see if the helpless damsel in distress works as a hot button for Mr. Weirdo Beardo.

"Oh. I thought you'd been here for a little while."

I shake my head. "Nope."

When he doesn't offer to show me around or make another comment, I decide this button isn't going to work with him. Maybe I should have just taken charge and picked a place I've heard of, faked my sense of the city. *Oh well. Too late.*

Our trip down to the ground floor is utterly silent. I wish I were better at small talk, but . . . *mmm* . . . no . . . I pretty much suck at it.

I've always depended on Amber and Rose for starting and keeping a conversation going. I literally cannot think of a single thing to say to this man.

What I really want to know is who this Sadie girl is, but I can't very well ask him about her again; that would be rude. Since he didn't answer me before when I asked and he managed to change the subject, I have to believe this is an off-limits topic . . . which of course makes me want to talk about that and only that until I get to the bottom of the mystery. She could be his girlfriend. Or a woman who broke his heart and left him in the dust. Or maybe she's his mom. I don't remember if Amber ever mentioned her when she was telling me about Ty.

When we get outside into the dark night, the cold air hits me and goes right down into my bones, making me wish I'd brought a jacket. Sam walks fast, and I struggle to keep up, ignoring the pain in my knee. I'm soon happy for his speed, though, because it's warming me up quickly.

"Do you know where you're going?" I ask, almost matching him stride for stride. I have to take an extra step for every three or four of his to not fall behind. The pain in my knee has disappeared. This may be because the cold has numbed my skin all the way through.

"I was thinking Central Park. I don't know when it closes, though." He pulls his phone out of his pocket and looks at it. "It's ten now."

"Does it close? I thought it was open twenty-four hours."

"I heard they had problems with crime in the park, so they started closing it at night."

"Oh. That's probably a good idea." My teeth chatter at the end of my sentence.

"Are you cold?" He slows down to look at me.

"No," I lie, trying to sound really convincing. "It feels great out here. Invigorating. It was getting really stuffy up in that room. I needed to get out."

"Yeah, in mine too."

Maybe I'm imagining it, but it seems like he slows down a little bit to make it easier for me. We're not at the point where we're strolling, but I also don't feel like I'm competing in a 5K anymore. I'm warm enough to fend off the chill without a jacket, but I'm also not sweating. *Nice.*

We get to the edge of the park and stop to read a little sign. "It's going to close in three hours," Sam says, looking left and then right. "Which way?"

There's live music coming from our right, so I gesture that way, feeling inspired for Sam. "Let's go over there." Maybe hearing somebody else playing will help motivate him to stop using his guitar as a baseball bat on his amp or his furniture or whatever. Watching somebody else paint does that for me sometimes. Other times it makes me feel completely unworthy to pick up a paintbrush, but hopefully that won't happen in the park tonight. The stuff someone is playing down the path from us doesn't sound particularly fabulous from here, so hopefully it'll just remind Sam how talented he is. I have to believe the sounds coming from his bedroom earlier were just him banging out his frustration with his life. Amber can't be *that* tone-deaf.

CHAPTER EIGHTEEN

We wander down the path together, other people passing by, some with dogs, some jogging alone, some as couples walking hand in hand. Two lovebirds walk by practically wound around each other, and I feel a little jealous of the affection between them. I do love my life, but sometimes I wish I had somebody to share it with. I can't help but glance at Sam as this thought flits through my mind.

His head is tilted down, and he looks like he's brooding again, his beard resting on his chest. The man I marry won't be anything like Sam. Not that Sam's a bad person or anything—I mean, as far as I know—but he's just too . . . overemotional. And he has a reckless way about him that makes me feel very . . . unsettled. He's too . . . too . . . just *too much* . . . of everything.

No, the man I fall in love with will be kind and serene. Easy to get along with. Sweet and gentlemanly. He'll love animals and children. I definitely want to have children someday.

"A nickel for some chalk," he says, still focused on the ground. I'm not sure that his comment is for me or that I even understood him properly until he finally looks at me expectantly.

"What? I'm sorry, I missed that."

He keeps looking at me for a few more seconds before shifting his gaze to the path ahead. "I said, a nickel for your thoughts."

"Oh." I laugh. "I thought you were trying to buy some chalk."

"What?" He looks at me again, half-smiling and confused.

No way do I want to tell him what I was just thinking. *Quick! Distraction!* "Since when are thoughts worth a nickel?" I'm charmed, imagining that my thoughts are more valuable to him than someone else's.

"Inflation."

"Oh. Inflation. Of course." So much for being charmed.

"Are your thoughts for sale?" he asks. He pulls something out of his pocket and hands it to me.

I take whatever it is without thinking. It's warm and heavy—an actual nickel. Does this mean he just paid for my thoughts and I have to share them? Because there is no way on God's green earth that I'm going to tell him the sappy, girly things that were just running through my mind. Not even for a whole quarter would I do that.

"Want to know what I was thinking?" he asks, making me realize that I left his question hanging without answering it.

I smile at the flirty tone in his voice and the fact that he's pretty much managing this entire conversation without any help from me. "Sure." It's a lot easier for me to listen to his thoughts than to share my own.

"I was thinking how cool it would be to be like those people." He nods at a couple headed in our direction.

"Who? Those people right there?" I point to clarify because I don't see anything special about them. They're just two people walking together, holding hands and chatting.

He reaches up and puts his hand on top of mine, pushing my arm down. "Yes. And next time, try to be more obvious about it so they can be absolutely sure we're talking about them."

Perhaps it's my imagination, but it seems like his hand rests on mine just a few seconds longer than it needs to before it disappears. It makes me warm all over. "Sorry. I wasn't sure I was understanding you correctly."

He doesn't say anything in response, but my curiosity is too piqued to let the conversation go at that. "Why would you want to be like them?" I do a further evaluation of the couple, trying to figure out the answer on my own, since he's taking his sweet time answering. They're both fit and good-looking, but so is Sam; he can't be jealous of their attractiveness. Or maybe he wants to move to New York permanently and wishes he fit in more; they look like native New Yorkers—both of them have very stylish haircuts and they're wearing really cool exercise clothing. Their sneakers are fluorescent. I could totally see them in an advertisement for a gym or a high-end yoga studio.

"I don't know," he says. "Maybe because they seem happy together."

I completely get what he's saying, and it makes me fall back into the dream I was having earlier, about what I would like my life to look like someday. "Yeah." My voice comes out dreamy as I picture myself walking with a man down this path, smiling about our life in Maine together. We'd be here on a vacation, visiting my sister, talking about how great our life is as we hold hands. I'd look up at him and he'd smile down at me. He'd have a beard . . .

Oh, shit. Stop that. I shake my head and say the first thing that comes to mind. "I was thinking the same thing."

He pauses and looks at me. "The same thing about them?"

I keep moving forward so he'll follow me and not stare at me so intently. "Yeah. Or whatever. I was just walking along here thinking how cool it would be to have a boyfriend . . . or whatever." *Oh God.* I can't believe I just said that out loud! Why don't I just pass him a note written in crayon: *Sam, would you please go out with me? Check Yes or No . . .*

"That's funny." He's not laughing. He sounds . . . *intrigued?*

Do I dare ask? "Why is that funny?" *Why, yes, I do dare.* I don't know who I am right now. The old me would have left it alone. The new me—the New York me—is looking for his buttons.

"That we were thinking the same thing."

"Oh. Yeah. That is funny." I'm so relieved he's not taking what I said as a hint that I want *him* to be my boyfriend, words start spilling out. "To be honest, I wouldn't have expected that to be something on your radar."

His voice is a little gruff. "Why? You think I want to be alone forever?"

"I don't know." I shrug, feeling out of my depth. "Guys don't think the same way girls do."

"Oh, yeah? How do guys think? Tell me."

Okay, so this is an embarrassing trap of my own making. Now I have to show him how incredibly uneducated I am about the male species. But I'm going to woman up and deal with it, because I'm enjoying the fact that we're actually having a conversation and not walking around in awkward silence anymore.

"Don't guys just think about getting laid, having fun, and partying?"

He chuckles.

"What's so funny?"

"You said 'getting laid.' It doesn't sound right coming out of your mouth."

I knew it. He thinks I'm a virgin. "I am just a touch offended by that," I say.

"Why? It was a compliment."

"It doesn't feel like a compliment to be called a complete prude."

"No, hey, I wasn't calling you a prude." He rests his hand on my shoulder for just a second or two before pulling it away. "You just seem like a really nice girl, is all."

I'm only slightly mollified. "Well, I am a nice girl, but it doesn't mean I'm a virgin."

He leans his head back and laughs before responding. "Fair enough."

I kick a stone off the path, imagining what I must look like to him, especially compared to all these people walking in the park around us. I fear I'm coming up short. "My life must seem really tame to you."

"No, not tame necessarily . . ." He takes a few more steps before continuing. "Just different. I'm actually kind of curious about it, if you want to know the truth."

"There's no need to stay curious," I say, not allowing the shyness to come in—the fear that wants to stop the conversation and send me back to the apartment alone. "Ask your questions. I'm happy to answer them." This I can do . . . talk about my life. If there were a scale of conversations to measure my abilities by, an impossible one would be about orgasms, and an easy one would be about the weather. The one he's introduced definitely falls more toward the weather end. In fact, it's probably the easiest conversation I could ever have with Sam. It certainly doesn't hurt to know that he seems interested in my life. Even if it's just polite interest, I'll take it.

"What do you do all day?" he asks. "What's a typical day in your life look like?"

He starts to turn down a path that will lead away from the music, but I gesture for him to follow me toward it. He comes along without a word.

"I would say it's very . . . tame . . . compared to New York City, anyway."

"In what way?"

"Well, it's very quiet, first of all. The only sounds I hear most of the time are birds chirping, bees buzzing, horses neighing, or goats bleating sometimes, and occasionally the dogs barking. Every once in a while there'll be people talking, but not always." I laugh, thinking about how strange it would seem to him, being from LA. Sometimes the people at the farm are so busy snoozing or meditating, I don't hear a single word uttered for days.

"It sounds pretty cool."

"It is pretty cool. I love my life." I can't help the smile that spreads across my face, even when I catch him looking at me.

"I guess I can see why you aren't too thrilled about being here in the city."

"It's not that bad." I'm admitting this to myself at the same time as I'm admitting it to him. "It's just a bit much. I wasn't planning on it. My sister kind of sprang the trip on me at the last minute, and I didn't have time to prepare myself for it mentally."

"Tell me more about your life," he says. "Your farm."

"Well, I get up every morning pretty early. Around seven."

He moans. "Oh, man. That is so not me."

I smile. "I'm not sure it's me either. It's just what I've had to do my whole life. I'm in charge of taking care of the animals, so I have to get up early and feed them. I don't like them to go hungry for too long. It's not good for their digestive systems, or so Rose tells me."

"Rose?"

"My sister. She works at an animal clinic."

"How many animals do you have?"

"The number varies. Sometimes we take in rescues and our numbers go up, and some of them pass away from either old age or illness, and our numbers go down. My sister isn't exactly a veterinarian, but she's really good at giving medical care to them, so they don't die from sickness very often. Usually, death happens when a rescue comes in that's in such bad condition there's nothing we can do to fix it up. But I would say we usually have around two or three dogs running around, several cats . . . I have a herd of six goats, two pigs, five horses, four cows, and I have, right now, I think, twenty-four chickens? Give or take?"

"Wow. That's a real farm."

"Well, yeah." I smile at his city-boy amazement. "We also grow some things. We have a really big garden, and we sell a lot of our produce at the farmers' market because we could never eat or can it all ourselves. And in the winter, we tap our maple trees for the syrup. We harvest our honey all summer long and sell it through the winter."

"That's so cool. Do you ever do tours?"

"What do you mean?"

"You know, like people come to your place and see all the things you do, and you give talks about it while you show them around."

He says this like I live at some kind of amusement park. I guess to someone from LA my life must look pretty silly. I try to use humor to brush off the little bit of sadness that his comment creates. "Why? Are you interested in a tour?"

He nods, not getting my joke at all. "I actually would be. I've never seen anything like that. I'm a city boy, born and bred." He seems serious.

"Well, you're in luck, because the farm is open to anyone who wants to come there. People can stay as long as they want, as long as they're contributing. It's an intentional-living community . . . Do you know what that means?" No one ever does, not even the people who frequent the farmers' market.

He shakes his head. "Nope. But it sounds cool."

I laugh. "Well, I don't know how cool it is. I think some people consider it pretty dorky, but what it means is our community is open to anybody who wants or needs to be there, so long as they share the same values and ideas about community as we do. You can pitch a tent on our land, or, if we have room, you can stay in the house. And in exchange for the space and the place to rest, you just have to do some work on the farm. Contribute."

"People contribute in what way?"

I shrug, trying to picture all the things I've seen people do around my home. "You can help in the garden, with the animals . . . or if you're good at repairing things, you can do handyman projects around the place. We have a lawyer who comes once a year who helps us with legal issues when we need it. There's always something that can be done; you don't have to be a skilled laborer to do it. We had one guy who just came up with activities to keep the kids busy while the adults were working. I loved it when he came. He always had fun games for us when we were younger, and he played guitar, too. We sang songs every night by an outdoor fire in the summer. I never got tired of it." It was so sad when he died. I still think of Wilbur often.

"You said it was intentional living. What does the word *intentional* mean? Where does that part fit in?"

I've never actually explained it to anyone, so I have to fish around in my brain to remember what my mothers have said to people who have asked at the farmers' market. People know us so well there, we don't get many questions anymore.

"Well, we try to have very low impact on the environment. We make sure that whatever we do is sustainable, so for example, if we cut down a tree, we plant two trees. We treat ourselves and others with respect and think about why we do what we do. People who stay with us need to agree that being kind to one another and at peace with ourselves and the world is the best way to be, whenever possible. We don't practice any specific religion, but I guess you could say we follow the Golden Rule . . . treating people the way you want to be treated and all that." Explaining this to Sam warms me, reminds me of how much I love my life at Glenhollow Farms. How could I ever be angry with my mothers for making the decisions they did way back in the day, when the result has been this life? I can't. I just can't blame them for anything because they gave me a gift that I will have for my entire existence.

"Does everyone eat vegan there or something?"

His comment makes me laugh. So many people equate our lifestyle with veganism, I'm not offended. I'm used to hearing this from people in town. "No, not as a rule. Some people who come to stay with us do, but my family eats meat. But we don't buy it anywhere because we don't know how those animals were treated. We raise the animals, and we have them slaughtered on our property by a professional butcher in the most stress-free and kind way possible. We try to be mindful of what we're doing with the animals and treat them right, since they're nourishing our bodies."

"That's cool. So the intentional thing is just to kind of think things all the way through?"

"Yeah, in a way. We take time out every day to center ourselves, to meditate and connect with our inner selves." I shrug as my face goes a little pink. "I can only imagine what this sounds like to a city boy like you. Pretty hokey, huh?"

"Nah, it sounds interesting. Nice. Really." His expression has gone really soft. He places his hand on my shoulder for couple seconds. "Thanks for telling me. I don't want you to think I'm judging you with my questions. It's not like that."

As he says it, I realize it's true. He could be sitting there making faces and laughing, but he's not. He seems sincerely interested. "You should come see it sometime," I say boldly, not realizing until the words are out that I'm going to say them. "You might like it. Maybe it would be a place for you to unwind a little bit." From what I heard coming out of that bedroom, it sure seems like he could use the time-out.

I won't tell him it's a place where he could write music, because I know what it's like to be an artist and to be told by someone that a certain place would be good for me to create in. Nobody knows what that place is but the artist, and thinking that someone is sitting there wondering why you're not painting a picture or writing a song is enough stress to stop the creative process altogether.

"Maybe I will," he says. "Someday." He doesn't sound very hopeful. Perhaps he doesn't really think intentional living is as cool as he said he said it was. *Oh well.* It's not for everyone, and that's okay with me. I wouldn't want it to become too popular; the farm could quickly become overrun like this city is.

I like my privacy. I need it, in fact. But if Sam wanted to come out to Glenhollow Farms and stay for a little while, I don't think it would be so bad. Not that I've spent a ton of time with him, but he seems pretty nice . . . not judgy, like he said. The more I think about it, the more I believe it might actually be fun to have him visit, to show him all the things I've described to him . . . these things that make me proud and happy. I get the feeling that he'd respect it, even if he didn't want that life for himself. It's too bad that's not in the cards for us. He's an LA guy, and I'm a hippie chick who lives on a farm in the middle of Maine. There aren't too many people who could be more opposite than we are.

CHAPTER NINETEEN

As we make our way around a bend in the path, we come upon a group of artists doing their thing. A couple of them are packing up to leave, but there's still a guy drawing portraits, a woman in rainbow-colored clothing juggling three bowling pins, and a guy in dreads strumming an acoustic guitar with a girl singing next to him.

We stop several yards away and watch in silence. The guy is playing a song that I remember from one of the many Red Hot albums my mothers have played over the years. I see movement out of the corner of my eye and look down to catch Sam's fingers playing an invisible guitar on his thigh. I don't even think he realizes he's doing it. Amber's voice plays in my head: *Find his buttons. Push them.*

"You should come out here and play sometime," I say casually.

His fingers stop moving, and he slides his hands into his front pockets. "Nah. It's not for me."

"Why not? I hear you're pretty good."

He turns his head toward me. The lamplight coming from our left hides the details of his face in shadows, but I can feel the intensity of his gaze. "Who told you that?"

"My sister. She told me you're going to write some music for the band, so you must be decent at it."

He shrugs and goes back to watching the people in front of us. "Maybe."

The person drawing a portrait by portable-lamp light is almost finished. It's not a terrible job, but I've seen better. He gets paid ten dollars for his efforts and then sits there looking around for his next customer. He catches my eye and wiggles his pencil at me. I shake my head no.

"You should give it a try," Sam says, a challenge in his voice.

"Go sit for that guy? Are you crazy?"

"No, not sit for him. Draw."

"Noooo way." I shake my head vigorously.

"Why not? I hear you're good."

He's mocking me with my own words, but he doesn't mean it in a cruel way. He's smiling too hard for that—the white of his teeth is reflected easily in the meager light. We might be flirting, but I'm not sure.

"Who'd you hear that from?" I'm feeling emboldened by the darkness.

"Your sister. When you were in your room. She told me all about you."

"Is that so?" Oh, how I wish my sister were here so that I could interrogate her for an hour and learn everything she told him. "What did she say?" *Please, God, don't let it be anything embarrassing!*

He shrugs as he looks at the portrait artist. "Well, based on what she said, you could wipe the floor with that guy's stuff."

I laugh. "My sister is my biggest fan. I'm not sure I'd believe what she says, if I were you."

"Yeah, well, sisters are like that."

"Do you have one?" *Maybe Sadie is a sibling?*

He shakes his head. "No, but I've got a brother, and that's close enough." His voice softens, like he's fallen into his own thoughts and doesn't realize he's still talking out loud. "Sometimes you think they'd jump into a fire to save you."

"Yeah." I get choked up thinking about it. My sisters would do that for me, and I would for them too. But I can't claim anymore what a big sacrifice it was for me to come to Manhattan for Amber, because I'm having too much fun now for it to be considered anything but pleasant. I realize in that moment that Sam makes me feel lucky to be here.

"I really admire those guys," Sam says, gesturing with his chin at the musicians.

"Because they're good?" I must be the one who's tone-deaf.

"No, not really. I wouldn't say they're outstanding based on what I'm listening to now, but I admire them being able to come out here and play for strangers . . . hoping to make a living at it but probably surviving on ramen."

"Yeah, that takes a special set of ball . . . zzz . . ." I can't believe I just said *balls* in front of a guy I've just met. I think I'm just a little *too* relaxed around him now.

"You said it." He disregards my choice of words like it's no big deal.

We stare at the guitarist for a little while longer before I build up the guts to speak again. "So, why don't you do it? You're a good musician. Maybe it would be more fun working out here than throwing things around in your bedroom."

I can see the stress taking over his body as his shoulders stiffen. "Hell no. Why don't you?" His voice has lost its earlier softness.

"Because I can't play a musical instrument? Trust me . . . no one wants to hear me strumming a tune. They'd probably take up a collection to make me stop." I smile at him, trying to take some of the pressure off.

"No, I'm serious." He turns to face me, and I do the same automatically. It feels like warm air currents are traveling between us, flowing back and forth, heating up the space around us. I'm a few degrees warmer already. *Damn.*

"Really," he says.

"What're you talking about?" My heart starts beating fast again. I cannot keep it under control with him this close and staring at me so intently. I can't even focus on what he's saying. My head is full of air right now. Helium, maybe.

"Why don't you come out here and draw something? It doesn't have to be a person's face. Why not draw that tree over there?" He points.

I look over my shoulder, following the direction of his finger. "It is a pretty tree, but no, thanks."

"Why not? You afraid?"

There is that damn word again: *afraid*. It makes my blood boil. Now there's a different kind of heat between us. A challenge is in the air. "No, I'm not afraid."

His smile becomes decidedly evil. "Prove it."

"*You* prove it." *Oy.* Here I am with my seven-year-old retorts again.

"I can't draw." He laughs, scoffing at the very idea, as if that's what I was talking about.

"No, not *draw*. Nice try. You know that's not what I meant. Why don't you come out here and play a song? Any song. You could play 'Row, Row, Row Your Boat.'"

He folds his arms around his top half like he's trying to get warm all of a sudden as he looks to the side. "I would never play that in public."

I try not to grin too hard. He looks like a little boy being stubborn. "Okay, so what *would* you play in public?"

He shrugs, looking around . . . anywhere but at me. "I don't know. I don't do that stuff."

"Why? Are you *afraid*?"

He glares at me. "No, I'm not afraid. I just don't do that shit."

I shrug, trying to act all casual, when inside I'm throwing a party. *I'm pushing buttons! Woo hoo!* "Sure seems like you are." I pause to look at the musicians. "Look at them . . . They're even younger than you are, and they don't seem to be very afraid."

"No, they don't. And neither does that guy drawing faces, and he's not even any good at it. The last one he did looked like Scooby-Doo, but you don't see him backing down."

I laugh, realizing as he says this that the portrait did bear a striking resemblance to a certain cartoon character. "Scooby is the dog. You're talking about Shaggy."

"See? You saw it too." He grins at me in triumph.

"Whatever." I shake my head, trying to get rid of my smile. I know where this is headed, and I need to stop it in its tracks before it gets too far. "Are you hungry for dinner by any chance?"

"What would you say about making a friendly wager?" he asks, ignoring my dinner invitation.

I can feel my blood pressure rising. *Uh-oh.* "What are you talking about?"

He takes a step closer to me, closing the distance between us and ratcheting up the heat. "I'll bet you a hundred bucks you won't come out here and draw a picture of anything. Not *anything*. Not a face, not a tree, nothing. Because you're too *afraid*."

I imagine myself sitting in a folding chair like that guy over there and sketching just an outline of a tree, and fear strikes me like a bolt of lightning, right in the heart. *Now who's pushing buttons?* "No thanks." I look away, shrugging, trying to convince Sam that none of this is affecting me.

"Too scared, huh?" His voice is soft, but it's no less sinister to my ears. He's the devil on my shoulder, daring me to give myself a heart attack. The angel on my other shoulder is telling me to run all the way back to the apartment and lock myself in my room, that it's okay to be afraid and to prefer my own company to that of strangers.

"I told you I'm not scared." I grit my teeth to keep them from chattering. It's suddenly very, very cold out here in Central Park.

"Then take the bet."

I hate that he's pushing me into a corner. We both know he's as scared shitless as I am. Well, fine. If he wants to play that game, I can play too.

"I will if you will," I say, staring him down.

Now he doesn't look quite so excited, as he takes a step back. "What?"

"I'll take the bet, but only if *you* take the bet too. We both go out. You play a song, I draw a picture."

"Nah. That's not the bet I said."

"So? Can't handle me upping the ante?"

"What do you know about antes?"

"I play poker at the farm." The contribution of one of our guests—Victor Lunel—was to teach all of us how to gamble. I'm actually pretty good at it; Amber says my innocent look allows me to get away with way too much bluffing. "Don't try to run and hide from me, Sam. Do we have a bet or not?" I think I know how the champion of the world poker tournament must feel when he takes the title. I totally called Sam's bluff, and now he's going to have to fold and beg for mercy.

"How do we know who's winning and who's losing?" he asks, caution flavoring his tone. I could be wrong, but it's possible he's considering taking me up on this ridiculous challenge. *Oh, crud.*

"Well, I guess if we both do it, we both win."

"And if I play a song and you bawk, bawk like a chicken and run away without drawing anything?" he asks.

"It won't happen, but in that case, I guess I'd have to give you two hundred bucks." I pause and then continue on a happier note. "But if *I* go out there and draw a picture and *you* chicken out and don't play a song, you pay *me* two hundred."

"I can handle it."

I hate how confident he sounds. I need to push him harder, make him back out before we're both pushed to the limit and peeing our pants in public. "And . . ." I hold up a finger.

He grins. "And?"

"And . . . when I win and you lose, you have to wear a sign on your chest and your back that says, 'I'm a lily-livered chicken' for an entire twenty-four-hour period; and you can't stay in the apartment all day either." I don't know who I am right now, but I like it! This new me isn't afraid of anything, openly flirting with this gorgeous man in the dark in Central Park. I think some crazy New York magic has happened to me. Either that or I've caught a virus and I'm feverish. I resist the urge to check my temperature.

He strokes his beard a few times as he checks me out. "Damn, girl. I thought you were a nice little hippie chick all about peace and harmony, loving thy neighbor, and all that jazz."

I can't stop grinning. "Nope. I'm one of those badass hippie chicks you've heard about, who you should never enter a bet with because they always win."

He drops his arm to hang by his side. "You know . . . I don't think I've ever heard of one of those before."

I hold my hand out for him to shake. "Hi, my name is Emerald Collins, badass hippie chick from Glenhollow Farms. Nice to meet you *and* it'll be nice to *beat* you too."

He slides his hand into mine and slowly tightens his grip. I'm tingling all over with this simple touch.

"It is *really* nice to meet you, badass hippie chick. My name is Sam . . . the man you will be paying two hundred bucks to tomorrow afternoon."

I snort. "You wish." We should stop shaking hands now, but we don't. Instead we stare at each other, the warmth from our skin making its way up my arm and into my heart. I can feel my pulse beating at my neck. He moves closer. And for a moment, I think he's going to lean down to kiss me, but then his cell phone buzzes and he backs away, dropping contact.

"Yeah?" he says to the caller. He walks away and continues his conversation in low tones I cannot discern as words. The funny, silly, warm mood that our bet created has dissipated, and in its place is this feeling of dread. I cannot *believe* I just agreed to come out to Central Park and draw something in front of a crowd of strangers. *What the hell!* I'm not a badass hippie chick! I'm a bawk, bawk, bawking chicken!

CHAPTER TWENTY

Sam turns around and walks back in the direction we came from, continuing his phone call. His voice is low, but I hear parts of it. I'm sad because it sounds like someone back home is trying to convince him to return.

"I can't do that. I can't leave. Not right now. Just . . . call Patty. Maybe she can help."

I think he's talking about Sadie. It's his girlfriend, it has to be. And if he has a girlfriend, I need to stop flirting with him.

Manhattan looks a lot more dismal to me now than it did thirty seconds ago. I wonder if our bet will still be on. I don't really want it to be, of course, because the idea of painting in front of anyone, let alone a park full of strangers, sends fear slicing through me. It's bad enough trying to create something all alone in my studio when my muse has abandoned me for parts unknown, but trying to come up with something worth looking at in front of a group of strangers in the middle of Manhattan? *Holy balls*. What made me say yes to that bet? To upping the ante? *Madness*. It had to be the connection I felt between Sam and me . . . the shared fear we have about performing in front of people who are expecting something great to come from our hands and minds. Somehow, that shared fear is easier to manage, I guess.

"Call me later and let me know how it goes," he says. "I've gotta go. I'll talk to you soon." He ends the call and slides his phone into his pocket.

He doesn't say anything about the conversation, and it doesn't feel right to question him about it. We walk along the path lit by streetlamps, Sam with his hands in his pockets and me with my arms folded over my chest. The temperature is dropping rapidly, and I can't stop shivering. We're both staring at the ground as we head out of the park.

"You hungry?" he asks, startling me. His voice sounds abnormally loud now that the park has mostly emptied and we've been quiet for so long.

"I wasn't hungry . . . earlier."

He glances at me briefly. "Does that mean you're hungry now?"

"I guess I could eat something. But I don't mind eating what's in the fridge back at the apartment."

"You on a budget or something?"

"Not exactly. I just don't know any place to eat around here. That hot dog wasn't so great, and I'd rather not repeat the experience."

"Yeah, I've had better, which is too bad because I had high hopes for New York."

I smile. "Yeah, me too. It's my sister's favorite place, though."

"What's up with her and that guy? The one outside the place."

"The homeless man? Ray?"

"Yeah, him."

"I don't know, really. My sister's the kind of person who sees a problem and then wants to solve it. I'm sure she took one look at that guy and decided she was going to help him out somehow." He definitely looked to me as though he needed help from someone.

"That was nice of her to buy him that blanket."

"Yeah, it was."

I can't think of anything else to say, so I focus on the rhythm of our footsteps on the sidewalk. We're out of the park now and headed back in the direction of the apartment. Maybe we're going to eat there after all.

"So, I guess my brother and her are pretty serious," Sam says.

"Yeah, I guess they are. They live together." I look at him, wondering if he's fishing for information, but I can't read the expression on his face; it's too dark out. "How much do you know about it?" I ask.

"Not much. Just that they're living together and that they met a few months ago."

"Oh. Well, you have the basics." I shrug, loath to divulge too much of my sister's business, even though it's his brother's business too. Maybe there's a reason they haven't shared details with him.

"How did they meet, exactly?" he asks.

He's looking at me, waiting for an answer, and I'm stuck in that place again where I want to keep conversing with him, but I don't want to reveal too much about our private lives. The band means nothing to me, and I'd really love to tell him why, but they're a group of men that he wants to work with, so I hesitate to say anything that will cause any negativity between them.

So . . . how do I explain how Amber and Ty met without revealing our big secret? *Argh.* I hate subterfuge; I'm so terrible at it when I'm not bluffing at the poker table. But I have to say something. "My sister got a job with the band, and Ty was kind of showing her around in the beginning, and they just . . . connected." I shrug, hoping this will be enough for him.

"But you said that she was living in Maine, right? With you?"

"Yes. But she always wanted something more. I guess she didn't realize it until she got here, but she was meant to live in the city."

"Unlike you?"

"Yes. Unlike me. I prefer a quieter life, I guess."

"Nothing wrong with that."

I nod.

"If you don't mind," Sam says hesitantly, "I'd rather grab something to eat outside the apartment. I saw some of the food your sister has in the fridge, and no offense, but I'm not sure it's my thing."

"Sure. No problem. And hey, you don't have to stick with me. If you want to go find something on your own, I'll just head back to the apartment by myself. It's no biggie." Actually, it is a biggie, but I'd never admit that to him.

He shakes his head. "No way. I'm not letting you walk around out here in the dark by yourself. This place isn't safe."

There are still plenty of people around, many of them walking down the sidewalk right next to us, so I don't know why he's feeling this way. "I'm not alone, as you can see." I gesture at all the strangers busy going somewhere. "And I'm not totally helpless either. One of our guests showed me some self-defense moves, so, you know . . ."

"Oh, yeah, I heard; you're one of those badass hippie chicks. I still can't let you go home alone when it's dark out. Sorry. Call me old-fashioned."

I'm flattered that he feels so protective toward me, and I'm hoping in a tiny corner of my heart that he knows full well I could catch a cab home and be perfectly safe. It's a little inconvenient, though, because I don't want to waste all my savings on restaurants in the most expensive city in the world, and I have no desire to spend Amber's money. So if we're going to eat together at a restaurant, I either have to order a tiny salad that'll probably cost me twenty bucks or tell him to take his chivalry and stuff it. "Okay, fine," I say. Despite my financial situation, the decision is easy; I'd rather spend another hour with Sam than assert my feminist power. "What are you in the mood to eat?"

"I don't want to *force* you to hang out with me," he says in a teasing tone.

"No, no." I wave away his concerns. "Ignore me. I was just worrying about my budget."

"How about pizza? I hear that's pretty cheap around these parts."

I smile, grateful he isn't mocking me. "I can handle that."

"Cool. I understand they're pretty good here, too."

"Like the hot dogs?"

He chuckles. "Let's hope not."

CHAPTER TWENTY-ONE

We go only three blocks before several choices for dinner appear. We pick the third one, enticed by the garlicky smell coming from inside. Even though it's almost eleven o'clock, they still have several tables full, and other people are coming in at the same time we are to start their meals.

"You want to share a pie?" Sam asks as we look over the menu.

"Sure." I'm looking at the prices: twenty bucks for a single pizza. "Order whatever you want. I can be adventurous." I flip my menu over and slide it to the edge of the table, folding my hands and resting them in my lap when I can't think of anything cooler to do with them. It sure is toasty in here. I feel like lying down on the bench seat of the booth and taking a nap. My cheeks are going warm as my body recovers from the cold that had started turning me into an icicle.

Sam peruses the offerings on his menu and then puts it to the side. "I'm ready. You want a beer?"

I shrug. "Sure, why not?" What's the worst that could happen, right? I've already spilled most of my secrets and showed him my hand—he now knows I'm deathly afraid of doing things in public that strangers will see, just like he is. And he'd have to be completely dense to miss the fact that I've been flirting with him for half the day. But I do need to stop doing that, assuming Sadie is his girlfriend.

"So . . . who is Sadie?" I ask, blurting out the question before bothering to weigh the consequences.

He sits back in the booth and looks left and right, almost as if he's searching for an escape hatch. He sighs when none appears. "She's a girl."

I chuckle. "Oh, because I was wondering if maybe she was the family dog or something."

His smile doesn't reach his eyes. "No, she's not the family dog. We were never allowed to have pets growing up."

Unfortunately for him, I'm going to save that comment for another conversation, since I'm too interested in this one to be distracted.

"She your girlfriend?" I'm smiling really hard, trying not to let him see how nervous I am. I'm terrible at conversation and small talk, and this isn't even small talk. This is *big* talk. I really want to know his answer, though, because if he says, "Yes, she's my girlfriend," it means there will be no more flirting coming from or accepted by me. I'll probably have to call off the bet, too. And that's good news in a way, but in another way it isn't so much; I was kind of looking forward to the extra two hundred bucks. All I have to do is paint a tree, right?

"No, she's not my girlfriend." Sam stares at me, his jaw muscles bouncing out several times before he speaks again. "What's your connection to the band?"

My hand goes up and touches my chest, my fingers trembling a little. He's just thrown down a gauntlet. Dare I pick it up? *Sadie's not his girlfriend!*

"My connection?" I try to laugh it off. "Why would *I* have a connection? I don't work for them."

"I don't know. You tell me." The intensity of his stare makes me think he can see right through me.

I shrug, hopefully looking way cooler than I feel. "My sister works for them. Apparently, she just got a promotion, too, so she's a really big deal. And I support her one hundred percent." I nod emphatically. This is all about her, not me.

He shakes his head, narrowing his eyes at me. "No, that's not it. There's something else going on."

"Not really." Technically speaking, there isn't; they offered me ten million bucks, and I turned them down. Our business together is over—it was over before it even started.

"I can tell by the look on your face that you're not telling me something," he says.

I roll my eyes. "Great." I have no idea how I can be so good at bluffing at poker when it seems like everyone who meets me can eventually read my mind.

His mouth quirks up in a half smile. "Why do you say that?"

"Because." I throw my hand up and let it come down to slap the table. "You're just one more person who can climb into my brain and read my thoughts. Do you know how annoying that is? To never be able to keep a secret from anyone?"

He smiles, somewhat sadly. "No, I don't know what that's like. Nobody ever gets in my head."

"Well, consider yourself lucky. I am *never* alone in mine."

"Lucky you," he says. "To never feel alone."

"Yeah, maybe." He's twisting the meaning of my words, but it does make me stop and think. I suppose there could be a benefit to being so open that people you care about can read you; there's less chance of a misunderstanding that way, less chance of hurt feelings . . .

The waitress arrives and takes our order as delivered by Sam. This will be my first pizza with anchovies. And now that we're alone again, I can continue to pursue my line of questioning. I am on a mission to get into Sam's head and find his buttons. *Yeah!*

"So, Sadie is not your girlfriend, and she is not the family dog." I play with my napkin, doing my best to keep my hands busy so I can seem cool and unaffected by his presence.

He leans forward, his voice dropping into a very suggestive, sexy tenor. "And you have something to do with the band other than your sister working for them."

I stop messing with the napkin and fold my hands in my lap. We sit there staring at each other, time slipping past, conversations flowing around us. The waitress delivers our drinks and I take a sip of my beer, trying to delay the inevitable.

If I want to know the answers to my questions about him, I'm going to have to give him the answers he seeks. *Ugh.* Why does everything with Sam always have to be all about give-and-take? Can't he just give me what I want and let me stay quiet, private, and living in my own world?

"Sadie is my daughter," he finally says. Then he takes a long pull from his beer, gulping several times before he puts the frosty mug down.

It takes me a few seconds to gather my thoughts enough to respond to his totally unexpected statement. "You have a daughter? Huh. Wow. I had no idea. Amber didn't say anything to me about this."

"Amber doesn't know."

This doesn't make any sense to me at all. "I can't believe Ty wouldn't tell her that he's an uncle."

"Ty doesn't know either."

CHAPTER TWENTY-TWO

It's like Sam dropped a bomb in the middle of the conversation. My jaw opens, and all I can do is stare at him.

"You think I'm an asshole, don't you?" He takes another drink of his beer, but he stares at me the entire time.

I shake my head, trying to get myself out of the weird daze I've fallen into. It can't be the beer; I've only had two sips so far. "No, I don't think that." I blink a few times, letting it settle in that this man sitting across from me has a child and he hasn't even bothered to tell his brother about it. I think their relationship is a lot more broken than Amber realizes.

Sam looks away, staring at the wall that has framed pictures of famous movie stars on it. The sadness I see in his face prompts me to quickly elaborate on my answer.

"No, really . . . I don't think that at all. I am confused, though. I mean, earlier . . ." How do I finish this sentence? *Damn,* I suck at this.

He looks at me. "Earlier?"

"Earlier . . . you said Ty would jump into a fire for you, so it just seems kind of strange . . ." I shrug pitifully. I'm making him feel bad, I know I am. When did I get so judgy? Is this New York's influence on me? Because if it is, I need to get out of here tomorrow.

"It's strange that he doesn't know I have a kid?"

I nod.

"Yeah, you're right, it is strange." He lets out a long sigh and then picks up his mug, finishing his beer. He lifts the empty glass toward the bar until the waitress recognizes what he's after and nods at him.

"What happened between you two?"

He shrugs. "It's kind of hard to say."

I wait, knowing that I could very easily say the wrong thing. I sip my beer instead, silently willing him to confess.

"We had a tough time growing up. We took a lot of abuse . . . watched our mother take a lot of it too. Ty was better at dealing with it. He found a way to push it off, but I couldn't."

I nod, totally getting what he's saying. Sam is a sensitive person. I could see him absorbing everything, much like I would. Amber is like Ty; she can see what happened with our mothers and compartmentalize it as their issue that happened in the past. I can't do that; I've taken what the men of Red Hot did—or didn't do—personally.

"Eventually, it got in the way of our relationship. I got angry with him just brushing it all off and never standing up for himself. We fought a lot. Said some things we shouldn't have. I couldn't stay and watch it anymore. I was so angry at everyone, and it was destroying me."

"So you moved away to save yourself. And you had a child."

"I guess." He shrugs, looking away.

"Wow. That must be really tough," I say.

"What? Having a kid?" His gaze comes back to me as he waits for my answer.

"Well, having a child, sure. But doing it without the support of your family? That must make it harder."

"Yeah, it's hard."

Time stretches between us again. Before it was charged with a happy, almost sexual energy, but now, not so much. There's a sadness . . . almost a hopelessness here, and I feel Sam pulling away emotionally. I can't let him go so easily.

"You want to know what my connection to the band is?" I can't *not* tell him now. That would be incredibly rude and hurtful. I know he's just shared something huge with me, and now I want to do the same for him.

"Yeah. What's the big secret?" He perks up, sitting straighter, resting his hands on either side of his empty beer mug.

I lower my voice, paranoid that some Red Hot fan will be listening in from a neighboring table. Amber says they're everywhere and that they love taking videos. "If I tell you, do you promise not to share the information with anyone?"

He leans forward and nods, dragging his empty mug toward his beard and resting his elbows on the table. "Sure. Your secret is safe with me."

I give him a half smile. "Before you said my secrets weren't safe with you."

He points a finger at me. "I said that they weren't before, that's true. But now I'm saying they are. You can trust me. I don't sell out my friends."

I smile shyly, my face going warm. We're flirting again, I think. It feels like we are, anyway. And he says we're friends, but I've had friends before and it doesn't feel like this. It probably doesn't hurt knowing that Sadie is not his girlfriend.

"Okay, so the big secret is . . . ," I try to breathe normally, but it's not working, ". . . that for twenty-five years, I lived on this hippie commune and I had no idea who my father was, and then one day this lawyer named Greg Lister showed up at our house to tell me that I was the long-lost love child of a Red Hot band member."

"Greg Lister?" Sam tilts his head. "That's the guy who works for Red Hot. He's the one who contacted me after I talked to Ty."

"Yes. The devil himself." I try to laugh my joke off, but it falls flat when Sam just stares at me, so I keep talking. "Anyway, he said that the members of the band just found out that we were alive, that we were all their *daughters*—Rose, Amber, and me—and they wanted to offer us some money."

"Money? What for?"

"An excellent question," I say a little too loudly. I take a sip of my beer, trying to calm myself down.

"How much?" He pauses. "Or should I not ask that question? Too personal, maybe . . ."

"You can ask. It's part of the secret, I guess." I take another sip of my beer and stare at the table. I hate this part of the story. "They offered each of us ten million dollars."

He lets out a long hiss of air before finally responding. "Daaaaamn."

"Yes, it's a lot of money. It makes me sick to my stomach."

"What are you going to do with all of it?"

"I'm not doing anything with it." I look up at him, angry at the very idea. "I wouldn't touch their money with a ten-million-foot-long pole."

"Are you insane?" He's staring at me with his eyes bugging out.

"No. I'm perfectly sane, thank you very much."

His response annoys me. He doesn't seem to notice, though, because he keeps on going. "But think of everything you could do with . . ."—he drops the volume of his voice—". . . ten million bucks. Hell, if you don't want it for yourself, you could give it away to charity."

He totally doesn't get it, which is so disappointing. "Yeah. Sure."

He shakes his head, sitting back in the booth and letting out a long breath, frowning so hard he looks almost angry. He runs his hands through his hair and then strokes his beard a few times, staring off into the distance. Then he looks at me and his face falls. His expression softens, almost turning him into a different man. "Sorry. I just got a little thrown off by that number."

I have nothing to say to that.

He's staring at me so intensely again, I have to look away. "You're not the type to be thrown off by money, are you?" he asks.

I shake my head.

"You're strong. I'm not sure I could say no to that kind of dough, even if it was the devil himself offering me some sort of payoff."

I guess I shouldn't fault him for being blown away by this information. It is pretty crazy. "I get it. Believe me, when we first heard the offer, it was shocking to us too. Never tempting, but shocking, yes."

"Probably not as shocking as finding out that your father is in Red Hot, I'll bet."

Sam's trying to cheer me up, and it would be completely stupid for me to resist his efforts. Besides . . . it feels good to be able to talk to someone outside of the family about this, especially now that it seems like he's figured out the problem I have with the money." *He called it a payoff, which is exactly what it is.* "You're right. That *was* the most shocking part."

"Which one is he? I mean, which one is your father?"

"I don't know." I shrug. "And I don't care."

"What do you mean, you don't know?"

I look around the room and then roll my eyes, a little embarrassed about this part of the story. "Our mothers—Rose's, Amber's, and mine—were groupies for the band, back in the day. There was a lot of free love and casual sex going on, and they kinda mixed it up a lot."

"No way." Sam laughs. I'm glad at least someone sees humor in the situation.

"Yeah way. And they all got pregnant right around the same time, and as a result, they don't know who the father is for any of us."

"That is un*real*," he says, shaking his head in amazement. "What are the chances of that happening?"

I find this part of the story especially annoying. "Probably about as good as us winning a really crappy lottery, but it happened. People win lotteries every day, you know."

"Yeah, I guess you're right." He's shaking his head in either disbelief or shock at my crazy story.

"And as soon as our mothers found out they were pregnant, they took off without saying anything to the band."

"They *took off*?" Sam throws his hands up. "Without saying anything? Why would they do that?"

"Yes. Thank you." I throw my hand out toward him in frustration, glad that someone else besides me thinks it's totally stupid. I focus on being charitable as I explain the rest of the story. "There were two things at play: First of all, our moms say they knew that motherhood and raising a family were not things they should be doing in that environment. *And* the second thing was that there was a guy named Ted who was the band manager . . ."

"Wait . . . *Ted*? I know a Ted. Is it the same guy? I talked to him on the phone, too. After Ty and Lister. He arranged my plane tickets and stuff."

"Yeah, it's the same guy. Ted was instrumental in getting our mothers some money so they could leave and start a new life without the band members finding out about it."

"They just took off, though? They didn't say anything to anybody?"

"Except for Ted and a guy named Darrell, who's no longer with the band, nope." I shrug. "I don't know that I would've handled it the same way if it were me, but that was twenty-five years ago, so it's hard to say. All three of our moms decided it was a good idea, and so they did it. End of story." They always told my sisters and me that there's no use crying over spilled milk, but I sure do feel like crying over this spill. What a freaking mess they made . . .

Sam is nodding slowly, like he's piecing it all together. "So, here you are, twenty-five years later, paying the price for their irresponsibility. No father to raise you but a stranger standing there with a fistful of dollars, telling you to take it and forget what happened . . . or what didn't happen, I guess."

"Exactly." I point at him and then let my hand fall to the table in a fist, banging it down. Suddenly, my mind is racing through memories of so many things: growing up on the farm, selling things at the farmers' market, arguing with the city council about the boundary limits of our property and what we're allowed to do on it, guests who have come and gone, the animals, my sisters and the growing up we did together. Seeing it all playing on a reel in my head like this makes it hard to stay mad at my mothers for very long. Yes, I grew up without a father . . . but how can you miss what you've never had? And I did have a good life. *No . . . a great life.* And that's because of the choices my mothers made.

"I really shouldn't be so harsh about the whole thing," I say, my body and heart softening. "We had a really great life, and these men appearing out of nowhere doesn't change anything."

"Looks like it's changed some things for Amber," he says softly.

A lump forms in my throat and I shake my head, unable to speak. *Yes.* My sister is gone and she's never coming back. I have to face it, as much as it hurts.

"Well, I see why you're so conflicted about the money. I guess it's not as easy as just saying 'I'll take it' and giving it to somebody else." He pauses, searching my face. "It would be like saying that the fact they stayed away for twenty-five years is okay with you. And it's not. It's definitely not."

I stare down at my beer and reflect on how nuts my life is in this moment. Sam totally gets me. It's a genuine relief to have someone like him sitting across from me instead of one of my sisters telling me to get over it. How crazy is that . . . that I'd rather be here with him than with Amber or Rose?

CHAPTER TWENTY-THREE

"I guess things are tough all over," Sam says.

I look up at him, sensing a double meaning in his words. "How so?"

His next beer appears, and he waits until the waitress is gone before he answers. "My daughter . . . She's not actually mine."

"What?" I'm not sure I understand, but I definitely want to. I sit up straighter and lean in to hear him better.

"Biologically speaking, she's not my daughter. But she is my daughter in my heart, you know?" He touches his fist to his chest a couple times and waits for me to respond.

"I think I get it," I say. "You must love her a lot. You tattooed her name on your body."

He looks at his arm that's covered in ink. "Yeah. I've got a lot of other ones that don't mean a whole lot compared to that one."

"It's all by itself there over your heart."

"Yes. She means everything to me."

"And she's back in LA?"

"Yeah."

"With her mother?"

He suddenly looks decidedly uncomfortable. "Yes and no."

I am so ready to question him further, but our pizza arrives, steaming-hot and smelling delicious. Although suspicious of the anchovies on top, I'm ready to dive in.

"Thanks," he says to the waitress, who hands us silverware and plates in a pile.

Sam serves me first and then himself. He takes two slices and turns them into a big pizza sandwich. We lapse into companionable silence as we try the food. The anchovies aren't bad. They add a little extra saltiness to the pizza, which helps the beer go down easier. I order a second drink and Sam orders a third.

"You want to ask me about Sadie's mother, don't you?"

I nod, using a napkin to wipe sauce off my lips before I answer. "Yes, but I don't want to be too nosy."

"That's all right. You shared your secret with me; I might as well share mine with you."

"Cool." I give him a thumbs-up and try to wink, but both of my eyes close; I've never been good at winking.

He laughs and shakes his head silently. He swallows his next bite of pizza before he continues the conversation. "I met Sadie's mom, Madison, a few years back, when we were both jamming with this group of people who were messing around, killing time in this old warehouse. She sings. She's pretty good, too, when she's not wasted."

"Oh." This sounds like the beginning of a very sad story. I munch on my pizza as I wait for the rest.

"We were never more than friends. She was always with different guys; she likes to sleep around. And she's had a bad drug problem for a long time."

I swallow with an exaggerated gulp when my throat suddenly goes dry. I wasn't expecting this. "I'm sorry to hear that."

"Yeah, well, some people are more prone to that stuff, I guess. She's very sensitive . . . easily influenced by the different shitheads she let into her life. I was always trying to help her out, but it didn't seem to matter what I did. She always fell back into the same trap, ending up with a guy who didn't treat her right, who encouraged her to party too much."

I wipe my mouth again, feeling sad for Madison and Sam. "Some people can't be helped. They're their own worst enemies. We occasionally see people like that out on the farm."

"Yeah. She's a sad case. I mean, I love her. She's a good girl inside, but she's just really messed up. She had a very bad childhood. She was abused by her father, and her mother knew about it but didn't do anything to stop it, so Madison doesn't really feel like she can trust anyone."

"Oh, that's terrible." My heart hurts for the poor girl.

"Anyway, she's seriously hooked on H and has been for a while."

"H? What's that?"

"Heroin."

"Oh." I get a chill down my spine. I don't know a lot about drugs, but I've heard that one is especially bad.

"Her friends and I have done everything we can to help her out, but it's to the point that I don't think there's anything we can do anymore. She doesn't want help and she's avoiding us, hiding where we can't find her."

"Oh, no. What about Sadie?" Tears fill my eyes—for Sam, for Madison, and most of all for Sadie. No little girl should have to live without her mom. I'm so lucky; I have three. They might not be perfect, but they love me more than anything in the world. They proved that when they walked away from Red Hot twenty-six years ago, giving up on the life they loved so much for the good of us kids. I wish they were here in this pizza place with me right now so I could hug the crap out of them.

"When Madison got pregnant, she had no idea who the father was, but the options were *not* good. It was either one of the junkies she was hanging out with or her dealer, and I didn't want any of those guys having anything to do with her. At least not more than they already did. I couldn't keep them away from her, but I was not going to let them get near Sadie."

"So what did you do?"

"I told her I wanted to put my name on the birth certificate. She agreed, and I took over dad duty."

"Wow." I put my pizza down. This conversation is way more interesting than the anchovies. "That's really huge."

"Yeah. I didn't realize how huge it was at the time, actually." He has a slight smile now. "She's a handful."

"Do you have a picture of her?" I can totally see him being a dad to a tiny girl, and it makes my heart melt into a puddle of goo. I'll bet she pulls on his beard, which makes me love it even more. I have to work hard to control my emotions so I don't start blubbering like a baby all over this pizza. Hot men with babies do something weird to my insides.

He leans forward to reach into his back pocket, pulling out a leather wallet. He opens it up and takes out a photo, sliding it over to me. "This is from about six months ago."

Sadie has curly blond hair and sparkly blue eyes. I can tell she's totally mischievous by her sassy expression. The picture was taken in a park; there are swings in the background. "She is absolutely beautiful."

"Yeah. So is her mom."

I hand the picture back to him and smile. "And you're trying to tell me that you never had a relationship with her mother?" I find that very hard to believe. Madison must be gorgeous.

He shakes his head. "Nah. She's not my type."

I pick up my pizza and take a bite. I really want to know what his type is, but it doesn't seem like the right thing to ask at this particular moment.

"I prefer women who are a little more chill than Madison is."

I chew my pizza slowly and nod, hoping he'll keep going if I encourage him silently.

"She's always out partying. The whole idea of having a kid freaked her out, but she didn't want to have an abortion either. The nine months she carried Sadie were the only clean months she ever had . . . as long as I've known her, anyway."

"If she's always out partying, who's taking care of Sadie?"

"Mostly me. Sometimes friends, if I can't because I'm working or whatever."

Do I dare ask my next question? I take a sip of courage—otherwise known as beer—and let it fly. "You've been getting some phone calls since you've been here. You sound stressed when you answer them. Is it about Madison or Sadie?"

His expression turns dark, and he drops his pizza crust on his plate, taking another gulp of his beer before he answers with a hoarse voice. "Madison. She's in trouble again."

"Is Sadie okay?"

"Yeah. I have a friend looking out for her. She's pretty much making sure Madison doesn't come around, keeping Sadie on her routine so she doesn't know anything weird is going on. Sadie is used to her mother going AWOL, so it doesn't bug her too much, but my friend has been a constant in her life since day one, so it's cool. Sadie's oblivious to all of it."

"Oh. That's terrible." My heart sinks for Sam and his daughter. "You have to keep them apart?"

"It's never good when Madison gets high. Sometimes she starts feeling really regretful, and she wants to come and be with Sadie, but she's so messed up she doesn't realize that she's scaring her. And it's not safe to let Madison come around when she's using because she sometimes gets violent. She never remembers any of it either. It's just . . . a huge, fucking mess."

I reach out and take his hand, pulling it toward me so I can stroke the top of it. "It sounds like you're doing everything you can for Sadie and Madison. You're a good friend and a great dad, Sam."

He looks down at me petting his hand. After a few seconds I become a little self-conscious and pull back, lacing my fingers in my lap. I'm treating him like a fussy hen.

"That's why I'm here," he says.

I'm confused. "You think being away from Sadie right now is better for her?"

He shakes his head. "No. That's why I'm here earning some money. I do all right back in LA, but the sick money they were offering me here was too good to say no to." He pauses. "They didn't offer me ten million bucks, but it was more than I normally make in a year back there. And I figured if I could get the work started sooner, maybe I could finish sooner and get back before . . ." He pauses and looks up at the ceiling before he finishes. "Before anything seriously bad happens with Madison that I need to deal with. I couldn't risk waiting and then not being able to come at all."

"Oh." Now I'm feeling just a little bit of regret over not taking that money Lister offered. It could make such a difference in the lives of people like Sam and Sadie. I know it's crazy to think that; I don't even know them. But it doesn't stop me from wanting to help them.

"Anyway, that's my sad, sorry tale. I didn't ask you to keep it a secret before, but if you'd do that for me, I'd really appreciate it. I haven't told Ty any of this, but I need to. And I'd rather he hear it from me than anyone else." He glances at me as he busies himself with preparing another pizza sandwich. I get the distinct impression he's uncomfortable now. I think he revealed more than he planned to.

"Your secrets are safe with me." I say this as cheerily as possible as I pick up my pizza again, hoping to dispel his worries. "This food is awesome. I'm not into the hot dogs, but the pizza is all right with me."

He holds his slices up at me, and I hold mine up at him, and we touch pizza corners together. "Cheers," he says. "Here's to keeping secrets."

"Cheers," I say, knowing that it's going to burn me up inside to not share this stuff with Amber. This is exactly the kind of thing she wanted me to find out for her, but there's no way I can tell her what I just learned without betraying Sam's confidence, and I'm not going to do that. When Sam decides that his brother needs to know these things, that's his place to do that, not mine. I wish I could talk to him more about him and Ty, but what he's said so far is so heavy, I hate to push him further. This vibe we have between us feels good but tenuous. I don't want to ruin it. Maybe the subject will come up later, and I'll be more comfortable with asking questions about his brother and their relationship.

We enjoy our pizza for a few more minutes without saying anything. The waitress comes over and leaves the check, and Sam starts digging into his back pocket.

"Let's split it," I say. Now that I know he's raising a child who's not even his own, there's no way I can let him treat me to dinner.

"Maybe next time," he says. "This one is mine."

I take his comment to mean that we're going to share another meal out. I can't stop the smile that takes over my face. "Thank you."

"No problem. You got anywhere else you need to go before we head back to the apartment?"

"No. I'm finally getting tired, so I think it's good that we go back now."

"Great. We can plan for our bet tomorrow on the way."

I tilt my head, looking as innocent as possible. "What bet?"

He smiles and winks at me. "Nice try. You're going down, hippie chick. Might as well wrap your brain around it now."

I gather up my dirty utensils and stack them on the plate, pushing the pile to the edge of the table. "There's only one person going down at this table, and it ain't me; it's you . . . the weirdo with the beardo."

He bursts out laughing, as my face flames red. I seriously need more practice at this conversation thing.

CHAPTER TWENTY-FOUR

My heart is surprisingly light as we leave the pizza place for the apartment. We talked about some heavy things in there, but it was worth it. I've learned so much about Sam, and I like all of it, even though it's complicated.

He's an incredible person. He volunteered to be the father of a child who's not even his, and it sounds like he's doing a lot of single parenting, too. I have tons of respect for him now that I know his story. It must be especially difficult for an artist like him, being that he's not able to fully exploit his talent by performing his music onstage. Talk about pressure . . . having to work while also worrying about feeding and caring for a child, and at the same time keeping her drug-addicted mother away when necessary? *Damn.*

I thought not being able to paint was heartbreaking, but it's nothing compared to what Sam is dealing with. Now I feel a little bit bad about this bet we made; he's got enough pressure on him without me adding to the problem. We're halfway back to the apartment when he stops and points to a boutique that's lit up from inside. The sign on the door says it's open until two a.m. for the Halloween season.

"You want to go in here?" he asks, looking at me.

"What is it?"

"It's a costume store."

I'm confused. "Are you planning on going to a Halloween party or something?"

"No, but maybe you'll want to wear a disguise tomorrow."

"A disguise? What for?" I think Sam's had too many beers.

He takes me by the elbow and walks us toward the door, opening it for me. "After you," he says, winking at me.

I have no idea what he's talking about, but he's in too good a mood for me to deny him. That phone call he got at the park bummed him out, so if going into a costume shop and trying on silly wigs or whatever will make him happy, then I'm going to do it. I don't feel tired anymore, anyway. Being with Sam energizes me. He walks ahead of me and I follow. We end up in an aisle filled with masks, fake hair, body paint, and various costume accessories.

"I was thinking," he says, looking over the items, "if you're too nervous to paint in public, you could probably wear a costume and it wouldn't be so bad."

"You've got to be kidding me." I laugh, sure he's pulling my leg. "It would make it worse."

He's looking over the shelves, picking up one thing after another. "There's this DJ named Dead Mouse who wears a giant mouse head when he performs in public."

"A *mouse* head?"

"Yeah. And it doesn't even look like a real mouse head either. It's like a giant cartoon. More like a big Styrofoam ball with some floppy ears and a nose stuck to it."

"He sounds . . . interesting." Sam sure hangs out with some characters—drug-addicted women and men who dress like dead mice? Man, he's going to fall asleep standing up out of sheer boredom if he ever visits the farm.

"I don't know him personally, but I hear he wears that costume because he's nervous about being in front of crowds."

"Stage fright? Wow. That's pretty inconvenient for a DJ."

"Exactly." He mumbles the rest of his sentence. "It's inconvenient for a guitarist, too."

"So . . . are we looking for a giant mouse head, then?"

He glances at me with a half grin. "Ha, ha. No, we're not looking for a giant mouse head, unless that's what you want to wear when you're painting."

"No, I think I'd prefer something like this." I slide on a pair of black-rimmed glasses that have a fake nose, eyebrows, and mustache attached. I look at Sam, lifting my chin. "What do you think?"

"That's hot. But I think you need a little something extra." He picks up a purple-sequined derby hat and sets it on my head.

I turn left and right, giving him a shot of both of my profiles. "What do you think? Am I awesome?"

He smiles big, revealing his mostly straight white teeth. "Yeah. It's cool. I would definitely go with that if I were you."

Getting into the spirit of things, I whip off the hat and the glasses and grab something else. "But what about *this*? Don't be too hasty in making your decision. *This* could be *more* awesome."

He checks me out in my new getup, which is a set of googly eyes that are falling out of black-framed glasses and a beard that's attached to my chin by an elastic strap around the back of my head.

He strokes his facial hair, pretending to be studying me closely. "Wow, you're right. This is a pretty hot look, too. It's tough; I can't decide which one I like better."

"What about you?" I point at his face. "You look pretty boring with just that beard right now."

He points at his chin. "You mean *this* beard? The weirdo beardo?"

The heat of embarrassment rises to my cheeks, but I don't back down. "Yeah. Your weirdo beardo."

"Fine. How about this?" He puts a giant Abraham Lincoln hat on his head and attaches a preacher's collar around his neck, complete with a black half shirt beneath.

"Oooh, I like that a lot, and I think the ladies are *really* going to be into it." I'm saying it like a joke, but he does actually look good in it. It's so bizarre to find out that I'm attracted to men who look like preachers born in the 1800s.

He looks up at his hat. "The ladies, huh? Well, then, I definitely need to buy it."

My heart skips a beat. It sounds like he's cool with finding a girlfriend. Jealousy takes over my brain, which is so, so crazy. Okay, I'll admit that I want to be with him. But it doesn't matter because I never could be. We live across the country from each other. He's a rocker who hangs out with party animals, and I'm a hippie who likes the quiet life. Our siblings are in love and could very well get married someday—or they could end up hating each other if things don't work out. It would complicate things immeasurably for us to get involved, regardless of how things went with Amber and Ty. Besides, Sam seems like a really cool friend. I should be happy with what we have and not try to change things and mess them up.

"Anything else you need?" He points to several items. "Vampire teeth? Fishnet stockings? Magic wand?"

I shake my head. "I think I'm good with these." I hold up the glasses with the nose and mustache attached. "I've got it all in just one piece. It suits my simple style."

"I agree. Let's go."

I walk ahead of him to the cash register, not caring if he stares at my butt this time. He's got his silly Abraham Lincoln hat that conveniently collapses down into a black disk, and I've got my glasses with nose and facial hair attached. We smile our way through the purchases. Even though we pay for our own stuff, the cashier puts everything in one bag and hands it to Sam. We leave the store and pause momentarily outside.

"You want to get a cab?" he asks.

"How far are we from the apartment?"

He shrugs. "A few blocks. I'm not sure, exactly."

I'm loath for the evening to end too quickly. "Let's walk. I still have some energy left to work off."

We start moving. "Yeah, me too," Sam says. "Which is weird, because I was really tired a little while ago."

"I guess the anchovies are kicking in."

"Are you bagging on my anchovies, young lady?"

I smile, my face going warm. "No, I liked the anchovies. It's the first time I've ever eaten them, though. I wasn't sure if I was going to be able to do it, but it wasn't bad at all."

"You've never eaten an anchovy before? Man . . . Is life on the farm a little too tame, maybe?"

"Hey. I've eaten a lot of *not* tame things on the farm. I'll bet I've eaten a lot of things *you've* never tried."

"Oh yeah? Like what?"

"Calf balls."

He laughs, but when he realizes I'm not laughing with him, he stops. "Are you serious?"

"Yeah." I shrug, now worried I sound like a complete lunatic. "We have to castrate the male calves, or they become full-grown bulls and way too aggressive. And you've gotta do something with their balls, so . . ."

"Couldn't you just throw them away?"

"Sure we could, but they're edible, so why not eat them?"

"Yeah, okay. Why not. I guess."

Maybe my life isn't so tame after all. I'm no longer embarrassed. Why should I be? I live my life by a set of rules, and they're good ones. I shouldn't be ashamed of that. "You think I'm crazy, don't you?"

"No. I think you're adventurous."

I have to laugh at that.

"You don't believe me?" he asks.

"No, not at all. But I appreciate you trying to fake it."

"No, man, I'm not faking it. You are adventurous."

"Because I eat balls."

"Well, yeah." He chuckles. "But also because you live in this different kind of community with an alternative lifestyle, sharing your home with total strangers, being close to the animals you eat. That's cool. And adventurous, too. Not a lot of people would do what you do."

I feel like he's giving me credit I don't deserve. "It's not like I have a choice. It's my mothers' place. I just live there."

"Yeah, but you're twenty-five; I mean, you could have left, but you stayed because it's a good life. You probably don't see it as being very wild because it's what you're used to; but trust me . . . it is. Where I live, we only eat out, and there's never anything like calf balls on the menu. Sushi is about as crazy as it gets. We lock our doors and we don't talk to strangers much. In fact, people never even go outside and walk around."

"What do you mean, they don't walk around?"

"Haven't you ever heard that song 'Walking in LA' by Missing Persons?"

"No."

"Well, it was from back in the eighties, so it was before our time. But it's pretty accurate. It's really hot, and everybody just drives when they need to go somewhere. The traffic is ridiculous."

"Oh. Well, things are probably pretty spread out there, right? Car travel is probably necessary."

"Yeah, it is. Not like your place. Anyway, maybe someday you can show me how the other half lives." He looks at me for a second and then goes back to staring straight ahead.

"I'd be happy to. You're welcome on the farm anytime."

That's the last of our conversation before we reach the apartment. I spend the entire trip back imagining Sam at Glenhollow, staying in my home. I think he might like it, and I'm pretty certain I'd like having him there.

CHAPTER TWENTY-FIVE

We make it on to the elevator without a problem. They have pictures of Sam and me at the front desk, so even though it's different people working there at this time of night, we have no issues with getting access. Sam uses his card key to get us up to Amber's floor. The doors open, and we step off the elevator, and then we stand there looking around the foyer together.

"I don't know what my brother was thinking with this stuff." Sam is shaking his head at the decor.

"I don't think either one of our siblings pays much attention to their surroundings. They were probably just looking for an apartment that was private and protected, and this place came already decorated like this."

"Yeah, I guess."

Our easy camaraderie slips away and leaves us with another awkward moment. I try to smile, but the expression feels stiff on my face, so I stop.

"So . . . ," I say, hoping more words will follow. Unfortunately, they don't. And now I know what it means when people say silence can be deafening.

"Yeah, so, thanks for hanging with me." Sam holds his hand out.

I look down at it, not knowing what I'm supposed to do. *Does he want to shake hands?* It feels like he's making a declaration . . . something like: *Don't think anything actually happened between us; we're just acquaintances, nothing else.*

His arm drops to his side. "Sorry. I don't know what the hell I'm doing." He runs his fingers through his hair, obviously nervous.

"We can shake hands if you want." I shrug, almost happy to know that he's feeling and acting as off-kilter as I am.

He shakes his head and lets out a long breath, looking at the floor. "I have no idea what's going on with me. To be honest, I feel completely out of my element. This is not normal for me." He looks up, his eyes dark and his stare intense.

I'm pretty sure I know what he's thinking. For the first time in my life I can read someone else's thoughts, and it's exhilarating. He's wondering what's going on between us; he has to be. I can't be dreaming all of this up . . . this connection we have . . . this desire to be in each other's company. We shared a lot tonight, and while I still don't know him that well, I'm almost positive he doesn't tell many other people what he told me tonight. He's a private person, like I am—but with each other, we open up.

"We could hug it out if you prefer," I say, hoping I can ease his discomfort with a little silliness. "We do a lot of hugging back at my house. I'm a pro."

The grin is slow to spread across his face, but when it does, it lights up the entire room. "I could definitely deal with a hug." He holds his arms out, the plastic bag holding our costumes hanging from one of his hands.

I take two steps toward him and walk into his embrace, wrapping my arms around his waist. His strong arms encircle my back and pull me in. *Damn.* Our bodies are touching from knees to shoulders, and this could very well be the best hug I've ever had in my entire life.

I'm holding my breath at first. When I finally let it out, I collapse in a little and he holds me tighter. Our bodies meld together, all heat and softness. He smells so good, like a combination of fresh air, cologne, pizza, and laundry soap. There's something else there too—the scent of a man. I try not to be obvious about inhaling it like a drug.

"This is way better than a handshake," he says into my neck, making goose bumps rise up my arm and leg.

"Yeah, it is."

The hug should probably be over by now, but I can't let go. I don't want to. I'm going to let him decide when it's time for it to end. This feels too good, and it's been so long since anyone has held me like this.

"Is this weird?" he asks a few seconds later.

"I don't think so." Maybe somebody else watching us would think we were strange, and maybe if it were anybody else with his arms around me, it would be, but with him it feels totally right.

"Good. I don't want things to be awkward between us."

"They won't be," I say, hoping with everything in me that I'm speaking the truth.

"How do you know?" he asks in a soft voice.

"Because." I speak with a confidence I don't necessarily feel. "I'm a hippie chick, remember? We give free hugs all the time. I'm a hugging expert. And anything goes with hippie chicks."

He chuckles deep in his chest. "That's good to know."

I realize then that he took what I said in a sexual way. "Well . . . not just *anything*. That's not what I meant."

He laughs harder. "Sure it isn't."

I pull away a little and look up at him. "Seriously. I'm not that kind of girl."

He leans back but doesn't let go. We're left standing in each other's arms, and it's very intimate. His face is mere inches away, his beard occasionally touching my chin and tickling me.

"I know you're not that kind of girl, Emerald."

I love the sound of my name coming from his mouth. And maybe I'm just imagining things, but there seems to be a special meaning in his words. I'm not sure I quite understand them, though.

"What kind of girl are *you* talking about?" I ask, not quite believing I have the audacity to do it. Being with Sam makes me braver.

He looks like he's trying not to grin. "I don't know. What kind of girl are *you* talking about?"

Now he's starting to frustrate me. "Would you stop teasing me?"

"I'm not teasing you."

"What do you call it?"

"I call it flirting."

Heat flashes up from my neck and goes straight to my forehead. My words come out almost as a whisper. "You're flirting with me?"

"Wasn't it obvious?"

"Maybe. But I wasn't sure."

He gives me the most endearing look. "Is it okay if I flirt with you a little?"

I shrug, trying so hard to be cool about something I want to scream over. "Yeah, I'm not complaining."

"Good."

We search other's eyes for several more long seconds. My heart is beating so hard, I know he can feel it through our shirts. *I can't believe it! He feels it too!* I wasn't just imagining the connection between us, and I'm not crazy. This is real and it's happening.

"I seriously want to kiss you right now," he says in a soft voice.

I can smell the beer and pizza on his breath. It's intoxicating, which is bizarre. I should be repulsed, but I'm not . . . not by a long shot. I am so attracted to this man right now, it's unbelievable.

"What's stopping you?" I ask. This is so not me, to be this bold. But I want him to kiss me more than anything in the world, and I'm not going to let fear ruin things for me.

He frowns just the slightest bit, worry furrowing his brow. "I don't want to mess things up."

I open my mouth to tell him there's nothing he could do to mess this up right now except walk away, but his phone rings and stops the words before they can leave my throat.

His body stiffens in my arms.

"You should answer that," I say. I pull away when I sense that he's going to disagree. "It could be about Sadie or Madison." I can't get in the middle of that. His real life comes before this . . . fantasy . . . or whatever it is we've got going on here.

He nods stiffly and steps back, taking his phone out of his pocket. "Yeah. What's up?"

I turn and start to walk out of the foyer, intending to leave him alone so he can have a private conversation, but he reaches out and takes my hand. I stop immediately and face him. We stand there together as he continues his conversation.

CHAPTER TWENTY-SIX

"No . . . *No.*" Sam's hold on my fingers tightens. I step closer and gather his hand into both of mine. Something terrible has happened; I can tell by his expression. His eyes are welling up with tears.

"Don't say that. You're fucking with me." His face twists with emotion. Moments later, he pulls the phone away from his ear and rests it on his forehead. He tips his head down in sorrow, his voice hoarse. "Goddammit. God*dammit,* I can't believe this is happening." He takes several long breaths that are meant to calm his emotions. He's struggling big-time, and watching it is breaking my heart.

I step closer and rub his arm, speaking in a near-whisper. "Whatever it is, I'm here for you."

He takes a deep breath to gather himself before putting the phone back to his ear. "I'll come. I'll be there as soon as I can." He nods a few times, his nostrils flaring and his lips trembling. A tear spills out of his right eye. "Okay . . . Call you when I get there." He pulls away from me, staring at his phone as if he's lost in thought. I wait with bated breath, twisting my hands together as I wonder and fear what he's going to say.

"I've gotta go." He sounds lost—sad and disconnected—as he continues to stare at the phone that delivered him some pretty bad news from the looks of it. "To leave. New York. I have to leave New York."

It feels like a knife was just plunged into my heart by an invisible hand. "Back to LA?"

"Yeah."

"For how long? What happened?" I pray this is something that can be easily fixed, that Sam will be coming back in a couple days so we can pick up where we'll be leaving off when he gets on the plane.

"Madison's in the hospital." He pauses to clear his throat. "They don't think she's going to make it."

My heart stops for a second. "What?" This is not at all what I was expecting to hear. I thought there was something bad going on, but not *this* bad. This is terrible. Devastating. Unreal. "Oh my god, Sam . . ."

"Yeah. She overdosed, apparently."

"Oh my god. Oh my *god*, that's just . . . That's just *horrible*. You have to go right away." I need to do something . . . anything but just stand here in the foyer getting ready to cry. I start walking toward the bedrooms and then stop, turning and rushing back to him, grabbing his arm. I'm so lost and confused, but I want to help him. I shake him, trying to wake him out of his stupor. "We need to get you a plane ticket, like, right now."

He finally looks up at me. "I don't know if any flights leave this late at night."

I feel like I'm channeling my sister Amber. *Sam has a problem and I am going to fix it, dammit!* "Yes, they do. The band has a private jet that can go whenever it wants. I think. You can take their plane."

He shakes his head and pulls out of my grasp. "No way, man. I can't do that."

I grab Sam's shoulders and shake him hard. "*Yes,* you can. And you're going to do it, and don't give me any sass about it either. I know you have your pride and all that, but this is an emergency. We don't have time for that man-crap."

Sam just stares at me, looking numb and shell-shocked.

I step away and wave my hand in his face. "You go pack your stuff." I point down the hall. "Right now. I'll take care of your travel plans."

Sam glares at me for a few seconds but then looks down at his phone and sighs. His body seems to sink in on itself. He reaches up to wipe the tears from his face as he slowly disappears down the hallway without another word.

I grab my purse and dig through it to find my phone. After dialing my sister's number, I wait for it to ring. I pray that she'll still be able to get calls when she's on the plane or in the airport. I'm not exactly sure where she is right now.

The first two rings are normal, but then there's a click and another ringing tone takes over. When she finally answers, it sounds like she's been asleep. "Hello?"

"Hi. It's me, Em. We're having an emergency right now, and I need your help."

"What? An emergency?" She's whispering loudly. From the sounds I'm hearing in the background, I'm guessing she's on the plane.

"Yes. Are you in flight right now? How are you getting my call?"

"I transferred all my calls to my Wi-Fi account. What's up?"

"I need you to tell me who I have to contact to get the private jet ready to go to LA tonight."

My sister's voice comes in much more clearly this time. "What are you talking about?"

"Listen, I can't give you all the details, but I need you to fly Sam back to LA tonight. It can't wait until tomorrow."

"What do you mean it can't wait? Why back to LA? Did you piss him off? I told you to *press* his buttons, not explode them!"

"This has nothing to do with me!" I yell. I have to take a moment to calm myself down before I continue. "This has to do with Sam's personal business back in LA. I promise, I wouldn't ask this of you if it weren't an absolute emergency." I lower my voice so Sam won't hear what I'm saying next. "I can't tell you all the details, but it's for real. He needs to get on a plane now, and all the commercial flights are gone for the day." I check the time on my phone just to be sure . . . It's past midnight, and by the time we get to JFK it'll be after one a.m. "This cannot wait until tomorrow morning. It's a life-or-death situation."

"Okay, I'm awake now. Fine. Whatever he needs." She yawns loudly.

"Sooo . . . what do I do to make this happen? I've never booked a private jet before." Heck, I've only purchased a regular airplane ticket a few times in my entire life.

"Don't worry, I'll take care of everything. I have all of Sam's personal details on my phone, so it's no big deal. You just need to get him to JFK ASAP. Mr. Blake knows where to go, and I'll be happy to wake his grouchy ass up."

"I told Sam to go pack a couple minutes ago. We'll be out of here in ten minutes."

"Okay. The plane will obviously wait for him to get there, but go as soon as you can. They don't like people leaving too late at night. Something about noise regulations or whatever."

"You got it. Thank you so much, Amber."

"Don't think this is the end of this conversation, Em. You have a lot of explaining to do."

She sounds annoyed with me, but I don't have time for that right now. "I promise, I will tell you everything I can . . . later. Right now my priority is to get Sam out of here."

"Are you going with him?"

"What?" Her question throws me for a loop.

"I said, are you going with him? On the flight plan, the pilot needs to indicate how many passengers there will be."

I hadn't even thought of going with Sam, but the idea is nuts, so the answer is simple: no, I am not going to LA with Sam. Yes, we had a connection today, but that doesn't equate to me suddenly being thrust into the middle of his life.

"Of course I'm not going with him. It's just Sam."

"Are you sure? Because if this is a life-or-death situation, if it's *that* bad, maybe you *should* go with him. Remember what I asked you to do,

Em. Nothing has changed. I need your help with him and Ty. I can't have Sam falling apart on me. He means a lot to the band right now. There's a lot riding on this." She drops her voice. "And Sam and Ty are on the edge of fixing their relationship, and I need that to continue forward, not move backward. They need to mend their fences."

I can't believe she's trying to recruit me into this nonsense. Yes, I care about Sam, but I cannot get involved in all his problems. And even if I wanted to, I'm sure he wouldn't want me there. That would be crazy. We're still practically strangers.

"No, he doesn't want me to go with him to LA; that's nuts."

"You can if you want," says a deep voice from behind me.

I spin around to find Sam standing in the entrance of the foyer with his fully loaded backpack in hand. He doesn't have either guitar I saw him come in with this afternoon.

"But . . ." I look first at him and then at the phone in my hand. "But I don't know anybody in LA," I say lamely.

"You don't need to know anybody in LA besides me."

I can't believe how scared he looks. This is not the Sam I've seen over the past twelve hours. His skin is as pale as paper, and he looks physically ill. Drained. Hopeless.

I don't know what to think about his statement. We're practically strangers. The only thing I *do* know about him is that he's a standup guy and that he stepped in to take care of a little girl who needed him because her mother was a mess. And I guess I know too that he's the brother of my sister's boyfriend. Maybe he's not as much of a stranger as I thought.

I feel my resolve weakening, my reasons for not going evaporating over this sense that we are somehow connected and fated to see this thing through . . . whatever this *thing* is. Friendship, probably. But friends aren't anything to discount. I don't have so many that I couldn't use one more.

Besides . . . do I need to know anything else about him? I'm sure he's got skeletons in his closet just like I do. Does any of that matter? He looks so vulnerable. Scared. And I know what that feels like, to know that you're alone in the world and that no one understands. Somebody he loves could be dying—the mother of his child, no less. The only thing is . . . I'm sure he's got a million friends back in LA, so why does he need me?

He stares at me, waiting for me to respond.

The risk seems huge. What we started together here in New York City is nice, but it could so easily go sideways in the wrong environment. LA? What could be more opposite from New York than LA?

"Do you *need* me to go with you?" I finally ask. Regardless of how I feel, I know one thing: Sam was there for a little girl who needed him, so I can be there for him when he needs somebody. *If* he needs somebody. I don't think it's in him to admit that he does. I've only known him for half a day, but I can see that the chip on his shoulder is the size of a boulder.

He gives me a brief shrug. "It might be nice to have some company."

I nod, knowing that's the best I'm going to get from him. But the small amount of vulnerability he lets slip through is all I have to see. "Okay, fine. I'll go." I change my focus to the telephone. "Put me on the flight plan. I'm going to LA with Sam."

"Wow. I never thought I would see the day," Amber says.

"What's that supposed to mean? What day?"

"The day that you would drop everything and take a spontaneous trip across the country for a guy you just met. New York sure has had an effect on you."

My heart plummets as Amber puts what I'm doing into perfect perspective. I'm such a rube. "Shut up. I have to go."

"It's only going to take you fifteen seconds to pack," she says, a smile in her voice. "We still have time to chat if you want."

"No, we don't. Gotta go." I hang up the phone before she can say anything else. I take a deep breath and let it out. Sam stares at me and I stare back.

"So . . . we're doing this?" he asks. "Together?"

"I guess we are." My heart is pounding to beat the band.

"Is this too freaky? Is it too much?" He looks almost pained asking his questions.

I think about it for a couple seconds before I shake my head. "No. It felt like it at first, but not now. But maybe it hasn't sunk in yet either." I stop trying to explain my feelings because they're too screwed up in my head to make sense of anyway. "I need to go pack."

"I'll be here," he says. He's staring at the floor when I walk out of the room.

CHAPTER TWENTY-SEVEN

"So," Sam says, standing in the foyer at the elevator doors. He's looking straight ahead and we have our bags next to us on the floor. "You're going to LA with me."

"I guess I am." Things were so easy with him just thirty minutes ago, but now they're complicated again. We need an escape hatch; the pressure is getting to be too much. Maybe he regrets asking me to go.

"But I don't have to," I say. "If you don't want me to go . . . if it makes you uncomfortable, all you have to do is say so. You don't have to worry about hurting my feelings or anything. The most important thing is that you get where you need to be with the least amount of hassle."

His mouth is set in a grim line. I wish I could read the emotions on his face, but I'm having no luck. I wait for his response with my heart pounding.

"I'm glad you're going." That's all he says as he presses the button to summon the elevator again.

"I'm going to call downstairs really quick and see if they'll get us a cab." I don't think my sister was serious when she said she was going to wake Mr. Blake up to take us.

Sam nods once as I turn around and walk as quickly as I can to the kitchen. Picking up the intercom, I chew on my lip. I still don't know if I'm doing the right thing by going. I don't want Sam to think I've glommed on to him like some kind of leech. And what the heck . . .

LA? At this point, I'm pretty much jumping out of the frying pan and into the fire. I'm not only going to a city that's completely different, I'm also going to the opposite corner of the country, three thousand miles away. I couldn't be farther away from my comfort zone—literally and figuratively—than LA.

Someone at the front desk answers—a young male voice. "Hi, this is George."

"Hi, George. This is Emerald, Amber's sister."

"Hello, Ms. Collins. We have your car ready for you down here."

"My car?"

"Yes. Your sister called ahead to make sure your driver would be here. He's waiting for you at the curb. Do you need one of us to come up and get your bags for you?"

"No. We'll be fine. We'll be right down." Thank goodness Amber thinks of everything.

I join Sam in the open elevator, and we ride down in silence. When the doors open, George is standing there gesturing toward my bag. "Let me help you."

I allow him to take over, even though my suitcase is as light as a feather. Like Amber predicted, it only took me fifteen seconds to pack. She must have told George how much of a rush we'd be in because he speeds ahead of me to get to the door and hold it open for us. We're loaded up in no time, Sam riding in the backseat with me.

Mr. Blake looks at us in the rearview mirror. "JFK?"

"Yes, sir," I say. Sam is too lost in thought to answer. "You sure got here fast. Thank you for that."

"I was just around the corner. You're welcome."

I wish I knew what to say to Sam. I want to reassure him that everything is going to be okay, but I really don't think it is. He said that Madison is a heroin addict and that she overdosed. I don't know much about drug addiction, but I'm pretty sure her chances of survival are very slim, which means he could very well soon become the sole caregiver of their child. He probably sees his career crumbling before his eyes, assuming he's even capable of thinking about that stuff right now.

"Amber and Ty will support you, no matter what," I say, hoping to be reassuring.

He nods once. I don't know if he's feeling too emotional to discuss it or he wants me to stop talking, so I leave it alone. We ride all the way to the airport without another word spoken between us. By the time we arrive at the curb, I'm pretty sure coming along was a mistake, but I can't very well abandon him at the airport, can I? That would be unforgivable. Here I am promising him, reassuring him that my sister and her boyfriend will support him, and I'm going to just leave him out in the cold? No. I can't do that, even though ninety-nine percent of me wants to leave in this car, go back to the apartment, and stay there until my trip is over.

I was right about myself and so was Sam: I am afraid. I'm afraid of change, I'm afraid of conflict, and I'm afraid of things I don't understand. And I definitely do not understand the kind of life that Sam has obviously led, where he hangs out with drug addicts and plays music with strangers and takes on the responsibilities of raising another man's child. It's all so *foreign*.

"Do you know where we go from here?" he asks as we arrive at the airport.

I shake my head, panic settling deep into my chest. *Great*. I got us tickets to a plane that's parked who knows where.

"I'll show you where to go," Mr. Blake says. He hangs a big plastic card on his rearview mirror and receives a nod from a police officer standing nearby. He gets us and our luggage out and quickly hustles us over to a special ticket counter that doesn't have a sign on it. Soon, we're whisked away in an electric cart and delivered to the steps of a small jet airplane.

Sam looks up at it and then at me. "Pretty nice."

"Yeah. I flew commercial into JFK."

"Me too," he says.

Without another word, we mount the steps. Inside the door, two pilots are waiting. One of them holds out her hand. "Hello. I'm sorry to say we don't have a flight attendant on board with us tonight, but once we do our takeoff, we can help you get settled."

I shake her hand first. "Don't worry about us. We'll probably just sleep the whole way."

Sam shakes her hand next and nods. "Thanks."

We bring our bags inside, and they're stowed in a couple of closets near the front of the plane. Sam and I sit across from each other, a small table between us. The seats are heavily cushioned and covered in soft leather, more like recliners than actual plane seats.

"Are you tired?" he asks.

The engines whine, and there's a bumping on the outside of the plane that makes my heart skip a beat. I buckle my seat belt, tightening it. "Yes." That's a lie, actually. I am so keyed up right now, I have no idea how I'm going to sleep. But I think a nap at the very least is the best option for Sam, and I don't want him staying awake just to be polite.

"I probably should sleep, but I doubt I'll be able to." He looks out the window. There's nothing to see out there other than runway lights.

"If you want to talk, just talk. I'm here." I shrug, at a loss for what else to say.

"Thanks." He sighs and looks down at his interlaced fingers. He seems nervous. "I'm just glad you're here. I really didn't want to do this alone. I think I knew this day would come, but imagining it and living through it are two different things."

I nod, feeling so sad for him. "I can't imagine what you're going through. I'm sorry, Sam. I wish I could make things easier for you."

He nods, his lips pressing together. He's trying really hard not to cry.

"It sounds like she's in the hospital, right?"

He nods again.

"Then that means she's getting the best care she can get. We'll just have to pray that everything works out okay."

He takes a long breath and lets out a trembling sigh. "See, that's the thing . . ." He hesitates. "I don't know what the best thing *is* for her. I mean, if I pray, what do I pray for?"

"What do you mean?"

He looks up at me, his eyes shining with unshed tears. "She's miserably unhappy. Everyone who cares about her has done everything they could to help her, and she just doesn't want the help."

"It sounds like she's depressed."

"She's more than depressed. She's completely addicted. She hits the bottom of the barrel over and over, and she doesn't try to pull herself back up. It's like she's trying to kill herself in the slowest, most painful way. She doesn't even care . . ." His voice hitches on the last words. ". . . about Sadie."

"We should talk about this with her doctor when we get to the hospital. They should treat her psychiatrically, too."

"Yeah. We've done that before . . . so many times I've lost count."

"I know it's tempting, Sam, but don't give up on her. She's going to need you to hang in there for her."

He nods more enthusiastically than he did before, his nostrils flaring a little. "Yeah, I know. You're right. I can do that." He takes a deep breath and seems to expand before my eyes. He was slumping before, but now he's sitting up straighter. "I can definitely do that for Madison."

I don't know Sam that well, but I'm really proud of him. He's got the weight of the world on his shoulders, but here he is thinking about how he's going to hang in there for this girl who sounds like a hopeless case. I'm sure he's panicking about what's going to happen with their child. He's probably worried about his music and the business agreement he has going with the band, too. I wish I could assure him with one-hundred-percent certainty that the band will hang in there with him and stand by him through these difficult times, but I can't do that. I don't have a lot of faith in those men, even though my sister does.

The plane starts moving and I grip the armrests of my seat, suddenly realizing that we're about to fly through the air in a machine that's smaller than my sister's apartment. This thing is tiny! What if it runs into a storm and gets hit by lightning? We'll fall out of the sky!

"Are you afraid to fly?" he asks, glancing down at my hands.

I follow his gaze and check out my white knuckles. "Not usually." I try to laugh, but the terror I'm feeling seeps in and makes me sound like a crazy witch, cackling over a spell's brew. *Double, double, toil and trouble* . . .

"Do you want to come and sit next to me?" he asks.

I shake my head. "No. I'm okay. Really. I'm great. Cool as a cucumber. Cooler than that. Like ice." Here I am acting like a damsel in distress when I'm *supposed* to be supporting him while he goes to the hospital to deal with his friend's heroin overdose. I just took a flight to New York this morning and I was fine, but now I'm freaking about the plane simply taking off? Wow, I'm going to be a lot of help.

He takes off his seat belt and gets up, walking around the table to stand next to me. "Scoot over."

I look up at him and around me. "What?"

"Scoot over." He points at the seat to my left. "Quick, before I get thrown on the floor."

I scramble to unbuckle my seat belt and take the other seat. As he settles into the one I was just occupying, I finally realize what this musical chairs business is all about: the guy's world is falling down around his ears, but he still manages to be concerned about me.

To say this man is charming would be the understatement of the year. Talk about a knight in shining armor. He's galloping off to save not just one but two damsels in distress . . . Three, if you include his daughter.

"That's better," he says, securing his seat belt. "I don't like these little planes. Not that sitting next to you is going to change anything, but I feel better about not dropping out of the sky having you close." He reaches over and squeezes my hand once before folding his arms over his chest.

I smile, charmed to the core. The spot where he touched me remains warm and tingly. "I was thinking the same thing. What holds this thing up in the air, anyway?"

"I think it's called a wing and a prayer."

I clasp my hands together and close my eyes. "Dear God, please keep this plane in the air until it's ready to land in LA." I pause, wondering if God would be so cruel as to use loopholes to get around my request. I decide it's worth being a little more detailed, just in case God is also a lawyer in his spare time. "And please don't let any lightning hit us. Or hail. Or wind. Or a hurricane. Or a tornado. Or a tidal wave. Or any weather that's dangerous. Or another plane. Or an alien ship." *There. That should cover it.*

"Good one," he says lazily. When I look over at him, he's leaning against his headrest and smiling with his eyes closed.

I decide to use his method and lay my head back too. I'm just going to close my eyes during the takeoff, and then once we're up in the air, we can have a conversation. What we'll talk about, I don't know, but I'm sure it'll be interesting, mysterious, and stimulating, because every conversation I've had with him since the moment I met him has been at least one of these things. A smile plays along my lips as I drift away and the plane points its nose toward the darkened sky.

CHAPTER TWENTY-EIGHT

Los Angeles is nothing like New York City. First of all, it's warmer. Much warmer. And the people here look really different. On the drive from the airport to the hospital, I see a bunch of luxury vehicles and convertibles. They're everywhere, even though it's super early. The people inside them are sparkling with jewelry, mostly blond, and stacked with cleavage. And Sam was right . . . nobody is walking around outside.

The taxi driver drops us off in the valet area of the hospital emergency room. The main door to the facility is closed this early in the morning. After checking in at the triage station, we're escorted to a curtained-off area in the intensive care unit. The beds are lined up in a row, each with several machines surrounding it. Short drapes hanging from tracks on the ceiling divide one patient off from another.

"Do you want me to wait outside?" I ask Sam.

He takes me by the hand. "No. Stay." He pauses and looks down at me. "Unless this is too much for you. I'll understand if it is."

I shake my head and squeeze his fingers a little. "No. I'm cool. I'm good. I help Rose with emergencies at her clinic all the time. I'm used to it." I'm saying this as much for my benefit as his, because I am very nervous. This isn't at all like taking care of dogs, cats, or owls. The smell of disinfectant and sick people is very strong. It doesn't turn my stomach, but it does make my blood pressure go up.

I'm so worried for Madison and Sam . . . and Sadie, too, of course. She's not here, and she has no idea what's going on. She's safely ensconced with one of Sam's friends who has two children that play with her often. She's probably sleeping away with a little smile on her face, dreaming of her daddy and his big, fluffy beard.

A nurse is standing at the foot of Madison's bed talking to Sam. She's murmuring, trying to maintain Madison's privacy. Even though I've detached myself from Sam's grasp and taken a step back, I'm still catching bits of what she's saying.

"She's peaceful now . . . it's all we can do for her . . ."

I catch a glimpse of Madison's arm above the covers. She's bone thin, and her skin is covered in red streaks that I think are from needles and the drugs they delivered into her body. I swallow with difficulty. As I step closer, her face comes into view. She's been intubated, but it doesn't hide the fact that this girl was very, very sick before she got here, long before she overdosed. She looks like a skeleton, her eyes sunken in and her lips gray. Her hair is greasy and stuck together in bunches; it looks like she hasn't seen a shower or a brush in weeks.

I stare at Sam in shock. How could he have left her like this? He said he took off from LA early because there was stuff going down, but it looks more like he abandoned Madison, left her behind when she obviously wasn't in any condition to be alone. This doesn't align at all with the image I had of him just thirty seconds ago.

A small female doctor in surgical scrubs walks over and shakes Sam's hand. "I assume you're Sam Stanz."

Sam nods.

"You're named as Madison's next of kin on her papers, and apparently you're the only one the hospital was able to identify as being family."

"Yeah. She doesn't have anyone else. Her parents both passed a while back, and her one brother died overseas last year."

"We've got her on a ventilator now, but things aren't good. She has no brain activity, and we don't expect her to gain any back. This is the end for her. We just need your permission to turn the ventilator off and let her go."

My jaw drops open in shock. Does this woman have zero bedside manner or what? "How can you say that?" I blurt out, without waiting for Sam to respond. "Just say it like that. Gosh, you didn't even introduce yourself first."

The woman looks over at me and shrugs. "I'm sorry, but I think you can see from her condition . . . I assume this is no surprise to you, Sam. She's been sick for a long time."

I feel like I've suddenly inherited Amber's gene for raising hell. I can't wait for Sam to respond. He looks too shell-shocked to do it, so I jump in again. "Maybe she doesn't look so great, sure"—I gesture at Madison's sad body—"but that doesn't mean you shouldn't treat her and Sam with some basic dignity." I wouldn't be surprised if steam started coming out of my ears, I'm that hot under the collar.

Sam lifts his hand and puts it on my shoulder briefly. "Let it go, babe. It's okay."

My heart flips at the endearment, but the effect lasts only for a split second. This seems all kinds of wrong to me, but Sam wants me to stop, and it's not my place to raise a fuss here. I take a deep breath in and out as I focus on Madison. She looks like death warmed over, and this woman standing next to us is a medical professional, even if she has a crappy bedside manner. Maybe the best thing for Sam is to hear the cold, hard truth.

"Can I spend some time with her first?" Sam asks. "Before we . . . pull the plug." His voice chokes on the last bit.

"Sure. Take all the time you need." The doctor starts to walk away, but then she stops and turns around. "I'm sorry for your loss. It can't have been easy, trying to help her."

Sam shakes his head. I'm going to go ahead and let this doctor walk away without any more fuss from me, because at least she had a little bit of empathy in the end. She's right, too. It could not have been easy to live with Madison. Is that why Sam left early? Maybe it wasn't just about getting the work with the band done faster. He's only human; maybe he just couldn't take it anymore. I've never watched someone I love kill herself slowly like he has. I probably shouldn't be so quick to judge. I hear my mothers' voices in my head telling me that I can never understand another person's trials and tribulations until I've walked a mile in his shoes. It sure looks like Sam's shoes have been to some scary, sad places.

I have so many questions that I want to ask him. There's too much mystery here. But all of that has to wait, because the important thing right now is for Sam to be able to spend some time with Madison before he has to make the awful decision to allow her to end her life.

There's one chair next to the bed, and Sam sits in it. I stand awkwardly near Madison's feet for a few moments, wondering what I should do. Sam has forgotten that I exist. He's resting his hand on hers, crying as he stares at her face.

I know he needs this private moment with her, so I step away. On either side of me, though, are other patients. One of them has a nurse tending to her, and the other has family nearby. So I stay just beyond the curtain, ten inches away from Madison's left foot. Being in this position, I can't help but overhear the conversation Sam has with her.

"Hi, Maddy. It's me . . . Sam. The guy with the ugly beard."

I smile through the tears that start pouring out of my eyes. I try my best to wipe them away, but more and more come.

His voice is raw with emotion. "I'm sorry I wasn't here for you. You disappeared and I didn't know where you went. When I went to the cops, they wouldn't look for you. You know how they are. You know they got tired of looking for you a long time ago."

I can't imagine the heartache he must've had to bear, wondering where she was, knowing he had a daughter to take care of and a future to secure at the same time. I could imagine he thought he'd go to New York and get the work done quicker than planned so he could get back to LA and try to find her, get her some help. Or maybe I'm just believing that story because I want him to be a good guy and not the kind of man who would leave a woman like Madison out in the cold.

"Sadie is okay. I made sure she was far away from Drake so he couldn't find her. And I left town, so he wouldn't go looking for me. Everybody you care about is safe, and I promise we're going to stay that way. We're not sticking around LA, okay? I'm going to find a nice place for Sadie to grow up. I promised you I'd take care of her before she was born, and I'm not going to go back on that promise ever. Daddy for life."

My heart is beating rapidly and I feel sick to my stomach. This man has a heart of gold, yes, but he has people after him? What does that mean for him? For Sadie? For me and my sister Amber? Are we in danger?

"The doctor told me you're already gone," Sam says after a long pause. He sniffs loudly before continuing. "You and I used to talk about people in comas being able to hear people talk around them, remember? I guess you're not in a coma, but if you can hear me, I just . . . I just want to tell you that I'm sorry . . ." His voice breaks, but he keeps talking as he cries. "I'm sorry that I could never get you out of that hole you were in. I really wanted you to wake up these past few years and open your eyes so that you could see how much love everyone had for you." His voice lowers and he sniffs. "But I know what your dad did broke something inside you that could never heal." I think he's done but then he talks again, softer this time. I can barely make out the words. "I'm always going to wonder if I tried hard enough to heal it for you, to help you heal yourself." There's a long silence before he finishes. "I'm never going to know, am I?"

I have to cover my mouth to keep from weeping out loud. I've never actually felt my heart breaking for another person before; it's incredibly painful.

Sam's voice is barely there. "The doctor says I have say when to turn off this machine that's keeping you breathing. But I don't think I can do it. I don't think I can be the one to decide that you don't get to breathe anymore." His voice wavers. "Could you give me a sign, Maddy? Can you tell me what to do? You were always so bossy. I've got to believe that even on your way up to heaven, you could manage to tell me what to do."

Oh, how I wish I had met Madison while she was still alive. I think I would've liked her. I'm so caught up in the emotion of the moment, I don't see the nurse moving out of the cubicle next to me. She turns around in a hurry and immediately starts running, slamming right into me. I scream, throwing my arms out to stop my fall, but she was going at a fast clip and she's a big girl, so there's no hope of me not making a grand entrance into Madison's cubicle.

The curtain flies up in my face and then slides across my cheek as the world turns sideways, and suddenly, I'm with Sam and Madison. And I'm tripping. A goofy sound flies out of my mouth.

"Whooo hooooo-oooo!"

I land across Madison's legs, grabbing the rail on the opposite side of her bed to keep myself from falling to the floor. When I finally stop moving, I'm lying there prone across her legs, hanging on to the metal railing for dear life, my mouth wide open as I stare at Sam's surprised face.

Holy shit! Could I be any more disrespectful of the dying?! No, I could not! I want to look away, but instead I cringe with a huge apology in my eyes. "Oh my god, Sam. I am *so* sorry."

Sam is astonished at first, but then he smiles. And then he laughs. His face is gaunt with sorrow and his cheeks are wet with tears, but he is laughing so hard he's having a hard time breathing. He picks up

Madison's hand and holds it against his cheek as he slowly calms down. I straighten myself and get to my feet, and he speaks to the mother of his child.

"Okay, girl. I hear you loud and clear. Consider it a done deal." He leans over and kisses her on the cheek and then stands, slowly placing her hand on her chest.

In the meantime, I do my best to smooth down her covers and then my skirt. *Holy shit.* I have been alive for twenty-five years, and I can remember every humiliating moment that has ever occurred in my lifetime, and I can safely say that *not one* of them even comes close to this one. My face is on fire with embarrassment. Sam is going to hate me.

Sam comes walking over to me and places his hand on my shoulder. I can't look at him.

"Thank you."

I can't believe I just heard those words coming from his mouth. I look up at him. "Excuse me?"

He takes my face in his hands very gently and looks deep into my eyes. His are still wet with tears, but I swear I can see joy radiating from his face. "Thank you for allowing Madison to communicate through you to me."

"Uhhh . . . you're welcome?" I'm pretty sure he's having a psychotic break right now, due to his grief and all, but I'm not going to mess up the moment for him. We can talk to the doctor about psychiatric counseling after.

He leans forward and kisses me on the forehead before pulling back. "I need to go find the doctor." He leaves me standing there at Madison's feet. I swallow and look around. All I can hear is the whooshing of air going into her body and the beeping that indicates her heart is still beating.

I walk over closer to her head, curious what she looked like when she wasn't destroying her body with drugs. I think I can see hints of Sadie's beautiful face in hers. The bone structure is there . . . easy to see as her skin sinks even farther in to reveal the skull beneath. The evidence is clear that she has no life left in her. Such a terrible tragedy. I wish there was something I could do . . . or say . . .

I'm seized by the desire to try to talk to her before anyone comes back. Maybe Sam was right; maybe a person on her deathbed can hear what people nearby are saying. Maybe Madison hasn't left this realm yet.

"Sam is a really great guy," I say, whispering by her ear. "But you know that already, of course. He's going to take great care of Sadie. And if he lets me, I'm going to be his friend." I don't want to make this woman any promises I can't keep. I wish I could tell her that I'm going to look out for them, that I'm going to help Sam get over his fear of performing in public, but I can't do that. I think those things may be beyond me. And I still need to know why he left her and his daughter. Does he think he was doing the best thing he could for them, or was he chickening out, leaving Madison to fend for herself because he was too shallow to get involved, and leaving Sadie in the care of some random woman? Until I know for sure, I cannot risk my own world to try to fix his.

I sigh as I sit down in the chair next to Madison. "I wish I had known you. I think if you were a friend of Sam's, you must've been pretty special." I pause, thinking about Sam and his issues. I guess Madison failed him as much as he failed her. "Maybe you could have told me why he can't play his music in front of people he doesn't know. Maybe together we could've helped him."

There's no sign whatsoever that she's hearing me. And talking to a person on a ventilator who's taking her last breaths should be a simple matter, but it's exhausting. I don't want to do the wrong thing. I want to be respectful. I stand, done trying to figure out Sam's secrets by talking to Madison. The sound of voices coming from behind me causes me to move back away from her bed a little more. The doctor is back with Sam.

Sam comes over to be next to me, putting his arm across my shoulders.

"As I said earlier," the doctor prompts, "my advice is that we turn off the ventilator. The question is whether any of her organs are viable for donation, something we have to determine before we do that. Looking at the medical records on her that we have access to, I have a feeling she's in pretty bad shape, but that doesn't mean there isn't something she could do to help someone else."

Sam nods. "She's been a heroin addict for a long time."

"Okay. Well, be that as it may, if it was her wish to be an organ donor, we'll do what we can."

"It was her wish," Sam says. "We talked about it."

"Great. I'm going to call the harvesting team in to do an evaluation. We'll keep the ventilator going until they've done what they need to do, as long as you give us your permission to do that."

Sam nods.

"Fine. Somebody from administration will be here very soon with paperwork for you. You can either wait here with Madison or you can step outside; it's your choice." The doctor walks away and stops at a cubicle a couple beds down.

I touch Sam's arm to get his attention. "Why don't you stay with her, and I'll go wait outside?"

He nods and takes a seat at her bedside without a word.

I leave him alone and go out into the waiting room. Pulling my phone from my purse, I stare at the screen. I need to call my sister and talk to her about what's going on, but I also need to keep Sam's confidence. How on earth did my life suddenly get so incredibly complicated? I just met this man eighteen hours ago!

CHAPTER TWENTY-NINE

I fret over what I'm going to say to Amber, but there's no point. She doesn't answer her phone; my call goes right into her voice mail. She's probably over the middle of the ocean or maybe stuck in transit somewhere. I rest my head against the wall in the waiting room, and then it feels like a moment later somebody is touching my shoulder and shaking me gently.

I open my eyes to find Sam standing over me.

"Did you get some sleep?" His smile is weak.

"I don't know. It feels like I just closed my eyes two seconds ago." I look at my phone and see that two hours have passed.

"Everything's over." Sam jams his hands into his front pockets and folds his shoulders inward. He stares at the toes of his boots. "Madison passed away."

I get to my feet and hold him tightly. "I'm so sorry, Sam. I know this is really hard for you."

"Yeah." His body is stiff, but I don't let go. We stand there for a long time. Eventually, his shoulders and back soften and his hands come out of his pockets. Then I feel his arms go around me and I slide mine up to be around his neck. I hold him tighter. "You're going to get through this, I promise."

He gives me one last squeeze and then releases me. We step away from each other, an awkwardness slipping in to steal the moment away from us. This is a different Sam standing before me. He's been stripped bare, shy and unsure of himself.

I can't let this happen to him. I move to stand next to him and lace my arm through his. "Why don't we go find some breakfast somewhere and then figure out what we're going to do next?"

"Good idea."

He lets me guide him out of the hospital and across the street to a café. He gets coffee and I get tea. I order a muffin and he gets a bagel with cream cheese. We take the corner table and sit with our backs to the crowd.

We eat in silence. I'm not going to push for conversation. He looks like he's been put through a wringer. His eyes are swollen and red rimmed, his shirt wrinkled and stained, his pants barely hanging on to his waist. He slowly chews his bagel, staring at the crumbs it leaves behind on the table.

"Would you like a bite?" I hold up my blueberry muffin.

He reaches up and breaks off a piece of it, popping it into his mouth. This is the first tiny signal I've had since we arrived in LA that his will to carry on is still in there somewhere. It gives me hope.

"Is there anything special you want to do first?" I ask. "We can arrange our day by priorities."

He sounds like a robot when he answers. "I've got to contact some people. I have to go get Sadie. And I need to arrange the funeral and memorial."

I nod. "Let me help. I can do the funeral stuff if you want."

"Yeah, sure." He pushes the rest of his bagel away and hunches over his coffee.

"How far away is Sadie from here?"

"About an hour."

I reach over and brush some crumbs from his beard. "You can go get her while I do the funeral arrangements if you want. Or I could go with you."

"It's probably better if you hang back." He looks up at me with an apology in his eyes. "It's not that I don't want to be with you . . ."

I wave away his concerns. "No, I get it. At some point you're going to have to break the news to Sadie that her mother is . . . gone. I don't know if you're going to do that now, but I have a feeling when you see her it's going to be tough. You'll probably want to be alone."

"Yeah. You've seen enough crying for one day, huh?"

"No, that's not what I meant." I shove him gently, trying to get a smile out of him. "You can cry all you want. I kinda like your eyes when they're all red and puffy like that." I point at his face.

A sad little smile lifts the side of his mouth for a second or two. "You're mean."

I reach over and put my arm around his shoulders, pulling him over to me. Our heads touch and we stay that way for a little while, decompressing from the sadness. "I'm not mean. I'm just trying to cheer you up, but I know it's not possible right now."

"Keep trying. It'll work eventually."

I kiss him on the forehead before withdrawing.

He places his hand on my arm, stopping me from gathering up our napkins and other garbage.

"What?" I look at him questioningly.

"Do that again."

"Do what again?" I feel my cheeks getting warm.

He puts his hand on the back of my head and pulls me to him. "Kiss me." His face is raw with emotion and there's a storm in his eyes. There's no way I can avoid this very public display of affection, and I don't want to.

My hand goes to his cheek as our lips touch. It's a gentle kiss, full of longing and sadness. We're in the middle of a coffee shop that's busting at the seams with customers, so it doesn't go too far, but it goes plenty far enough. When we pull apart I'm on fire.

"Well." That's all I've got: *Well.* Sam has destroyed my ability to converse with a single kiss.

"That was nice," he says. "Thanks."

"Sure." Butterflies are flitting around in my stomach. I busy myself with cleaning up our mess. It helps take my mind off the fact that what should have been a perfectly innocent kiss has me dreaming of the day that I can have him in my bed. This day will probably never come to be, but I'm not going to let that stop me from fantasizing. Besides . . . stranger things have happened, and life is too short to be afraid of taking risks all the time.

"You ready to go?" he asks, getting to his feet.

I stand and take my purse from the back of the chair, throwing it over my shoulder before gathering up our trash to bring over to the bins. He takes the pile from me and waits for my answer.

"Yes, I'm ready. Where're we going?"

"My place."

Sam's mind is occupied with the tragedy that just occurred in this life, so I know he's not thinking what I am when he says, "My place," which is: *sex, naked man, sex!* I'm picturing his bedroom, his bed, and him in it—no clothes on and ready to rock 'n' roll . . . and I don't mean with a guitar either.

My body heats up as we make our way out to the curb and get a ride using an app Sam has on his telephone. I pray this will be the one time that he isn't able to read my mind, because while I'm ready to throw caution to the wind for the first time in my life, I really don't want him to think that I don't care about his sadness or the tragedy that's befallen him and his daughter. There's a time and a place for the sexy stuff, and I know this isn't it. I just wish my libido would get on board with that.

CHAPTER THIRTY

Sam's apartment is nothing special. It does have two bedrooms, though, and one of them is definitely furnished for a little girl. It's got pink and purple everywhere with highlights of yellow. There are toys in a big plastic bin in the corner, and a tiny bed with a Disney princess painted on the headboard. It smells like a little girl, too . . . a mix of strawberries and cotton candy.

He opens his fridge. "Sorry . . . I don't have any food or anything to drink in here."

"That's okay. I'm not hungry or thirsty."

He leaves the kitchen and goes into his bedroom. I follow him, stopping in the threshold. He's thrown both my bag and his down on his bed. My heart leaps into my throat seeing our things together like that. *Is he expecting me to sleep with him in here?*

"You can take the bed and I'll grab the couch tonight," he says, catching the look on my face. "I don't think we can leave until tomorrow at the very earliest. I need to get Sadie."

I shake my head. "If you want to stick around for the funeral, which I assume you will, we're probably going to be here for the next several days."

He pauses and stares off into nowhere. "Yeah. You're right. I hadn't thought about that." He turns to look at me, his face set with pain. "For a second, I forgot that she died."

I walk into the room and put my arms around him. He returns the hug without hesitation. It's starting to feel normal to do this with Sam . . . to hold each other in a warm embrace as we wait for a sad moment to pass. How strange it is, not only that I'm doing this, but also that I'm so comfortable doing it with a man I just met. *Was it New York that changed me, or was it Sam?*

"I think it's going to take a while for her death to sink in," I say.

"Yeah, but how could I just forget? I'm such a shit."

"No, you're not a shit. Don't be mean to yourself like that. You're a human being. Madison has been in your life for a long time. She was just a natural part of it, like your arm is part of your body. And now this natural part of your life has been cut away with no warning, like an amputation of that limb. It's going to take a while for you to adapt to the idea that she's not here anymore. I mean, she's here in spirit, and she's here in Sadie . . . she's just not going to be here in person anymore."

"I don't know if I believe in the afterlife," he says.

"That's okay. Even if you don't believe in that, you know that when she was here, you did your best by her."

"That's the problem; I'm not sure that I did." He pulls away from me and goes over to his bag, opening the top and digging some things out.

"I don't know you that well, but what I've learned since I met you yesterday is that you cared about her and you tried really hard to help her out."

"I should've tried harder."

We're going to go round and round on this, with him trying to convince me he's a jerk and me trying to convince him he's not. What a colossal waste of time. "Is there really any point to this?" I ask.

He stops digging in his bag and looks at me. "To what?"

"To beating yourself up? Will it change anything?"

He seems mad now. "No, it won't. She's dead and that's not going to change."

I take a step closer. "Yes. But she's not dead because of *you*, Sam. She's not dead because you chose that ending for her. She's dead because of the choices that *she* made."

His expression turns dark, and he goes back to messing with his bag. "Sure. Whatever. Thanks for trying to help, but I don't really need a lecture about it right now."

The temptation to snap back at him and tell him that I'm not lecturing him is great, but this is not the time or the place to have that argument. He's hurting and my words aren't helping, that much is clear. I turn and leave the room in silence, refusing to take his anger personally. He's not mad at me; he's mad at himself, and right now me talking sense to him isn't going to do any good.

I spend the next fifteen minutes sitting on his couch and twiddling my thumbs. There's a permanent dip in the center cushion; somebody has spent a lot of time there. Maybe Sam likes playing video games, but the game console I see under the TV is covered in a thick layer of dust, and the controllers are buried under wires. They obviously haven't been used in a long time.

There's evidence of Sadie everywhere around the room . . . a toy here, a little girl's blanket there, a pink article of clothing draped over the arm of a chair across the room. Viewing his world from this perspective, I can see Sam more fully now, as not just a really good-looking guy, but also as a man with a child . . . a father with a life that revolved around a tiny girl and her sad mother.

As I take in all the evidence of his life, I realize that I need to try to control my need to fix Sam's sadness. He has to go through the process of mourning the loss of his friend and the mother of his child so he can move on eventually. It will be painful, but every person who experiences the death of a loved one must get through the pain of that loss to reach the happiness on the other side . . . the closure we crave as humans, the sign that life will go on, even when it deals us a shitty hand and shuts us down temporarily.

I can't even imagine what must be going through Sam's mind right now. He's a single dad for real, not just temporarily. I'm sure he had hoped in the back of his mind all along that Madison would get herself together and become a true mother to Sadie. Now there's no chance of that happening, and he's on his own with this little girl to raise.

And as if that weren't tough enough, apparently there's some bad guy out there who wants to get in touch with Madison or Sam. *What was his name . . . Drake?* I can handle the death of a friend or the prospect of babysitting a little girl I don't know for a few days, but dealing with bad guys? No, thank you. I'm not okay with that.

A noise to my left catches my attention. Sam is standing at the entrance to the living room. "Sorry," he says, leaning on the wall with his hands in his front pockets.

"You have nothing to be sorry for."

"I snapped at you and was rude. You were just trying to help."

I stand and walk over, stopping a couple feet away. "I was trying to help, but I was also out of line. I know you need time to get through this stuff. I probably don't know you well enough to say the right thing anyway, so I'm just going to shut up now and let you do your thing."

He comes closer and picks up my hands, holding them between us. His fingers intertwine with mine a little. "That's the thing . . . You *do* know the right thing to say." He stares into my eyes, the vulnerability I see there piercing my heart. "I might not want to hear it, but what you're saying makes complete sense. I've had a hard time my whole life letting people in. I don't trust anyone. I guess maybe that's why Madison and I got along so well; we'd both been burned pretty bad, so we had high walls and we understood each other and our limitations. But I don't want to push you away. You're a special person, and I'd like to keep you in my life . . . if you want to be there, that is."

I squeeze his hands. "Of course I do. I think you're really awesome too."

His smile is sad. "I can't imagine why."

"Stop fishing for compliments." I shake his hands a little to wake him up out of his sad stupor. "When I tell you you're awesome, you just have to accept it."

"Yes, ma'am."

I glance at the door to his bedroom. "And FYI, nobody is sleeping on the couch in this apartment." I'm feeling super bold right now, like nothing I say could go wrong.

"Is that so?" he asks, his eyebrow arching.

"Yes, it is. You've just been through a terrible time, and I'm not going to make you get a backache on top of everything else. And I'm not going to let myself get one either. We'll just share the bed. We can be platonic buddies who share a mattress." I hold up our hands, still locked together, for him to see. "Right?"

He shakes his head slowly. "I don't know about that."

"Why? Don't you want to be my friend?" A little sliver of panic comes in. Maybe I took things too far. Maybe he doesn't see us as being anything but two people who have siblings who date.

He's still shaking his head. "No, not really."

I try to drop his hands as my face warms with embarrassment, but he hangs on tighter.

"Don't run away." His voice is liquid heat. He pulls me closer.

"Why would I run away?" The realization that he's flirting hits me and sends my heart fluttering.

"Because I'm scaring you right now."

"No, you're not." I lift my chin. "It's going to take a lot more than a little flirting to scare me away."

"So . . . if I get closer to you, that's not going to scare you?" He takes one step.

"Don't be silly." Part of me wants to run; he's right. Maybe he knows me better than I thought he did. But I want to stay, too. I want to see how far this will go. I want to heal his pain, and there's a crazy side of me that thinks physical intimacy could help. It could be that I'm just being selfish to think that. It's true that I want to feel his naked body against mine more than anything in the world right now. Hell, I've been staring at him for most of the past twenty-four hours and dreaming of it pretty much constantly the entire time. It's clear I cannot trust my motivations where he's concerned.

"You sure about that?" He takes another step, leaving mere inches between us.

My heart is beating wildly, but I'm too far gone to stop. "I'm sure. I told you before . . . I'm not a virgin."

He chuckles low in his throat. "I do remember you mentioning that." Now his body is touching mine, hip to hip. He reaches up to stroke my arms. "Maybe it's wrong, but I really want to take you to bed."

"Why would it be wrong?" I ask in a whisper. My pulse is pounding loud enough that I can hear it inside my head.

"We don't know each other that well," he says, his mouth moving toward mine.

"We know each other well enough, Sam."

CHAPTER THIRTY-ONE

I put my arms around his neck and pull him to me. Our lips meet with a crash. Then his hands are all over me, and we're stumbling into the bedroom.

I imagined our first encounter together would be soft and hesitant, both of us fumbling around and shy, but boy, was I wrong. His hands are *everywhere* . . . my bottom, chest, my stomach, between my legs . . . his fingers sliding along my most intimate parts.

I'm out of my clothes in a matter of seconds, and I don't even realize how it happened. I'm naked, and so is he. We're sitting at the edge of his bed, touching each other all over, kissing, licking, both of us moaning. His hand is on my rear end pulling me toward him, his arousal strong and hard.

"Do you have a condom?" I ask. If he doesn't, I do, but I'm going to hate having to run into the other room to get it.

He reaches over and yanks on a drawer, pulling it out completely. Several condoms fall to the floor along with various other things. He bends down to grab a foil packet, quickly ripping it open.

I stroke him while he removes the condom and throws the packaging off to the side. He pauses to kiss me some more before putting it on.

His fingers move across my thigh and slide down into my folds. "Are you ready for me?"

I hold his face in my hands, breathing heavily through my arousal. "I have never been more ready for someone in my entire life."

"That's what I wanted to hear."

He pushes me backward and I fall across the bed. I scoot over to make room for him. He joins me, his giant body looming over mine. I rub my hands over his chest, looking up at him. When I see the ragged look of his face and tear-swollen eyes, a brief flash of guilt hits me. Am I taking advantage of a man who's too full of sadness to make good decisions?

"Are you sure you want to do this?" I ask, breathing heavily, praying he won't say no.

"I was just going to ask you the same thing." He lowers himself slowly down to me, the muscles of his arms bulging with the effort. I close my eyes in a mixture of relief and pleasure as I realize he's giving me his answer. *He's sure.*

He goes slowly, gently pushing against and into me. My body is slick down there, but he's big and it's been a really long time for me.

"You are so tight," he says with a hiss.

"You're too big," I say, and not just to pump his ego.

"Here, let me help you." He lifts one of my legs, spreading me open. He eases in a bit and then out, very gently, teasing away the tension I was feeling, making it easier for both of us. My hips start to move with him, welcoming his thrusts and opening for him.

When he's finally buried to the hilt, we moan together in pleasure and relief. He stays that way for several seconds, pausing to kiss me for a bit before pulling out and burying himself inside me again. The super-slow rhythm he's using is killing me. I know I should probably just relax and enjoy it, but I'm having trouble doing that. The sensations are building too quickly. I've never been in such a hurry to reach orgasm before.

"It's been a while for me," he says, grunting with the effort of speaking and exercising extreme control over his movements. "I'm not going to last very long; you feel too good." His eyes are closed and the muscles in his face show the tremendous strain he's under.

Just hearing those words excites me even more, and I was already half over the moon. "Don't worry about me," I say breathlessly. "I'm ready to go too."

He picks up his rhythm and I join him. With each thrust he delivers, my hips rise off the bed, taking his force and pulling it in. I hold on to him, my body rocking faster and faster as we seek climax together. I'm so close, a warm, tickling sensation building between my legs.

Sweat rolls down his face and drips onto my chest. "I'm so close, babe. I can't hold it anymore."

I grab his back, holding on for dear life. "Come for me, Sam. Let go."

His body starts to tremble as he thrusts forward hard against me, three . . . four . . . then five times. His back arches and he shouts. My nails score his back and ribs as he slams into me over and over again and I try to hang on.

I wasn't expecting the strength of his lovemaking or the effect it would have on me. The end takes me by surprise, his body and movements somehow managing to rip the orgasm out of me. I scream as my world crashes in on me and then explodes outward.

He pulsates inside me as he comes to the end of the line, giving me chills from the inside out. All I can think is, *Thank God he was wearing protection, or I would've surely gotten pregnant.* I can't believe what we just did together; it was so incredible. I've never come this quickly in my life, and never with a man this amazing in bed.

Sam's movements finally slow to a stop. His chest heaves as he tries to breathe, propped up on his elbows above me. I pull in a long breath of air, hoping to calm myself down. It feels like I just ran a race around the entire city.

"Damn, girl," he says, leaning down to kiss me. His beard tickles my face and neck. "Sorry, I'm sweaty." He leans away.

"Come back here," I say, pulling his face down and forcing him to kiss me again. Our tongues tangle together, and the connection between us deepens. I feel something growing hard between my legs and realize he's getting another erection.

I stop and look down between us. "Are you kidding me?"

He chuckles. "I can't help it. You're hot."

I push on his chest until he rolls over. "Get outta here." I have never in my life been called *hot* by anyone. It makes me giggle like a schoolgirl.

He sits up and busies himself with removing the used condom and putting it down on the nightstand. I'm on my back, and he joins me on his side, tracing circles around my breasts. The air that's blowing over us from the air-conditioning vent above feels amazing.

"That was cool," he finally says.

"Yeah. Cool." I giggle.

"What are you laughing at?" He leans in and snuggles my neck with that fluffy weirdo beardo of his, making me laugh harder.

"Stop. You're going to make me get goose bumps."

"So? I like goose bumps," he mumbles in my neck.

"They'll make the hair on my legs grow," I whine, pretending to try and push him away. I'm not using much force, though.

He pauses for a minute. "What?"

"I *said* you need to stop, or you're going to make the hair on my legs grow."

He lifts the covers at my waist to look at my legs. "You shave your legs? I thought hippies lived au naturel."

I grab the covers from his hand and yank them over my body. "Not this hippie."

He leans down again and kisses me gently. "I was just kidding."

"Okay. I forgive you."

"Forgive me for what?"

I sigh in fake frustration. "For making the hair on my legs grow."

He takes a few moments to push the sweaty hair off my forehead and the side of my face. "So what do you think of LA?" he asks.

He's trying to act like this is a casual question, but I know better. I can tell by the way his jaw is tensing that my answer matters.

"Do you want me to be honest?"

His lips press together for a few seconds before he answers. "Always. Never say something that's not totally true just because you don't want to hurt my feelings."

I take a deep breath before I give him my answer. I know it will complicate things between us. "Well, it's a little warm, and I'm not a fan of the traffic."

"Me neither."

"Which one?" I ask.

"You mean the heat or the traffic?"

"Yes."

"Both."

I frown at him. "If you don't like it, why do you live here?"

One of his shoulder lifts in a casual shrug. "Don't know. Maybe because it was far away."

"Far away from your parents?"

"Far away from my father."

I reach up and brush a sweat droplet from his temple. "Tell me about him."

Sam gets a pained expression. "Do I have to?"

I pinch his cheek. "No, you don't have to. Not if you don't want to." *Not today, anyway . . . but someday.*

He falls back onto the bed with a sigh. "Okay, fine. Twist my arm."

I can't stop smiling.

"My father was a dick of the highest degree."

"The highest degree, huh? That's pretty bad."

"Yeah, tell me about it. He drank a lot. And when he drank a lot, he punched a lot."

"Oh. Damn. My sister didn't tell me that."

He looks at me sideways. "Your sister tells you all of Ty's secrets?"

"Not all of them, apparently. She told me that he had a difficult relationship with his father. I guess I didn't realize how bad it was."

Sam is on his back staring at the ceiling, casually stroking his abdomen with his hands as he speaks. "Yeah, he was abusive, but it wasn't the worst part of our relationship."

"How could that not be the worst part?" I turn my head to look at him more fully. Seeing his sad face makes me want to envelop him in another one of my hugs, but I don't want to stop him from telling me his story. I feel as though I'm acting as his therapist right now.

"He was bound and determined to make us famous."

"Famous as musicians?"

"Yeah. He put instruments in our hands when we were just babies. That's why Sadie doesn't have a guitar."

"Because you don't want her to learn to play?"

"No, it's not that. I'd love for her to learn, but I want it to be her idea, not mine."

"You feel like your father forced you into becoming a musician?"

"He absolutely did, there's no question about it. I had no choice in the matter."

"Well, you have a choice now." I wait for his answer. It's a long time coming.

"Not really," he finally says.

"What do you mean? Is he still making you do it?"

He frowns. "No, nothing like that. He's not a part of my life."

"Then what is it?" I nudge him with my elbow. "Tell me."

"He's always there in my head, you know?" He looks at me briefly before continuing. "He's in there telling me I have a talent that God gave me and I need to use it. That the world is waiting for all the things I'm going to create. That I need to support my family with what God gave me and not be selfish."

"Was he a good supporter? For the family? Was that a big thing for your father?"

"Yeah, I guess . . . if the only measure of being a good supporter is how much money you bring in. He did okay. But he spent half of it on booze, and he spent the other half shoving Ty and me into music careers."

"Not that I'm saying your dad was right or anything, because I believe you when you say he's a dick, but it did seem to work out pretty well for Ty, right?"

"I don't know. Did it?" He looks at me intently.

I shrug. "To be honest, I don't really know him. He's been a fan of Red Hot his whole life. That's what my sister told me, anyway. And now he's playing with them."

"Yeah, that much is true." Sam sighs, back to looking at the ceiling. "I'm a fan too. Don't get me wrong . . . don't think I don't love the music. I *do* love it. And I do love playing the guitar. It's just . . . I don't know."

I try to help him out. "It's just that it was never your idea. The person who put the idea in your brain is not somebody you respect."

He turns over on his side to face me fully. "Exactly. I've never been able to really acknowledge that to myself or put it into words before, but that's *exactly* how I feel. It's like somebody else is pulling the strings in my life. Like I'm just my father's puppet."

"But you love the music and you love the guitar," I say, ready to test out a theory.

"Yeah. I do, but . . ."

"I think maybe you just need a change of perspective."

"What do you mean?" Sam starts playing with my breasts, gently drawing shapes on them with the tip of his finger, causing my nipples to harden.

I wiggle a little, trying to get comfortable, but the sexual arousal he's bringing up in me is making it pretty difficult. I push his hand away so I can finish my thought. "You've always looked at music through your father's eyes, as something you *had* to do, that you're forced to do because you were given a gift. But maybe if you could see it in a different way, it wouldn't have all those terrible, negative feelings attached to it."

"Maybe." He leans in to kiss me. His lips are warm, and his tongue is soft and hot.

"Are we done talking about this?" I ask, smiling against his kiss.

"I think so. I've got something better in mind, if you're interested." His tongue comes out to tangle with mine some more.

I grab him and hold him close. "What's that?" I ask as he moves his lips from my jawline down to my neck and then my chest.

"This weirdo with the beardo wants to sex you up again."

I start giggling. "I am *so* sorry I called you that. You're not a weirdo."

He sits up on his elbows above me. "Oh, don't worry. I know my beard is weird. I keep it because Sadie likes it." He uses it to brush my chin.

"You're a nice daddy." I grab his face and pull him down to me. "Now kiss me and sex me up, would you?"

"With pleasure," he growls.

CHAPTER THIRTY-TWO

The rest of the day passes swiftly, as we catch up on our sleep and I busy myself with locating funeral homes and services for Madison. Sam makes arrangements to pick up Sadie at his friend's house later, and we enjoy lunch together in his tiny kitchen followed by another round of sex.

I'm having a hard time keeping my hands off him. He is so beautiful, and his sadness acts like a magnet drawing me in. I don't want him to suffer this way. I want him to feel the joy in life again. I know he will eventually, but at odd moments during the day, I find him in the other room crying or staring off into the distance, no doubt thinking about Madison. He believes he shoulders some of the blame for her death, and no amount of me talking sense to him about it is going to change his mind.

When I'm cleaning up our lunch dishes from the takeout we ordered, his cell phone rings and he answers it, his expression going dark immediately. He moves off into the next room, but I follow behind, keeping out of sight. I'm being a nosey parker, but I can't help it. I need to know what's going on in his life if I'm going to be out here with him for the next few days. I'm still worried about that guy he mentioned—*Drake*. I haven't worked up the courage to ask Sam about him yet, though. I haven't wanted to bring a dark cloud over the semi-happy place we've found together.

"What do you want?"

There's an angry male voice coming from the other end of the line, but I can't make out his words.

"Yeah, she passed away and there's nothing you can do about that. It's over."

Sam's back muscles are rigid and his free hand is balled into a fist. "Nah, man, you can go to hell about that shit. I don't owe you anything."

Sam pulls the phone away from his ear and looks like he's going to throw it across the room, but then he puts it back. "Listen, man, my best friend in the entire world died today, and I'm the one who had to pull the plug. I don't want to talk to you about this shit now or ever again. Whatever deal you had going with her died with her today. You can leave me and Sadie out of it."

The voice from the other end of the conversation comes through loud and clear. I can hear it even though Sam has the phone to his ear.

"You'll pay me what she owes me, or I'm going to come after you, Sam. You can't hide from me forever. You owe me."

Sam's voice goes very low and sounds dangerous as hell. "You come anywhere near me or Sadie, and you'll go to jail for the rest your life if you're lucky. Don't call me ever again." He hangs up the phone and slides it into his pocket. Then he turns around and catches me standing there, three feet away.

CHAPTER THIRTY-THREE

We stare at each other, him still angry, and me both worried and embarrassed to be caught listening in. "Yes, I heard all of it." I figure I might as well just be up-front about the fact that I eavesdropped.

"Oh."

"Can you tell me what's going on?"

"I'd rather not." He looks like he's annoyed at me now, but I'm not going to let that sway me.

"I know you'd rather not, and I get the fact that we've got a really good thing going on right now between us and you don't want to bring the mood down; but you know, that man sounded like an angry person who still wants to be in your life for some reason, and I'm in your life right now too, so . . ." I look around the apartment and shrug.

Sam looks like he's deflating from the inside as his shoulders sag and his head drops. His beard is resting against his bare chest.

"Please don't be sad or angry with me. I don't mean to be pushy. I'm just worried about my safety."

He holds his hand up to stop me. "I get it. Just give me a minute." He turns around and goes into his bedroom and shuts the door.

I stand in the hallway for a few seconds and then turn around and go back to the kitchen, my heart heavy with worry and disappointment. It's like he doesn't care about me in the least, and I would have thought, after what we've been through over the last day or so together, that I deserved *some* kind of thoughtful emotion from the man. I'm not asking for the guy to pledge his love to me, but come on . . . something? Anything?

I keep myself busy by cleaning up the rest of the mess we left behind with our lunch a couple hours ago. The monotonous task and the small amount of time it takes me to complete it helps to put things into perspective. Considering all that Sam has been through today, it's pretty amazing that he's doing as well as he is. I need to give him the time necessary to get his stuff straightened out, and that's probably going to take a while; one day isn't going to cut it. But I'm also not going to stay here tonight if I don't feel safe. I can get a hotel, no problem. I can be supportive from a distance. The idea of being apart from him makes me sad, though.

The bedroom door opens, and he comes out with a fresh shirt on and his hair combed. He sits down at the table and points to the chair opposite him. "Why don't you have a seat and I'll explain everything."

My heart leaps with happiness. "Great." I quickly go to the kitchen and grab two glasses of water and bring them back with me, setting them down between us before I take a chair. "I'm all ears," I say with a smile. I push a glass of water toward him. We had a lot of sex and he needs to hydrate.

"Drake is Madison's dealer. And, apparently, she was into him for about twenty grand."

"Twenty grand? That's a lot of drugs, right?" My eyebrows are up in my hairline. No wonder she passed away from an overdose. It's not like I know the going rates for heroin, but for a woman who's an out-of-work musician, it seems like an awful lot of money for way too many drugs.

"Yeah. I think she was dealing, too."

"Oh, damn. That sucks big-time."

"Yeah, it's bad. And, apparently, Drake seems to think that Madison's debt didn't die with her . . . that it's now my job to pay him back."

"That's wrong. How did he come up with that rule?"

"Drake doesn't give anybody any free rides, even the dead. He knows we share Sadie together, so in his mind, that means I share Madison's mistakes, too."

"What are you going to do?"

"There's not a lot I can do. I don't have twenty grand, and even if I did, I sure as hell wouldn't give it to a drug dealer. I just need to stay out of his way until he gives up looking for me."

"Does this mean you'll be going back to New York?"

He shrugs. "I don't really have a choice, do I? I promised to come out and do some work with the band. I signed a contract. I assume I'm still going unless you think I shouldn't."

"No, of course you should go. And Sadie too." I have to work to hide my excitement about him being in New York with me again. The fact that Sadie will be there too is something I'm going to disregard for now, because it complicates things, and life is already complicated enough. "Does Drake know where you live?" I ask.

"I moved here recently. As far as I know, he doesn't know about it, but he has friends in high places, so I wouldn't put it past him to figure it out eventually."

Panic hits me. I stand. "We need to go. We need to check into a hotel or something."

He takes my hand and gestures for me to sit down. "He's not going to do anything right now. He believes he's put the fear in me, and now he assumes I'm going to be busy looking around for some money. If he comes in here and messes with me now, he won't get anything but heat from the cops. We're in no danger."

"We should call the police, though."

He nods. "I will. And I have before. The problem is, they don't bother with Madison's problems anymore, and according to them, Drake is her problem. Last time she went missing, they wouldn't even go looking for her. She was a junkie, and junkies don't rate very high on their list."

"Oh, that's really sad." I slowly sit down, and for the first time, I kind of understand the defeat Sam felt toward her. When even the cops don't care, it probably feels completely hopeless.

Sam taps the table a few times with his fingertips. "Anyway, Drake is a bad dude, and he throws a lot of threats around, but he's also busy. He has a pretty big operation that needs constant attention. Madison was just one of many issues he deals with regularly. What I mean is, I'm not top priority for him right now; we have time to get things done. Why don't we just wrap things up here and then we'll head out?"

"Where are we going?"

"To get Sadie."

"I thought you wanted to do that alone."

He reaches over and strokes the back of my hand, making me feel like a crazy chicken needing calming. "I did. But that was before."

"And now something has changed?" I sound like I'm fishing for compliments, but I need to understand what's happening in his head. I don't want to assume anything. Is he saying he wants me to be with him because he likes my company or because there's a danger in staying in this apartment?

"I think I would feel better if you were with me." He looks up. "But if that's too much to ask, just tell me. I've been leaning on you a lot, and I don't know if that's really fair of me to keep doing that."

"Lean on me all you need to. That's why I'm here."

It doesn't matter what his motivations are. I can support him however he needs me to, and I can also decide to leave this place whenever it suits me. If I feel threatened or unsafe, I'll go; it's that simple. And right now, his explanation makes sense and I don't feel the extreme urge to find other accommodations, so I stand.

He looks up at me. "Where are you going?"

"I'm going to go shower and brush my teeth and hair so we can head out."

He nods, staring at me but saying nothing.

"A nickel for your thoughts," I say.

His smile is sad. "I was thinking how I just met you yesterday, but it feels like a lifetime ago. It's crazy."

"I know. It is." I lean over and kiss him gently on the lips. "I'll be ready to go in twenty minutes, tops."

As I'm walking away he calls out, "Have I mentioned how cool it is that you're so low-maintenance?"

I spin around to see if he's joking, but he's wearing a serious expression.

"No," I say, frowning, "and I'm trying to decide if I should be offended by that."

He shakes his head. "No, don't be. I'm used to hanging around chicks who take two hours to get ready. It's nice not having to do that with you."

I slowly turn back and head toward his bedroom, feeling both complimented and gawky. I think my sister was right; I should've gone clothes shopping while I was in New York. Sam said he likes that it only takes me ten minutes to get ready, but how could he possibly mean that? No man on the planet wants to be with a woman who wears the same four outfits all month long, who doesn't wear makeup, and who styles her hair simply by brushing it. What's wrong with me? Why don't I make more of an effort? I sigh as I stare at my reflection in the mirror above his dresser.

I will get another chance to shop if I want it. If we pick up Sadie today and the funeral goes through like it's supposed to in two days, I'll be back in Manhattan for another week. That's plenty of time to upgrade my look just a notch or two. The idea makes me happy. Just because I live with a bunch of hippies and regularly muck out horse stalls, it doesn't mean I have to look like a farmhand all the time.

The more I think about it, the more I'm actually liking the idea of a new me. I can hardly believe it, but it feels like I've already changed in some fundamental way since leaving the farm. Yes, it's only been two days since I temporarily put my life in my rearview mirror, but clearly a lot can happen in forty-eight hours. Heck . . . I'm in Los Angeles of all places! I think a lot of this sensation I'm experiencing has to do with Sam. I've never been so open with someone I've just met, and I've definitely never felt this energized or excited by a man before. For the first time in my life I've been bold, decisive, and unafraid. Well . . . mostly unafraid. At least I haven't let my fear get the better of me, and that's a big improvement. It's like a miracle or something.

Imagining myself back in the apartment in New York with both Sam and Sadie kind of blows my mind. It occupies all my thoughts as I shower, change into clean clothes, brush my teeth, and fix my hair. The apartment isn't really a great place for a little girl. There's so much trouble she could get into, so many breakables and no toys at all. Will Sam and Sadie stay there, or will they go somewhere else? Is he still going to work for the band? Maybe he'll decide he has to stay here or go somewhere totally different to avoid that Drake guy.

I haven't asked him any of these questions yet, and now I'm burning to get the answers. *And* I really need to talk to my sister. I hope she calls me back soon.

CHAPTER THIRTY-FOUR

I am way more nervous than I should be. Sadie is just a tiny little girl, so why am I having these paranoid delusions that she's going to be mean to me and make me cry? My nerves are so on edge, I'm imagining worst-case scenarios left and right. What if she points at me and yells, "Get that ugly lady away from me!" or "You're not my mommy and I hate you!" No kid has ever done that to me before, but anything could happen. Nothing in my life is going like it usually does, so I can't imagine why this situation would be any different. Abnormal is my new normal.

Sam seems completely relaxed and looking forward to picking up his daughter. I imagine being with her will make him feel more hopeful about his future. I hear kids can do that for a person. We've had enough of them visit the farm over the years with their parents. I just hope she doesn't somehow figure out that her dad and I have become close and then get jealous enough to try to destroy it. I hear kids do that sometimes too.

The driver who brings us to Sadie's babysitter does a great job of chitchatting, keeping my mind off the upcoming meeting in favor of a discussion about the local music scene. He has all kinds of opinions about whose show is worth watching and whose isn't.

Sam joins in the conversation, being very knowledgeable about the scene himself. Of course the driver doesn't recognize Sam because Sam's never performed in public. Sam acts kind of incognito, hearing this man's opinions about people he could very likely be jamming with on their off days. It's kind of sad in a way, that people will never talk about Sam like this man is talking about these other musicians. I wonder if it bothers him to always be anonymous with his talent.

After a while, I let their words wash over me and instead focus on the conversation I'm going to have with my sister Amber. It will go down in history as one of the stranger ones we've had. *Yes, Amber, I met your boyfriend's brother and slept with him the very next day. We've had crazy sex over and over again, while trying to deal with the pain of losing his best friend to a heroin overdose. Oh, and by the way, Sam has a little girl, and we're going to go pick her up and bring her back to your apartment in New York, 'kay?*

"You ready?" Sam asks.

His words break me out of the daze I was in, and I realize that we're sitting in the driveway at somebody's house. I grab my purse. "Oh. Yeah. Sure. I'm ready."

I am so not ready. I am not ready *at all*. We're in suburbia, somewhere an hour outside of LA. All the houses look the same with identical façades and front lawns. I can hear children playing in the backyard of the one we're parked in front of; they're squealing with laughter. Poor, sweet little Sadie. I don't know when Sam is going to share the news of her mother's passing with her, but it seems a shame to have to do it anytime soon. She sounds like she's having a lot of fun.

"Don't be nervous." Sam takes me by the elbow and walks me up the driveway to the front door.

"I'm not nervous. I'm fine." I quickly smooth my hair down as best I can. It's still a little wet from my shower.

"Sure you are."

I lower my voice. "Just because we've been intimate doesn't mean you can read my mind now."

"We've been intimate, like, *eight* times," he says, tickling me by poking me in the ribs.

"Still . . . you can't read my mind."

"Okay, if you say so."

He rings the doorbell and winks at me. I so want to yank his beard and wipe that satisfied look off his face, but I hear footsteps coming. My window of opportunity closes when the door opens and a woman with short red hair sticking out in all directions is standing on the threshold smiling at us.

"Welcome back," she says, stepping out to give Sam a hug. She claps him on the back a few times and then lets go to look at me. "And who is this pretty little thing?"

Sam rests his hand on my shoulder. "This is my friend Emerald. You can call her Em."

This woman, whoever she is, grabs me into a hug and squeezes the stuffing out of me before letting me go abruptly. "And you can call me Patricia, or Patty, if you prefer." She backs up and gestures into her house. "After you, guys. I'll grab the door."

We walk inside, and I try to keep my jaw from hitting the floor. It looks like a toy factory exploded inside her living room. Primary colors molded into a thousand different plastic shapes are spread around every square inch of the room. She must let her kids have toy wars; it's the only explanation for it. There are toy parts even in the potted plants. I suppose it makes her a cool mom, but what a nightmare to clean up after.

"Excuse the mess," she says, laughing. "You know my house is usually so clean."

"Yeah, sure it is," Sam says, laughing along with her.

I follow them into the kitchen and then to the back door. There's a whole group of kids of different ages playing in the yard together. Some of them are on a swing set, some are in a little baby pool, and others are climbing around in a pile of dirt.

Patty cups her hands around her mouth and yells, "Sadie! Your dad is here!"

A little girl in the dirt pile stands up straight and screams at the top of her lungs, "Daddy!" Her curls are so grungy they don't look blond anymore. She comes running over, wearing a mismatched outfit of red, purple, and orange. When she gets closer, I notice a small princess crown sitting lopsided on her head, held there with a knot of tangled hair.

"Sorry about the mess," Patty says, gesturing at the outfit Sadie is wearing. "We had a little accident, so she had to borrow some of Cassie's clothes."

"That's okay." Sam bends down with his arms open and grabs his little girl as she throws herself against him. He hugs her close, his eyes shutting as he buries his nose in her neck and inhales deeply.

I have to look away. It tugs my heartstrings not only to see how much he loves her but to know that he's going to have to share some horrible news with her soon. Poor little thing lost her momma. My mothers' faces flash before my eyes and take my breath away.

Sadie pulls back from her father and stares up at me. She gets a suspicious look in her eye. "Who's that?"

Sam stands, holding her hand. "That's my friend Emerald."

"Emerald is a color," Sadie says, looking me up and down. "She's not a color. She's a lady."

He reaches down and taps her gently on the nose. "That's right. Emerald is a color, but it's also somebody's name, so please be nice and say hello."

"Hello," she says begrudgingly.

"Hello, Sadie. It's nice to meet you. I like your crown."

"Can you say thank you?" Sam asks.

"Thank you." She gives me a few more suspicious once-overs before turning her attention to the interior of the house. "My backpack is over there. I'll get it." She runs off to retrieve it from the couch where there's a pile of them in several different colors. She picks out a pink one with a princess printed on the outside of it.

"Thanks so much for taking care of her, Patty. I owe you one."

She holds her hand out. "Actually, you owe me a hundred ones. Madison hadn't paid me in weeks."

He smiles sadly, reaching deep into his pocket and pulling out a wad of cash. He counts out some twenties and puts them in her hand. "Now we're square. Don't ask me to watch *your* kid anytime soon."

She laughs and pinches his cheek. "I know you'll babysit if I ask you to." She takes some keys off the counter. "Your car is parked down the street."

"Thanks for keeping an eye on it for me." He lowers his voice. "Listen, we're going to be out of town for a while. Same place."

She nods, also quieting down. "I get it. It's cool. Just let me know if you need anything." She shoves the money into her back pocket. "Good luck." She looks at Sadie, at Sam, and finally at me. "Looks like you guys've got your work cut out for you."

I try to smile, but I know it's not really working. Talk about awkward.

"Just try to keep where we're going on the down-low, if you could," Sam says. "I don't want any bad news following us over there."

She nods and pretends to zip her lips and throw away the key.

Sam pulls her into a hug. "You've been a great friend to Madison and me. And Sadie. We appreciate it."

She rubs his back, talking softly so Sadie won't hear. "It's been my pleasure. You've got a great little family here, Sam. I know it just got a little smaller, but don't let it get you too down. Madison is in a better place now. She's finally found the peace she was looking for all her life."

He nods. When he pulls back, he has tears in his eyes.

Patty faces me and smiles, cupping my cheeks in her hands. "You are so pretty. I don't know where Sam found you, but I'm glad he did."

I don't know what to say to that. I wasn't privy to the phone conversation Sam had with her before we got here, but I can't imagine he was able to tell her too much about me; he hardly knows me himself. The people of LA must really be into my hippie-chick vibe or something. I decide it's best to just keep things simple when responding to her compliment. "Thank you."

Patty glances over at Sam, who's helping Sadie get her backpack on. She leaves her hand resting on my shoulder. "Don't let him get too bratty on you." She lowers her voice. "He can be real stubborn. He doesn't like letting people into his big, fat heart, but don't let that stop you from trying."

"Okay." I don't think Patty realizes that Sam and I just met. Our siblings are in love, but that doesn't mean we are. We're going back to New York together—at least I think we are—but then a few days later I'm going to leave Sam there. I'll be going back to the farm, and he'll be staying in Manhattan to work—end of story. My heart hurts a little as I acknowledge these facts to myself.

"Ready?" Sam asks, leading Sadie over.

I nod, moving out of Patty's grasp. "Ready."

"Send me a text with the details of the you-know-what," she says to Sam as we make our way to the front door. I assume she's hinting about the funeral.

"Will do."

"Great. Drive safe. See you soon."

Out at the car, Sam takes his time buckling Sadie into a seat that he pulls from the trunk.

"I don't need a baby seat anymore," she says, struggling with him a little. "I'm a big girl now."

"Yes, I know how big you are, but you still need the car seat, according to the policeman." He holds her hand out of the way so he can insert the buckle.

"There's no policeman here," she says, making a big show of looking around.

"Yeah, well, maybe not here, but they're always out there somewhere watching out for people trying to break the law, and I don't want them catching me being a bad dad."

Sadie taps him on the top of the head and then starts playing with his beard. "You're not a bad daddy. You're a good daddy."

I get into the front seat and wait for Sam to join me there. I want to turn around and watch his interactions with his daughter, but I feel like it might be too nosy.

Sadie whispers, "Why is she here?"

"Because I asked her to be here," Sam responds, also in a whisper.

"She has a pretty skirt."

"Why don't you tell her that?"

"Because I don't want to."

"Okay. Maybe later you can tell her."

"Maybe." Sadie doesn't seem convinced that it's a good idea.

Her sass makes me smile. I think the little girl has inherited some stubbornness from her dad. They might not have the same DNA, but you'd never know it from watching them together.

Sam joins me in the front seat and we're soon headed back into the city. The drive takes almost twice as long as it did coming out, with the traffic that has grown in our absence. By the time we're back at Sam's apartment, we should be eating dinner, but I'm too exhausted. Maybe it's all the sex Sam and I had or the emotions running so high for the past twenty-four hours or the jet lag, but I'm ready for bed by eight o'clock.

Sam feeds Sadie some chicken nuggets and apples that we grabbed at a corner store before putting her to bed in her room. He shuts the door behind him and joins me in the kitchen.

"Are you sure we should sleep together in the same room?" I ask, worried she'll get up in the middle of the night and find me in there.

"It's fine, trust me. She sleeps like a hibernating bear."

"Okay." I stand and he takes my hand.

"Are you ready for bed?" he asks.

I give him a pained expression. "I am. Is that totally lame or what?"

He smiles and leans in to give me a sweet kiss. "I was actually hoping you would say that. I'm dead on my feet right now."

I move in close and wrap my arms around his neck, hugging him to me. "Let's go to bed."

"You think we could actually get some sleep this time?" He pulls me against him and his hands slide down to my rear end and squeeze.

"Why don't we just see how things go?" I suggest, feeling the heat starting to build between us.

We pull apart and slowly walk to the bedroom, holding hands as we go. Once inside with the door shut, I watch him strip off his shirt and pants, getting down to his boxers. I swear I was ready to pass out from exhaustion two minutes ago, but now I'm suddenly awake and my body is tingling all over.

When he turns around and gives me that look, his eyes dark and his jaw tensing, I know we're not going to be sleeping anytime soon. I turn around and lock the door. When I face him again, he's naked and ready for me. I slowly drop my skirt and step out of it.

CHAPTER THIRTY-FIVE

Sam isn't ready to tell his daughter that her mother has passed away, and he can't very well bring her to the funeral, so she stays in the apartment with me. She isn't too keen on the idea at first, but once I show her that I can stack a mean set of blocks and don't mind when she kicks them over, she accepts me as a babysitter.

"What's your name?" she asks me.

"My name is Emerald, remember?" You'd think after two days of having this conversation, she'd finally have it straight in her head, but no . . . *Here we go again.*

She shakes her head, making her curls bounce. "I mean your *real* name." She watches as I stack another block on top of the others.

"That *is* my real name."

"No, that's a color. I mean your *real* name."

I smile at this stubborn little stinker who's well on her way to stealing my heart. Watching her bond with and tease her dad for the past two days has shown me what a sweet and sassy angel she is. Life is never boring with this kid around.

"That *is* my real name. My name is Emerald Grace Collins."

She thinks about that for a few seconds. "Grace isn't a real name either. It's what a ballerina has. Ballerinas are *graceful*."

"You're right." I nod, never realizing before how incorrect my name was. "Ballerinas can be graceful. And they wear tutus."

She giggles. "That would be funny if your name was Emerald Tutu."

I can't help but smile. "Yes, that would be funny."

"Where did my daddy go?"

I put up a few more blocks before I answer. "He had to go out with some friends for a meeting."

"Is he jamming?"

I'm trying to look as serious as possible. This kid's vocabulary is something else. Sometimes I feel like I'm talking to an adult. "Yes. I think he's jamming."

"Well, where was his guitar? He didn't have it when he left."

I shrug, feeling like I'm being interrogated under a hot lamp at the police station. "I don't know. Maybe he had it out in his car." I don't know if Sadie's aware of her father's trip to New York, so I'm not going to tell her that this is where at least one of his guitars is.

She shakes her head. "My daddy never leaves his guitar in the car. He says people will steal it. There are lots of stealers here."

"Maybe your daddy's friend has it at his house."

"Why would my daddy's friend have his guitar?"

"Maybe he borrowed it." I start using two hands to stack the blocks. I need to get this damn thing built so Sadie can start focusing on knocking it over instead of grilling me about her father. She's relentless and I'm running out of stories.

"My daddy never lets anybody use his guitar. He says they'll screw it up."

"Well, that's not very nice for someone to screw up his guitar, is it?"

She puts her hands on her hips, tilting her head at me. "It's not. When you borrow somebody's stuff, you should be nice with it. And not break it, also."

"I agree one hundred percent." I gesture at the tower that's now almost as tall as she is. "Are you ready to knock this sucker over?"

She folds her arms across her chest and studies it intently. "No. I don't think so. I think it needs to be taller."

"You're ready to cause some mayhem, aren't you?"

She looks at me, all innocence. "What is mayhem?"

"It means a big, giant mess."

She smiles and nods, her little blond curls bouncing all over the place. "Yes! I'm going to cause some maydem. But I need this tower to be a lot taller first."

I salute her. "Yes, ma'am. And taller it shall be. And the word is may*hem*, not may*dem*."

"Mayhem, mayhem, mayhem," she mumbles under her breath as she helps me by handing me the next block she wants me to use.

I spend the next couple minutes making sure it's perfect. Then I stand up and step back. "Are you ready to cause some mayhem now, Miss Sadie?" *Little Miss Mayhem is more like it.*

She takes a few steps back, adjusts her shoulders, and nods once. "I am *ready*."

"Should I do a countdown?" Before she would just rush the towers and blast them apart with her little foot, but it seems like this one needs a little more pomp and circumstance. The thing is taller than she is. I'm actually a little fearful she's going to hurt herself.

"Yes," she says. "Count down."

"Okay . . . ready . . . set . . . ten, nine . . ."

The doorbell rings.

I pause my countdown.

"Just ignore it," Sadie says. She has all of her focus on those blocks. "Do the countdown."

I glance toward the door to Sadie's room and out into the hallway but do as I'm told. "Eight, seven, six . . ."

The bell rings again, several times, and then there's a pounding on the door. Someone really wants to talk to Sam, but all of his friends are at the funeral. Paranoia and fear trickle into my heart.

"Just ignore it." She looks up at me, clearly frustrated. "We don't answer the door."

"We don't?"

"No. We never *ever* answer the door. That's the rule."

I'm now officially freaking out. *Is that really the rule here? Why?* Do they get a lot of annoying salespeople, or should I be worried about who's on the other side of that door? I'm so happy Sadie has the vertical blinds closed over her window.

"Sadie, why do you have a rule that you don't answer the door here?" I pick up a block, trying to act casual as I weigh my options: I can continue to hide in Sadie's bedroom, or I can go to the door and confront whoever is there. Neither sounds like a good idea.

"Because. It's gonna be those Jedobah Witniks again." When she shakes her head and rolls her eyes, I can completely see her father in her expression.

It takes me a few seconds to translate Jedobah Witniks into its proper form. I feel marginally better after hearing and understanding her explanation. "Oh. Okay. So if it's a *Jehovah's Witness*, we don't answer the door, but what if it's somebody else?"

"Who else would come here? When my daddy jams, everyone goes there." She walks around the stack of blocks carefully and stands next to me. Then she gestures for me to bend down. I fold in half and put my face close to hers.

She leans in and whispers into my ear, cupping her hands around her mouth. "Maybe it's the bad people."

Fear strikes my heart like a lightning bolt. I whisper back, "Bad people?"

She nods and then puts her finger to her lips. She gestures for me to follow her as she goes over to her closet.

"What are we doing?" I ask in a whisper.

"Hiding from the bad people." She climbs into the closet and crouches down in the corner, pulling a blanket over her bent knees. She motions for me to join her.

My heart breaks right in half. "Sweetie . . . who taught you how to hide from the bad people?"

She looks up at me, her eyes wide, full of both innocence and a healthy dose of fear. "My mommy did."

I immediately stand up straight. There's no way in hell I'm going to let this tiny girl be afraid in her own house. This is ridiculous. Sam said that Drake guy isn't going to come by here, and I believe him. I'm just going to go tell whoever it is to go away.

"You stay here. I'm going to go look through the peephole and see who it is. I'm sure it's probably just the Jehovah's Witnesses with some pamphlets."

She's still whispering. "Okay. I'll stay here." As I start to walk away, she speaks again. "Wait!"

I turn around and she whispers at me, "Don't open the door."

CHAPTER THIRTY-SIX

By the time I get to the front door, there's no one there, but I am nearly peeing my pants with fear. There's no way in hell I'm staying in this apartment another minute; I don't care if it was Jedobah Witniks ringing that bell or not. I have to get out of here and take Sadie with me. I don't feel safe, and a sweet little princess like her should never have to hide in a closet in fear while she's whispering about bad guys.

I dial Sam's number, but it goes immediately to voice mail. He's probably in the middle of the memorial service. Should I call one of my sisters? *No.* We still haven't talked about what happened yet, so this would be too much of a shock. We keep missing each other and leaving voice mails. Amber is super busy with the band in Japan, not only working but also doing a ton of sightseeing, and Rose is up to her ears in sick animals. I can't scare either one of them with stuff they can do nothing about. I also can't call my mothers because it'll have the exact same effect.

So, instead of alerting the entire world that I'm scared out of my wits, I leave a voice mail for Sam with details of my plan, and I call a cab. While we wait for the car to arrive, Sadie and I pack her little backpack with clothing and toiletries, grab my suitcase, and head out to the waiting vehicle. Sam can get his own bag; it's too heavy for me to carry anyway.

"Please take us to one of the hotels that's right next to the airport," I say to the cabdriver.

"We talking LAX?" the driver asks.

"Yes, exactly."

"Why are we going to the airport?" Sadie asks, her eyes going wide. "Am I going on an airplane?"

"No, not right away. But would you like to someday?"

We're holding hands in the backseat. It was her idea, not mine. It feels nice, having her tiny hand there. I need to keep her safe, and holding on to her makes me feel like I'm doing that in some small way.

"I don't know," she says. "Maybe. But maybe not."

"It's really fun," I say, trying to head off the future temper tantrum I see with Sam asking her to get on the plane and her refusing. I have a feeling Sam is going to want to get her on one sooner rather than later, once he hears about the visitor at his apartment.

"But what if they crash?" She looks at me with worry in her eyes. "My mommy says that planes crash."

"No, they don't." I shake my head. "They're very safe."

"My mommy lied?"

Damn. She got me on that one. "No, she didn't lie, because they *used* to crash; but they don't anymore."

The cabdriver looks at me in the rearview mirror and shakes his head slowly. I guess, according to him, I'm screwing up. *Well, hell's bells, buddy! I'm new to this stuff and I have no idea what I'm doing! Don't judge me!*

"Hey, what's that?" I ask, pointing at nothing outside the cab.

Sadie puts her hands on the windowsill and pushes her nose against the glass. "What? Where?"

"Something blue," I say, trying to tempt her into playing a car game with me.

"I don't see it," she says, her breath fogging up the window. The condensation she made fascinates her enough that she makes more of it and then tries to draw pictures in it with her fingertip. I'm glad for the break in the conversation; I was seriously screwing it up. I refuse to look up at the cabbie to see if he approves.

My phone rings and I glance down at it. *Amber.* I don't really want to have a conversation with her in front of Sadie, because there are a lot of things I need to say to her that a little girl shouldn't hear, but maybe I can give her some basics by talking in code. I need to hear her voice if nothing else. I answer the call and put the phone up to my ear.

"Finally," I say.

"I know, right? It has been absolute madness over here. Madness, I'm telling you. But the Japanese people are *amazing.*" The smile and excitement in her voice are impossible to miss.

Her happiness immediately lightens my mood. "That's really cool. How are the moms taking it?"

"Oh my god, they are on cloud nine. You wouldn't even recognize them right now; they've all had makeovers. They don't even look like themselves anymore."

My heart feels like it's shriveling up in my chest as I picture my mothers turning into jet-setting frou-frou witches who no longer want to can beans and make jam. "Seriously? And you're happy about that?"

"Why wouldn't I be? They look fantastic. They've dropped ten years from their looks. I've never seen them this happy."

"Oh." My heart sinks even further.

"Oh, come on, Em. Stop feeling sorry for yourself."

"What? For myself? Give me a break. It doesn't bother you, even in the slightest, that our mothers are happier being gone from their lives?"

"No, and it shouldn't bother you either. They're moving on to another era, just like you are. Life doesn't have to stay stagnant all the time, Em. It can change and still be good."

"I'm not moving on from an era of my life. I'm *in* my life. My *only* life. My life is not changing."

She laughs. "You could've fooled me. Where are you right now?"

Okay, so she has a teeny, tiny point. "I'm in LA. But I'm headed back to New York soon and then I'll be going home, to Maine, where I belong." I glance over at Sadie, but she's too busy drawing little faces and flowers in her hot-breath fog on the window to pay me any attention.

"See? You just proved my point. If I told you a week ago that you'd be out in LA running around with a guitarist, you would've told me I was nuts."

"I'm not running around"—I lower my voice is much as I possibly can—"with a guitarist."

"Oh. You're not out there with Sam?"

I let out a sigh. "Yes, I am."

"Okay, then, I'm right, and you're wrong. Ha, ha. Ten points for me."

I can totally picture Amber giving herself a high five right now. "Anyway . . . whatever. I have news, but I'm not in a great position to be talking about it now, so we probably should have another phone call at a later time."

"No!" she exclaims. "You need to tell me everything now; this is the only break I'm going to get."

"This is your only break? What about going to the bathroom? Don't they let you do that?"

"You want me to call you when I'm sitting on the toilet?" She giggles.

"Okay, no. Please don't do that."

She sighs happily. "Just tell me, don't be coy."

"I'm not being coy."

"You're not? You sound serious. Oh, wait . . . Is there somebody there listening? Is that why you can't talk now?"

"Bingo."

"Who is it? Is it Sam? Oooh, cool, let's girl-talk about a boy while he's sitting right next to you."

"No, actually, it's not Sam."

The sound of her father's name catches Sadie's attention. She spins around and stares at me. "Are you talking about my daddy?"

There's a gasp on the other end of the line. "Who was that? What did she just say?"

Dammit! I'm so not sly at all! "It's nobody. She didn't say anything."

"Yes, I did," Sadie insists, her voice rising. "Are you talking to my daddy?"

I pat her on the shoulder. "No, I'm not talking to your daddy. I'm talking to my sister."

"Who is she talking about?" Amber asks. Her cheerful tone is completely gone. "Is she talking about *Sam*? Does Sam have a *child*?"

Oh, crudbuckets. This conversation is not going at all how I wanted it to. "Would you calm down, please?"

"No, I'm not going to calm down. This is *huge*. Are you telling me Sam has a kid, and I'm just finding out about it now by *accident*?"

"No, I'm not saying that. Well . . . maybe I am kind of saying that, but no. Not like that." I shake my head and then rest it against the window. This is hopeless.

"Em, you seriously have to tell me what's going on *right now*. If he has a child . . . I need to know about that stuff."

I lift my head off the window. "Why do you need to know about it? How is it even relevant?" I glance over at Sadie. She's staring straight ahead, but I'm pretty sure she's listening to every word I'm saying.

"Because, it could change everything." Amber's voice suddenly sounds devoid of emotion.

Panic hits me like a sledgehammer in the chest. I cannot screw up this deal with the band for Sam. "No, don't say that. Everything is going forward as planned. I'm doing exactly what you told me to do, and everything is going to be fine. I'm handling it."

"Since when do you handle things?" she demands.

"Since when do I *not*?"

She snorts. "Since the beginning of your life on this earth. You always run away when things get difficult."

I gasp in offense. "I do *not*! That is such a lie." Geez, could she be more insulting? She's the one who told me to take care of Sam and get to the bottom of his issues. And am I not doing *exactly* that?

"No, it's not a lie, and you know it. *I'm* the one who runs headlong into problems. *You're* the one who runs in the other direction. Avoid, avoid, avoid . . . that's your motto."

I turn my face toward the window and lower my voice as much as I can, hoping Sadie won't hear me. She doesn't need to experience grown-ups not getting along. "I'm here, aren't I? And I was in New York for you, too. So don't give me that nonsense about being afraid. I'm anything but that. Now, if you don't have anything nice to say to me, then I'm getting off this phone right now and you can just talk to me later."

There's a long silence before she finally answers. "Okay. Fine. Maybe you're not as afraid as you used to be."

I know this is Amber's lame attempt at an apology, but it still sucks. "You're going to have to try a *lot* harder than that before I forgive you."

She sighs really loudly. "Fine. I'm sorry, okay? I'm just . . . under a lot of pressure here."

"Regardless, it doesn't mean you can be rude to me."

"You're right. And I'm sorry, sorry, *sorry*, so please forgive me." She doesn't wait for me to do that before continuing. "So . . . how old is this little person you're sitting next to?"

I glance over at Sadie, who's still listening in on my conversation. "This little girl I am sitting next to is four years old. And she's pretty amazing. You should see her knock over a tower of blocks like a giant King Kong princess. She's aaall about the mayhem."

That earns me a very slight smile. She's pretending not to listen, though, because she doesn't even glance at me. She's playing with the strap on her backpack, twisting it around her tiny finger.

"So, Sam has had a child for the last *four years* and he hasn't said anything to anyone, not even his own brother. Ty is going to blow a nut over this one. Probably two nuts."

"I hope not. I think he's probably going to need those at some point." Amber doesn't laugh at my tasteless joke, which is all I need to know about her mood; she's all business now.

"Sooo . . . I guess Sam is pretty sensitive about it?" Amber asks.

"You could say that. There's a long backstory."

"I can't wait to hear it. *All* of it. When are you going to be alone?"

"Not for the foreseeable future. I'll have to let you know on that."

"Okay, well, just so you know, I'm going to be dying to know what's going on and it will be eating away at my very soul to not know it, so you'd better hurry up and find someplace you can hide away and talk to me about it really soon. Before I die from the not knowing."

I'm relieved that she's back to being ridiculous and not so serious. "Well, that's not likely, because Sam is not here with us right now; but when he is, I'll do my best."

"Where's Sam?"

"I can't say right now."

"Did he take off? Did he just *leave* you with his kid?"

"No, stop. Stop saying that stuff. I have to go." Talking to Amber is exhausting. I feel like a child who's done something wrong and has to explain herself to an angry parent.

"No, don't go. I want to share my news."

"Great. I'd love to hear your news." Yes, I would be thrilled to have the spotlight on her for a change.

"Well, the crowds here are absolutely fantastic. People are practically turning themselves inside out when they hear the music. They know all the words to all the songs. I had no idea we were so big in Japan."

"That's great." *Ugh.* She said "we."

"And Ty is doing really fab. Nobody here is giving him a single boo. I think he likes Japan better than the United States."

"That's nice. I don't think anybody should be booing anybody."

"Believe me, I agree. Our moms have been backstage every night, and they are just *loving* it. They want to go out on the rest of the tour."

"They do? Are they actually going to do that?" It literally nauseates me to imagine them being gone that long, let alone with *them*.

"I don't think so. It's fun having them here, but they do kind of interfere with what we're trying to get done. The band is finding it hard to concentrate, more fixated on reminiscing than keeping to schedules. I think the guys are going to gently tell them no."

"Oh, I get it. Because our moms are cramping the band's style with the other, younger groupies?"

She snorts. "Hardly. I mean, yeah, those groupies are probably out there, but they're not allowed backstage. They're not allowed anywhere near the band, actually."

"Because our mothers are blocking them?"

"No, because of *them* . . . the band. They don't have any interest in that shit anymore."

"Why not? I thought old dudes like to get it on as much as young ones do."

"Maybe, but these old dudes are feeling a lot of regret over the way they treated women in the past, so they've turned over a new leaf." She sounds very proud of that supposed fact.

What a load of donkey poo. "Yeah, right. Whatever." My sister is so naïve. She thinks those men aren't having sex with groupies anymore because they've turned over new leaves? *Ha! As if!* Amber may be a very sophisticated woman in some ways, but she still has a lot to learn about life. Those men may not be doing the nasty in front of her, and they may be pausing that kind of activity while our mothers are with them, but they haven't stopped. A leopard can't change its spots.

"You got any more good news for me?" I ask, wanting to hurry the conversation along.

"Wellll . . . I have one other bit of news, but I don't know if I want to share it with you right now because you're being so rude to me."

I sigh. "I'm sorry. I've been under a lot of stress too these last few days, and a lot of shit has been going—I mean a lot of *poop* has been going on, so you'll just have to try to forgive me."

"Okay, good. I forgive you, because I'm so excited about this I can't *not* tell you anymore."

"Well, what is it? Don't keep me in suspense."

"I really should wait until I see you in person . . ."

"Amber, don't play; you know you want to tell me. What is it? Did Ty ask you to marry him or something?" I wouldn't put it past him. They're moving so fast in that relationship as it is.

"No. But you're on the right track."

I mull that one over for a few seconds, but I'm not coming up with anything. "I don't get it. I'm lost." With all of the stuff happening with Sam, my brain is exhausted.

"Hold on. I just need to go into the other room."

I hear a door shutting, footsteps, and then some muffled sounds before my sister's back on the phone.

"Are you ready to hear the biggest news of the century?" she asks in a whisper.

"Yes, I'm ready." I'm already bored with this conversation. I know she's going to say something I don't want to hear, like she got another promotion and is never coming back to New York. She's probably going to tell me they're all moving to LA, our mothers included. *Please, God, no.*

"I'm pregnant."

Suddenly, the scenery that I was driving past becomes a mere blur. I get a tickle in my nose and feel like I'm going to sneeze. My ears start ringing. I'm ill. I'm instantly sick, every cell in my body crying out to be medicated.

"Did you hear me? I just told you I'm pregnant."

"What?" My voice comes out a lot louder than I mean for it to. Sadie looks at me with fear in her eyes. I reach over and pat her on the leg, telling her silently not to worry.

"Yes, you heard me right. I am *pregnant*. The other day when I was in the bathroom, when you thought I was building a log cabin, I was taking a pregnancy test."

"You mean you *knew* you were pre . . . the p-word . . . when you were there with me, but you didn't tell me?"

"Yes. But I couldn't tell you until I told Ty first, right? Plus, I had to have a blood test to be sure."

I don't know whether to be happy or sad about this. "No, I guess. Maybe."

"I've surprised you, haven't I?"

"Yeah, a little." My sister knows what birth control is, so she has to have done this on purpose. But why? What was she thinking? Isn't her life crazy enough? "I don't get it, though. How could this happen?"

"Believe me, I don't get it either. I was on the pill, as you know. I've been on the pill for years to regulate my periods." She sighs happily. "But it happened. It was meant to be."

"That's insane." It's finally sinking in that my sister is actually going to have a baby. With Ty. With *Sam's brother*. Holy shit, Sam and I are practically related now! We're both going to have the same niece or nephew. I have only one question: *Does this mean we have to stop sleeping together?*

"I know, right? I haven't told anybody except Ty and you."

"What about Rose?"

"Nope, not even her. She's been too busy. But I'm going to tell her as soon as I hang up with you."

"What about our moms?" This really surprises me, that she hasn't told them yet. It seems like they would've been the first people she shared her news with, even before Ty.

"Nope. They're going to go nuts over it—beyond insane. I want them to just enjoy this trip without thinking about me or you or anything else that's going on. Ty and I decided it's better to let them in on it later."

I nod. "That's probably a good idea." I feel a hand on my leg and look down. Sadie is tapping me with her finger.

"Hold on a second." I look at Sadie. "What's the matter, honey? Do you need something?"

"I want to talk on the phone." She holds out her hand.

"You want to talk on *this* phone?" I point at it.

"Yes, I want to talk on your phone because I don't have my own phone."

"How about we call your daddy and we can talk to him on the phone?"

She shakes her head. "No, I want to talk on the phone *now*. To your *sister*."

I go back to the call. "Amber, do you have a minute to talk to Sadie?"

"By Sadie, you mean the little girl you're sitting with right now? Sam's daughter?"

"Uh, yeah." I wish I could tell her that I know how awkward this is and that she doesn't have to do it if she doesn't want to, but I don't want to hurt Sadie's feelings.

"Sure," Amber says, full of spunk. "Put her on the phone."

"Okay." I hand my cell over to Sadie and help her get it up to her ear.

"Hello," Sadie says, with the sweet voice of a tiny angel.

I hear my sister's answer. "Hello, Sadie. It's nice to meet you. I'm Amber."

"Oh. Hi, Amber. What are you doing?"

I can't hear my sister's response. Sadie lets go of the strap of her backpack. "Oh." She pauses. "Do you want to know what I'm doing?"

She waits for a minute and then continues. "I'm riding in a car with Emerald. You know her name isn't a real one. Her name is a *color*. It looks like green but it's more shiny."

There's a long pause and then Sadie looks up at me. She puts the phone on her chest. "Did you know that *Amber* is a color too?"

I nod as I smile. "I did know that."

Sadie puts the phone on her ear again. "How come your mommy named you colors?"

I don't hear Amber's answer, but it seems to satisfy Sadie. "Okay. That's all I want to say. Bye-bye." Sadie presses a button on the phone and hands it back to me.

I put my ear to it but there's no one there. "You hung up." I look at her in surprise.

"I know." She looks at me like I'm crazy. "I was done talking."

"Well, okay then." This kid is too much. I slide the phone into my purse and try really hard not to laugh. All this time when Sam was talking to me about Sadie, I was seeing her as a job he had to do—a very difficult burden he was going to have to shoulder for the rest of his life. But after spending a couple days in her company, I'm definitely seeing her in a different light. She's a joy to be around. A real hoot, actually. And I can imagine how she could actually lighten his load rather than make it heavier. The single-dad thing is not going to be easy for him for sure, but it's not going to be awful either. Not with a little girl like Sadie around.

"You're looking at me funny," Sadie says.

"Am I?" I cross my eyes and stick my tongue out, using my hands next to my ears to make floppy reindeer antlers. "How about this look? Is this funny enough for ya?"

She giggles and then tries to imitate my movements. "What about this?!" she shrieks.

"Oh, hold that face . . . I need to get a picture of that."

We spent the next thirty minutes making the ugliest faces we can come up with and taking pictures of them with my phone. By the time we reach the pinnacle of silliness, we're pulling into the parking lot of a hotel next to the airport.

"That'll be sixty-five bucks, on the nose," the driver says, shutting off the engine.

Sadie quickly unzips the front of her backpack and pulls out a quarter, handing it to me.

"What's this?" I ask, holding it up.

"Sixty-five bucks for his nose," she says, turning to face straight ahead with her chin up.

I reach over the seat and hand it to the guy. "Here you go. Sixty-five bucks for your nose."

Sadie starts laughing into her hand and snorts a little, glancing at me with a coconspirator's glee. I give her a quick, gentle pinch on the cheek and then dig through my bag to come up with the rest of the fare plus tip we owe him. I hand that over too as the man rolls his eyes at us.

Sadie and I get out together at the sidewalk and grab my suitcase before walking hand in hand up to the hotel reception desk.

"This is a fun adventure," Sadie says.

"It sure is." I can't stop grinning.

CHAPTER THIRTY-SEVEN

After hearing from Sam and confirming that he can meet us out at the airport hotel in the next two hours, and that he does indeed still want to go back to his brother's apartment in Manhattan with Sadie, I use a chunk of my savings to purchase three airplane tickets to New York City, leaving the next day. I could probably call for the private jet again, but I don't like the feeling of owing the band any more than I probably already do for that last trip.

There are flights departing today, but Sam is going to be mentally exhausted, and Sadie has been playing all day. I decide it would be better for them to have a quiet evening together before we go on such a stressful trip. He can take the time to decompress from the funeral, and Sadie can forget about the scary doorbell that rang earlier today.

Sadie and I are resting on one of the queen beds in the hotel room when there's a knock at the door. She doesn't hear it because she's zonked out. I get up quickly to answer it. Looking through the peephole, I find Sam standing there. He's wearing a suit, and although his swollen, red eyes tell me he's been crying, he's still pretty damn stunning. *Holy hell.* How am I not going to have sex with him now?

"What's the secret password?" I ask, stalling so I can get control of my sex drive.

"Weirdo beardo."

I open the door and lean on it, smiling. "I like that suit."

"I'm glad to hear that, because I bought this for you." He holds up a white paper bag with black handles.

When I reach out to take it from him, he grabs me around the waist, kissing me before letting me have it. Shivers go up and down my spine, but then he's in the room, leaving me behind to shut the door.

"What's this?" I ask, holding up the long-sleeved black dress I find inside the bag.

He shrugs. "I don't know. I figured we could go out to dinner tonight."

"We have Sadie, though." I follow him into the room.

He stops at the foot of the bed, looking down at her. "I know. There's a dress in there for her, too."

I reach inside and pull out another outfit. This one is purple with a fluffy skirt.

"Is there any particular reason why we're getting all dressed up?"

He shrugs. "I guess I didn't want to be the only one."

I get it now. He's tired of feeling alone and he needs a connection. I put the bag on the bed and hold the dress against me. "How did you know my size?" It's not a dress I would have bought for myself, but I have a feeling Amber would approve.

"I asked Patty."

I place the dress on the bed and put my hand on his arm. He's still staring at his daughter, almost as if he's mesmerized by her tiny form under the covers. "Did everything go okay today?" I ask.

He finally looks away and runs his hands through his hair as he sighs. "It was rough, but we got through it."

"Did a lot of people come?"

His eyebrows go up as he nods. "Surprisingly, yes. I would say there were about . . . I don't know . . . fifty or sixty people there? It's more than I expected. She'd alienated a lot of people toward the end, but they forgave her." He pauses. "Thanks for arranging everything. It was great. Really perfect."

"I was happy to do it. And I'm glad to know a lot of people came, too. That's nice. Nice for you and for her."

Sam looks around the room. "So, you really hated my apartment that much?" He slides his jacket off and places it on the bed.

"Not exactly." I glance at Sadie. She hasn't moved, but I don't trust that she's not listening; she's pretty sly. "Can we talk outside for a minute?"

"Sure." He puts his hand on my lower back and escorts me to the foyer. "What's going on?"

I wait until we're outside the room with the door only slightly ajar before I respond in hushed tones. "Someone came to the door of your apartment today, and I didn't get a chance to see who it was before they left, but it really scared us."

"Why? Did they do or say something?"

"No, not really. But they kept ringing the doorbell and banging on the door over and over, and Sadie was pretty freaked out about it."

"She was scared, huh?"

"No, not just scared. Freaked."

He frowns in concern. "What do you mean? What did she do?"

"She told me not to answer it because it could be the Bad People. And then she hid in the closet. She told me her mommy taught her how to do that."

Sam stares at me for a few seconds and then slowly closes his eyes, shaking his head. "I guess it was worse than I thought."

"What was?"

He hisses out his frustration before answering. "I was talking to some people at the memorial service. Apparently, that guy Drake was a lot more present in her life than she led me to believe he was."

Sam has just confirmed my worst fear—that it was probably Drake at the apartment today. I'm so glad we left when we did. "You think he came around Madison's place on a regular basis?"

"Yeah, I'm pretty sure he did. I always thought he did it when Sadie wasn't there—that's what Madison always told me—but now, I'm not so sure. I always believed Maddy when she said she kept him out of Sadie's life, but I shouldn't have."

"You think she was lying?" Why would she lie? Maybe because Sadie is Drake's biological daughter and Madison thought he should be allowed to be around her? A shiver of fear runs through me again, imagining that Sadie will never be free of him.

"Yeah." He sighs with sadness. "She was an addict. Looking back now, I'm pretty sure she lied to me about almost everything. I knew about some of it but not all of it."

I pull him in for a hug. "I'm so sorry. That's not a nice thing to find out about her at her funeral."

The door slowly opens, and Sadie is standing there with her hair a mess and her face puffy from sleep. "What's a funeral?"

It feels like my heart has jumped up into my chest and blocked my throat. I can hardly breathe.

Sam points to the inside of the room. "Back in bed, young lady. I need you to take a nap so we can go out to dinner together soon."

"I already did. What's a funeral?" She reaches up and scratches her head. She looks like a life-size doll, so sweet and innocent.

Sam pushes the door open all the way and herds her into the room. "Go on inside and I'll tell you."

I follow them in, dreading the conversation they're about to have. What's he going to tell her? The definition of a funeral in a general sense or the reason for this particular funeral? Am I going to witness the moment this sweet little girl finds out her mother has died? I can think of a thousand other things I'd rather do than that, but of course I'm not going to leave. If Sam decides that now is the time to have this conversation with his daughter, I'm going to support him. I just wish I could do it without feeling like I was going to throw up.

"Why don't you sit on the bed, and Daddy will help you put on your new dress?"

"I have a new dress?" A small smile appears on Sadie's face.

Now I see the real reason for Sam's shopping trip. He told me before how much he hates shopping, but he's hoping he can soften the blow of bad news with some frills and lace. My heart melts a little at his attempt.

"Yeah. I bought it for you today. It's purple."

She pouts. "But I like pink."

"But your second-favorite color is purple, right? So, I got you a purple one because they were all out of pink." He removes it from the bag.

She looks at it, jumping on the bed in anticipation. "Okay. I do like purple."

He holds it up to her. "What do you think?"

She stops bouncing and presses it against her tummy. "It's pretty fabaluss," she says, nodding seriously.

"I thought it was pretty fabaluss too when I saw it." He glances up at me and winks before turning his attention back to his daughter. "Ready to take off those dirty, stinky clothes and hop into the bath first?"

"I probably need about two or three or four baths," she says, rolling her eyes and sighing dramatically. "I was playing in the dirt a lot today."

"How about if Emerald goes and draws that bath for you while you and I have a little talk?"

"Okay." She looks up at me. "Not too hot. Hot water is dangerous for childrens."

I don't want to say that I run out of the room, but I do move pretty quickly. Sam is giving me an escape hatch, and hell yes, I'm taking it.

Fine . . . I'll admit it; I'm afraid. I'm afraid of the emotion. I'm afraid of the pain these two are going to suffer together. I lost my father before I even knew I had one. In comparison, that was easy. I can only imagine what it would be like to be told that my parent, who I'd known about and loved all my life, was suddenly gone. I don't even like to *think* about one of my mothers passing away. I know it's going to happen someday, obviously, but hopefully not for a very long time. I'm not going to handle it well, that's for sure. Yeah . . . it's better that I hide in the bathroom when Sam breaks the news to Sadie; I won't be any help to either of them in there if I'm blubbering like a baby.

I focus on filling up the bathtub and making some bubbles with the shower gel that came with the room. When I was little, I loooved me some bubble baths. Maybe lacy dresses and bubbles will help ease Sadie's pain. I'm willing to try anything.

I hear crying in the other room. And as much as I want to stay away, I step out and stand silently in the little hallway between the front door and the bedroom. I don't want them to think I don't care.

Sadie is standing next to the bed with tears running down her cheeks, and Sam is on one knee in front of her.

"But why?" she asks.

Sam's voice cracks. "I don't know. I guess God decided that he wanted her back early."

"But doesn't God know that I need her here? I'm too little to be alone."

Tears rush to my eyes as my heart breaks for her. Every little girl needs her mama; she's right. This is so unfair for all of them.

Sam tries to explain. "You're not alone, sweetie; you have me, and I'm not going anywhere."

"But I need my mommy too. Doesn't God know that?"

"Yes, God knows that, but sometimes people are so sick, they just can't stay here anymore."

"My mommy was sick." Sadie says it like a statement, not a question. Maybe she knew.

"Yes, she was. She was very, very sick. But she's not anymore. Now she's really healthy."

Sadie sniffs, sounding hopeful. "Then maybe she can come back if she's not sick anymore."

Sam wipes the tears from her cheeks. "That's not how it works, baby girl. Once someone goes to heaven, they can't come back here."

"Maybe I'll go there and be with her," Sadie says, more tears streaming down her cheeks. "So she won't be alone. Mommy doesn't like to be alone."

Sam shakes his head, pressing his lips together. His chin is trembling, making his beard move too. "No, baby," is all he manages to get out.

Sam isn't able to say anything else, and the look on his face compels me forward. "She's not alone," I say, moving toward them.

Sadie looks up at me. "She's not?"

I bend down to look her in the eye. "No. There's all kinds of people and animals there waiting for her."

"What people?"

I look at Sam. "Well, her mommy and daddy?"

Sam nods, joining in. "Yeah. And her brother, your Uncle Hank who died last year, remember?"

She nods and then turns her attention to me. "What animals?"

I open my eyes wide. "Oh, *all* the animals. Sooo many animals."

"Which ones?"

I can't believe the pressure a tiny kid can put on an adult. I scramble for names. "Well, I had this goat named Frisky who was really silly and fun and very sweet. He's in heaven now, so if I ask him, he could probably hang out with your mom while she's getting her wings."

Sadie frowns in confusion. "What wings?" She swipes her hand under her nose, spreading boogies across her cheek. I have to look away to ease the insta-nausea that takes over my stomach.

Sam takes a handkerchief from his pocket and wipes her face as I answer.

"Well, she's an angel now, so she's going to have wings and be able to fly."

I glance at Sam and he's nodding at me. I guess it's okay if I sell Sadie on this idea of the afterlife, even though he doesn't believe in it himself.

"What other animals are there?" Sadie asks.

"Well, I also had a horse named Henry who's there. Do you want me to talk to him about your mom too?"

She nods. "Yes. Especially if he's a unicorn horse."

"I'm pretty sure he is. You know, I didn't see a horn on his head when he was with me, but I think unicorns keep their horns invisible so nobody tries to catch them and put them in a zoo."

Sadie nods at me, her eyes lighting up. "I think you're prolly right about that. Unicorns are very magic."

"Yes. They are." Sam pats her on the chest. "Do you still want to put on your fancy dress and go to dinner with Daddy and Emerald?"

Sadie looks around the room, puts her hands on her cheeks, and nods. She takes a deep breath in and out, and then lets her arms fall to dangle by her sides. "I'm really sad right now, but maybe if I have some chicken nuggets, I won't be so sad after."

I have to look away as my throat closes up. Poor, sweet little thing. She's still going to be sad, even after she eats those chicken nuggets, but I like the idea of her getting a temporary reprieve if nothing else.

"That's the spirit," Sam says. "Why don't we go have that bath now?"

"Can it have bubbles in it?" she asks, taking her dad's hand.

"I already took care of it," I say, proud that I can read the mind of a four-year-old.

Sadie pauses and looks up at me. "How did you know I like bubble baths?"

"Because I was a four-year-old once too."

She looks me up and down. "That must've been a really, really long time ago because you're really old now."

Sam hides his laugh behind the back of his hand.

"You're right. I'm twenty-five and that is pretty old, now that you mention it. Some days I feel like I'm a hundred." *Like today.*

"That's okay." She slides her free hand into mine. "I still like you, even though you're old."

We all walk toward bathroom, squeezing through the very narrow hallway together.

"Good. Because I like you too, even though you're young."

"If you want, you can marry my daddy," Sadie says.

My eyeballs almost fall out of my head hearing that. I can't see Sam's face, but he's frozen in his tracks, just like I am.

"Okay, well . . . that's good to know." I let her hand go. "I'm going to go in the other room and watch TV while you take your bath."

She spins around. "No. You have to stay with me and wash my back. It's dangerous to leave a child alone in the bathtub."

I work to get my voice even, still freaked out about the marriage comment. "Your daddy can watch over you."

She presses her hands on her hips and gives me a look that I'm pretty sure she learned from one of her parents. "You *both* can watch me."

"Fine. We can both watch you," Sam says. "Just get your clothes off and stop your yappin'." He points toward the bathroom, avoiding making eye contact with me, thank goodness.

I walk over to the tub, lowering myself down onto my knees next to it. I talk to myself inside my head the entire time. *I can get through this. I am not afraid of a four-year-old—not even one who sees too much and somehow manages to say exactly the most embarrassing thing at exactly the worst moment.*

Pfff. Who am I kidding? Of course I'm afraid.

Amber was right about me; I'm afraid of the feelings I have for Sam and his little girl, of how they can evoke this need to protect them both when I hardly know them. I'm afraid of the sadness that overwhelms me when I realize that our time together is going to be short-lived because they'll be staying in New York and I'll be moving on. I'm afraid that I'm never going to meet a guy as attractive to me as Sam is out in the middle of nowhere in Maine, or anywhere else for that matter. I'm sitting here next to this bathtub, watching a sassy little princess make a bubble beard that "looks just like Daddy's," and I want to run for the hills . . . Because love is *scary*. I swallow with difficulty as that word floats through my mind. *Love . . .*

CHAPTER THIRTY-EIGHT

We make it through the bubble bath and dinner without any incidents or too many tears. Sadie knows herself better than I do; she was right about those chicken nuggets helping her feel less sad. Sadie falls asleep on our way back up to the room, snuggled in Sam's arms. He puts her to bed, and her whispery snore keeps a steady rhythm as we remove our clothing and change into pajamas. I'm wearing flannel pants and a T-shirt, and Sam is in basketball shorts. I have to look away from his muscular chest to keep from wanting to run my hands all over it.

"I really want to sleep with you tonight," he whispers. He comes over to hold me while we're standing at the foot of the other bed. His masculine smell and presence nearly overwhelm me and make me want to forget every rule of decency I ever learned.

"But we can't," I whisper back. I push out of his embrace, worried he's going to ignore the fact that his little girl is sound asleep next to us. Yes, I really want to have sex with him, feel his hardness penetrate me and make me forget at least temporarily all the sad things we dealt with today, but there's no way I'm going to risk getting discovered by Sadie.

This little girl is so impressionable, and she sees *everything*. She kept the entire conversation going during dinner with her crazy banter, and from the stories she told, it's clear that she understands a lot more about her mother's lifestyle then Sam ever realized. He feels guilty enough about that; we don't need to add anything else to his list of regrets.

"How about if I sleep with her?" I suggest. "That way you can spread out tonight in your own bed."

"No, I'll sleep with her. You paid for the room, so you should have your own space. And by the way, I'm going to pay you back for this."

"Don't worry about it. Let's just get back to New York and worry about everything then."

He takes my hand. "Are you scared?"

"About what?"

"About marrying me."

I release his hand and step back, my mouth dropping open in shock.

He giggles like a girl, hiding his smile behind his hand. I can see his stupid weirdo beardo quivering with his laughter.

"Stop that." My face is flaming hot. I slap him gently on the arm. I'd hit him harder, but I don't want to wake Sadie.

"I'm sorry. I couldn't help myself." He laughs some more.

"You are so bold." I shake my head at him. One thing I can say about Sam: he sure knows how to bring down the temperature in a room. My blood is now running cold from the shock, when before it was ready to boil over from staring at his gorgeous body.

"What else am I gonna do? My four-year-old thinks she needs to make moves on chicks for me. She must think I'm pretty lame."

"Well, she's a pretty smart little girl; you are lame." I busy myself with putting my clothing in my suitcase, trying hard not to smile but failing miserably.

"Seriously, though." His voice is no longer teasing. "Are you okay? Are you worried about anything? Are we cool?"

"I'm not worried about anything anymore." I close my suitcase and turn to face him. "We're safe out here at this no-name hotel, and we're leaving tomorrow. What's there to be afraid of?"

He takes my hand again. "Are you freaked out about what's going on otherwise . . . like, between us?"

I shrug. "Maybe a little." Being able to admit my feelings to him somehow makes the fear recede, seem more manageable. It helps that he's being so open and talking about it. I've never been in a relationship like this with a man before.

"I worry about you being afraid, you know," he says.

"Why?"

"Because. Some people make snap decisions when they're afraid of something, and it may not always be the best option in the long run."

"What kind of decisions are you talking about?"

He stares at me for a while before answering. "The kind where you choose between sticking around and running away."

I fold my arms, slightly offended that he'd think this about me. "I was just relocating, not running."

"I'm not talking about your decision to come to this hotel."

Oh. His meaning hits me like a smack upside the head. He thinks I'm so afraid of what's going on between us, I'm going to run from *him*. "I thought you knew me better than that by now." It's true that we will probably end up apart, but it won't be because I was afraid and took off; it'll be because life circumstances dictate that he be in one place and I be in another, either because of work or because we decide we don't get along anymore.

"I think I do know you, Em."

I cross my arms over my chest so I can keep from doing something we'll both regret. "What happened the last time you told me I was afraid?"

"I don't remember." He tries not to smile, which is smart of him because if I even get an inkling that he's mocking me, I am going to make him very sorry; I see a serious beard-tugging in his future.

"You ended up in a bet with me that you still need to fulfill, by the way. You're going to owe me two hundred bucks."

His grin is huge. "I can't wait. Maybe I can get Sadie to play tambourine."

I lift my chin. "Perfect. I can't wait either." I turn away and pull my toothbrush out of my bag, moving toward the bathroom.

Even while brushing my teeth, I'm fighting off a grin. I love hanging out with Sam and Sadie, even when things are emotionally charged or sad. I never realized before that four-year-olds could be cool. Even though she majorly embarrassed me with that marriage comment, it still turned out okay. Sam can joke about it, and that's exactly what we need—humor . . . laughter . . . the things that will get us past these bumps of sorrow that we're running over.

If we can hang on to our smiles and our senses of humor, everything's going to be okay. One step at a time, we'll get past the death of Sadie's mom, and one day at a time, I'll get over missing these beautiful people who will eventually move on. It doesn't matter that I'm falling in love with this man. I won't let it destroy my world. I'll just deal with the inevitable pain when it comes and move on.

At that thought, my smile fades and is replaced by a frown. I'm afraid that while Sam and Sadie will become a part of my past, the sadness of losing them will remain forever a part of my present.

CHAPTER THIRTY-NINE

Sadie has never been on an airplane before, so she's terribly excited. All she can do is talk, for the entire trip. I don't think she pauses even once in the conversation except to breathe. She doesn't really need anyone to respond either, which is convenient since both Sam and I are exhausted. Sexual frustration is never conducive to a good night's sleep.

The passengers in nearby seats look over from time to time and smile at us. I feel like I should apologize to them, because maybe they expected a quieter journey, but nobody seems to be bothered by her. Sam just nods and grunts in response to her questions as he thumbs through magazines. I manage to catch a few minutes of sleep somehow, and as far as I can tell, Sadie doesn't even notice or stop talking to me when I'm completely zonked.

"Where are we going?" Sadie asks, as we make our way from the airport to the taxi stand.

"We're going to a really fancy apartment," Sam says.

"Is it your apartment?" she asks me.

I shake my head. "No, it's my sister's. And it's your Uncle Ty's, too."

When Sam looks at me sharply, I realize I just let the cat out of the bag without his permission. *Oops.*

"Who's Uncle Ty? I don't have an uncle Ty. And that's not a name. That's something you do with your shoelace. You tie your shoelaces. I don't know how to tie my shoelaces yet. I'm too little."

Sam interrupts whatever her next conversational volley was going to be. "Actually, sweetie, you do have an uncle named Ty, which is a real name that is short for Tyler. Daddy will tell you all about him in the cab."

She stares up at her dad and then at me, frowning in disapproval. "I think you're telling a lie."

I shake my head. "No, I promise. Your dad wouldn't lie to you."

She pulls her tiny rolling backpack behind her and surges ahead of us, stomping her feet.

"What does that mean?" I ask, watching her go.

"I think this is her way of saying that she's been told a lot of lies in her life and she thinks this is going to be another one to add to the pile." Sam sighs in defeat.

"Oh. That sucks." My moms were always very fixated on the truth. I wonder now if that makes them hypocrites, because they sure did lie to our fathers, if omissions are considered lies, anyway. But our fathers never bothered to ask why our mothers left, so is not telling them really a lie by omission or just a part of our mothers' story they never shared?

Ugh. Why does everything have to be so twisted and complicated all the time? I feel like Sadie does. I just want to stomp my way through the airport and yell at somebody. But who would I yell at? My moms said they did the best they could at the time. And I have a feeling that Sam is going to lie to his daughter about matters from time to time too, because that's what he has to do. She'll be too young to know the truth of some things, like the fact that her mother didn't die because she was sick, she died because she overdosed on drugs. Sadie knows part of her mother's truth today, and maybe someday she'll know all of it.

I was only ever told part of the truth about my life. The question is, would I be better off knowing the whole truth, or is part of it enough? Knowing Madison died of a drug overdose versus from illness won't change the fact for Sadie that her mom is never coming back. If what Amber says about our fathers is true—that they were innocent and never could have known about us—will it make any difference? I still will have grown up without a father, and they still will have grown old without having raised me. Truth can be so cruel and ugly. Sometimes I think the lies are more comfortable.

Sam catches up to his daughter and takes her by the hand. She lets him, and together they make their way through the airport. I watch from a few steps back, my heart aching over how sweet they are and how tough things will sometimes be for them. Parenting is so hard. This is the first time in my life that I've actually been able to truly appreciate that concept.

We catch a cab and ride to the apartment in silence because Sadie finally falls asleep and neither of us wants to disturb her. All that yammering on the plane finally caught up with her, giving our brains a rest. I stare out the window, dozing off too. Sadie and I only wake when we're at the curb outside the apartment building and Sam is pulling our bags out of the car.

"Are we here?" Sadie asks as I help her out of the cab.

"Yep. This is the place."

She stands at the curb bending backward with her hands on her butt so she can see to the top of the building. "Wow. That's really tall." She looks at her dad, her eyes big and round. "It's like in space."

"What do you mean?" He takes her little bag and hooks it over his arm. It's both hilarious and heartwarming to see such a tough-looking guy with a pink princess mini suitcase on his shoulder.

"It's like a space building," she explains. "Like in the movie."

"Yeah. Sure. Whatever you say, Sadie. Can we go now?" Sam is waiting impatiently for her to get moving toward the door.

She looks at me. "Is your sister home?"

I shake my head. "No, my sister isn't home right now, but she gave me a key and she told me I can go in whenever I want."

Sadie puts her hand in mine. "Okay. But I hope she doesn't get mad at me."

"Why would she get mad at you?" I lead her toward the front door.

"Because some people don't like kids."

"That's silly. I don't know anybody who doesn't like kids."

"Drake doesn't."

I pause for a moment and look at Sam. He's furious, that much is clear. I decide that distraction is the best defense against the storm I see brewing in his eyes, so I point through the glass. "You see those guys in there?"

Sadie stops and nods.

"They are the bosses of this whole building. They put a photo of our faces—mine and your daddy's—in their computer before we could be allowed to go upstairs into the apartment. Only the owners of the apartment can say if it's okay for someone to put their picture in the computer. No strangers allowed." I'm hoping that will banish any thoughts she might have of the bad men—aka Drake—coming to the front door of Amber's place.

She looks up at me. "Do you think they'll like me?"

I nod vigorously. "I'm absolutely sure of it."

She tilts her head at me. "How are you sure?"

"Because you're so adorable and you're Sam's little girl. And your uncle lives up there too, and he can't wait to meet you."

Sadie takes her time thinking it over but eventually nods. "Okay. I'm ready to meet my uncle."

Sam holds the door open for us and I usher Sadie in. "Your Uncle Ty isn't here now either, but there are some pictures of him and my sister up there, and I'm going to show you."

Sam pinches my butt on his way past me. Before I can retaliate, he runs forward and grabs Sadie up in his arms to swing her around. She giggles in delight, which means he's instantly forgiven for that pinch. His techniques for distracting Sadie—frilly dresses and acrobatics—work way better than my technique of trying to discuss my way out of things. I have a lot to learn from him.

I wave to the two young men behind the counter, recognizing them as the ones who were there a few days ago. They smile and wave back as Sam goes over to call the elevator down. I know it's strange, but I feel like I'm starting another chapter of my life right now. Going up to my sister's apartment and walking into her golden, be-feathered foyer with this little girl and her dad means something.

This is some scary shit, this commitment I feel I'm making by bringing them both here and staying together, the three of us. There's a part of me that's tempted to do a one-eighty and go back to that cab so I can hop a ride to the airport and fly home. Sam has a lot of baggage, and some of it is four years old and vulnerable as hell. I could really screw things up for both of them. Heck, I just told the girl she has an uncle she's never heard of when it should've been Sam's decision when and how to do that.

As I watch them disappear into the elevator and realize that they could be going up there alone without me, I hurry to catch up. The fear of losing them is greater than the fear of leaving them. I never realized before that there's a difference between making a choice to walk away and making a choice to let someone walk away. It's subtle, but it's huge. One is running, the other is risking loss . . . and I'm tired of running.

Starting another chapter of my life with these two is a frightening thing, but I still want to risk it. Because I'm not really afraid. Maybe it's fair to say that I'm timid or shy . . . I'm definitely an introvert. But it's *not* fair to say that I'm a coward. I've shown that I can woman up when the situation calls for it. And I'm no dummy; I see happiness on the horizon. I can feel the warmth of that sun on my skin. I know there are no guarantees, that maybe my future will have these two people in it and maybe it won't, but I'll never know if I run now, will I?

I walk over briskly and enter the elevator with them. Sam is waiting with his key card in the slot.

"I wasn't sure you were coming," he says, vulnerability shading his tone.

I shrug. "Why wouldn't I?"

"Because this is some big shit."

Sadie looks up at her dad. "You're not s'posed to say that word."

He looks down at her and nods. "You're right." He looks up at me. "Because this is some big doodoo."

I can't help but giggle with Sadie. "That's okay. I have a lot of experience with big doodoo."

"Because she has a horse named Henry!" Sadie says, jumping up and down. "I hope I get to meet your horses and your goats. Not the dead ones, though. I only want to meet the alive animals. I don't want to be an angel yet."

I have to stare straight ahead at the doors as they close because I cannot bear to look at the precious little girl at my feet. I can't promise her that she's going to come meet my animals when it's possible she never will. I don't want to be another one of the adults in her life who lies to her. I glance over at Sam, but his expression is unreadable.

CHAPTER FORTY

Sam and I both had high hopes, thinking we could hang out here in the apartment until Amber and Ty got back from Japan, but it's just not happening. It's been three days, but Sadie is still more than a handful; she's ten of 'em. She's on a warpath from the minute she wakes up until the moment she falls into an exhausted sleep, refusing to nap, refusing to eat anything healthy, refusing to take baths. Any fantasies we had about her dealing calmly with her mother's death have gone right out the window and landed splat on the sidewalk fifty floors below us. She's not doing well *at all*.

After finally getting her down to sleep, Sam and I are sitting on the couch having a glass of wine together. He's not even drinking a beer, too exhausted to do anything but grab the nearest alcohol. He looks into the glass and sighs. "You know my life is complete shit when I'm drinking white wine at seven o'clock at night, wondering if I can sneak off to bed without having sex with the gorgeous girl sitting next to me."

"What are we going to do?" I whine, shaking my head. I'm too exhausted for sex too, and that's just criminal when we're so damn good at it together and we have more than enough bedrooms with locks on them to ensure our privacy. I try to run my fingers through my hair but stop when they hit a knot. I don't remember the last time I used a brush. Parenting a child in mourning is way too much work.

"Why does she hate it here so much?" he asks, sounding bewildered. "She's usually so easy."

"I don't think it's this place. Or maybe part of it is this place, because it's all new to her, but I think it's her mom. She misses her. Her behavior is totally normal." *I think.*

"You're right." He sighs distractedly. "I shouldn't be so hard on her." He gulps half his wine and winces, glaring at the glass. "Jesus, this stuff is terrible."

I nudge him with my toe. "You haven't been hard on her at all; you've been incredibly patient." I really admire him for that patience, too. There have been times that I've wanted to rip my hair out of my head, and yet he just calmly steers her in another direction to distract her. Unfortunately, none of the distractions he's come up with have lasted more than ten minutes before she's out looking for trouble again.

"I think she just needs more space to spread out or something," he says. "It's just been so rainy here . . ."

I look around. "There's lots of space in the apartment, but . . ."

"Yeah, but everything is breakable." He points with his glass over to the vase we tried to glue back together. Despite our best efforts, it's going to be permanently lopsided. "That's probably going to cost half my paycheck to replace."

"I don't think Amber or Ty are going to care about that thing, but I get your point," I say. "She's going to bring the house down around our ears if we don't do something."

"Maybe I should get a hotel room." He looks pained at the idea.

"No, that's crazy. The hotels around here are way too expensive, and it won't be any different from here other than being much smaller."

He shakes his head and sighs, slowly sinking deeper into the couch. "I'm at my wits' end. I don't know what to do." He closes his eyes and rests his head against the cushions.

I take the glass of wine out of his hand and put it on the table next to mine. "I know exactly what we're going to do." The idea comes to me like a flash of lightning, brightening up the sky. I can't believe I didn't think of it sooner. The question is whether Sam will see it as me asking for more commitment. I don't think I am. It just makes sense . . . way more sense than staying here watching Sadie become more and more miserable as the hours tick by.

He opens one eye to look at me. "Just tell me what it is and I'll do it."

"We're going to the farm."

He turns his head toward me and opens his other eye. "Say that again?"

"You heard me." I lean over and push on his shoulder. "We should go to the farm. Why not?" I stand up, quickly warming to the idea. I pace back and forth in front of him. "We have all the room in the world, twenty other adults who can help keep an eye on her, and the animals. She'll *love* it." My heart beats quickly with excitement. This could work. I know we'd be so much happier there. Why was I resisting before? I've already made a commitment to being with them during this mourning period—this is the first time I'm officially acknowledging that to myself, actually, but it feels right—so why not be with them in a nicer place? Once Sadie has settled down and Sam is ready to go back to work, we can move on and go our separate ways or whatever. I'm not going to think about that right now, though; we have plenty of time for making those kinds of decisions. "The animals will keep her busy. She won't even think about destroying things because she'll be having so much fun playing with them."

"Is that safe?" He leans forward, his gaze more intense.

"Safe? Of course it's safe. Chickens aren't going to hurt anybody."

"What about the goats? Don't they like to headbutt things?"

"Yeah, sometimes, but we have pygmy goats. They can't do a whole lot, and we'll keep an eye on her."

"It's going to be an awful lot of work," he says hesitantly, sounding like he's warming to the idea.

"Believe me, we have kids out at the farm all the time. My sisters and I were born and raised there. Everybody who comes to Glenhollow is used to children being around and getting into trouble. It's no big deal. We're hippies, remember?" I give him my biggest smile.

"What about . . ." He looks around the room.

"It can be just for a few days, to help her work out whatever she needs to work out. You can come back when the band returns from Japan. You'll be right on schedule, writing music and everything, just like you agreed."

He looks down at his hands, rubbing his palms with his thumbs. "But what about you?"

"What about me?" His question confuses me.

"What are you going to do? Are you going to stay there or come back here after?"

"I'm going to stay there." This seems like a question he should already know the answer to. "Why would I come back here? I don't live here."

"Oh."

I realize when I hear the defeat in his tone what he's saying. He's worried it will mean the end of "us," whatever "us" is right now. A part of me is thrilled to know he's thinking of a future with me in it, but the other part of me is trying to be realistic. Is it fair to imagine moving forward together as a couple when there are so many unknowns? When our futures seem to be going in different directions?

I go over to sit next to him, putting my hand on his arm. "Don't worry about me. Everything is going to be cool; you'll see." I have to trust that everything is going to work out the way it should. It's the belief system that our mothers raised us within: the Universe provides. We just need to go with the flow and be open-minded.

"Yeah, sure." He stands and walks over to the kitchen, taking a beer out of the fridge. He pops the top off and takes a long drink.

I twist around to look at him. "What's wrong? Why are you angry all of a sudden?"

"I'm not angry." Sam walks over and leans on the edge of the counter, the couch maintaining distance between us. "I'm cool."

"You're not cool." I get up and walk over, taking the beer away from him and putting it on the counter. "Tell me what's going on in your head right now. A nickel for your thoughts."

He stands up straighter, his presence dark and smoldering with emotion I can't translate. "They're going to be more expensive than a nickel this time."

I lift my chin. "Fine. A quarter for your thoughts. A dollar."

"Whatever it takes?" He looks like he's trying to smile but can't quite get there.

"Yeah. Whatever it takes. Ten million bucks for your thoughts." My heart lurches at the idea.

He leans in and kisses me on the mouth, the dark emotion he was sending out dissipating into nothingness. "Don't ever do that. Don't sell your soul to the devil for me."

I take him by the chin, wiggling it a little, trying to shake the melancholy out of his silly brain. "I won't have to if you'll just confess." I let him go and wait, staring at him, trying to tell him silently that he can trust me.

It takes him a long time to finally answer. "I was just kind of hoping you could stick around with us for a little while. Things are good between us, you know? That's new for me. I like it. I don't want to lose something when it's this good."

My heart does flips inside my chest, cartwheels of happiness. Sam is not the kind of guy to expose his feelings to just anyone. I think this is the Universe talking to me through him. "I could do that." My ears burn with the idea of what we're actually saying . . . that we both have feelings for each other and that we aren't ready to say goodbye.

"But I don't really like the idea of begging you to do it." Sam looks disgusted with himself.

"You're not begging me, silly; you're just telling me how you feel, that you want to hang out with me. That's cool. I want to hang out with you too."

"That's going to be pretty difficult if you're in Maine and I'm here in New York." He looks sad.

The solution comes to me immediately. It seems crystal clear now. He wants to be with me . . . I want to be with him . . . it doesn't need to be this difficult. "You'll just have to stay at the farm, then." I grin big. My heart feels like it's going to explode. I have never been so daring in my life.

"How's that going to work?" He picks up his beer, looks at it, and places it back down on the counter, folding his arms over his chest.

"Doesn't writing music require a quiet place?" I have no idea if this is the case, since I've never been around anybody writing music, but it makes sense to me. I could never paint in a loud environment.

"Yeah, generally speaking. At least in the beginning of the process, for me."

"Well, you're in luck, because that's pretty much all we have out at the farm—quiet spaces. You can use my studio. It's a painting studio, but it's very private. There's plenty of room for you in there."

"I'm pretty sure the band wants me to be here with them, to be in on some jam sessions and whatever."

"When you're done doing what you need to do with them, you come back to the farm and work on more songs. It's not like they're hurting for money. They can pay for you to fly back and forth. People in business do that all the time."

"I don't like taking advantage of people like that."

"Listen." I put my hands on his shoulders and stare him right in the eye, shaking him a little. "According to Amber, you're a hot commodity. They need you, so they're going to have to do whatever is necessary in order to make this work." I pray that everything Amber says about those men is true . . . that they're kind people and interested in having a relationship with us. Because I'm not above using that potential relationship to help Sam and Sadie. "It's not just about you anymore. You have Sadie to think of. When you made this original deal with the band, you didn't have a little girl full-time in the picture. You were just going to be here for a short while, for a temporary gig. That's not the case anymore." I shake him again. "You told Patty you weren't going to stay in LA. Why don't you just move out here permanently? You couldn't get any farther from California than the East Coast. You could be totally anonymous in this giant city." My pulse is pounding wildly over the fact that I just asked a man I've only known for a very short while to move out to the East Coast . . . where I am. Talk about bold!

"But I don't like the city. I don't think it's good for Sadie." He searches my eyes, I think waiting for me to take another step forward.

In for a penny, in for a pound . . . "Great." I swallow with effort, trying to force the lump out of my throat. "Come out to the country. Maybe after you visit our farm you'll like it so much, you'll find a place nearby." God, it sounds like I'm asking him to marry me! I hurry to clarify. "Or maybe you'll want to move to Upstate New York or Pennsylvania. I don't know. But you'll never find out if you don't at least try."

"What if . . . I'm . . . afraid?" He shrugs, looking embarrassed.

I step back, dropping his arms. "Are you kidding me? You're not afraid of anything."

"I'm afraid to perform my music in front of people."

I know this fear like I know my own bones, but I can't let it rule him like it so often does me. "Pish-posh. Baloney. Nonsense. You made a bet with me to do it, and you know you're going to follow through. Don't play games with me."

He twists his mouth around in an almost-smile, making his beard move. "You gonna make me do it, Bossy Pants?"

I put my hands on my hips. "No. You're going to do it on your own. And for your information, I'm a very non-bossy person with other people. You make me bossy."

He stares at me long enough that it makes me uncomfortable.

"What?" I finally ask.

"Nothing. Just checking you out."

"Well, stop. You're making me nervous." I resist the urge to fold my arms over my chest.

"Why would it make you nervous to have somebody admiring you?"

"Because. I don't like it."

"Tell me why."

I shrug. "It feels weird to be saying this out loud . . . I don't know." I stare at the floor because his gaze is too intense. "I guess I imagine that you're staring at me and coming up with a list of things you don't like about me. All my faults, like being bossy." I never before realized how much Amber and I can be alike. When I'm with her I let her take over because it's easier, but when I'm with Sam, I feel . . . stronger. More independent and opinionated.

He laughs for a second before he realizes that I'm serious and stops. "That's ridiculous. Why can't I be looking at you and coming up with a list of things I *do* like about you?" His voice softens. "*Like* your bossiness, for example."

My heart feels like he's got his fist around it and he's squeezing. "Because it's not realistic?" I finally look up and see him gesturing at me.

"Of course it is. Look at you."

I tip my head down and see my out-of-fashion hippie skirt and the raggedy top I probably should've put in a Goodwill bin a few years ago. "Yeah. So?"

"What do you see?" he asks.

"I see a tired wardrobe and a tired woman who's been chasing after a four-year-old for three days nonstop."

"Do you want to know what I see?"

I stand there facing him as my face turns pink. I can't answer.

"I see a giving woman. Somebody who cares about other people more than herself. I see somebody who will drop whatever she's doing at a moment's notice to take care of somebody in need. I see somebody very sexy and smart. I see somebody who's bold and rare. I see somebody who's completely courageous and capable."

"Wow," I say, totally embarrassed, but in love with this vision he's painted. I wish I really were this person; she sounds amazing. "You're seeing a lot."

He smiles. "Yeah. Pretty much the whole package."

I wave him away and turn sideways. "Stop. You're making me blush."

He walks over and takes my hand. "If I take you into my bedroom, I'll show you what I think about this body of yours, too." He traces the outline of my exposed collarbone, giving me shivers. "Words can't do it justice . . . what we do in the bedroom together is really something special."

For two seconds I think about pulling away, but then I realize how stupid that would be. He's right about how good we are together sexually. And he's allowed to compliment me. He's allowed to think nice things about me. He's allowed to see the same things in me that my sisters and mothers see in me. It's just such a revelation to know that there's a man out there like him, and he's standing right in front of me asking me to take a chance on him.

"I think I could be talked into that," I say, finally facing him.

He looks into my eyes. "I like you. A lot. I'd like to spend some time with you in the place where you grew up. Can Sadie and I come out to your farm for a little while?"

"As long as you don't mind pitching in, you're welcome anytime." I smile, imagining him shoveling horse poop out of the stables.

His eyes narrow. "Why do I suddenly get the impression I'm going to regret inviting myself over?"

I shrug innocently. "I have no idea. I'm sure we'll find something you can do there that won't be too difficult."

He pulls me close and kisses me thoroughly, leaving me a little dizzy when he pulls away.

I put my hand up to my forehead. "I think I've had too much wine."

He grins lazily, unbuttoning my top button. "I think you've had too *little* of *me*."

When I see the bulge in his pants, I can't help but grin. "I think you might be right about that."

CHAPTER FORTY-ONE

Sadie is excited about the idea of finally meeting all of my animals. On the short plane ride to central Maine, she insists that I list all of them by name, over and over, until she has them memorized. By the time we reach our destination, I'm sick and tired of the poor creatures in my care at Glenhollow Farms.

"And I'm going to take Bessie the baby goat, and I'm going to comb her hair with my pink brush." She's looking out the window as the landscape flies by. The only one available at the farm to pick us up was Smitty, supposedly. I try not to glare at the back of his head. He is so nosy. I know very well Harold was there, and he could've driven out to the airport to get us, but Smitty inserted himself into the situation, and now here he is sitting in the pickup truck, smiling his stupid head off as he chats with Sam. I'm in the small backseat with Sadie.

"How many brushes do you have?" Sadie asks, pulling me out of my mean thoughts about Smitty.

"For animals or paint?"

"Animals."

"I have lots and lots of them. I don't think I've ever counted. But you could do that if you want. You can count all of them for me."

"I'm very good at counting. Ask my daddy." She pauses and then shouts, "Daddy! Dad, Dad, Dad!"

Sam turns around with exaggerated patience. "Is someone calling me back there?"

"Tell Emerald how good I can count."

Sam glances at me, twisting his head halfway around to do it. "She's the best. She's the best counter ever. In the whole wide world. No one counts better than Sadie. You've never seen someone count like her. It's incredible." He winks at me.

Sadie smiles up at me. "Told ya."

"I can't wait to see you in action." I smile encouragingly, imagining that I'll have a brief reprieve before I actually have to experience her doing her counting thing, since my animal brushes are all in the barn that's full of other junk.

I should have known better. The next thing I know, she's counting trees. By the time we get to the farm she's accounted for over a hundred. She's missed some numbers on the way, but rather than point it out, I just go with the flow. It's mesmerizing in a way, her voice droning on and on in a pattern like that. I'm almost asleep, but then the potholes in the driveway jar me out of my daze and wake me up.

There are a lot more people camped out around the house than there were when I left just a week ago. *Has it only been a week?* It seems like a lot longer. Harold comes down the front porch steps, smiling. The truck stops just in front of him, and Smitty puts it in park. He turns around and grins at me. "Home, sweet home; farm, sweet farm."

I roll my eyes at his corniness. "Thanks for the lift."

"Don't mention it." He winks and then chuckles as he faces the steering wheel again. Sam works on getting our bags from the truck bed while Sadie and I climb down.

Sadie and I go over to the front steps. She looks around, her eyes wide and her expression solemn.

"What's the matter?" I ask.

"This place is really big."

"Is it? I guess I never noticed."

"Why?"

"I don't know. Maybe because I grew up here and saw it all the time."

She looks up at me. "It is big. It really is. Do I get to stay in there?" She points at the front door.

"Yes, you do. If you go inside and up the stairs, you'll find a bedroom at the end of the hall that has a pink rose pillow on the bed. That can be your room, if you want."

"Really?" She looks like I just offered to buy her a pony. She runs into the house, hooting and hollering.

Sam joins me on the stoop. "What did you just say to her?"

"I promise I did not just tell her I was going to buy her a pony."

He laughs. "Thank you. Please don't ever do that."

"I told her which room she can sleep in."

"You sure you don't want us to pitch a tent out here?" He looks over his shoulder at the other campers.

"No, you can stay in the house. I'm sure there's a free bedroom or two available."

Sam takes Sadie's and his stuff up the porch stairs, and I start to follow, but a hand on my arm stops me. I find Smitty standing there in his flannel shirt and beat-up jeans. I sigh. I've been rude to him, and although part of the reason he's being so helpful is because he's nosy, it doesn't change the fact that he's done me a lot of favors since I left, looking out for the animals and other visitors so I could go to New York.

"Thanks for everything, Smitty. For the ride and for watching over things."

"Sure. No problem." He takes his baseball hat off and scratches his head. "So . . . you here to stay?"

"Where else would I go? This is my home." I walk to the top of the stairs, leaving him below.

"What about him? He staying too?"

"For a little while. Why?" I turn around to see his reaction.

He shrugs. "Just wondering." He waves at me and walks off, putting his hat back on as he heads up the road.

"Where're you going?" I call out after him.

"Help Rose at the clinic."

"Would you tell her I'm here?" My earlier calls to her went unanswered. All we've been able to do since I flew out to LA and back is exchange voice messages. She's busier than she's ever been at the clinic, and my life hasn't exactly been boring. I make a mental note to go down there later after Sam and Sadie are settled in to give her a hand. It's been way too long since we've talked.

"Will do," Smitty shouts.

I walk inside and take Sam by the hand.

"Where are we going?" he asks as I lead him to the stairs.

"To my bedroom."

"Am I sharing with you?"

"It's up to you," I say as we mount the stairs. "You can share with me or Sadie."

Sam leans in, taking me from behind in a warm hug, as he whispers in my ear, "Show me to your bed."

CHAPTER FORTY-TWO

Getting Sadie and Sam acclimated to the atmosphere of the farm is a lot easier than I was expecting it to be. She's a natural with the animals, very gentle and kind, and open to learning about them. And Sam is learning to unwind. His favorite place is the meditation meadow. He's spent almost every afternoon there since we arrived over a week ago.

Having both of them occupied to some degree has allowed Rose and me a chance to reconnect. Not only is she fully supportive of my budding relationship with Sam, she's as patient with Sadie as her father is, even taking some time with her at the clinic to teach her about basic veterinary care. I've been able to slide right back into my routine of taking care of the farm's animals with hardly a hitch. I hate to jinx things by being too positive about everything, but Sam and Sadie sure do fit in well here.

Sadie and I make our way between all the tents and around the gardens to join Sam in the meadow. We have a picnic basket with one of his favorite sandwiches inside.

"Why is Daddy out here again?" she asks.

"I think he likes it because it makes him feel peaceful inside."

"Do you think he's worried about my mommy?"

"I don't know if he's worried, but I know he thinks about her a lot. And he misses her."

Sadie gives an exaggerated sigh. "I miss her too. Sometimes. But not all the time. Sometimes I'm too busy."

"I'm glad you don't miss her all the time, because it would be sad if that's all you could do."

"Yeah. I'm still sad. But sometimes I think about other things."

"Like what other things?" I'm curious how a four-year-old girl gets over the loss of her mother. She seems to be adjusting pretty well, all things considered. I can't imagine I'd do half as well.

"I think about the chickens. I think about Boris the pig a lot, because he likes me to scratch his back a special way, and so I haffa do that *every day.*" She says it like it's a factory job and she's been forced to work double overtime.

I try to take her seriously. "That's something nice to think about. I'm sure Boris appreciates it."

"And I haffa do it in a *special* way, and if I don't do it like that, then he doesn't get his special back scratch that is his very favorite. And he gets sad. And he cries. He really *needs* it." She looks up at me with a pitiful expression.

I could be wrong, but it sounds like she's angling for a longer stay. "You think so?" I don't want to lead her into thinking that this is going to last forever. We're doing really well right now, but that doesn't mean Sam isn't going to want to move on eventually. We haven't talked about it, both of us trying really hard to appreciate what we have and not put undue pressure on things. He's mourning Madison and I'm giving him the space to do that. And regardless of whether he wants to move on or not, the reality of his business deal with the band remains. He may not be able to stay here, as much as he might want to. The idea fills me with sadness because I'm having so much fun with him and Sadie. I'm to the point that I can't imagine my life without them anymore.

Most days I spend with Sadie or at least have her nearby while Sam works on his music in the studio shed. But every night is for him and me alone, and we couldn't be more perfectly suited to each other. Our bodies fit together like they were made from the same mold, two halves pulled apart and set down on opposite ends of the country to be brought back together again by fate.

"And you know Fleur?" Sadie asks.

"Yes, I know Fleur the chicken. What about her?"

"Well, she's missing some feathers on her butt. I think we need to take her to see Rosie."

"You may be right about that. Maybe she has mites." Good thing I have Rose around to help me take care of those kinds of things, although unless I have a sick animal or a spare hour to help out at the clinic, I hardly see her. She's taking all her meals out there now and sleeping there often, too. The best we've been able to do is a few midnight chats, but they're good enough for me. I'd never demand that Rose spend time with me when she has patients who need her.

"Maybe we can go see her after we have our lunch," Sadie suggests.

"Maybe." I bend down and point out the man sitting under the tree she hasn't yet noticed. "Look. There's your dad."

Sadie gets ready to run, but I grab her hand and hold her back. "Go softly. Maybe he's meditating. We don't want to interrupt his peaceful moment."

She starts tiptoeing, making a big show of listening to me. It's hilarious because she's making such a ruckus, Sam has no hope of any peace now that his daughter is in the meadow.

When he turns around and sees her coming, a grin lights up his face. He stands and opens his arms. She runs right into them. I pause for a moment to enjoy the scene. He's got a thick sweater on to protect against the coming winter, and the skin of his face and hands has a healthy glow from all the time he's spent outside. As it turns out, Sam is pretty handy with a hammer. He's been fixing fences all over the property. It's made his hands rougher, but I like it. I feel like I'm in bed with a real workingman when he touches my skin with his callused hands.

When I get closer, I hear Sadie chattering on about the picnic basket's contents. Sam acts as though he's really excited about his ham-and-cheese sandwich.

"I'm sure it'll be the best one I've ever had," he says. He smiles at me. "I hear I'm in for a gourmet lunch today."

"You bet." I set the basket down and pull out the rolled-up blanket from inside, spreading it under the tree. Soon enough, I have the whole thing unpacked and we're munching away. Sadie's favorites are the tiny carrots dipped in ranch dressing.

"I think I'm ready to write some music," Sam says. He's staring out into the meadow.

"Really? That's great."

"I've been working out some things in my head."

"I can't wait to hear it." So far I haven't been privy to anything he's been working on, but I have high hopes that he'll let me do that one day.

He faces me. "I'm glad you said that, because I have a plan."

"What is it?" Now I'm suspicious; he's got an evil glint in his eye.

"We still have that bet, remember?"

"No, I don't remember. I don't know what you're talking about." I look around, refusing to meet his eyes.

"Here's the plan. We're going to do it here. I play, you paint."

I gesture around. "Here? No problem."

He shakes his head. "No. In town."

My sandwich gets caught in my throat, and I have to cough to release it. "What?"

"In town. At the farmers' market."

"You're nuts." He went to the market with me one time, and all he did was complain about how cold it was.

"Yeah, I was thinking we could get this bet out of the way, and then I could use the two hundred bucks I'll win to buy a couple new T-shirts I saw."

"Don't tell me you're into hemp now." I saw him eyeing the things last week, but I can't believe he'd actually buy one. Besides, he doesn't need that bet money from me if he wants to change his wardrobe. I know he has some from the band. Amber made sure the deal was still solid between them, and he's already gotten a percentage of his fee.

"Hey, it's natural fibers, man. You gotta be friendly to the environment." He holds out his hands and frowns at me. "Hello? Intentional-living community? Sound familiar?"

I laugh, totally charmed by his attempts to fit in. And those attempts are working. All the regulars have accepted him as one of the family, especially when they see how much effort he puts in. The only one who seems a little reticent is Smitty, but I don't care what he thinks. He's just bummed that he's not going to be getting any booty calls from me. Not that he ever did.

"I don't know," I say.

Sam shrugs. "Or you could just forfeit the two hundred bucks. Save us both the humiliation."

I shake my head. No way am I letting him get away with not performing his music. "Forget it. It's on."

He slaps his hands and laughs. "Yeah!"

"Why did you say, 'Yeah,' Daddy?" Sadie asks.

He jumps up and grabs Sadie, swinging her around in the air. "Because I'm happy!" he shouts.

She shrieks with glee.

"You don't need to be *that* happy about it," I say, trying to sound grouchy. Truth is, I'm a little nervous about painting in front of the people at the market. I know a lot of them, but I'd rather not expose that part of myself to them. I almost think it would be easier doing it in Central Park, a place full of strangers.

Sadie's face is pink and she's giggling her head off. "That makes my tummy tickle," she says gaily.

"Oh, yeah?" He throws her high up into the air. "How about that? Does it make your tummy tickle too?"

A shriek is her answer. Her arms are spread like eagle wings. "Do it again, Daddy!"

I spend the rest of my lunch break watching the two of them be silly, running around the meadow, playing tag, spinning in circles, and falling exhausted to the cold ground. This trip has been so good for them. I really don't want them to leave, but everyone is due back from Japan tomorrow, and I know our time together here is coming to a close. Sam will need to go to New York to work with the band. Ty and Amber have offered him and Sadie rooms in their apartment.

Neither of us has mentioned what comes next, and my upbringing tells me to just let things lie. Around here, we don't do the commitment thing. People come and go as their moods and the weather change. It was easy for me to say all kinds of things about our future when I was temporarily living outside of my normal life, but now that we're here and my world has mostly gone back to normal, it's hard to be that "other" Emerald anymore. I belong here. I have no desire whatsoever to move to Manhattan.

My heart is heavy and aching over it. I don't really see an easy solution to our dilemma. In order for Sam to write music for the band, he needs to be in New York with them pretty often. Sadie doesn't do well there, but it's not like he can leave her with me. I'm not her mother, and although I love her, I'm not ready to be a single mother to the child of a man I just met. Maybe that's coldhearted of me, but I really believe she needs to be with her dad right now. She lost her mom, and although she's doing okay, she still needs to talk about it and work her way through it. And she needs to do that with Sam, not me. She's only four years old. She needs stability in her life. Her dad going back and forth and leaving her behind doesn't fit in with that program. Maybe when he's done working with them, he can think about living somewhere else . . . maybe somewhere close by. But then again, maybe not. There's not much call for professional musicians out here in the middle of nowhere.

I sigh, collecting all of our picnic things. I wish the Universe would offer me a solution, but so far all it has done is show me how sad I'm going to be in about forty-eight hours.

CHAPTER FORTY-THREE

I thought I would be ready for my mothers' homecoming, but when a giant tour bus pulls up onto the property, I nearly pee my pants in panic. *What the hell is going on?!*

I stand out on the front porch holding Sadie's hand. She's jumping up and down, using my arm as leverage to go higher and higher. I look down, hoping if I focus on her, I'll be less likely to have an accident in my pants. "Are you excited?"

"Yes, yes, yes! I'm gonna see a circus!"

I blink at her a few times. "A circus?"

She points at the big, colorful bus. "That's a circus."

I shake my head, mumbling under my breath. "I think you're right about that. We're about to see some clowns come out, too, I'll bet."

Sam is suddenly behind me, resting his hand on my shoulder. "What's this all about?"

"Your guess is as good as mine." I feel better having him there with me.

The door opens with a bang and a hiss of steam. People start piling out. The first one to exit is Amber, and she comes running straight for me. She's wearing ridiculously high heels and almost trips in the dust before she makes it to the stairs and grabs the railing.

She looks up at me, smiling like a loon. "Holy crap, I almost bit it out there." She climbs the stairs, clomping all the way up in her heels.

She stops near the top and bends down to look right at Sadie, the little imp who's suddenly become very un-Sadie-like. She's trying to hide behind my legs.

"You must be Sadie."

She peeks out. "I am Sadie. Are you a clown?"

Amber snorts. "A clown? I don't think so." She looks up at me. "Am I a clown?"

I can't help but laugh. "Yes, you are." I turn my attention to my little buddy, who's still glued to me. "Sweetie, this is my sister Amber. We stayed in her apartment in New York, remember? I showed you pictures of her?"

"Hi, Amber," Sadie says, coming out a bit more.

"Hello, Sadie. It's so nice to meet you. I think I *might* have a present for you on that bus. Maybe you could go find it."

Sadie looks conflicted, and I know exactly what she's thinking: she wants that present, but she's worried about attack clowns lying in wait.

"Is that a circus bus?" she asks.

Amber glances up at me, but I just shrug. She's going to be a mom soon; let's see how she handles it.

"I guess you could call the tour bus a circus bus," she says. "It gets pretty crazy in there sometimes. Maybe your daddy can show you the inside." She stands straight and waits for Sam to make his move.

He looks at me and shrugs, taking Sadie by the hand. They walk down the stairs together, weave their way around the groups of people who just got off the bus, and climb inside.

Amber steps up to be on the same level as me and stands at my side, staring at the bus. "Don't freak out," she says in softer tones.

"Why would I freak out about a tour bus in the middle of my front lawn?" I'm trying not to be mad at her. She could have called and warned me, so I know she decided at some point along the way that a sneak attack was a better idea.

"Hey . . . if Mohammed won't come to the mountain, the mountain has to come to Mohammed."

I look at her. "What's that supposed to mean?"

She sighs and drapes her arm over my shoulders. "I know that you aren't ready for Sam to go back to New York, and everybody's really whipped from the tour, so I figured, why not come out here and relax for a little while before we go back? Maybe talk a little bit, work some things out . . ."

I stiffen, my entire body going rock hard. "You think that's going to be relaxing?"

"Yes, I do." She rubs my back vigorously. "You just need to let go a little bit."

I step away to release myself from her hold. "Let go of *what*?"

"Let go of your bitterness. *Jesus*." She frowns at me. "Are you wound tight, or what?"

I ignore the fact that she just bought me more time with Sam and Sadie and focus on the part of the story that's giving me an ulcer just thinking about it. "You say that as if this is just a decision I need to make, like, *presto bango*, I'm no longer uncomfortable about the idea of spending time with . . . *certain people*."

"It *is* a decision. And it's an easy one; all you have to do is bother to get to know them just the tiniest bit." She shrugs and looks out at the bus. "But hey . . . maybe you're too afraid to do that. Maybe it's easier for you to be angry and offended over things that *didn't* happen than to face that fear."

I feel like slapping her. "I'm *not* afraid. I'm not afraid of *them*, and I'm not afraid of *you*. I know all I need to know about those men, and you're not going to bully me into doing anything I don't want to."

"I'm not a bully." She grits her teeth.

I fold my arms. "That's funny, because you're doing a great imitation of one right now."

She stares at me with her nostrils flaring for a few seconds, but then her face falls and tears well up in her eyes. "I'm really not a bully. I just love you so much, and I want everyone to be happy."

I want to say nothing and let her stew in her guilt, but watching her crumble in front of me makes that impossible. "You need to let it alone," I say, putting my arms around her.

She's pregnant. I can't believe I temporarily forgot that. Maybe I should try harder to keep my opinions to myself while she's in such a delicate state. It's just that she makes me so mad trying to force a relationship with those men on me.

She sighs and pulls out of my embrace, looking at the door of the tour bus with me as she wipes her eyes. More people are coming out. "Well, I'm afraid it might be a little too late for that."

Guys wearing jeans and leather jackets emerge. I recognize them—even though they're old, gray-haired, and wrinkled, with slightly updated haircuts—as the men who grace the album covers in my mothers' living room. They're quickly surrounded by our moms, three women who used to give a hoot about me, but who cannot be bothered to even say hello before they're over there throwing themselves at their feet. It seems like after that overseas trip and the bus ride, they could spare a minute for the daughter they haven't seen in almost two weeks.

"Screw this," I growl, spinning on my heel and stomping into the house. I go straight to my bedroom and lock the door. Amber invited those turds to our home without even talking to me first, but *I'm* the one who still lives here. Don't I deserve at least the respect of a phone call? What was she thinking? She knows very well that I don't want them here. This is Amber forcing her solutions on me, as if my problems are her problems. Well, I've got news for her: they're *not*.

And that goes for my mothers, too. They're in on this little plan of hers. It's all a conspiracy to pressure me into doing what they want me to do, feeling what they want me to feel. But I'm not going to do it. Not this time. I'm my own person and I'm not afraid of them. And I'm not afraid of hurting their feelings by standing my ground either.

Amber decided to set up her life with the band so she could try to foster some kind of new relationship with them, but I am not interested in that. I don't need them in my life. I don't need their money and I don't need their complications. I know everybody else loves them, but I don't, and nothing they say or do is going to change that. And if Sam joins their team and tries to get me to suck up to those guys, then he can just go back to New York and take Sadie with him.

Just thinking those words makes my heart ache, but I do my best to steel myself against the pain. I am not going to compromise this time. I have my principles, and I'm going to stand on them. If you love somebody, you do the right thing by them. These men either did not love my mothers and are therefore lying about that, or their love for my mothers was less than their love for themselves; and in that case, they aren't my kind of people.

When our mothers walked away all those years ago, those men should've followed them or at least tracked them down and asked why they left without saying goodbye. They didn't, though, and that tells me all I need to know, which is that they didn't care about our mothers then and they don't care about them now. They just like how our mothers worship the ground they walk on. My moms are better women than this, and it frustrates me to no end to see them acting like brainless twits.

Their old-men egos probably need that adoration to keep their hearts pumping. Amber says they regret the choices they made, and maybe that's true, but that doesn't undo them. Those mistakes still happened. I grew up without a father, and when I see Sam with Sadie, I realize all that I missed. It's a tragedy is what it is—a preventable one.

I am not ready to forgive now, and maybe I never will be; but I certainly won't be forgiving anybody who forces himself on me. Those men can't be that clueless; they know they've come into my territory without my approval. So, fine. I don't need to see them. They can live their lives and I'll live mine. This farm is two hundred acres big, and I can easily disappear on it.

I cry until I don't have any tears left and my eyelids are too heavy to hold open anymore. The world goes black, and that's just perfect as far as I'm concerned.

CHAPTER FORTY-FOUR

I wake up two hours later to the sound of someone knocking. Sam's voice comes through the door. "Hey, babe? Everybody's getting ready to have dinner outside together. Will you please come out and join us? I know it's not going to be easy, but maybe it's worth doing anyway."

I get up and walk over to the door, cracking it open. "I'm not interested in having dinner with those people."

His handsome brown eyes look concerned. "Why not?"

I really want to slam the door in his face because he's asking me dumb questions I'm not in the mood to answer, but I resist. "I think you know why."

"I know you don't want to have a relationship with them, but could you just come out anyway? For your moms' and your sisters' sake? You know . . . just be polite or whatever."

I'm being guilt-tripped and lectured by the guy who threw things around and bashed up amplifiers in my sister's apartment mere hours after he met her. "Polite? Are you kidding me? What's polite about people showing up at my front door, thinking they can stay here without talking to me first?"

Sam glances down before answering. "Isn't that what everybody does around here?"

"It's not the same, Sam, and you know it." I hate that he's mostly right.

"I really don't think they know how upset you are. I don't think they came here trying to make you mad."

"Amber knew."

"Yeah, about that . . . I don't know her very well, but I kind of get the impression that she's not telling them everything. They're really excited to meet you, actually."

I feel myself start to soften, but I ignore my traitor heart. "Well, they can forget it, because I'm not excited about meeting them at all. In fact, I'd rather kiss the ass end of a warthog than meet them."

Sam chuckles. "I think you're being a little overly dramatic."

I shut the door in his face. "Then I guess you won't want to have dinner with me either, since I'm so overly dramatic."

His fingers tap on the door. "Come on now, don't get me wrong. I like the drama. It's exciting. Why don't you let me in there so I can take your clothes off? You're getting me all excited with your spitfire attitude. I've never seen you like this, but I have to say, it's pretty sexy."

I'm trying really hard to stay mad at him, while my heart melts into goo. I know what he's trying to do, but it's not going to work. "Go away. I'm not getting naked with you."

"Please. I really miss you. You've been gone all day."

"No." I regret my words as soon as they're gone from my mouth, but I'm not taking them back. I'm not in the mood to have my ruffled feathers smoothed down.

"I wrote a new song. I'd love for you to hear it. I'm going to play it at dinner tonight."

My heart leaps. I crack the door open. "You are not."

He points at me. "Gotcha."

I try to slam the door in his face, but he puts his foot in the way and blocks it. He reaches in with his arm and slides it around my waist, pressing the door open more and pulling me up against him. He kisses me right on the mouth and then glares at me. "Get your butt downstairs and come say hi to these people. They're guests at the farm, and you're supposed to be nice to them. And besides . . . I know you'll regret not doing it. You're a good girl and you love your family."

I narrow my eyes at him. "Those men are *not* my family."

"I was talking about your sisters and moms, sassy girl." He gives me a playful spank on the butt.

All I can think about is mutiny, saying no, and maybe even slapping his silly handsome face just for good measure, but then he kisses me again, softer this time. And then again and again. Pretty soon I'm mush in his arms.

"I don't think they're very nice people," I finally say when he gives me a moment to speak.

"Maybe they're not, but you'll never know if you don't go out and see for yourself."

I frown in frustration. "Why is everybody trying to make me do things I don't want to do?"

"Nobody's going to *make* you do anything. But the people who love you are going to encourage you to do the right thing. Just like you do for me, just like you do for your sisters."

"I'm feeling very manipulated right now."

"Love can be a great manipulator at times, that's for sure. But I'm not going to trick you into doing anything that's wrong for you; you can trust me on that."

His words ring so true, I cannot ignore them. He's the only one who's been willing to listen to me and actually talk to me about how I feel. He left me up here to work this out on my own, but now he's here working through it *with* me, and I know it wasn't easy for him to deal with all those people—the band, my mothers, my sisters, and Sadie—on his own.

We hold hands, our fingers lacing together, and I stare into his eyes. "Why do you care so much?"

"I don't know. Why do you care so much about me?"

"Don't turn my question back on me; just answer it."

He sighs and looks at me with such tenderness that it almost makes me weep. "I care about you because you're special. You're not like other women. Remember? You told me that the first time I met you."

I can't help but smile. He is so crafty. "I told you so." I pause. "Did you talk to your brother?"

"Yes, I did." He smiles.

"Are you going to tell me what you said? And what he said?"

"Maybe later." He reaches around and smacks my butt again. "Come on. Brush your ratty hair and then come downstairs and say hello."

"Hey. Don't talk about my hair like that." I reach up and touch my head, finding a big knot in the back. "Oh, damn."

He pinches my cheek and walks away. "I'll be waiting for you." He goes down the stairs, and his footsteps trace across the living room floor to the front door before I lose track of the sound of them.

Sam is not the most outgoing person in the world, but he's down there mingling with these people who are offering him a chance at a whole new life that will make it possible for him to raise Sadie without financial worries. It can't be easy for him, all that pressure. And I've been up here feeling sorry for myself and leaving him to do it all on his own. I'm ashamed of myself, thinking of how stubborn and unbending I've been. I believe Sam's impression of Amber . . . that she hasn't been totally forthright with the band about my feelings. It would be just like her to try and trick all of us into having a conversation I've been avoiding.

I hate her and I love her for her actions. I know why she's doing it; she thinks she's helping me move past my anger. She's doing this out of love for me. But it distresses me that she doesn't respect me enough to listen to what I'm saying and do as I ask. She and I are going to have to have a conversation about that. The time has passed in our lives when she can do this to me. It was fine when we were girls, but we're not kids anymore. I'm my own person, and it's high time she respected that.

I don't want to go down there and mingle with our guests, but I do want to be there for Sam. That's what gets my feet moving toward the bathroom so I can brush my teeth and my hair. I even go back to my room and put on a fresh pair of jeans and a T-shirt. I'm not going to wear anything too nice... I'm not interested in showing off for anyone, but I don't need to embarrass myself either.

I'm going to go out there and be myself—the real Emerald... shy and quiet, but determined to live her life on her own terms. I'll show the members of Red Hot that they walked away from somebody pretty special when they let my mom leave without a word. It's something they can never get back, and it's sad, but it's our reality, and I'm not going to hide from it anymore. I'm not going to be afraid of it any longer either. And I am not going to let it rule my feelings, thoughts, or emotions anymore. *Watch out Red Hot, because here I come.*

CHAPTER FORTY-FIVE

The entire front yard is a hive of activity. Each of my moms squeals when they see me, running over to give me a group hug. Somebody must've told them to leave me alone when I was up in my room, because I can tell by this welcome that they were chomping at the bit to see me. It eases some of the pain in my chest.

They look amazing, just like Amber said. They each have a new hairstyle, all of them way more modern and attractive than what I've seen the whole time I've known them. Sally has even gotten rid of her braids, her hair so short now that there's no chance of flyaway frizzies framing her face. I kind of miss her lost and confused look, actually. She's still my mom, but then again, she's kind of not anymore; she's a sophisticated woman, very alive and animated, talking nonstop about their trip and the music. I can't get a word in edgewise. They're wearing new clothing, too; my mother Carol even has high heels on, which is a first as far as I can remember.

Several of the guests who are seasonal regulars are busy carrying platters of food out the front door. Rather than get caught up in greeting everyone else who got off the circus bus, I detach myself from the moms and walk back to the house and into the kitchen.

"Can I help?" I ask a man who's turned away from me.

He spins around, and I find myself face-to-face with Greg Lister. I'm taken aback. *What's he doing here?*

He points at the table in the middle of the room. "I think those dishes need to be taken outside."

The last time I saw him, he was wearing a three-piece suit and driving a really fancy car, but today he's in jeans and a collared shirt. I almost don't recognize him. I walk past him, weirded out by his total change, grabbing the biggest casserole I can lift and taking it out without a word. It seems that nothing is the same anymore, not even the stuffed shirt.

Smitty comes to the door and smiles at me as I pass by. "Hello, Sleeping Beauty. You finally decided to join us, eh?"

Okay . . . so some things haven't changed. Smitty is still underfoot and nosy. I pause to whisper loudly at him, "What are you doing here?"

"I've been hanging out here since I was five, remember?" He shakes his head. "You have such a terrible memory."

I roll my eyes. "You're impossible."

He acts like he's trying to get around me but is trapped, jogging left and then right with big arm motions. I stand still and wait for him to stop being a fool, until he finally gives up and laughs, going around me. "Don't trip on the stairs."

I swear to God that guy is a curse. I never should've gone out with him. He's like an annoying older brother, not dating material. Our one night in bed together was proof of that—a mistake I have worked for a couple years to forget without much success. I walk very carefully, almost worried that he's put some kind of voodoo curse on me that'll cause me to do a face-plant right in front of everybody. That would be just the icing I need on my cake for today.

There are five or six picnic tables all pushed together and covered in a motley mix of tablecloths. There's already a lot of food out here and much more coming from the kitchen. I don't know who put this thing together on such short notice, but it's a heck of a feast. There's a separate table with beverages and a cake. Somebody in a leather jacket is working the pump on a keg. I recognize him as the bass player in the band. I look away. I don't want to see any of those men, and they're so busy chatting among themselves they don't even notice me.

I put the casserole down on the table and turn around to go back in the kitchen. I feel someone's hand on my back and look over my shoulder, fearing who I'll find there. But it's Rose, and she grabs me into a quick hug. Relief floods through me.

"I'm so glad you came down," she says next to my ear.

"Yeah, sure."

She stops and looks closely at me, touching my cheek. "You're not happy about it, but you're here. That's what's important."

"What are you doing here?" I ask. "Shouldn't you be hiding in your clinic?"

She gives me a disapproving look. "Neither one of us needs to do any hiding; you know that." She links her arm with mine and marches us back up the stairs. "Come on, let's bring more stuff out."

Thankfully, we don't have the time or the personal space to discuss it; I'm not in the mood to dredge up the conversations I've been having in my head. I just want this night to be over with. We spend the next ten minutes clearing out the kitchen and setting up the tables outside. Everyone but us five food runners is standing around in groups, waiting for the work to be finished. The band members are part of those groups, of course—the crown princes of Asshat Nation, too good to do manual labor. For men who claim to want to get to know me, they're doing an awful good job of acting like they couldn't care less about my presence.

All three of our mothers are also a part of the do-nothing group. Apparently, their two weeks in Japan have not only caused them to forget our community spirit, it also seems to have fanned the flames of their shared passion. Seeing the way they're hanging on the band members, it's easy to imagine that they were intimate again while on tour together—groupie love 2.0.

The mean-spirited part of me thinks it's sad, how easy they are . . . how easy it is for them to forget the past as long as Red Hot is there whispering nonsense in their ears. But then the part of me that isn't so mean, the part who loves my moms with all her heart, is glad to see them so happy. They deserve that. I just wish it wasn't those turds making it happen for them.

"If everybody could grab a drink and take a seat, that would be great," Amber yells out.

The crowd moves to follow her instructions, some of them headed for a seat at the tables and others to the beverage area. I make sure to choose a spot as far away from the band members and Lister as possible. They're gathered on the far left end and I'm at the right. Sam is next to me and Sadie next to him. Rose is on my other side.

Amber chooses a seat across the table from us but doesn't look at me. I think she's avoiding eye contact, so I stare, willing her to look at me . . . willing her to explain herself. I know this is her doing, this big meal being served up family style, where everyone pretends everything is hunky-dory. She might think she's created a Thanksgiving-type feast, but it feels more like a Last Supper to me.

Ignoring me completely, Amber stands behind her chair and grabs her drink, banging on it with her fork. Everyone pipes down and looks at her.

"I just want to thank everybody for coming tonight. We put this thing together at the last minute, but it looks like it turned out pretty well anyway. Thanks to all of our cooks." She lifts her drink at several of the guests who apparently helped make the food. Everybody cheers except me.

"I want to issue a very special welcome to the members of Red Hot, my moms' favorite band from waaaay back in the day."

More cheers go up, but none of them are coming from me or Rose this time. I love the sister solidarity, especially because I thought it had gone forever.

"I'd also like to especially welcome Sam and Sadie." She looks directly at them and then at me. Then she lifts her eyes to the group.

"Sam is going to be doing some really exciting work with the band, and we're thrilled he's found a nice, tranquil place to do his thing. Welcome to Glenhollow Farms."

She raises her drink to Sam, and he returns the gesture. He glances at me and puts his hand on my thigh, squeezing it a couple times before he takes a sip of his beer. I grudgingly lift my glass and do the same.

"I want to invite everybody to dig in, and then, after dinner, we have a really special surprise." She looks out over the group of diners before resting her gaze on Sam. "Sam has agreed to play a new song for us. Something he *just* finished writing today."

I nearly drop my glass, I'm so surprised. Sam lifts his beer at Amber and then at the band.

"You weren't joking?" I ask softly.

He shakes his head. "I told you. Now's your chance to give me my two hundred bucks."

"What do you mean?" I hiss. "This isn't the farmers' market!"

"I play a song, you draw a picture. A deal's a deal." He winks at me.

"What?" *Bamboozled.* I've been totally bamboozled. And Amber's in on it too, I know she is. She's purposely avoiding eye contact with me, but I know she hears what he's saying.

Sadie leans over and taps me on the arm. "Are you going to draw a picture?"

I want to say no, but she looks so excited, I force myself to smile. "Maybe?"

She grins big. "I want to make a picture too. Can I draw a picture with you?"

How can I say no to that? I look at Sam, but he's shrugging. I don't think he had anything to do with this part of the ambush. "Sure, Sadie," I say, my heart shrinking down to the size of a raisin. "You can draw a picture with me." In front of all these people. In front of *them.*

For the rest of the meal, I panic about exposing my innermost self to this huge group of strangers—not the least of whom are the daughter abandoners—while Sadie prattles on about what her picture will contain. By the time dessert comes, a warm apple cobbler served with vanilla ice cream, we know that her picture will include all of the animals on the farm and several of the people as well. I'm not sure I have a big enough piece of paper for her.

"You ready to rock 'n' roll?" Sam asks, squeezing my thigh as he pushes his empty dessert plate away.

I elbow him in the ribs.

He jumps in surprise. "Yowza, watch the elbows, lady." He's rubbing his side as he smiles deviously at me. "What's the matter? You nervous?"

I busy myself with folding my napkin and organizing the dirty dishes around me as I prepare myself to fight back. I feel like I'm going to vomit. "Nervous? Ha! You'd better have your game face on, butthead. I'm going to draw a kick-ass picture, no problem, but when you get up there in the limelight, you're gonna freeze and not be able to sing your song, and then what are you gonna do? Pay me two hundred bucks, *that's* what."

I expect him to trash-talk me back, but nothing comes. I look at him and find stark fear on his face.

My heart plummets. I am a complete jackass, letting my nerves turn me into a spiteful witch. "Sam, I'm so sorry. I was only kidding. You're going to be fine."

He shakes his head and forces a smile. "What? Yeah. It's fine. I'm cool. I'm totally going to win this bet." He does not sound confident at all.

I want to comfort him and apologize a thousand times, but I know that'll only make things worse. Without another word, I get up from the table as everybody else is finishing their dessert. As soon as I get inside the house, I run up the stairs to my bedroom and scramble through my bag until I find what I'm looking for.

I shove the two items I located into the pocket of a big jacket that I put over my shoulders. It's getting cold outside and I'll soon be freezing my buns off. I grab a sweater and a blanket for Sadie before heading downstairs and out to my painting studio.

I collect two canvases, a rag, several paintbrushes, two empty plastic cups, and several tubes of paint for me and Sadie. Neither of us is going to create a masterpiece tonight, but it doesn't matter. All that matters is that we show up. Sam needs us, and we're not going to let him down. I bring all the stuff out to a clear area next to the picnic tables and set the canvases down, taking my time to balance them on chairs that serve as makeshift easels.

Sadie comes over, hopping like a bunny, her face glowing with excitement. "Is that for me? Is that for *me*?" She points at the canvas and squeals.

"Yep. Here." I hand her the cups, hoping that giving her a job will help calm her down. "Go fill these halfway with water and then come right back. We need to get started soon before it gets too dark."

She races off, yelling at the top of her lungs, "Water, water, water!"

There are enough adults around that I don't need to worry about her accomplishing her mission. Instead, I focus on what I need to do, which is getting the acrylics ready for both of us.

I'm probably going to regret this; there's going to be paint everywhere. But the important thing is that Sam is able to pull off his thing tonight. Just a few notes performed in public would be better than nothing, especially because the band is here. They need to see that he can deliver. Anything but silence followed by retreat will be a success in my book. I ignore my nerves, which are jangling, and my spiking blood pressure. I've been painting all my life. I can do this. *I am not afraid. Okay, so I'm terrified. But I'm not going to let my fear stop me. Not this time.*

CHAPTER FORTY-SIX

Sam sets a chair down next to me and lowers himself into it, his guitar in his lap. He works on tuning it. Ty comes over and drops a chair next to Sam's. He also has a guitar. Sam glances up at his brother, and at first he seems angry to see him there, but then his expression smooths out, replaced by a half smile. Sam lifts his beer and the brothers touch bottles, taking long swigs before they settle in with their guitar tuning again.

There's electricity in the air, making my skin feel especially sensitive and tingly. I'm nervous both for him and myself. A crowd starts to gather as the guys play a couple chords.

Sadie arrives with the water, walking very carefully and handing it to me when she gets close. I set the cups down on a tree stump between us, and she sits next to me in her chair. I make sure she has her sweater on and the blanket over her legs before I let her pick up a paintbrush.

"Imagine what you want to paint before you start," I say. "Make outlines and then fill them in."

She holds her paintbrush out at the canvas and nods sagely. "I know. I did this before, a million and twenty times."

I leave Little Picasso to her own devices and focus on the blank canvas in front of me. It suddenly hits me that a couple dozen eyes are staring at me and I've never let anyone watch me work before. I think

I now know what it feels like to stand at the top of a very high cliff in a bathing suit, preparing to take a fifty-foot dive. I'm panicking. My ears are on fire. I think I'm going to barf. Or pee. Or both.

And then someone plays something discordant. I glance over and see that it's Sam. He's frowning down at his guitar. I think he feels sick like me. When the note finally stops ringing out, his body goes completely tense, and it looks like he's about to get up and run.

"Tonight!" I announce loudly to the group. "I am going to paint . . . a tree!" I point with my paintbrush like Babe Ruth did with his bat to signify the home run he was about to hit. "That tree, right over there." Everyone turns away from Sam to see what I'm gesturing at, leaving him to play without their scrutiny.

I quickly dig into my jacket pockets and pull out the items I took from the bag in my room. One of them I put on my face, and the other I pop into its full size and use to tap Sam's arm.

He looks over at me in confusion, surprise, and then in slow happiness. He takes the Abraham Lincoln hat from me and places it on his head. "Thanks, babe."

"I've got your back," I say, pushing the black plastic glasses up on the bridge of my nose. The fake mustache tickles my upper lip, and the rubber nose stinks like something I don't want to think about, but I'm keeping it on, no matter what. Sam was right . . . it helps to hide behind a mask when fifty people are staring at you and expecting you to perform.

I go back to my canvas and Sam begins to strum his guitar. Ty joins in, playing backup. I take my paintbrush and pull up some dark paint, brown mixed with black. My plan is to start with the tree's roots and work my way up. Just like I'm doing with myself. First I learn to harness my fear, and then I alone define who I have become. Easy peasy, lemon squeezy.

"I like your new glasses," Sadie says. "Can I try?"

I pause to let her wear them. She can't see her masterpiece through the big, furry eyebrows, though, so she returns them. "Here you go. I have to paint now."

I put the disguise back on, ignoring the titters and stares, and continue with my painting. I find courage in Sam sitting next to me battling his demons. More music comes from the guitars, not just chords now but an organized melody. I've never heard this tune before, but it instantly catches my attention, making me think of the first time I met Sam and the strange feelings he kindled in me from the moment he walked into my sister's foyer. My drawing of the tree comes out of nowhere while most of my attention rests on the music. Painting has never come so easy to me before, and here I am doing it in front of people for the first time in my life. I'm participating in what feels like a true miracle.

The song is beautiful. I'm stunned by how well these two men play together when they haven't done it in years and Ty's never heard the song before. Heck, as far as I know, they haven't even had time to have a meaningful conversation yet, let alone time to heal the wounds between them. It must come from the years of playing together and growing up in the same environment, sharing the same history.

Sam is angry with his father for how he forced them to play all those years, but there is a bright side to his misery; the magical connection between these brothers is undeniable, and it's hard to imagine it could have grown from anything other than all those hours they spent practicing and learning together.

I'm working on the branches of my tree, the bark lumpy and twisted. They reach toward the sky, searching for something. Sustenance. Something they can't live without. It makes me wonder what sustains me. Is it this place? The love of my family? The feelings I have for Sam and Sadie? It sure feels like it. I use shadows to bring out extra dimension, because nothing can be bright without some darkness to make it stand out in relief. Several people move around behind our chairs to watch over my shoulder, but it doesn't bother me, because I'm more interested in the music than what they're thinking about my work. Inspiration has struck; my muse has returned to my life and she's come in the form of a man and his child and the boundless love they've shared with me. My brushstrokes are effortless.

Sam starts to sing, and my heart stops beating for a few moments. *God, his voice is gorgeous.* And he can't perform in public? What a horrible, rotten shame. The world should be able to hear what I'm hearing right now. It's beautiful. He's speaking about darkness and pain and then light and hope. In my heart I know he's remembering Madison. His lyrics say he's dreaming of the day he'll feel the warmth of love on his skin again, like the sun on a tree's leaves.

I look at what I'm painting, and I see both Sam and myself there on the canvas. For us to be like this strong tree, surviving all the seasons year after year, we need to put down strong roots and reach for the sky. We need to stretch out of our comfort zones to find that sustenance, the things that keep us alive. Not just living but really *alive*. I feel very alive right now . . . probably more than I ever have before. And it's all because this weirdo beardo guy made me a bet and took a chance on following me out to Glenhollow.

Ty begins to harmonize, and what was already wonderful becomes unbelievable. Why have these men not been making music together their whole lives? What split them apart and made them live on opposite sides of the country and not speak to each other? What was so awful between them that Sam didn't tell Ty he was an uncle? They must have some serious regrets right now, hearing the beauty that they're creating together. They could have just chosen to deal with their problems sooner and avoided all the pain they've lived with instead of holding on to it.

Something tickles the back of my mind. *Regrets.* Life can be so full of them, but it's all just a choice. We don't have to have them; it's a choice we make. I pause my painting and look up. Four men are staring at me, all of them wearing leather jackets.

I go back to my canvas, flustered. I need to focus on getting this thing done. There are only a few leaves left on the original tree. The season is almost over, and it's losing parts of itself as a result. Does this tree regret the changing of the seasons? Does it wish summer would go on forever? Somehow I think the answer is no. I think the tree is smarter than I am. It knows that life must go on and we can't hold on to the past. We need to move forward into an uncertain future trusting that the seasons will keep cycling through and the leaves will come again. Beauty will reappear in another form.

I tip the few remaining leaves on my tree's branches with yellow-gold. The sun is setting around us, making everything seem a little magical. Sam and Ty's song comes to a close, and the applause it brings is even louder than the music was. People are whistling, and some have lifted their cigarette lighters up to the sky.

Now I know why the band needed Sam. He'll bring something to Red Hot's music that they've never had before. And the band will give Sam a creative outlet, a way to contribute and benefit from the fruits of his labor and the gifts God gave him. Amber was right: they need each other. And the only way it's going to happen is if everybody respects one another and can get along.

I look over at Sadie's picture to see what she's done. A huge lump rises in my throat when I see what's on the canvas: a little girl in a purple dress holding the hand of a lady with a black dress who's holding the hand of a man in a suit. There's a pig on the ground and a unicorn in the sky being ridden by a blond woman with wings and high heels.

I put my paintbrush down and fold my hands in my lap, doing my best to calm my thoughts and emotions. Sadie leans over and puts her hand on mine. "I like your tree. It's really pretty."

"Thank you. I love your picture too. Is that your mommy flying in the sky?"

Sadie nods. "And that's you and me there, with our party dresses on."

"I love your picture. I think it's much better than mine."

Sadie squints at my painting and nods. "I think so too. Maybe you should make it with more colors."

I smile and lean over so I can hug her. "I think you're right. What color should I use next?"

She picks up the purple paint and hands it to me. "Purple is my second favorite. But I think it could look really nice anyway."

I hold my paintbrush out and use it to point at the canvas. "Tell me where."

She points at the lower corner nearest her. "Right there. You need more flowers."

I dab the paint on the canvas as she instructed. "You're absolutely right. This picture is way too boring. I need more flowers in my life."

She giggles. "Not in your life, silly. On your paper."

"Oh, yeah. Silly me. On my paper."

She stops grinning and looks up at me. "But maybe in your life, too. People can be like flowers, right?"

I lean over and touch her nose. "Yes. You are a very pretty flower. A pink and purple one."

She points at my painting. "Right by your tree."

Emotion hits me right in the gut. This dark and twisted tree, sad over losing its leaves, looks so much happier with a pretty little flower under it.

I can't paint anymore; it's just too much for me. But this painting is done enough, so that's okay. Rome wasn't built in a day, right? I put my paintbrush down and quickly wipe the tears from under the silly glasses before anyone notices they're there.

Sam leans over to look at what I've done. "I guess we'll have to call this a draw."

Seized by emotion toward Sam and his daughter, I grab him by the cheeks and kiss him right on the mouth. We get lots of catcalls and whistles. "Yeah, I guess it's a draw," I say when we pull apart. I take my disguise off and set it to the side of my makeshift easel.

We're suddenly surrounded by everybody exclaiming over the multimedia performance, even the band members. I accept the compliments about my painting but move away as soon as I can. I know they mean well and they're being very kind, but it's just too overwhelming for me. I feel like my life is tumbling down a hill, turning into a giant snowball. It's not that this is a terrible thing, but it's just a lot to take in, especially for someone whose life—up until she met Sam Stanz anyway—was ever so predictable and unexciting.

I walk up the front steps to the house, stopping on the porch to look out over the crowd, amazed at what's happening to my life. My moms are mingling with the men they've loved their whole lives, even from afar . . . the ones they kept from being our fathers for twenty-five years. My pregnant sister Amber is hugging her man to her—a guy she met mere months ago—and kissing him right on the mouth in front of everyone, not at all ashamed of her feelings for him. Rose is deep in conversation with Greg Lister—the attorney who arrived in our lives three months ago as the bearer of bad news—neither of them paying attention to the craziness around them. Children are playing tag, Sadie at the center of it. Various other adults are busy eating apple cobbler, drinking coffee, and enjoying the relaxing night together. Someone is strumming a guitar.

I'm standing off to the side because I'm more comfortable not being the center of attention, but I know I belong here. These are my people. Right now, no one in this crowd is excluded from that group either. When the Universe talks to me, I need to listen, and right now it's telling me that I am being handed a gift . . . a way to move out from under a pile of regrets . . . if only I will take a risk and let people in. There's nowhere else in the world that I'd rather be than here. I just hope it doesn't mean that I have to be without Sam and Sadie, because they are my people too. I want them in my life for more than just a few more days; tonight proved that to me.

Sam is the golden sun outlining the tips of the leaves on my tree of life, and Sadie is the little purple flower at the base of it. Without them, my life would be boring and lonely, and I'm tired of having that kind of existence. Comfortable and scared is no longer going to cut it for me.

CHAPTER FORTY-SEVEN

I'm so mesmerized by the view that I don't realize there's a man standing below me until he speaks. "Rapunzel, Rapunzel, throw down your long hair."

"Go away, Smitty." I can't be mad at him; he's too goofy.

"What're you doing up there? How come you're not down here with your boyfriend?"

"I'm just taking a break."

He walks up a couple of the stairs, stopping at the one just below where I am. It puts us at eye level. "You really like that guy, don't you?"

"Yes, I do." It feels good to admit that out loud to someone, even if it's only Smitty.

"I'm happy for you."

"Are you?" I look at him, trying to read his thoughts. He sounds genuine, but you never know with him. He likes to tease and mess around.

"Yeah, sure I am. I mean, if it doesn't work out, and I'm not seeing anyone, maybe we can go out again; but, hey, if you're happy, I'm happy."

I roll my eyes. *Typical Smitty*.

Another voice comes from a spot below where Smitty is standing. "Hey, man. You moving in on my woman?" Sam is there, looking flushed from his win.

I hold out my hand toward him. "Come up here and see what you did."

Sam climbs the steps, slapping Smitty on the back pretty hard on his way up. "Sorry, man. Looks like I got the girl."

Smitty shrugs him off, smiling good-naturedly. "That's fine. You two look good together, and everyone knows Em has a soft spot for guitar players. Have a good one." Smitty wanders back into the crowd and picks up a cup of beer.

Sam stands next to me, putting his arm around my waist and looking out over the group. "What's he talking about?"

"Oh, he's just being a fool. He used to tease me about going into the bar in town to listen to the music. He tried to learn to play guitar, but he was all thumbs."

"You still have feelings for him?"

I laugh. "No. I never really did. He was just . . . there. Besides, he's just messing around. He's dating a girl in town named Tanya." I point to the crowd below. "Look."

"What are we looking at?"

"We're looking at your people." I fold my arms over my waist, feeling very content.

"My people?"

"Yes. Every one of them was listening to you play, and they were loving it. They're your fans. They get you."

He looks down at me. "I don't give a damn what they thought about my song; I only care what *you* thought."

I look at him so he knows I'm being honest. "I loved it. Really, it was amazing. It helped me paint that tree. I thought I was going to have to run, but the music helped me through it. I had no idea you were so talented." I pause to take his hand. "And I know you're angry with your father for forcing you to play all those years, but he was right about one thing: you have a gift from the heavens, and it would be a crying shame not to share it with the world. It was really brave of you to stick it out. I know performing in front of them wasn't easy for you."

He shrugs. "It was no big deal."

"*Please*. You aren't fooling me for a second." I sigh and shake my head. *Men*. "You were scared shitless. You almost took off."

He laughs good-naturedly. "I can't put anything over on you, can I?"

"Nope."

"That was a nice save, by the way. Making everybody look over at that tree. Good call."

I shrug. "I do what I can. Some people call me an artist, some people call me a superhero. I don't like to put labels on it."

He turns me around so we're facing each other and wraps his arms around me. "I like this place. I hope you'll let me stay for a while."

I want to shout and cheer, but I remain cool. "Well, *you* can stay, but I don't know about that other riffraff over there." I tilt my head toward the band's bus. I smile so he knows I'm mostly kidding.

He rubs my back for a few seconds and then pulls away, resting his hands on my shoulders as he looks into my eyes. "If it's okay with you, they're hoping to stay for a couple weeks too. Your moms invited them. They're not going to stay forever; it's just so we can jam a bit and see where it goes."

I sigh, knowing I have no choice. I've been outvoted by my moms and Sam has asked; there's no way I can say no to either of them. And I'm not even sure that I want to anymore. "That's fine. Whatever." I break away and start walking toward the house, but his hand on my arm pulls me back.

"Will you do me one favor?" he asks.

"Maybe."

He tugs my arm. "Hmmm. Maybe? That's not good enough. What if I promise to love your body all over tonight, at least two times? Will you do me a favor then?"

How can I say no to that? I try not to grin but fail. "Okay, yes. I can *try*." *Ugh, I'm so easy.* But he does have a way with those hands and that tongue of his, so I can't be blamed.

"Would you just hear them out? I'm not saying that you should believe them, or that what they're going to say makes any sense . . . I just want you to give it one fair chance so you won't have any regrets later."

He's looking at me with what could be love in his eyes. Amber's glancing up at me from the crowd and looking so hopeful. Rose is staring at me too, giving me a thumbs-up. It's like the whole world is conspiring to make me a better person, to force me into letting go of my bitterness and turn the page.

"Fine. I'll do it for you." *And for them. And for me.*

He pulls me into a big hug and kisses the top of my head. I'm thinking about begging him to come to the bedroom with me now, even though the party is only half over, when there's a commotion out in the driveway that grabs our attention.

Sam pulls out of our embrace, and we walk over to the edge of the porch to see what's going on.

CHAPTER FORTY-EIGHT

Amber comes up the stairs with a strange look in her eye, holding out her arm toward me. "Go inside."

Rose is right behind her.

"Why? Who is that?" A man in a leather jacket and jeans with long, ratty hair gets out of a sports car that's parked in the driveway behind the tour bus. He looks familiar, but I don't know why because I'm pretty sure I've never met him.

"Just go inside," Amber says. "He'll be leaving very soon."

The band members and Lister head straight for him, and even though we're losing what little daylight we have left, I can still see that none of them are happy.

I stand firm. "I'm not going anywhere until someone tells me what's going on." It's not like the guy has a gun on him or anything. I don't think he could even fit a knife in pants that tight.

Amber stops at the top of the stairs and waits for Rose to join her before she speaks again. "You said you didn't want to get involved in their stuff and you didn't want to talk about the past."

"So?" Amber is making no sense. "What's that guy got to do with any of that?"

Sam leaves us to run down the stairs, going over to join his brother, who's standing at the back of the group of men in front of the newcomer. Rose is on my right and Amber is on my left.

"That," says Amber, "is the man who ruined our lives. His name is Darrell Ford."

"It's the guy who told the media about you," Rose says to Amber.

"The one who was in the band for the first couple years," I say, understanding dawning.

"Yes. And he's here to cause trouble, so if you don't want to be involved in all that, just go inside and let us deal with it."

I turn to frown at Amber, my bossy-pants, know-it-all sister. "I don't need to be anywhere but here, thank you very much."

She shrugs. "Fine. It's up to you. But you're going to end up hearing things you don't want to if you stick around." She moves in close and puts her arm around my waist. Rose does the same from the other side. "I'm not saying you have to go anywhere. I'm just trying to understand and respect your wishes."

I sigh, feeling defeated by her kindness. "It's not that, okay? It's just . . ." I can't explain myself. Everything I was thinking earlier seems stupid to me now.

Amber looks at me, her expression softening. "Tell me. I'm listening."

"Me too," Rose says. "If you've figured any of this out for yourself, I'd love to hear it, because I'm clueless about what to do."

"Give me your hands," I say, wiggling myself out of their sisterly hugs. They obey and slide their palms into mine. I feel stronger and steadier with them standing here. We used to go down the front steps holding hands like this all the time when we were little, running off to play together. And I know it's time to act like a grown-up, but as I delve into my feelings and innermost thoughts, I feel like I'm going to need the extra support.

"I think that life is too short to live with regrets. Our mothers have been doing it for over twenty years, and what a rotten shame that is."

Amber nods but says nothing, which I'm grateful for, because it would be so easy for me to let her take over this conversation.

"I'm hurt over the idea that a man who fathered me and supposedly loved my mother would be so casual about letting her walk out of his life. But I've spent some time with Sam, a man who lived a very sad life for a lot of years, and I see how people who weren't brought up the way we were, and who are in the throes of a huge career upswing, might lose track of what's important."

"They were manipulated," Amber says.

I close my eyes and sigh. "Amber . . . you are their biggest champion . . ."

She opens her mouth to protest, but I cut her off. "No . . . let me finish." I take a breath before continuing. "You are their biggest champion, but I trust you. You and Rose are my rocks, and you have been since we were born. That's never going to change."

Amber sniffs, but I can't look at her or I'll never finish. I stare at the tree I did this evening so I can get through it. "If you believe they are kind men, I will believe it until they give me firsthand reason not to. I will hear them out. I promised Sam I would do that. But you need to understand that I am not you. I am not an extrovert who feels like she can solve everyone's problems. I'm just me. So I can't promise that I'm going to believe them or that I'm going to forgive them for not being a part of our lives or that I'm going to make much of an effort beyond just listening."

Rose squeezes my hand and I take that as support.

"We all know that we had a great life here. So much better than many other people. But I can't help wondering what it could have been like if they had known we were alive. If they had bothered to just say, 'Screw all the fame and fortune,' and come after our moms all those years ago."

"Can I say something?" Rose asks.

"Yes." I nod and look at her. Her eyes are full of tears.

"You and I have been on the same page since the beginning of this mess. I think we're more reserved when it comes to people we don't know in general, but I've also been very busy with work and not really willing to let this stuff take up space in my head. But with the way things are going . . . with Amber pregnant and Ty being a part of the band and maybe Sam too in some way . . . I think it would be a mistake to continue to remain indifferent. Or to try to remain indifferent. I don't think either of us was unaffected by this, even though it's been taking place for the most part in another state or another country altogether."

"So you agree that the band should be given a chance to share their side of the story with you?" Amber asks.

I wait for Rose's confirmation. It sure seems like that's what she's saying.

"Yes. But I'd also like to talk to Ted, because it seems like he was the key player in this fiasco. I believe he has more insight than anyone."

"Unfortunately, I'm not sure that's ever going to happen," Amber says.

"Why?" I ask.

"Because. He got fired. He's not going to want to talk to anyone. In fact, we just got word that he's suing the band for wrongful termination."

I snort in disgust. "Good luck with that."

"I know," Amber says. "And the kicker is, he's asking for thirty million bucks."

"That can't be a coincidence," Rose says.

"No, of course it isn't. I guess he figures if we're worth thirty mil, he is too."

"What a pig," I say. As if the value of our stolen fathers could equal his punishment of being fired for being a homewrecker extraordinaire.

"But you can talk to the band and you can talk to Lister too. Lister wasn't around when everything went down, but he's been with them for a long time, and he knows Darrell."

We all look over at the man who's in a heated discussion with Red Wylde, the band's singer and head decision-maker.

"What is he doing here?" Rose asks Amber. "Do you know?"

"What he's always doing when he comes around: causing trouble."

He yells something, and everyone stops talking to turn around and look at us. The crowd is silent.

"What did he just say?" I ask.

"I don't know," Amber says, letting go of my hand. "But I'm going to go find out."

"Not without me, you're not," I say, hurrying to catch up with her.

"Hey! Wait for me!" Rose whisper-yells, clomping down the stairs behind me.

CHAPTER FORTY-NINE

When we arrive at the scene, the band looks like they're ready to fight this guy Darrell Ford. But he's not afraid; he's standing his ground, pointing his finger at Red's face while Lister and Ty hold them apart.

"What's going on?" Amber demands, pushing past our mothers, who are standing on the outskirts of the crowd, looking not just concerned but fascinated. I can't tell if it's their groupie reaction to seeing Darrell again or just their interest in the drama. I suppose they stand to learn some new things about their pasts, too, assuming Darrell is here to spill some beans.

"Babe, it's probably better if you guys just go inside the house and wait," Ty says, grunting with the effort of holding on to Red. Two more members of the band join him.

"Don't you dare tell me to go be a quiet little girl in the other room," she says, hands on her hips. "Surely you know me better than *that*." She turns her attention to Darrell. "What are you doing here? I don't remember inviting you."

"Since when does anyone need to be invited to Glenhollow Farms?" His smile is more of a sneer. His voice is rough, but I don't think it's from emotion. It's more likely from a heavy-duty smoking habit from the sound of it.

"Since today. So you can head out right now, because you're not welcome."

"I think my daughter might say different." He looks right at me.

Everyone freezes for a few seconds. Then they all twist their heads and stare at me.

I point at my chest. "Who . . . me?"

"Yeah, you, Rose. You're my daughter."

I bark out a laugh of relief. "Ha!" My hand flies up to my mouth and I feel my eyes bug out of my head as I turn to look at Rose. Her nostrils are flaring and her eyes narrowing.

"You are not my father," Rose says in a low, angry tone.

He frowns. "What?"

I point at my sister. "That's Rose. I'm Emerald."

Darrell sags a little. "Oh. Well, fine then. I'll ask her." He looks at Rose. "You mind if I hang out for a while at the farm?"

She shakes her head slowly from side to side for a few seconds, but then she stops, shocking the you-know-what out of me with her next words. "Actually . . . I'd like to speak with you. Why don't you come inside?" She gestures at him and then turns, heading for the house.

"You can't be serious," Ty says as Rose walks by.

"Oh, yes I can," Rose says, sounding as determined as she did the day she announced that she was going to open a clinic in a rickety old outbuilding on the edge of our property that the city was trying to condemn.

The crowd dissipates as Darrell is allowed to follow Rose. I run to get past him and reach my sister as she's opening the front door and stepping inside.

"What's the plan?" I ask, trying and failing to catch my breath.

"I have no idea," she says, her voice shaking.

I grab her hand and lead her over to the couch, pulling her down beside me. "We've got this. I'm with you." Of course I'd rather be up in my room with the door locked, but there is no way in hell I'd abandon my sister right now. How this guy can think he's her father is a big mystery, but we are soon going to find out what's going on in his head, at least. I'm actually glad that Rose had the foresight to give him a chance to explain himself. Maybe he can help solve some of the riddles that have plagued our lives without us even knowing.

She squeezes my hand, and we both look up to see not only Darrell, but Lister, Ty, the rest of the band, and our mothers and Amber walking in too. It's standing-room only for the final showdown at Glenhollow Farms.

CHAPTER FIFTY

Darrell holds out his hands toward the three of us sisters. "I'm going to start out by saying that I'm sorry if I ruined your big event here." He glances over his shoulder toward the front door and the rest of the guests who are milling around outside.

Just then Sam appears in the doorway holding Sadie on his hip. He walks in and holds up his free hand. "Sorry. Just coming through. Got to put the little one to bed." He touches my shoulder on the way past, and I reach up to pat his fingers and let him know I'm okay before he continues on.

Darrell waits until Sam is gone before he speaks again. "I know you all want me gone from here, and I get it. I've been a thorn in some of your sides for a long time." He glances at his former bandmates.

Red grunts but doesn't look at him.

I go back to staring at Darrell, wondering if any of his features remind me of my sister. It's hard to say. Maybe they have the same face shape . . .

"But there's a reason for me being here. I need to speak my piece." He looks right at Rose as he explains. "Back when Sally and the others were around, things were good for us." He glances at Rose's mom—who's looking a little shell-shocked with her mouth hanging partway open—before going back to his story. "Maybe too good. We were riding high on emotion and good times, writing good music together, living the life . . . but then it all caught up to us."

Red opens his mouth to speak, but a hand on his arm stops him. This time it's Ty putting on the brakes as he slowly shakes his head and warns his bandmate to let Darrell have his say. I'm amazed when Red listens.

"We started making waves with our music. A lot of money and offers were coming in. Drugs were being handed out like candy." He glares at the band members, almost daring them to deny it; but they say nothing. Mooch looks like he feels a little guilty over that statement, which lends it more credence in my mind.

"Ted and I talked a lot about it," Darrell says. "We both thought the environment was getting toxic."

"That wasn't their fault," Red blurts out. "The girls had nothing to do with that."

For a moment I think he's talking about us, but then I realize when our mothers share a look that he means them. My heart hurts for them, that a man they cared about saw them as a problem.

"I'm not saying it was their fault, but they were a part of it," Darrell insists, his voice rising. "They didn't bring the drugs in, but they participated. They encouraged the whole . . . environment or whatever. And you did too." He runs his hand over his head, clearly frustrated as he glares at Red. "You can deny it all you want now, but I remember, and so does Ted."

I'm not surprised by Darrell's statements. The fact that our mothers were smoking pot and being very free with themselves and their time with these men is not news to me. Our mothers have been very honest about what happened . . . or they have been since Lister entered our lives. I refuse to be angry with them over their past lies by omission. My mother once said that motherhood makes liars of us all, and I get it. Sometimes it's better if kids don't know the truth about things like

Santa Claus, the Tooth Fairy, and rocker fathers who didn't want them around.

"It still doesn't make it okay," Cash says.

Darrell responds. "All I did was point out to you guys that having the girls around was keeping all of you . . . all of *us* . . . from doing our best work. They used to inspire us to write, but then they just inspired us to party."

Barbara and Carol wipe tears from their eyes, but Sally is staring at the floor. I wish I could see what's going through her mind as she wrings her hands and taps her foot. I'd like to hug all of them right now. This is a part of their shared pasts that obviously makes them feel terrible. What I see is a tragedy. So much of this pain they all caused—both the band and our mothers—could have been avoided if they had all just communicated better . . . and more lovingly. The men carelessly threw around the statement that wives and children would never be welcome in their lives, and our mothers selfishly kept the existence of their pregnancies to themselves. There are no innocent parties in this, other than my sisters and me, of course.

Guilt niggles at me when I realize that I can only be putting myself in that innocent category if I'm not one of the people making the problem continue or making it worse, which means I have to ensure that I'm not repeating their mistakes. In other words, I need to be a better communicator, or I'm no better than they were twenty-six years ago. The idea makes a knot form in the pit of my stomach.

"That's not fair," Red says in a low voice. "They didn't make us do anything. We all partied by choice. Grown men make choices about doing drugs; they aren't forced into things."

"Fair has nothing to do with it." Darrell focuses on Rose, Amber, and me. "You have to understand . . . Life back then for us was nuts. We were young. Too young to be dealing with the pressure being put on us. Ted was just as young as we were. When he found out your mothers were pregnant, he came to me with an idea and I agreed it was the best thing for everyone."

"You knew and you didn't tell us!" Red yells, right before leaping on him.

It takes three men to pull him off and five minutes of shouting to calm things down enough for Darrell to be able to speak again.

He pulls down the bottom of his jacket and makes a big show of smoothing his hair before he starts again. "Yeah. I knew they were pregnant. And I also knew if they kept spending time around all those drugs, they were going to be tempted to use them while they were carrying those babies, and it was going to be the end of everything."

"You were involved in sending them away," Red says, his voice hoarse with emotion. "I'm glad we kicked your ass out of the band. A thousand times glad." All his bandmates are nodding, even Ty.

Sally lifts her head and steps forward, holding out her hand. "Stop."

I blink a few times, wondering where this is going. Sally never makes herself the center of attention.

Rose squeezes my hand so hard it cracks one of my knuckles. "Sorry," she whispers.

"Listen . . . ," Sally says, "I can see where this is headed, and I don't think it's going to help anyone to point fingers and play the blame game. Fact is, Barbara, Carol, and I knew what we were doing. We were pregnant and we weren't going to stay. We always knew our time with the band was temporary." Her smile is both endearing and sad. "It was the greatest time of our lives, except for all the moments we've spent being mothers to our three girls. Those were better. Greater. Much more important in the grand scheme of things." She holds her hands out to us and waves a little.

We wave back. I have to wipe tears from my eyes. I always thought that Red Hot came first in their minds, but I guess I was wrong. I never held it against them, but it's nice to know my sisters and I were always their favorite group.

"Ted did us a big favor," Barbara says, stepping forward to join Sally, putting her arm around her best friend's waist in support. "And Darrell did too." She glances at him and nods once. "We knew if we told you that we were pregnant that you would try to convince us to stay. And we knew we had to go. We did what we thought was right by our children." She sighs, looking down. "Maybe it was a mistake, but it doesn't feel like it."

"It wasn't," I say, filled with love for my mothers and the sacrifices they made for us. It couldn't have been easy to be that young and have to make such adult, mature decisions, particularly when I think about the environment they were living in. "We've had great lives here, and now that I've been to New York and LA, I can say with confidence that I, for one, don't belong in those places."

My sisters laugh quietly.

"Darrell," Rose says, "why do you think I'm your daughter?"

He lifts his chin. "Because I was sleeping with Sally when she got pregnant."

Red shrugs. "So was I."

Mooch lifts his finger. "Guilty."

Cash stares at the ceiling and whistles off-key.

Darrell frowns at them. "She told me she was exclusive to me."

Sally looks up, a guilty, awkward smile affixed to her face. "It's the only way I could get you to take your clothes off."

The entire room bursts out laughing, with the exception of Darrell. He just looks confused. And then he looks deflated. I elbow Rose and she elbows me back. I don't think she knew any better than I did what a vixen her mom can be. It's actually kind of hilarious to imagine sweet, scatterbrained Sally being so sneaky, just so she could get it on with a rocker.

"So, what you're saying, Mom, is that he *could* be my father," Rose states emphatically.

Everyone stops laughing.

Sally nods. "Yes. He could be."

Rose stands and shrugs. "That's all I need to know." She looks right at the man in leather. "Darrell, you are welcome to stay at Glenhollow Farms. So long as you follow the rules here, you can remain as long as you'd like." She nods once, silently daring anyone to contradict her.

I stand next to her and hold her hand. "Darrell, I don't know if my mom slept with you or not, but I don't care. If you could be my sister's father, then that's good enough for me." I look at the other men. "And as for the rest of you, I hope you won't take me ignoring you all night as a sign that you aren't welcome, because you are. I'm not going to lie and say that I want to be your best friend or anything, but I am curious about your lives and the choices you made, and I hope one of these days soon you'll take the time to share your thoughts and histories with me."

"It'd be my honor," Red says, putting his hand on his heart.

"And mine," Mooch says.

"Add me to the mix," Cash says. "And even though Keith is no longer with us, I know right now he's looking down on us and smiling. He'd be proud of you right now. All of you girls. And your moms."

Amber stands and holds on to my other hand. She looks at me and leans in to kiss my cheek. "Thank you," she whispers.

I don't say anything. I'm not doing this just for her. I'm doing this for all of us—her, Rose, me, our mothers . . . these men who had daughters taken from them without knowing, or so I hear. Our story is complicated and messy, made up of layer upon layer of lies and misunderstandings. But it's a story that needs to be told and unwound. It's only fair that each of us knows where we came from.

One of the band members comes over to me and holds out his hand. "Hi there, Emerald. I'm Mooch."

I shake his hand, feeling suddenly nervous. "Hi, Mooch." He could be my father, and that's no small thing.

"It's such a pleasure to see you again." His eyes well up with tears, which makes me want to cry immediately. This man is revered by literally millions of people, and he's brought to tears at seeing me? *Craziness.* He moves on to Rose, and then another band member walks up.

"Remember me? I'm Cash," says the man, coming up behind Mooch. "So great to be here with you. You're as pretty as an emerald, that's for sure. We didn't get a chance to talk last time, but maybe this trip it can be different." He shakes my hand too.

"Thanks. Sure." I look down, too shy to comment any more than that.

He looks over his shoulder. "You remember Red." He turns to talk to Rose, and I'm left with Red approaching. He stops in front of me. I shake the tall man's hand and look into his eyes. I've seen those eyes before, but not on him. It makes my heart skip a beat.

"Nice to see you again, young lady. And can I say how much I admire the painting you did out there? You have true talent. I'm jealous. I've always wanted to be able to create something like that."

I try to smile, but my lips are quivering too much. "Thank you. It's really not a big deal."

"And she's humble too," he says softly over his shoulder to the people behind him.

I can't look at him anymore; it feels like he's seeing right into my soul.

"Paul," says a smaller man behind Red. "Not your dad, but happy to be here nonetheless." He grins big and shakes my hand as Red moves over to talk to Rose. "I joined the band after Darrell left, so I wasn't around for all the fun stuff."

Everyone laughs at that, and I have to smile too.

"So," Darrell says, clapping his hands together and rubbing them, "you got any room at the inn for me?" He looks longingly at the stairs.

"No way," Ty says, surprising everyone. "Not in the house, man."

Darrell frowns at him. "What's it to you?"

"He's right," Carol says, motioning at the door. "All of you . . . out."

Paul is smiling. Mooch and Red are frowning. Darrell looks resigned. Ty is grinning in satisfaction until my mother points at him. "That means you, too."

"But . . ."

"But nothing. The house is for ladies only. We'll see you all tomorrow. We girls need to have a powwow."

The staircase creaks and everyone turns around to see who's there. *Sam.*

"Hey!" Ty says. "If I can't stay, neither can he." He points at his brother.

Sam looks down the stairs with a guilty smile. "Say what?"

"He's an exception," Barbara says. "His baby is in the house. He needs to keep an eye on her."

Sam looks relieved for about two seconds before I speak. "No, that's okay. I can watch her."

His jaw drops as he stares at me. I can't help but laugh.

"Oh, man. She's kicking me to the curb already." He comes down the stairs smiling and joins the rest of the band in the foyer.

"Don't let the door hit you on the butts on the way out," Amber says, giggling when they grumble back at her.

CHAPTER FIFTY-ONE

When the last of them are gone, Sally shuts the front door and locks it.

"We never lock the door," Rose says, sounding a little shocked.

"I wouldn't put it past those two younger ones to try and sneak in later," she says, eyeing Amber and me.

Rose snorts. "I don't think you need to worry about them sneaking in as much as you need to worry about my sisters unlocking that door for them."

I exchange glances with Amber and smile. I'm not going to deny the fact that after everyone else is asleep I'm going to find Sam and bring him back into my bed. It's where he belongs, after all. How long he'll be able to stay there, I don't know, but what I do know is that I can't imagine ever wanting to sleep without him again.

"So, where do we go from here?" Carol asks.

"Let's sit down and talk it out," Amber says, looking excited about the prospect.

I moan. "Must we?"

Rose yawns. "I'm with Em. I'm exhausted."

"It won't take long. I just want to clear the air about a few things and get some questions answered," Barbara says. She looks as serious as I've ever seen her.

We all find seats and wait. Carol speaks first. "I know a lot of information is flying around, all of it over twenty years old. After spending two weeks with the band in Japan, a lot of things became clear to us. We made mistakes. They made mistakes. But I think we've all agreed . . ." She waits for her girlfriends to nod before continuing. "That it's pointless to try to figure out who's to blame for what. We just didn't communicate with the men we loved, and that was our biggest error. It's the one thing we will always regret."

"I don't think you should," I say.

"Why's that?" she asks. All of our mothers lean in to hear my answer.

"Because. Look at our lives." I gesture all around us. "We grew up in paradise. We're educated. We're surrounded by love and always have been. We've been allowed our privacy and safety." I pause to look at Amber, who nods. "Now we can choose how to move forward. No one is making the choice for us."

"So you're glad we came out here and lived the way we did?" Sally asks.

I nod. "Yes, I am. I wouldn't trade it for anything. Would I have loved to have a father, too? Maybe. Probably. But having those men as fathers comes with strings."

"Strings?" Carol asks.

"Yeah. Like a lack of privacy," Amber says. "You can't truly value it until it's been taken from you."

I nod, remembering how freaked out Amber was when the press was hounding her about Ty and the band. She knows how to handle them now, but in the beginning it was messy.

"I don't regret anything either," Rose says. "I'm very happy, fathers present or not." She pauses, looking at each of us in turn before continuing. "Plenty of people have fathers around who they don't like . . . men who've squashed their spirit or independence. I'm not saying these men of Red Hot would have done that, but what if they had? Or what if they were gone all the time touring and we had to live with the fact that their careers were more important to them than being with us was? Whatever . . . there are so many issues we could have had to deal with that we just didn't . . . because you all chose to leave. I love the way I was raised, and I wouldn't change that for anything."

I nod. Rose is saying exactly what's in my heart. "I second that emotion."

"And you?" Barbara asks Amber.

"I agree. I agree with all of you. Regret gets us nowhere. I don't believe any of you acted with malice, including Darrell. He was young too, don't forget, with stars in his eyes and big plans for his future. And no matter what you think about him as a person, thanks to him, we got this life together." She pauses while that sinks in. I'm almost persuaded to like the guy, even though I'm pretty sure everyone else hates him.

"Without Darrell being the jerk he was at the time . . . without the rest of the band being so self-centered . . . without our moms deciding it was best to take Ted's advice and leave without sharing their secrets . . . I never would have met Ty." She puts her hand on her belly. "And I wouldn't be having this baby." She looks up with tears in her eyes. "How can I possibly regret any of it?"

I put my arms around her and then Rose hugs us. Our moms come over and join in.

"You are such a smart little girl, my Amber," Barbara says.

"Our Amber," Carol insists.

"Yes. Ours," Sally says. "All three girls are my girls and your girls and our girls. We are the luckiest family I know."

A tiny voice comes from the stairs.

"Why is everybody hugging?"

The hug breaks up and the women wipe their wet faces as I climb a few steps to Sadie and pick her up. "Did we wake you, sweetie?"

She rubs her eyes. "Yes." She looks around. "Where's my daddy?"

"He's still outside. Do you want to see him?"

All the women are watching us, but I'm not nervous. Being with Sadie seems as natural to me as being with my sisters or my mothers.

"Can he come inside and read me a story? I miss my mommy."

"Of course he can," says Barbara, walking quickly to the door. "Sam!" she yells, after unlocking the door and throwing it open. "Sadie needs you!"

I roll my eyes as the sound of pounding feet comes to my ears. Sam mounts the steps in record time and appears red-faced in the threshold. "What's the matter?"

Sadie hangs on to my neck but holds one arm out at him. "Hug."

His face instantly relaxes as he strides over and joins our little love-fest. My heart swells to ten times its normal size, feeling like it's going to bust right out of my chest cavity as his arms wrap gently around us. Life with Sam is so good right now; I don't want it to end.

"Hey, if he gets to sleep inside, so does Ty," Amber says, pretending to sound put out.

"Fine. Call your man in. But no one else," Carol says, a smile in her voice.

"Ty! No bus for you! Come inside."

A chorus of boos follows him up. He turns around at the door and yells behind him, "See ya later, suckas!" He slams the door shut and strides over to Amber, picking her up and spinning her around. She squeals in delight and then they stop so they can make out.

"Let's get out of here," I whisper.

Sadie giggles. "They're kissing."

"I know. Gross, right?" We run over to the stairs, Sadie bouncing on my hip.

"I saw you kiss my daddy," she says, giggling some more.

"Uh-oh," I say, feeling a little guilty about that.

She puts her hands on my cheeks, making me stop our ascent up the stairs halfway. "That's okay. Because I love you and he loves you, and when people love each other, they kiss." She leans in and kisses me right on the eye.

"Oh. Okay. Now I can't see anything, but that's all right." My heart is a puddle of goo. It's both scary and amazing to have Sadie declare her love for me like this. In this moment, my life is awesome, but it could go very bad, very quickly. What will happen when she's forced to leave me, when Sam finds a place to live? It could be all the way in New York... or California, even. I have no idea what the future holds, but I'm hoping it won't need to change too much. I really love this little nugget in my arms.

She laughs and laughs, kissing me all over my face as I feel my way up the stairs.

"Somebody woke up in a good mood," Sam says.

When we get to Sadie's room, I hand her over to her dad. "Actually, this little girl woke up missing her momma, so you have been asked to read her a bedtime story before she goes back to sleep." I don't want to be so wrapped up in her love for me that I forget she's in mourning right now. My top priority, for as long as I have a say in the matter, anyway, is to make sure she's moving past her mother's death in a healthy way.

I start to leave the room, but Sam stops me by taking my hand. "Do I really get to stay?"

I nod. "I'll see you down the hall when you're done."

He nods, and there's no mistaking the smoldering look he gives me. I resist the urge to rush back to my room, walking gracefully instead. And I take my time in the bathroom, too, showering, brushing my teeth and hair, getting ready for a night like no other.

My life has taken so many twists and turns these past few weeks, it's almost unbelievable. But I handled it. And even though I was afraid throughout much of it, I stuck it out and came out okay. I'm a little bruised, but not broken. And whatever hurt I felt is going to fade out under the bright light of Sam's and Sadie's kindness and love. No matter how long this thing between us lasts, I will not regret taking this chance on them, because they are worth it and so am I.

CHAPTER FIFTY-TWO

I'm waiting naked in bed when Sam arrives. I was going to wear my silk nightie but then decided we might as well cut to the chase. And I'm so glad I did, because I can see how hard he already is through his jeans. There's doubt in his eyes, though, and maybe fear, too. Maybe he's wondering about our family meeting and what was said.

"Come in here," I say, holding out my hands.

He whips off his shirt and unzips his pants and drops them on the floor at the side of the bed. He's not wearing underwear tonight. His raging hard-on bounces out.

"Condom," I say, pointing at my nightstand.

He puts one on in record time and climbs into the bed, throwing the covers off onto the floor.

"What if I get cold?" I ask as he lowers himself down to me.

"I'll keep you warm," he says, pressing his lips to mine. His hand drags down my ribs to my waist and thigh. His work-roughened palm slides over the top of my thigh and moves to the space between my legs, his fingers delving into the warm, wet folds and stroking. It doesn't take long for me to be pulsating with need.

"Sam, I'm going to come if you keep doing that."

"Not without me, you're not," he says, falling onto his back. "Come over here, girl."

He wants me to get on top. We haven't done that yet, but I'm game. I take a moment to enjoy the view of his amazing body and hard length waiting to please me. "You are so gorgeous," I say, rolling up onto my side.

He takes my hand and kisses my fingers. "Beautiful girl. You turn me on so much."

"I do?" I know this is true, but I like to hear him say it anyway.

"Yes, you do. Now get up on here, would you? You're torturing me lying there like that."

Grinning from ear to ear, I get up on my knees and then straddle him. Looking down at him, I'm amazed at the fact that he's here, that we're here together and that fate saw fit to put him in my life. So many things had to line up just right for that to happen. The tour in Japan . . . our mothers going . . . Amber needing me at her place . . . Madison's addiction driving Sam to New York early . . . I have a lot of people to thank for this joy I'm about to receive.

"Nickel for your thoughts," he says as I position myself to take him inside me.

"I was just thinking how glad and lucky I am to have you in my life." There's a tinge of sadness to my words as I silently acknowledge that this could all be temporary.

As he lifts his hips and pushes himself into me, I groan. It feels too damn good, transporting me to another place . . . a secret world full of silky, sexy darkness. I won't think about him leaving . . . not right now anyway. This moment is too good to spoil with thoughts of reality.

"Want to know what I'm thinking right now?" he whispers.

Our bodies are fully joined, the length of him buried inside me. I move my hips, bringing myself extra pleasure. I look down at his beautiful face and see a vulnerability there.

"Yes," I say, sitting up so I can bring him in and out. I move up and down, setting our pace.

He rests his hands on my hips, closing his eyes as he grits his teeth in concentration.

"Well . . . ?" I ask, losing my breath a little. "Are you going to tell me?"

"Can't . . . losing my mind . . . ," he grunts.

I can tell by the way he's clenching his jaw that he's about to go. His control is slipping fast. I lean down and push faster. "I'm going to make you come, aren't I?"

His eyes fly open and he growls, two seconds before he surprises the crud out of me by flipping me over and coming down over me.

"No, babe. I'm going to make *you* come." He plunges into me, reaching around and grabbing my thigh, pulling it up. He somehow knows exactly where to touch me and how to move, and in just three strokes, I'm calling out his name.

"Sam! Oh, no!"

"Oh, *yes*," he growls, pushing faster and faster. "Come, babe. Come for me."

I hang on to him for dear life as that sexy darkness swallows me whole and sends me swirling around inside my own head. The pulsing orgasm takes over my whole body, making me buck and cry out, seeking release from its grip.

Sam slams into me, starting the cycle of sensation all over again for me as he finds his release. I cry out as the last spasms shake my entire being to the core. He falls on top of me, exhausted and breathing like he's about to die from overexertion.

After I'm finally able to breathe properly again, I tap him on the shoulder. "I believe I paid a nickel for someone's thoughts."

He lifts himself up onto his elbows and looks at my face, finally stopping his gaze on my eyes. "You sure you want to know what I'm thinking?" He gently moves wet hair from my sweaty forehead.

I nod. "Always." A special thrill runs through me at the idea that he's about to share his innermost thoughts with me. I pray it's something that will make me smile and not cry.

He takes a breath. "I was just thinking . . . when I saw you standing there in the hallway . . . that I love you. That I think you're amazing. That I hope I get to hang out with you for a lot longer than two weeks."

My heart nearly stops at the L-word and his declaration of desire for a shared future. "You love me?"

"Yeah. I do. Lame, huh?"

I laugh. "How is that lame?"

He looks down at my chest, maybe embarrassed to meet my gaze. "We just met. I sound desperate."

I pick his face up by his hairy chin. "Hey. If you're desperate, what does that make me?"

"What do you mean?" he asks, a small smile moving his beard.

"I pretty much loved you a week ago." I realize it's true as I say it. Love? Of course it's love that makes me want to see him first thing every morning and right before my eyes fall shut at night. It's love that makes me want to build a future with him in it. It's love that helped me get over my fear and take charge of my independence. I'm stronger with Sam in my life, but I'm also happier. He gets me, and that's saying a lot. Most people don't.

He laughs. "What happened a week ago to cause you to suffer this madness?"

I shrug. "I don't know. Seeing you with Sadie is some pretty potent magic, I think."

He nods. "I love that kid."

"I do too. She's really something special."

He kisses me, slow and soft this time, making my heart go pitter-patter.

"What do you think is going to happen tomorrow?" he asks, rolling over onto his back. "What do you want to happen?"

"I have no idea. I'm not going to try to guess or force anything. My life has been utterly nuts since I met you, and I don't expect it to be any different for as long as you're in it."

"You do realize you're the only woman in the entire world who doesn't want to plan every moment of her future, right?"

I smile and give him a sweet kiss. "As long as you and Sadie are there with me, I'm sure everything will work out just fine."

"Oh, shit," he says, his good mood disappearing in an instant as he looks down at his waist.

"What's wrong?" I frown at his sudden change in demeanor.

He holds up the condom. It's in two parts. "It ripped."

My heart literally stops beating.

"What's the date on these things?" he asks, sitting up to grab the box.

"I don't know." Now that I think about it, though, they are pretty old.

He reads something on the packaging. "They expired over a year ago."

I try to smile through my anxiety. "Oops."

CHAPTER FIFTY-THREE

Sam and I are coming back from the meditation meadow together, hand in hand, knowing that Sadie will be waking from her nap soon and will want to see us. The last three weeks have been full of music, painting, babysitting, laughing, eating big meals, and getting to know not just each other but the members of Red Hot. After they realized how well they jam together when they're out here on the farm, away from all the hectic hustle and bustle of the city, they decided to stay on for a while. I thought I would hate the idea, but I don't. Not at all, really.

It's been easier since Darrell left. The two days he spent here had us all riding an emotional roller coaster that only came to an end when he finally acknowledged that some mistakes from the past cannot be totally forgiven . . . at least not by Red. I don't know really how our mothers feel about it—their moods rise and fall on a daily basis as memories come and go—but Rose, Amber, and I aren't ready to write Darrell off. There will be another time in the future for us to talk about what happened in the past and what might happen moving forward, but none of us is in a rush to get there. Darrell is the one band member who knew we existed all along and yet made a conscious decision to be absent. That's not something we're taking lightly.

Since the band settled in, things have been . . . incredible. Exhausting. Unforgettable. I can now understand how our mothers got so wrapped up in them before. Even at their age, the men of Red Hot are magnetic and compelling, easily sweeping us into their orbits. It makes sense that Sam fits in so well with their group. Although not a member of the band, he's so much like them. To me, anyway. I couldn't resist him if I tried . . . not that I'm trying.

Sam has a contract with Red Hot now, working for them as an independent songwriter, because of course he's a brilliant musician, and with him on board, Red Hot is going to be at the top of the charts again. It was an easy decision for all of them, and now he no longer has to worry about how he's going to support his child.

As Sam and I walk along, hand in hand, he breaks the silence we've been sharing for the last hour. "So . . . I know you took that test this morning. I don't want to push you, but it's kind of driving me nuts wondering what the result was."

I stop, forcing him to draw up and face me. "Why didn't you say something, silly? I didn't mean to torture you by keeping it a secret." Being in the meditation meadow kind of suggests a person prefers silence, but it's not a hard-and-fast rule or anything. He went there to clear his head and I went there to find him. I want to tell him what happened just an hour ago. The news is burning me up inside. I just don't know how he's going to take it. It's making me nauseated to imagine him being upset.

"I didn't want to harsh your vibe or whatever," he says.

I pull him into a hug. "You could never do that. You are my haven from the craziness." I breathe in his scent, knowing I'll never tire of it for as long as I live. We are connected now, forever. The test I took this morning proves it.

He kisses the top of my head. "So are you going to tell me, or are you going to keep me in suspense?"

I want to tell him. I want to shout it from the rooftops and tell the world, but something is stopping me. I think it's my mothers. Over two decades ago they made a rash decision that affected so many lives. We're trying not to regret their choices as a family, but sometimes it's hard. I don't want to repeat their mistakes. I don't want to hurt the people I love. I need to be absolutely sure I'm doing the right thing.

"I'm going to tell you." I pull away, hanging on to his hands. "Are you ready to hear some big news?"

He grins. "Hell yeah."

My stomach feels like it's full of knots. "You know that condom that broke?"

"Yeah . . ." He grins harder.

"Well, apparently, it broke at exactly the wrong time of the month for me." My face heats up with embarrassment. I pray he doesn't think I somehow trapped him into this. Anyone could accidentally use an expired box of condoms, right?

He loses a bit of his smile. "What do you mean? Are you pregnant or not?"

I nod, worried about his response. He doesn't look happy anymore. "I am." I feel sick saying it. I hadn't intended this to happen. I don't want Sam to be with me just because of this.

He rolls his eyes heavenward. "Oh, shit."

"What?" I try to pull back, but he hangs on to my fingers.

"Don't go." He draws me toward him, putting his arms around my waist. My hands linger at his hips. I don't know what he's going to say next, but my heart is pounding.

"I didn't mean it like that. Please don't think anything negative."

"It's kind of hard not to when your response is to swear."

He reaches up and moves my hair away from my face. "You are so beautiful. Have I told you that lately?"

"Yes, but you're not answering my question."

"What was your question?" He stops messing with my hair and stares at me. I can't read his expression.

Now I'm confused. "I don't know. Maybe I didn't have one. Why are you mad about this? Do you think I meant for it to happen?"

"I'm not mad." He puts his hands on either side of my face. "Are you crazy? I'm thrilled." His nostrils flare and his eyes turn red.

"You look like you're about to go all Incredible Hulk on me or something." I've never seen this look on Sam's face.

His voice is gruff when he answers. "This is me about to fall apart, babe."

"Me being pregnant is making you fall apart? That can't be good."

He squeezes his eyes shut and then holds me against him. "I'm such an idiot. I'm not expressing myself well at all." He sighs over my shoulder. "I could write you a song that would tell you exactly how I'm feeling, but I can't say the words in a normal conversation. What the hell is wrong with me?"

I pat him on the back, finally understanding a little of what he's experiencing. "It's a lot to take in."

He pulls back and searches my eyes. "What does it mean for *us*, though?"

I shrug, afraid to be the one to say what needs to be said but knowing it has to happen. I'm going to be a mom now; I no longer can afford the luxury of letting fear stop me from being the bravest person I can be. "Well, I suppose you have a choice. You can either stick around and help me raise this child, or you can choose not to do that." I try not to let the ache in my throat become tears in my eyes.

He looks anguished. "How could you think I wouldn't want to participate in this adventure with you? This miracle?"

His clarified response is a glimmer of hope. "I don't want you to feel forced. I don't want this to ruin what we've started."

He rubs my upper arms, sounding more confident by the second. "It can't do that. It's only going to make it better. We're good for each other, Em. We make each other better. Stronger. More confident and comfortable. I've looked for that feeling all my life, and I finally found it with you. I'd be a complete fool to let that go or walk away from it."

"Really? You really think that?" My heart soars. This pregnancy isn't going to toll the death knell of our relationship; it's a new beginning! I had no idea that I could mean this to another human being. It makes me feel as though I'm reaching a potential I didn't even know I was capable of attaining. It gives me a confidence I've never felt with anyone before, not even my sisters. This is some crazy magic Sam is working on me.

He nods. "I do. I really do." He leans forward and kisses me very gently on the lips, his beard tickling me. "You are so courageous and loving and smart. How did I get so lucky to have you in my life?"

I hug him to me fiercely, so glad I took a chance on his man. "We're both lucky."

He chuckles. "I'm not sure if you're exactly lucky, but you're stuck with me now." He puts his lips right up to my ear and whispers, "We made a baby together."

I giggle. "Stop, you're giving me goose bumps."

He kisses me on the neck and then moves us in the direction of the house again. We're walking arm in arm, our sides practically glued together . . . me a pregnant girl and him the father of my baby. I thought my sister was crazy moving in with a man she just met, but look at me now; I'm even crazier than she is. And I wouldn't change it for the world.

"I don't want you to worry about me working far away," he says as we reach the front of the house.

I pause to hear the rest of what he has to say. "What do you mean?" I pray he means what I think he does. Our living apart was the big wrench in the works of our relationship. I cannot live in New York City. I know it will slowly eat away at the core of who I am to be surrounded by all that noise, all those people, and a complete lack of what I enjoy here on the farm. But he has to work with the band, and their permanent home is there.

He faces me. "I've already thought it all through. I was going to talk to you about it after meditating. I can work here with the band as long as they'll stay, and then I'll work from here alone. I can send them my work as MP3 files and take occasional trips down there if they need me to be there in person."

I tremble with happiness at the idea that he had already worked this out in his mind, before he knew I was pregnant. "Are you sure you want to do that?"

"Are you kidding me?" He pauses to look around us. "You're asking me if I'll regret living in paradise? With the woman I love and the baby we made together . . . and her big sister?"

"My big sister?"

"Well, yeah, Rose too, but I was talking about Sadie. I love all my girls . . . Sadie, you, your sisters, your moms. They're my family now . . . as long as you want me to be a part of it."

He loves my sisters and my moms too. Could a man be more perfect for me? *Nope.* We smile at each other like a couple of simple fools. "Are you kidding?" I ask. "You don't doubt that, do you? That I want you to be a part of my family?"

"No. Not one bit. All of you have been nothing but kind and loving toward me and Sadie. I couldn't ask for better people to have in my life."

I can't get over how much I love this man. He's said all the right things, and he's not doing it to manipulate me. "You think the farm is paradise?"

"It is for me. It is for Sadie. You don't want to leave, do you?" He moves in closer. "Don't tell me after all this time with the band you're suddenly feeling the need to move to Manhattan . . ."

"Oh, God, no." I put my hand to my throat as I laugh. I feel like my heart is going to burst. "I'm very happy right here . . . as long as you and Sadie are by my side."

"When are we going to tell Sadie?" he asks.

"Normally, people don't say anything to kids until more time has passed, but I'm worried my sisters will say something in front of her and let the cat out of the bag. And with everything that happened with Madison, I don't want her getting big news from anyone but us."

"Your sisters?"

"Yes. I have to tell them. We don't keep secrets from one another." I can just see their reactions in my mind. They are going to flip out.

"I agree that's probably best, then. We'll tell her together."

"Tonight," I agree. "I don't think I can wait to share the news. You, me, and Sadie are going to be a family." I want to sing with joy.

"And our baby," he says, moving in to kiss me again. "What are we going to name her?"

I can't stop smiling. "What if it's a boy?"

"Boys are trouble." He leans down and talks to my belly button. "Hey, baby. Can you hear me in there? You need to come out with girl parts, not boy parts."

Neither of us notices Red standing at the top of the stairs until he speaks. "Looks like somebody has some big news." He's wearing his standard leather jacket and biker boots, his thumbs tucked into the waistband of his jeans.

Sam stands up straight, losing his happy expression instantly. My face is suddenly very hot, the autumn cold no longer affecting me. Sam looks at me, an apology in his eyes. I slowly shake my head at him. This isn't his fault. He was just being an excited dad.

"Maybe," I say, mounting the steps. Sam is right behind me.

"Do you have a minute?" Red asks me, ignoring Sam. "I'd love to talk to you, one on one, if you think that'd be cool."

I shrug. Red has been waiting in the wings for a very long time to talk to me, and at this point it feels just plain mean to keep denying him. I can no longer claim I'm too busy with the animals or Sadie or cooking or cleaning. It's time to put all our cards on the table and have a heart-to-heart. "Sure. Let's walk to the clinic to visit Rose."

"Excellent. I was just headed there myself."

I put my hand on Sam's arm and smile. "See you later?"

He searches my face. "As long as you're good with this."

I nod. "I am. Thanks, babe."

He kisses me and I literally can feel the love he has for me, transferred into my body through his touch. I know now what it means to be high on life.

Red comes down the stairs, and I turn to face the road to the clinic. Our footsteps make the gravel crunch beneath our shoes. I wait for him to start talking, to say whatever it is he's been burning to say to me probably from the moment he found out that I exist.

CHAPTER FIFTY-FOUR

"I'm really happy you agreed to have a chat with me. I've been wanting to talk to you for a long time."

"I know." I hold in the sigh that wants to burst out. I've been childishly keeping myself separate from him. It's actually easier for me to chat with Cash or Mooch than with him.

"It's tough in such a busy house to find any private moments."

"Sometimes. Yeah."

"But you love it here. I can see that."

"I do." I look at him but he's staring straight ahead. I think he's making an effort to not put pressure on me with too much eye contact, and I appreciate it. Just standing next to him is difficult for me. It's like being too close to the sun or something.

"Your sister Amber is happy here, but I think she really likes New York a lot."

"Yes, you're right. She does." My heartbeat hitches. She's relocated for good, my sister. She'll visit the farm from time to time, but her days of living here permanently are over. Time has changed us. Time and the band.

"Are you upset about that?" He looks at me, waiting for my answer.

I don't know if he's asking me if I'm upset about her wanting to live there or her being okay with sharing the same address as the band, but regardless, it doesn't change my answer. "Not really. I miss her when she's there, of course, but I would never want to stop her from living the life that makes her happy."

"That's how I feel."

I look at him, again not sure what he means. "About Amber?"

He glances at me for a second before answering. "About all of you. I just want you all to be happy."

I nod, not sure I can respond without letting too much emotion get in the way. All I can think about is whether I would have been happier to have him in my life all those years growing up. I'll never know and it makes me so sad.

"Cool," I finally say, not wanting him to think badly of me. I'm not a brat trying to punish a grown man for things he said and did a long time ago. I'm going to be a mom soon, and he was denied the chance to be a father—by decisions, by circumstances, by the actions of others, by his own actions . . . Life can be so unfair sometimes. This is the first time I've actually seen our whole situation as being unfair to him. I imagine taking off and leaving Sam without a word because I don't want to ruin his career, and all I feel is a burning pain in my chest. *How could our mothers have done that?*

Red derails my train of thought by speaking. "We really love being out here, but I know this is your home. And I don't want you to feel uncomfortable in your home."

I shrug. "I'm not uncomfortable."

He stops walking. I stop too and turn to face him.

"I'd leave tomorrow if I knew it was causing you pain for me to be here." The leather of his jacket creaks as he moves to rub his hands together. He looks nervous, which is really strange considering who he is.

I try to be polite and smile, but I can't. My face twists as emotions crash into me. "What about Amber?"

"Amber works for us and she lives nearby. I talk to her every day. That won't change."

"And Rose?"

"I haven't had a chance to talk to her, but she seems like a pretty even-keeled person. I have hope that we can find a way to communicate."

"I'm not even-keeled?" Does he think I'm an emotional basket case or something?

He holds out his hands. "You are, absolutely. That's not what I meant. I think you're just . . . a very sensitive person. An artist, like me." He shares a half smile. "We tend to take everything to heart, you know?"

I want to cry over the truth of that and the idea that we share this trait. "Yeah. We do."

He looks around, as if searching for words . . . or maybe for the courage to say them. I know exactly how he feels.

"If it's okay with you, I'd really like to get to know you better," he says.

I swallow with difficulty; my throat has gone dry. One of the most famous people in the world, literally adored by millions, wants to get to know me. He might even be my father. And here I am standing in front of him, speechless.

"I know it's a lot to ask. I know you're angry with me and the guys. I know you wish things had gone differently. Hell, so do I. I really do." He moves closer. I can see his bloodshot eyes and weathered skin clearly now. "I'm an old man. I don't know how much time I've got left on this earth, but I'll tell you one thing I do know." He pauses, staring me in the eye. "I'd give everything away . . . give it all up . . . just to have a relationship with you, your sisters, and your mothers. All of it. None of the money or the fame is worth having lost you."

I can't stop the tears now. They are flowing freely down my cheeks, and I'm trembling too hard to wipe them away. I want to run, to fly from this place up into the sky and look down on it from a hundred miles above. But I can't; I'm stuck here, facing my fears, dog-paddling in this pool of emotions that feels like it's going to drown me in its depths.

"You haven't lost anything," I say in a shaky voice. "You can't lose what you never had."

"I'd like a second chance at it," he says, his voice steeled against the pain he's obviously suffering. "But I can only get that second chance if you agree to give it to me. I can't force you, and I wouldn't even if I could. It's all up to you, child. I'm at your mercy."

Jesus Christ, this guy knows how to grab my heartstrings and tug the hell out of them. I say the first and only thing that comes to mind. "I'm afraid you'll hurt me and my family."

He drops down to one knee, reaching up for my hand. I let him take it, mesmerized by the tortured emotions on his face. "I would rather die than do anything that would hurt you or your family. Please believe me." He places his free hand on his heart, his thick, chunky rings catching my eye. I don't think this man gets on his knees very often, if ever.

I nod at his gesture. Love is ringing in my soul like a clanging bell. I know he means what he says; the truth is shining out from his eyes. "Okay." I nearly pass out saying that one word, but I can't stop there. "You can have that second chance. But if you do hurt us, if you're careless with our love, you will regret it. I will make absolutely damn sure of that."

He stands and steps toward me with his arms out. "I will never, *ever* go back to living with regret, I can promise you."

I can't stay away from him anymore. His eyes pull me in like a magnet, and then I'm in his arms. He's holding me tightly and his body is trembling, just like mine is. "I hope you're my daughter. I think you're really something special. But if you're not, I'm still going to treat you like you are, because DNA test results don't matter to me."

"Me neither," I say, overwhelmed by the idea that Red and I could have this in common. I have a hard time talking through my tears, but I have something that still needs to be said. "I don't need to know who my father is. I just want one; that's all I know. I want a father." My entire body is going haywire. I'm hot and then cold, scared and then brave, wanting to cry and then sing. I have never fully admitted this fact to myself until this moment, and now that it's here, I realize what my future holds: love.

"Then I'm your man," he says, his voice gruff. "I'm ready to be the best damn daddy a girl ever had. And so are Cash and Mooch. We're ready."

"Okay," is all I can manage.

"And being a grandpa is cool with me too. I'm ready to spoil grandkids like you've never seen."

I can't say anything to that. All the words I want to say are stuck behind a huge lump in my throat. But he knows from my tears that I'm on board with all of this. I am *so* on board.

We stand there for the longest time, and when the embrace is finally over, I feel as though I could take a week-long nap. I've never felt so exhausted and yet happy in my entire life.

CHAPTER FIFTY-FIVE

Dinner is a heck of a meal, with all of our available picnic tables pushed together and people taking up every seat. It's cold outside, but we manage to stay warm with hot food and lots of wine and laughing. I take a moment to look out over the crowd and smile. These are my people. This is my family. I have three moms and four dads, and a man who loves me who comes with a beautiful little girl I have learned to love as my own. And I'm carrying his baby. Life could not be better. I want to share our news with the group, but there's someone who needs to know it before all of them do.

Sam and I nod at each other, and he leans over to speak in Sadie's ear. "Want to go for a walk?"

"No, it's too cold."

"Okay, let's go inside and sit by the fire," he says. We all get up and head toward the house. I signal to my sisters to keep everyone out for just a few minutes. They get it and both nod. I haven't told them our news yet, but I will very shortly.

After Sadie and I are settled on the couch, and Sam is on his knee in front of us, he takes his daughter by the hand. "Baby girl . . . we have some news we want to share with you."

"Is it sad news like when my mommy died?"

"No, no," I say quickly, wanting to dispel that idea from her mind as fast as possible. "It's the opposite, really. Something very good." Hopefully, she will agree.

She looks up at her dad with her big blue eyes, her little curls framing her face. "Am I getting a puppy?"

He smiles, reaching up to pet her head. "No, baby. Something even better than a puppy."

"Rosie says I can play with Banana any time I want, so I kind of have a puppy anyway." She looks at me. "Right?"

I nod. "Absolutely. And you have Boris, also."

She sighs. "Yes. He's a lot of work, but I love him, so I do it."

I bite my lip to keep from laughing. Boris sleeps twenty-three out of twenty-four hours a day and hardly wakes when he's getting one of Sadie's famous back scratches.

"Baby, this is big news. Like the biggest news you'll ever hear."

Her eyes go big and round. "Are you getting married? Will I be a flower girl?"

Sam loses a bit of his smile. "Uh, no. That wasn't it."

Her happy expression falls away. "Oh. Well, it's probably not the best news, then."

I rest my hand on her tiny knee. "How would you feel about being a big sister?"

Her eyes narrow at me and then at Sam. "Why?"

He leans in. "Because. You're going to be one, that's why."

She looks at both of us, clearly confused. "Are we going to buy one?"

He laughs. "You can't buy a baby, silly."

"You can buy baby goats. And cows and horses. And pigs. Em'rald told me." She looks at me accusatorily.

"That's true. You can do that. But you can't buy baby people." I pat her knee.

"How do you get a baby, then?"

I look at the ceiling. I can't believe we are about to have a bird-and-bees conversation right now. I'm totally unprepared for this.

Sam surprises me with his answer. "Emerald and I made one together. We got together and we love each other and together with love we made a baby."

"Oh. Where is it?" Sadie asks, looking around. She climbs on the back of the couch and looks behind it. "Can I hold it?"

Sam pulls her back down into a sitting position. "It's in Emerald's belly right now."

"He or she won't be born for about eight months," I explain. "That's a really long time."

Sadie looks at my stomach. "How did you put a baby in there?"

"I think a better question is, what are we going to name it?" Sam says, faster than me on the draw with the distraction questions.

"Well. We could name it Boris."

I have to look away to hide my laugh. This pregnancy is going to be quite the adventure, I can already tell. And I am so very, very happy about that.

"We wanted to tell you first before we told anyone else," Sam says, stroking her hand. "Are you cool with it?"

She nods. "Yes. I'm cool. I like babies. Maybe I could teach the baby how to play guitar someday."

Sam nods. "Sure. But maybe you should learn to play yourself, first." He glances up at me. "If that's what you want to do."

She shrugs. "I don't know. I can either play guitar or paint. I have options."

Sam and I burst out laughing as he pulls us into a group hug. "Yes, you do. You have all kinds of options, sweet girl."

CHAPTER FIFTY-SIX

Later in bed that night, Sam and I are reflecting on our moments together as he holds me in his arms. "It's crazy, right?" Sam asks. "That all this happened in such a short period of time?"

"Yes. Crazy is one way of putting it." Nuts . . . loony tunes . . . ridiculous . . . insane . . . take your pick of synonyms.

"You don't regret it, do you?" He looks down at me.

I angle my head up so I can look into his eyes. I want him to see how truthful I'm being. "Never. I could never regret any moment I've had with you."

"Even the ones when I was rude?"

"You were never rude."

"Yes, I was." He sounds sad and his eyes have gone dark and moody. "When we first met. I had such a big chip on my shoulder. I took it out on everyone, but especially you. There was just something about you . . . I wanted you to care, I think."

"Yeah, I saw that chip there . . ." I play with his beard as I think back on that time. "But I ignored it. I figured you had your reasons. And you were easy to care about. I got a strong sense that you were someone special, right from the first time I saw you."

He kisses my head, his mood lightening. "I'm glad I finally talked to Ty about everything that went on back home . . . back when we were kids growing up. That helped me get rid of the anger I'd been harboring toward him."

"I'm glad for both of you. It's hard when you're young. You look at what someone's doing, like Ty staying friendly with your parents even after all the abuse you suffered, and sometimes it's impossible not to take it personally. You feel like they're being disloyal to you or agreeing with the abuse."

"It was hard for me, but I should have known better. Our father was worse on Ty than he was on me. Ty was just sticking it out for our mom. But I couldn't. I was so mad at her for letting it happen . . . for being so weak. I was disappointed in her and then in myself for being so cold. I thought I didn't have a heart. Not until I fell for Sadie, anyway. And then I thought it was only limited to her."

I feel a tiny nanoparticle of doubt sneak in. His mother was weak and I can be weak too. "You're not worried that I'm like her, are you?"

He pulls away so he can see me better. "Are you kidding me? You're the strongest woman I know."

I laugh at his sorry attempt to placate me. "Ha, ha."

"No, seriously." He gets up on his side, propping his upper body on his bent arm. "You are . . . incredible. I mean, look at you." He shakes his head, ignoring my reddening face. "You're beautiful, yeah, but you're *you*; you're independent, smart, brave . . ."

I have to stop him right there. "Brave? No, Amber's brave. I'm a lily-livered chicken poop."

"Bullshit. You're fierce. You do what needs to be done, and you don't let fear get in the way. Someone who never has fear in the first place isn't brave when they do things; they're just being who they are. You take fear and make it your bitch. I admire the hell out of that."

I giggle like a little girl. He really knows how to flatter me. "I was scared shitless when I thought Drake was at your door."

"Yeah, sure, but you didn't let it stop you, did you? You packed up and got the hell out of there instead of panicking and hiding in the closet. I get the fear, believe me. I know I didn't help the situation by telling you he was after me. But it doesn't matter anymore; he's in jail now and he's going to stay there. Patty sent me an email with the link to that news story, and I confirmed it with the detective on the case, so it's done."

"But they're saying he killed someone."

"Yeah. Another drug-dealing gangbanger who probably deserved it, and he got caught red-handed. The only thing that matters is we're safe. Madison's debts are not my debts, and the man who was claiming otherwise is gone."

"He'll get out eventually."

"Maybe in thirty years if he's lucky. They're throwing the book at him. He's a career criminal they've been trying to get off the streets for over a decade. Trust me, we're fine."

"I know we are." I reach up to kiss him. "We have each other."

"And we're creating a family together," he says, his voice dropping and his hand coming down to rub my belly. "I'm totally committed to you and our kids. And one day I want to marry you, but only when you're ready."

I want to weep with happiness. We have plenty of time for the marriage stuff. I'm still not quite believing the fact that I even found this man in the first place. "I love you, Sam. Thank you for helping me find my courage."

"I love you more, Emerald Collins. Thank you for helping me find peace and love in my life."

We move in closer and our lips touch. His tongue comes out to lick me and sends a spark right into my heart.

"You know . . . we have to get up really early to do the chores," I say, smiling against his mouth. "We should probably go to sleep."

"I can be quick," he whispers, smiling back devilishly.

"Well, then, what's stopping you?"

He leaps onto me and growls into my neck, sending peals of my laughter out into our bedroom. I am so in love with this incredibly talented, complicated, and emotional music man, and I'm overjoyed to have finally found my place in the world. I thank the Lord above and all the Fates with a hand in my destiny that my place—the place where I feel free and confident about who I am, the place where I will raise my own family and get to know the one I was denied for twenty-five years—turned out to be right here at Glenhollow Farms.

BRIGHT LIGHTS. BIG CITY.
RED HOT LOVE.

A handsome stranger offers Rose some help. Does she risk accepting? What if he has ulterior motives?

Coming July 2018. Order now.

ABOUT THE AUTHOR

Elle Casey, a former attorney and teacher, is a prolific *New York Times* and *USA Today* bestselling American author who lives in southwest France with her husband, the youngest of her three children, and a bunch of cats, dogs, and horses. She writes in several genres, including romance, suspense, urban fantasy, paranormal, science fiction, dystopian, and action/adventure.

Made in the USA
Columbia, SC
28 March 2025